# CHRISTOPHER ROSOW

# EPIC INJUSTICE

## BEN PORTER SERIES **BOOK FIVE**

EPIC INJUSTICE
Ben Porter Series – Book Five



For information about this title, contact the publisher:

Quadrant Publishing, LLC
354 Pequot Avenue, Southport CT 06890
QuadrantPublishing@gmail.com

Library of Congress Control Number: 2023907735
ISBN: 979-8-9882567-0-0 (Print Edition)
ISBN: 979-8-9882567-2-4 (Barnes & Noble Press Special Edition)
ISBN: 979-8-9882567-1-7 (E-book Edition)

1 2 4 5 6 7 8 9 0

# AUTHOR'S NOTE

**WHILE THIS STORY** is constructed in the real world, including but not limited to referencing actual companies, places, news outlets and articles, events, and things, it is a novel, and it is a work of fiction.

However, it's not entirely far-fetched.

# FRIDAY
# OCTOBER 21, 2022

**THIRTEEN DAYS** *BEFORE THE VOTE*

# CHAPTER

# 1



**THESE STORIES TYPICALLY START** with something thrilling: a foreboding, foreshadowing murky scene at sea, a sensational decapitation, or perhaps an exciting, careening car chase—you know, scenes and set pieces that grab your attention. "The Rules" demand an opener with a hook: a catchy first sentence, first paragraph, first chapter.

I'm breaking those rules.

Come to think of it, I've become adept at routinely breaking the rules.

My name is Ben Porter. I'm a Special Agent of the Federal Bureau of Investigation, and instead of being on a case hunting down a villain, I'm standing at a makeshift gravesite.

Yeah, I know. That's kind of a depressing opener. But I think that sometimes, it should be okay to face reality: we don't live in the Instagram world (or whatever varnished and filtered and polished social media-type universe you can relate to), and there comes a time when we need to adjust our lenses to see the occasional harshness of life. Now is one of those times.

You see, at only thirty-two years old, I've already faced risk to my own life, but I've never faced this: a funeral service for a dear friend—murdered about eighteen months ago because of my decisions.

It's a terrible weight to bear. And this is the third such funeral.

They're not getting any easier.

Three weeks ago, on the last day of September 2022, I found myself in Cohasset, Massachusetts, where a man named Miles Lockwood was laid to rest. Then, a week later, a similar service was held for Bradford Macallister in Boston.

And now, I'm one of the five people standing at Walley Park, at two in the afternoon on a Friday toward the end of October, on the shores of Narragansett Bay in Bristol, Rhode Island, to remember Anastasia Volkov.

Three of my closest friends—dead because my ego had been stroked, and because I thought that I could solve any case.

I'd enjoyed a pretty good run . . . until now.

Until Lockwood, Macallister, and Volkov all perished. Those people, once so important to my life and to my stories—all gone.

Or so I thought, because what I believed was a final chapter was actually a new first chapter—and the rules would no longer matter.

# CHAPTER 2



## *SAME TIME — NEW YORK CITY*

**AT THE SAME TIME** and roughly 155 miles to the west, a woman and a man seated themselves in front of a flickering, outdoor gas fireplace that was the centerpiece of a seven hundred square foot rooftop terrace overlooking Manhattan's West Village.

Tiled with white terra cotta and surrounded by a black iron railing, the terrace offered a commodity rare in the bustle of New York City: privacy. Even the entrance to the four-story townhouse below, which had grown substantially from its original footprint as a carriage house on Cornelia Street, was private; a vehicle could pass through a twin-leafed, arched top outswing door, constructed from heavy, wormholed oak timbers, and passengers were able to disembark invisibly inside the garage hidden behind the doors.

With fifty million followers on Instagram, privacy was a necessity for the occupant of the townhouse. With her fortune in the billion-dollar range, security, too, was a requirement, and the 5,500-square-foot townhouse offered both features to the woman.

The opulent surroundings, however, did not guarantee her success, and her frustration was evident as she asked her guest, "Do we have a deal, or not?"

From the sofa opposite, upholstered in a white, outdoor-rated fabric and covered by staff in inclement weather, the man drawled in his Texan accent, "I think you should take that contract and soak it in your pool, Hanna. Turn it to pulp. That's all it's worth." He paused, crossing a leg. "This place has got a pool in the basement, right? Isn't that what you told me?"

Hanna Mo'Nique Isaac smiled, exposing artificially whitened teeth that contrasted against her rich, dark brown face, and she said chirpily, "Indeed, it does, Virgil. The pool is not quite six feet deep, and it's not quite lap length. But it's lovely. Such a refuge. You know, the basalt tile that surrounds the pool was imported from the Azores."

Virgil Preston smiled in return, but the expression was one of polite disinterest. "Should I be impressed?"

"Not as impressed as you should be by the terms of my offer to buy your company."

"As I've told you many times previously, I don't care," the Texan said. For emphasis, he repeated, "I don't care for your offer. I won't take it. Aximerva is not for sale."

"I don't think you have a choice. I know you're overextended."

The Texan scoffed, "You might call it overextended, but I call it an investment. You gotta spend money to make money." Preston angled his head slightly, and in a patronizing tone, he added, "You buy companies. I understand that. But have you ever built anything, Missus Isaac?" He drew out the final words in his Texas twang: *Miss-usss Eye-sayck.*

"You've borrowed more than your company is worth today," Isaac replied evenly.

"You didn't answer my question," Preston complained. "You see, Aximerva is investing in itself. We will produce the most advanced semiconductors right here in the United States, but that doesn't come cheaply. You know, my plant—my chip foundry—will be ten thousand times cleaner than a typical hospital operating room. The chips are etched in a pure nitrogen environment. The foundry will use extreme ultraviolet photolithography. And our product is minuscule—there are 25.4 million nanometers in a single inch, and Aximerva is gonna be manufacturing seven nanometer chips. This is cutting-edge technology. There's only one other place in the world that can make those chips, and it is—"

"It is Taiwan," Isaac interrupted. "Yes, I've been there."

"To Taiwan?" Preston's tone was one of incredulity.

"Yes, Virgil," the investor sighed. "Hong Kong and China, too. My interest in Aximerva is very much informed by the advanced production capabilities of the so-called Middle Kingdom. And, in comparison, your plan is not only competitive, but it is also impressive." Her voice rose as she added, emphatically, "But you cannot afford it!"

"I sure can, ma'am."

"The vultures are circling, Virgil. I'm your only potential savior."

"I may have a short-term liquidity problem and a handful of, um, legal issues," Preston admitted. "However, I also got myself some very good protection from those, uh, vultures."

The woman's expression morphed from bright and reasonably friendly to fiery anger in an instant, and she snarled, "I think I've explained myself quite clearly. You simply do not have a choice in the matter. This is not a negotiation. Aximerva will not build the new factory that you've proposed. Not here in America. Not in Mexico. Not anywhere. And your only out is my very generous offer."

Preston snorted. "Not a negotiation? Bullshit, as we say on the ranch."

Isaac tossed her sweeping, shoulder-length black hair petulantly. "You don't want to do this, Virgil. You don't want to cross me." She sighed, staring at the Texan, and she added softly, "We've been going in circles on this for weeks. Months, maybe. I thought a one-on-one meeting, in private, just you and me, and you'd see the value in the offer that I proposed. In what I outlined, again, just moments ago. I hoped—"

"Enough," Preston snapped. "We're goin' in circles because you don't like my answer, which was and is still a firm no. A non-negotiable no. I'm not backin' down."

He leaned forward to the white coffee table that was positioned in front of the outdoor fireplace, and he pushed the half-inch thick stack of paper toward his hostess. "If you're not gonna drown this worthless contract—this garbage—in your fancy underground, indoor pool, maybe you should burn it in this here fire. Hmm?"

Isaac tugged her stylish shearling coat tighter as she reclined into the sofa. Her expression hardened. "Virgil Preston. Ranch hand turned tech tycoon. You've enjoyed a very successful career, haven't you?"

"I could say the same thing about you," Preston replied evenly. "You're married to a United States Senator, and yet you were once a poor girl from Los Angeles, who wrote her own ticket to become an acclaimed investor who owns a fancy New York townhouse with its own indoor swimmin' hole." He whistled appreciatively, "Shee-yit, this place is suitable for a pop star."

Isaac nodded, almost imperceptibly. "Yes. Yes, we can agree on that. We both did well for ourselves." She looked over the West Village view before drawing her eyes back to the tall Texan. "Except, there's this one little thing." Reaching into a pocket of the shearling coat, Isaac withdrew a USB flash drive, garishly emblazoned with the name of a big-box electronics chain, and she tossed it casually on the top of the document stack.

Preston growled, "What's that?"

"The clincher."

"Hmph. I doubt it." Preston ran a hand through his thick, sun-whitened hair before picking up the cowboy hat that lay next to him on the sofa. "As I've made clear, no deal. I'm not interested in any government handouts as proposed by your Senator husband, and I'm not stupid enough to realize you're trying to do an end run on his behalf by buying my company. By trying to buy me off to silence my opposition to your husband's pork-for-votes bill."

Preston stood to his six-foot-three-inch height, towering over the woman seated on the sofa. "You've got nothing more to offer, and I don't want or need any of your money, Hanna." He snorted as he looked over the New York skyline before drawing his attention back to Isaac. "Thank you for the tour. Nice place, but I prefer the prairie."

Isaac made no move to stand. Instead, she said softly, "It's evidence."

"Evidence of what?"

"Take the drive. Take it with you, open it up, and you'll find out."

Chuckling, Preston snorted, "Not a chance. A virus? Tracking code? Key logger? If you think I'm gonna touch that thing, you're outta your mind."

Isaac was nodding. "Oh, it could be all those things. Therefore, I'd suggest you purchase a new computer, which of all people, certainly you have access to, and open the drive with that."

Taken aback by her transparency, Preston muttered, "Save me the trouble. Whaddya got?"

Isaac's mouth curled into a sneer. "I've got you, and I've got the United States Attorney General. I've got evidence of your collusion with Bart Williams, the highest lawyer in the land, conspiring with you and your company to break the law. I know he's illegally protecting you from the vultures."

She exhaled with exasperation. "My offer remains straightforward, Virgil. I'm offering fair market value for Aximerva, and my suggestion is this: you take the deal. You take the cash, you do what you want with it, and I get your company."

"And if I don't sign?" Preston's voice, however, had lost its bluster, and he fiddled with the hat in his hands.

"I leak the contents of the drive. The AG, as you've probably already guessed, has insulated himself well. You take the fall. You go to jail. You lose it all. Your company, your reputation, and my offer. Because, at that point, I'll be able to pick up Aximerva for a song. No one will want to touch that steaming pile of shit with a ten-foot pole."

Preston sank back down into the sofa. "Gimme one thing. How did you get this information?"

Isaac didn't waver the slightest, holding her gaze firm and not making even the slightest movement. "You'll see my evidence is unimpeachable, after you review it, of course. But I'll agree to your terms. I'll disclose my sources after you sign." She stood, signaling that she was taking command of the discussion. "Lunch? I know just the perfect place. It's fabulous. Let's say, um, Tuesday, next week? That will give you plenty of time to review the information on the drive, and I know you're staying in

New York this weekend because you're booked on a television program on Sunday morning. I can't wait to watch," she concluded sardonically.

Tentatively and wordlessly, Preston stretched his right hand toward the flash drive. He blinked, and then palmed the device—but he made no effort to also pick up the thick stack of paper. With a sniff, he rose unsteadily and whispered hoarsely, "This ain't over."

Keeping his options open, the Texan composed himself and added politely, "I'll consider your materials, and maybe I'll see you for lunch on Tuesday."

# CHAPTER 3



**FIVE FIGURES** were gathered at the seawall of a peaceful, seaside park in the quaint, historic town of Bristol, Rhode Island, at two in the afternoon on a gorgeous, crisp, New England fall day with bright sunshine, a comfortable temperature at sixty-five degrees with low humidity. Despite the late October date, summer seemed like it was still hanging around, and stirred by a warm, gentle, early afternoon southwesterly breeze, wavelets sparkled on Narragansett Bay like millions of diamonds.

Five.

Only five individuals cared enough to spend a moment remembering a woman named Anastasia Volkov. Given her value to the United States and to the FBI, I expected that more mourners would have paid their respects—until I realized that I selfishly preferred the solitude and the privacy.

To say that my relationship with Volkov was complicated really understates the word "complicated." Volkov was a friend, but then she became a foe who tried to kill me. Like, literally was going to shoot me, with a gun, and I shot back. Not the makings of a productive relationship, you'd think.

We realized that the differences that begat our duel were resolvable. I would discover that her capacity for self-reflection was immense and that her desire for redemption was sincere. In due course, Volkov became one of my staunchest allies. We developed mutual respect, and though we never talked about our relationship openly, it was one of those things that needed no discussion. We just . . . *knew*. We knew that our bond was deep and was perhaps strengthened by the challenges that we'd faced together. That we'd overcome, together.

*Complicated, indeed*, I thought, contemplating the glittering water as I listened to Jennifer Appleton, the Special Agent in Charge of the Boston Division Field Office of the FBI, reciting "Requiem," a poem penned by Robert Lewis Stevenson:

*"Under the wide and starry sky,*
  *"Dig the grave and let me lie.*
*"Glad did I live and gladly die,*
  *"And I laid me down with a will."*

Appleton absently brushed her left hand through her conservatively styled, shoulder-length auburn hair. A silver bracelet twinkled, briefly catching the sunlight, as the SAC inhaled and began anew:

*"This be the verse you grave for me:*
  *"Here she lies where she longed to be;*
*"Home is the sailor, home from sea,*
  *"And the hunter home from the hill."*

Concluding the poem, Appleton adjusted her black, calf-length, long-sleeved, formal dress, took a half step to the seawall, and dropped a single white rose from her right hand into the water. She retreated slowly by two paces, wordlessly.

FBI Special Agent Leroy Havens took her spot on the seawall, the sun glinting off his dark, shaved scalp. Like Appleton, he let a white rose fall from his hand, and in his deep baritone, he muttered, "Rest in peace."

Havens turned, yanked at the lapels of his charcoal suit coat, and simultaneously cleared his throat while adjusting the half-Windsor knot on his nightshade purple tie. The big, powerfully built agent then joined Appleton as Intelligence Analyst Louis Lewis walked forward to the seawall.

Typically, Lewis would be garbed in some outrageously uncoordinated outfit, his spiky blond hair askew and accented by brightly colored eyeglass frames. Today, however, he was clad in a navy-blue suit, his hair gelled into complicity, and his eyeglasses a demure brown tortoiseshell. He looked like a proper G man until the illusion was broken when he spoke in his nasal twang, "Volkov, you were the best coder that there was. Now it's my turn to take the top spot. So long, and thanks for all the fish."

"Not appropriate," Appleton murmured, just loudly enough for her subordinate to hear.

Lewis snorted. "You just don't get it." He flipped a white rose into the waves.

Appleton raised an eyebrow. "Fine. Perhaps you'll enlighten me later?"

"Sure." Sniffing, Lewis took a position next to Havens, allowing the fourth mourner in our small group to pace toward the water.

My sister, Grace Porter, stepped to the wall and said, "I barely knew you, but I already miss you. I'm sorry for all that happened." Pausing and wiping her cheeks, she spoke again, "From the night we met, I knew there was something special about you."

Grace let her flower fall from her hand and then reflexively pulled a black shawl tightly around her shoulders. Despite the warm air and gentle wind, she visibly shivered; I stepped to my sister and enveloped her in a hug.

Appleton, sharp and insightful as always, knew better than to say anything; she would have guessed that my hug was only a diversion meant to shield my tears. Blinking rapidly, I pivoted away from Grace and faced the water. Gulping, I composed my thoughts. I wanted to say so much, but ultimately, I could only manage only one, awkwardly-choked-out word.

"Goodbye."

My rose joined the four other flowers being swept slowly away by the outgoing tide. I watched them drift . . . to the south, perhaps eventually to the mouth of Narragansett Bay, out to the open waters of the Atlantic Ocean.

I waited for the breeze to dry the tears on my cheeks before I turned to face the group. "Time to go." My tone left no room for debate.

Appleton nodded once and said softly, "Ben, call me when you're ready. Okay?"

I grunted a non-verbal affirmation of the SAC's command. Appleton turned her back to me and slowly walked to her black, Bureau-issued Chevrolet Tahoe, parked curbside to the green grass. Havens and Lewis followed and boarded a black Chevrolet Suburban.

As the two vehicles pulled away, Grace and I began the short walk to her Cape-style home, just three blocks away on a Bristol side street.

I felt my sense of loss in my shoulders, and as we walked that feeling seemed to morph into anger and bitterness. "When you're ready," I whispered to myself, quietly enough so that Grace wouldn't hear me repeating Appleton's words.

"What if I'm never ready?"

"What?" Grace's startled voice said, and I realized that I'd asked that question of myself in my normal tone of voice.

I decided to confide with my sister. "I've been fumbling around on minor cases for well over a year. You heard Appleton. She said for me to call her when I'm ready. But what if that day never comes?"

Reaching the corner of her street, Grace stopped in her tracks. "That's bullshit, Ben. I mean, I get it. Mourn your friends for a while. But they're not coming back, so that means that you better grow some balls and get back to work. Like Volkov once did."

She folded her arms defiantly across her chest as I repeated, "Like Volkov once did."

Grace was right, as usual. Calm, cool, and collected under pressure, my sister had encountered Volkov in a moment of confusion and fear, and yet neither woman bowed to the pressure. Instead, they found common ground and built a relationship from there.

"You're right, of course," I conceded. "But I don't think I'm ready."

"No, you're hangry. Let's make a nice dinner, get drunk, and then you go save the world again tomorrow."

"I'll be hungover."

"You'll be fine, Benbro. We'll all be fine."

"Hangry, huh?"

"Yeah." She poked at my belly, which to my satisfaction was not as rounded as it used to be, but Grace had a point. I did better thinking when I was well-fed, and of late, I've not been enjoying food.

I squinted at my sister, who confidently returned my stare as I said, "Maybe I've been starving my emotions."

Grace rolled her eyes. "Maybe you're also being immature. And maybe, no matter how drunk we're gonna get tonight, you should call Appleton tomorrow and get back into the game."

For the first time in eighteen months, I began to feel a sense of purpose. I waited for a beat and offered with a smile, "That sounds promising."

# CHAPTER
## 4



**BY THE TIME** SAC Jennifer Appleton said her goodbyes at the makeshift gravesite in Bristol and completed the two-hour drive north to Boston, the day had darkened to dusk. The SAC parked her black, Bureau-issued, Chevrolet Tahoe in a reserved space at the FBI's Boston Field Office—not quite in Boston, but close by in the suburb of Chelsea.

Glancing at her silver wristwatch, the SAC scowled, thinking, *I'm late.*

Normally precise, the efficient and composed Special Agent in Charge disliked anomalies of any sort. She demanded exactitude—of herself and her agents.

"This is a surprise," a deep male voice boomed as Appleton swept through a glass door into the conference room in the SAC's private suite of offices. United States Attorney General Bart Williams rose from his seat to his six-foot height and chuckled, "A whole five minutes behind schedule."

"Apologies, sir," Appleton replied sincerely, extending her right hand. "As you know, I'm typically punctual."

"No apology required." Accepting the firm handshake, Williams apprised at the Boston SAC with his deeply set, dark, almost black, eyes. "It's good to see you in person. Video conferencing is no match for a face-to-face discussion." The AG shrugged off his gray suit coat, which almost matched his short, gray hair, and rubbed his dark-skinned face as he sat. "We have much to discuss. Let's begin."

Appleton sank into a chair at the polished mahogany conference table. "Can you start, please, by explaining my role? Why me? Why Boston? From what you described to me on the phone, the matter of concern took place in New York, which I would think is the rightful jurisdiction. Shouldn't this case be assigned to Jacinda Burns in the New York Field Office?"

"Burns is a very capable Special Agent in Charge," Williams said, nodding. "But as soon as I heard about the meeting in New York, I flew from Washington to Boston to meet with you privately."

"In your voice message, you mentioned that—a meeting in New York. I assume you're going to divulge the details?"

"Of course." Williams pursed his lips. "The meeting occurred at about two in the afternoon today and—"

"Two in the afternoon? Earlier today? And you're already here now?" Appleton's voice cracked with incredulity.

"Yes," Williams replied. "As I said, I immediately reserved and then boarded a Department of Justice jet. My urgency is not misplaced, I assure you. We need to get ahead of this."

"Okay. Get ahead of what?"

"The meeting involved only two participants, Virgil Preston and Hanna Mo'Nique Isaac."

Ever the investigator, Appleton demanded, "If there were only two people there, how do you know about it?"

"Virgil Preston has been very forthright with me. He told me about the meeting, because I know him personally, and we've enjoyed a long relationship with each other. He's a solid citizen and an astute businessman. Exceedingly successful, in fact. With his brand of charisma, he'd be a good politician, except that he's quite abrupt." Shrugging, the

AG added, "Though that characteristic makes him transparent and honorable, in my opinion."

"I've heard of Preston," Appleton said contemplatively. "A colorful character who's always wearing a cowboy hat. The chief executive officer of the Texas-based tech company called, um—"

"Aximerva," the AG clarified. "It's a private company that manufactures and distributes semiconductors and computer parts, founded and wholly owned by Preston."

"Right," Appleton nodded. "Preston has been in the news recently with his outspoken opposition to the EPIC act—the, uh," the SAC looked at the ceiling for a moment, recalling the acronymized words before completing her sentence, "the Enhanced Production of Integrated Circuits bill, or something like that. Two-hundred-and-eighty-billion dollars to support the domestic semiconductor industry."

"You've got it exactly," the AG offered complimentarily. "Preston opposes the EPIC act because he thinks it's government overreach," Williams explained. "Aximerva doesn't need or want the assistance."

Appleton raised her left hand. "Whoa. I'm seeing a conflict here. EPIC is sponsored—and has been championed, negotiated, and maneuvered through both houses of Congress—by a Senator from California. By Merritt Coate." Appleton rubbed her chin. "He chairs the Committee on Homeland Security and Governmental Affairs. He's also quite popular—though he's registered as a Republican, he often crossed the aisle as a centrist."

Williams hummed his approval. "Mmm. Very good. You're correct, of course. Coate connects very well with voters. He talks often about his upbringing near the geographic center of the United States in Lansing, Kansas. He's tactful, thoughtful, and impeccably polite, and he uses his down-home charm to his significant advantage. He's also widely assumed to be a viable candidate for President, and a possible successor to the current, aging Oval Office occupant who is expected to serve only a single term."

Appleton clicked her tongue and shook her head reproachfully. "And the Senator's wife— the private investor, who's done quite well for herself in becoming a billionaire—that's Hanna Mo'Nique Isaac, and she is the individual who is meeting privately with Virgil Preston? What could they possibly be discussing?"

The AG pursed his lips. "Troubling, isn't it? Preston tells me that Isaac has been persistently attempting to buy Preston's company. At their meeting earlier today, he again declined her offer, but he informed me that she's applying a great deal of pressure."

Placing an elbow on the table and leaning forward, Appleton cautioned, "I'd be wary of crossing a line there, sir. This Preston may be a good guy, but that's immaterial. The Department of Justice and the FBI aren't intended to meddle in politics or business."

"That's true," the AG agreed. "But in this case, there's another angle—which is concerning. Look at it from a legal perspective. Is it lawful for a congressman, indirectly, via his wife as an intermediary, to silence his opposition with cash?"

"No."

"Exactly," the AG stated emphatically.

"But," Appleton argued, "is it lawful for the Department of Justice to interfere? For in this instance, if the congressman is at arm's length from his spouse's business dealings, there's no issue other than appearances." The tempo of her voice gained speed with rapid-fire questions. "Or is this all conjecture? Do you have any evidence? Have any laws been broken?"

The AG rubbed his scalp and admitted, "No. Not to my knowledge. And, yes, you've correctly identified a gray area. Do we act now to prevent what may be an illegal act, or do we wait for an illegal act to take place and then act?"

Appleton was silent as she considered the AG's dilemma.

The Attorney General, however, didn't wait for an answer. "The solution that I envision, SAC Appleton, resolves that gray area. But I'm sorry to say, it involves operating in a manner of absolute deniability, up against individuals that have an unsavory reputation for doing whatever it takes to achieve their goals. That, Appleton, may well be dangerous."

He compressed his lips to telegraph the importance of his message, and he spoke slowly. "I require someone independent for this investigation and given our prior work together as well as the discussions we've had about this sort of thing, I immediately knew that we must expeditiously formalize the outlines that we've toyed with before. You are the ideal individual for this assignment. And, given the outcomes that we've seen so far, I also would like to task one of your Special Agents that you oversee here in Boston. Ben Porter."

"I saw Porter at Volkov's memorial, earlier this afternoon," Appleton commented with an absent expression. "He's, um, detached. He's suffering."

"I don't mean this unkindly, but he needs to get over it. It's been eighteen months. You're authorized to do whatever it takes to push him along," the AG ordered.

"Okay," Appleton agreed. "I'll come up with something that will catalyze Porter. I've got to get him out of his funk."

"Good. Think quickly. Time is of the essence." He consulted his bulky wristwatch, squinting his dark eyes as he read the small number that indicated the date. "Today is October 21st. The vote on Coate's EPIC bill is scheduled for November 3rd. That gives us thirteen days." Tapping the face of the watch, he continued, "And in eighteen days, it's Election Day. The midterms. Don't think for a second that Coate's vote isn't purposely scheduled to precede Election Day by some happy coincidence."

"I see the significance of expediency," Appleton confirmed.

The AG sat back in his chair, placed his hands on the conference table, and rumbled, his eyes focused carefully on Appleton, "Bear in mind, SAC Appleton, what I will ask of you, and eventually of Agent Porter—well, I'm not certain that either one of you will like it."

# CHAPTER 5



**AFTER GRACE AND I** departed the simple memorial for Volkov, and after my sister's pep talk, we regrouped at her tidy, Cape-style home, only three easily walkable blocks from Walley Park.

We changed clothes for less formal outfits and headed to the market in Grace's equally tidy Subaru. We bought ourselves a bottle of chardonnay, a six-pack of beer, two New York strip steaks, two Idaho potatoes, salad makings, a couple of fresh-baked chocolate cookies, and some locally-made New England clam chowder. And, in memory of Volkov, a bottle of vodka.

Back at Grace's place, my sister shouldered me out of her way as she puttered around her kitchen, leaving me to tip back a few nicely chilled vodka cocktails as I sat at her kitchen island, idly tracing the veins on the spotless Carrara marble countertop. I suppose I was in a bit of a reverie when I heard a ceramic bowl tap onto the surface in front of me. "Potatoes are in the oven, so we got a little time before we need to grill the steaks. Let's have some chowder." She eyed me with sibling concern. "You look like hell, Ben. Want to talk about it? Or are you bound by confidentiality as usual?"

Placing her bowl on the island, she settled into the stool next to me.

I inhaled and muttered, "They're gone, so I suppose I can reveal a little bit."

"It's okay if you don't want to," she reassured me. "But you've been in a funk for well over a year. Maybe it's time to get it off your chest. Unload a little."

I drained my glass of vodka and stood. As I walked to the fridge, I considered Grace's invitation. *I do need to talk. Maybe she can help me. And who would she tell, anyway?*

Opening the fridge, I pulled out a chilled can of the local Narragansett beer. Reading the iconic slogan on the side of the sixteen-ounce can, I recited with friendly familiarity, "Hi neighbor," as I popped the top. Wiping the goofy expression off my face, I looked at Grace and added seriously, "We're in the cone of silence here. Okay?"

Grace grinned. "You realize the cone of silence wasn't really that effective. I mean, they couldn't hear each other. But, yeah, I got it. Who would I tell, anyway?"

"Exactly what I was thinking," I snickered. "Well, here I go, breaching national security." I plopped onto the stool and spooned chowder between my lips. It was creamy, with chunks of boiled potato and slivers of clams, seasoned with just enough salt and pepper for a tiny kick.

Licking my lips, I began. "A few years ago, the Bureau confiscated a 235-foot expedition-style superyacht from a criminal. The yacht was named *Almaz*. We used it for a few operations, and I lived aboard it. The boat was swank—think of a floating, mobile, high-tech platform equipped with computers and satellite connections and cars and helicopters and a few armaments . . ." My voice trailed off as I remembered details about the yacht that I'd once known as a home.

As Grace nodded her understanding, I sipped my Narragansett before continuing. "In March of last year, about eighteen months ago, the yacht was headed from America to Europe. Volkov, Lockwood, Macallister, and four crewmembers were aboard." I paused and looked at the countertop before sadly saying, "All seven of those souls drowned when *Almaz* sank in the North Atlantic Ocean."

"Holy shit," Grace whispered. "But—you—why weren't you there?"

"I can't go into that story of deception. Suffice it to say, I accepted a mission without doing my homework, and then . . . that happened. Seven people perished when the yacht broke apart and plummeted to the sea floor 11,370 feet below the relentless waves of the Atlantic." I snorted unhappily. "*Relentless*. My guilt has been relentless since then."

"I'm so sorry."

"It gets worse. A few weeks after the yacht sank, an automatically-deployed life raft—damaged, charred by fire, and empty—was discovered on a rocky beach in the Azores, some 175 miles south of the wreck site. The raft was flown to the United States for analysis."

Chowder forgotten and cooling, Grace was spellbound. "And? Was anything revealed?"

I stared at my sister and added quietly, "There was a streak made by a finger on the outside of the raft. There were fingerprints."

Grace gasped. "Prints? Someone got out before the yacht sank? Who?"

"Volkov and Lockwood."

"I don't understand," Grace confessed. "What happened to them? Where are they?"

I pushed my beer away. "The Bureau does this investigating stuff really well, of course. There was a classified, top-secret report, and it contained exhaustive detail that was backed up by simulations, even recreations, of what happened on the yacht and on the raft."

I inhaled and closed my eyes. "The Bureau concluded that Volkov and Lockwood reached the raft after *Almaz* sunk. They tried to grab for it—evidenced by the streak on the outside of it where they touched it—but they didn't make it onto the raft. They probably drowned within sight of salvation."

# CHAPTER

## 6



**BY UNSPOKEN AGREEMENT,** Grace and I paused my sibling therapy session as we completed our dinner preparations.

And by *our*, I mean Grace. Pretty much all I did was mope about lost hope.

Oh, and switch back to vodka.

As I poured myself a fresh round at the bar after we finished our meals, Grace asked, "I can't believe that happened. They drowned?"

"Yeah," I confirmed bitterly. "I'm sorry, but I can't go into the details of the report. It's—it's just awful." I sniffed involuntarily. "The report was issued this summer, well over a year after the, uh, incident, and the evidence was conclusive enough to show that they faced something called imminent peril. Typically, if someone goes missing, the law dictates that you wait seven years before they are presumed to be dead, but because of this imminent peril concept, the people aboard *Almaz* were declared as deceased." Sighing in conclusion, I said, "Hence, these funerals and memorial services were scheduled, and here we are."

Grace said reflectively, "I remember Volkov, of course. But—I never knew Miles Lockwood. When did you meet him?"

I closed my eyes. "2017. I was an unknown, and my interview with him, back then, put me on the map, so to speak, at the FBI. And two weeks ago, on the last day of September, Lockwood was laid to rest in Cohasset, Massachusetts."

Grace tipped back her wine glass in a contemplative manner. "What do you—what is there to—is there a casket? He was lost at sea. Did they . . . did you . . . bury him?"

I shook my head. "No. It was a memorial service at a headstone that overlooked the waters of Cohasset's brackish Little Harbor. It was pouring rain. The only thing I can remember was all the umbrellas." I paused and admitted, "It was a misty blur, because I was distracted, knowing that five days later, I'd be at a second service for Bradford Macallister."

Standing, I cleared our plates. Grace accepted the silent cue, and we tidied up without another word. It was only until we settled into her living room, her on the sofa and me on a recliner, and I clicked on the television, that my therapy session began anew.

The television was tuned to a news channel showing an interview. Since the audio was muted, I read the text that crawled across the bottom of the screen:

Senator Merritt Coate Discusses the EPIC Act

"Hey, Grace," I announced, "I saw that guy a couple of weeks ago."
"Who?"
"You know, this is a good way to watch a politician. Muted." I sniggered at my joke as I reexamined my empty glass. "This glass is defective. Must have a leak."

Grace giggled and offered, "I'll get this round of refills. But what politician are you talking about?"

"Look. On TV. It's that bigshot senator from California. Merritt Coate."

She laughed. "Oh, yeah, the sandy fox. He's good-looking. Doesn't look his age. What's he, like, late forties? And why are you interested in him?"

"I think he's early fifties," I replied, slurring my words a little. "They say he's a future candidate for president. And he was at Macallister's funeral. In Boston, a couple of weeks ago. It was a big deal." I paused. "You met Macallister once. You remember him, right?"

"Oh, sure. Your first boss at the Bureau. Natty guy, always well-coiffed and sharply dressed."

"Yeah. Macallister started as a Special Agent, then was a Supervisory Special Agent, served a stint as Acting Special Agent in Charge, and finally rose to the near-highest echelon of power as a Deputy Assistant Director working out of the Bureau's Washington, DC headquarters. When a company man with a resume like that goes down in service, the Bureau comes out en masse. You know, mourners, respect-payors, and quite a few folks who were only there to be seen."

"Sounds like a scene," Grace said, returning from the bar with two topped-off drinks, another highball for me, and a goblet of white wine for her.

"It was a throng of dark-suited people. A sea of sameness reflected by the flock of similar-looking black SUVs in the parking areas." I paused and squinted at my sister. "Do SUVs flock?" She cocked her head sideways as I slurped my vodka and continued, "Never mind that. It was an impressive turnout of power players and head honchos. All the bigwigs showed up."

Grace observed, "But Senator Coate is, like, beyond a bigwig. Why would he bother?"

"Entirely on point, if you ask me. He's the current majority leader of the US Senate, but he's a centrist, and so he's wildly and widely popular. He's also an outspoken supporter of law enforcement and the military, and he makes every effort to appeal to that base of voters." I waved my glass in the air to emphasize my point. "Ergo, there he was, at Macallister's funeral, surrounded by security staff and lessor senators, sitting in the front row."

Grace ogled the TV image of the famous, six-foot-two, surfer-tanned, sandy-haired Senator as he grinned broadly at the interviewer, a blonde woman who was a fixture on CNN. "I'd totally vote for him," Grace said firmly and happily. "Just what we need. A new face, a younger voice . . . and someone who crosses the aisle. And his wife—the one with the, like, lyrical name—Hanna Mo'Nique Isaac—she's got some serious style. Gorgeous and chic. I follow her on Insta."

"Yeah, I've seen her. She's also got some serious dough."

"Well, her husband Senator Coate likes you law enforcement types," Grace cackled. "Maybe you'll get a raise."

"I'll drink to that," I agreed, draining my cocktail. I weaved to the bar for a freshie. I dropped a handful of ice cubes in my glass, each one making a slightly different noise. *Clink. Clunk. Dink.* "Thank you. I needed this—you know, like an evening to unload." I poured out the last of the vodka, dribbling it over the frosty cubes. "I finally feel like I have clarity. Macallister and Lockwood—they got funerals and headstones. But Volkov—she got nothing."

"I don't follow, Benbro," Grace said softly.

"She deserves more," I replied, looking into my clear glass of clear vodka. "I owe her that." I looked up at my sister. "I've been dodging that feeling since the report was issued, but I recognize it, now. I need closure, and I feel like the only way I get that is to go to where that raft landed. To put a stone or something tangible there, for her."

With the strongest conviction I'd felt in a while, I announced, "I'm going to the Azores."

# SATURDAY
# OCTOBER 22, 2022

**TWELVE DAYS** *BEFORE THE VOTE*

# CHAPTER

# 7



**I'LL CONFESS** that as our convivial sibling evening progressed, I may have been too generous with my pours, eventually switching back over to beers. You know what they say—"beer before liquor, never sicker, but liquor before beer, you're in the clear"—but that definitely does not apply in quantity. I was not in the best of shape when I picked up my phone to call Appleton the following morning.

It didn't matter, though; she didn't answer—and that's when I realized it was a Saturday, and I figured even the SAC takes a day off occasionally.

I was wrong. Just before noon on Saturday morning, my phone chimed with a text from Appleton, who had presumably seen a missed call notification from me.

        Special Agent Porter, what's on your mind?

That Appleton addressed me as "Special Agent" indicated that not only was she in no mood for games, but also that the SAC expected me to engage fully in my duties in her Field Office. I replied:

        I'm ready to get back to work in earnest,

```
ma'am. But I'd like authorization to go to
the Azores first.
```

Her reply had been swift and succinct:

```
Why?
```

I took my time composing a response, deleting several attempts at explanation. In the end, I decided to be brief and to the point:

```
I want to see where the Almaz raft was
found.
```

This time, Appleton's response arrived several minutes after my transmission. I was beginning to sweat, though that could have been attributed to my hangover. As I guzzled yet another glass of water, my phone chimed with a text notification:

```
For what purpose? You don't have forensic
skills. You cannot contribute or add to
that investigatory work.
```

*Ouch*, I thought. The SAC and I enjoyed a solid, productive relationship, but even I wasn't above her typical perfunctory and cold attitude to her subordinates. Appleton was nothing if not efficient and direct.

But, before I could answer, my phone dinged again:

```
Or is this something personal?
```

So that she wouldn't have time to ask another question, I two-thumbed my reply as quickly as I could:

```
I'm sure the investigation was thoroughly.
But I Ned see all of it. Foreclosing.
```

I tapped the *Send* icon and muttered, "Stupid autocorrect." Tapping again, and racing the animated ellipse that indicated that Appleton, too, was typing, I sent:

```
* thorough. And I need to see all of it,
for closure.
```

The animated ellipse disappeared for a moment, and then reappeared as Appleton composed her reply:

```
I think I understand. I'll authorize the
trip.
```

Reading the words, I wiped my brow—this time, the sweat was definitely not induced by the booze.

*That was too easy,* I thought. *She didn't even argue.*

Knowing the SAC as I did, I was concerned; her normal reply would have demanded more details—a schedule, at the very least, or some other rationale to justify my request.

But then I thought, *Well, this is good news, right? She's gonna let me go. Show some foresight and offer gratitude.*

I typed:

```
    Thank  you  very  much.  I'll  create  an
    itinerary and send it to you on Monday.
```

I set my phone on the coffee table, and I was stretching my hand toward my glass when my device dinged with Appleton's reply:

```
    Don't  send  your  itinerary.  Bring  it  to
    me, and I'll decide if it works. Be in the
    office on Monday at 9. We have other items
    to discuss.
```

Pausing mid-reach, I stared at my almost-empty water glass dripping with accumulated condensation onto my sister's perfectly-lacquered coffee table, and I startled myself with the realization of a critically important item: *I forgot to use a coaster. My sister is going to kill me.*

Instead, I should have focused on Appleton's concluding sentence, because a missing coaster would be the least of my worries.

# SUNDAY
# OCTOBER 23, 2022

**ELEVEN DAYS** *BEFORE THE VOTE*

# CHAPTER

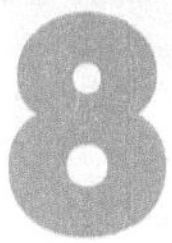



## *MID-MORNING — NEW YORK CITY*

**VIRGIL PRESTON SCOWLED** as the television production assistant balanced on her tiptoes as she fidgeted with the clip of a lapel microphone, attempting to secure the tiny device to Preston's thick, saddle-brown, herringbone-patterned blazer.

With a relieved sigh, the PA dropped to her heels and announced, "Done. Test guest audio."

A voice from the darkened rear of the television newscasting studio confirmed, "Guest audio, good level. Let's go."

The show host, dapper in a navy-blue suit with his dark, grayless hair gelled into impeccable order, and his tanned, clean-shaven cheeks just barely rouged with concealer, strode to the dais where two armchairs, upholstered in a tasteful, non-offensive, off-white fabric, were arranged before a green screen. He was eagerly trailed by yet another assistant who frantically tugged at the host's makeup cape, finally removing the protective item as the talent reached his guest.

Extending a hand, the host announced, "Mister Preston, I'm Cleveland Bauer." He threw his shoulders back, attempting futilely to match the six-foot-three-inch height of his guest, but knowing that once they were seated, the carefully calibrated seat height of the host's chair would compensate. "Good to see you on set again."

"I know who you are, Cleveland," Preston chided. "What's with the 'Mister Preston' nonsense? You pretendin' like we never met?"

Bauer laughed good-naturedly. "Sorry, sorry. Just a habit, I suppose. You know, Virgil, when you've been on television for as long as me, sometimes you just fall into the routine."

Preston's lips wrinkled into a faint smile. "Well, you're the best, Cleveland. And thanks for havin' me. It's mah pleasure to be here this morning."

"Well, Virgil, are you ready? Have a seat." Bauer offered a friendly gesture toward the opposite chair. "Make yourself comfortable. You know the drill."

The two men settled in the chairs as more assistants fretted with last-second wardrobe adjustments. A voice from the back of the set called, "Clear stage. Rolling in five—four—"

The remaining seconds were signaled by hand, and Bauer began enthusiastically, "Good Sunday morning, America. I'm your host, Cleveland Bauer, and I'm joining you for your morning cup of coffee with my guest, the chief executive officer of Aximerva, Virgil Preston. Welcome to the show, Virgil."

With confident and practiced ease, Preston smoothly and subtly turned his eyes toward the television camera that showed a red light above its round lens as he grinned. "Ah, it's mah honor to be with y'all today. Thank you for havin' me in your homes this mornin'." Angling his gaze to meet the eyes of the host, Preston added, "And thank you for having me on your program."

"Well, we've been together before, Virgil, but for those viewers who haven't tuned in previously, can you tell us a little about your company, Aximerva?"

"Sure can, Cleveland," Preston replied, crossing his legs to indicate that he was comfortable under the glare of the studio lights and in the unblinking eye of the camera. "Aximerva is an upstart in high-tech manufacturing. We build computer chips. Semiconductors, sometimes called integrated circuits." He spoke the words with an approachable emphasis on syllables—like *int-tah-great-ted*.

"Upstart, huh?" Bauer smiled. "Explain what you mean by that."

"Well, for one, Aximerva is a private company. I'm the sole shareholder. And we're relatively new. Been around only, what, twelve, thirteen years." Preston cocked his head sideways. "We're just the little guy compared to the big 'uns like Intel, or Nvidia, or even—from mah home state—Texas Instruments."

"A little guy, you said, but with a big reach. The, uh, Wall Street *Journal* termed Aximerva as *aspirational*," Bauer noted. "What do they mean by that?"

"I'm very proud of my company—my team—for never takin' no for an answer. That's why we, little Aximerva, are poised to do what none of the big companies are ready to do. We're currently sourcing our products from overseas, like my competition and my peers, but we're gonna change that. We're gonna be building a new plant, investing over twelve billion dollars right here in North America, and we're gonna build the most advanced semiconductors in the world—right here on our own soil."

"That's terrific," Bauer oozed. "And yet, that gets us to the heart of the recent controversy in Washington, and your—dare I say—strong opposition to the EPIC act."

Preston allowed a quiet guffaw as he readjusted his frame in the armchair. Seeking out the correct camera with a quick glance, he offered, "Ah, yes. EPIC. A tortured combination of words so that the big-shot legislators can give their bills a cutesy name to make 'em catchy—and media friendly." He waited for a half-beat before slowly, and somewhat mockingly, saying, "An Act for the Enhanced Production of Integrated Circuits."

Preston snorted his derision.

Bauer, ever the unbiased newsman, didn't bite, instead commenting evenly, "The EPIC bill has gotten quite a lot of non-partisan support in Congress, and seems to be very popular among voters because it contemplates a $280 billion investment by the United States government to bolster domestic production of semiconductors here in the homeland."

"Right." Preston rubbed his chin contemplatively. "The basic notion is to decrease reliance on overseas manufacturers, specifically China and Taiwan, but also some European countries. And the bill accomplishes that by, like so many government initiatives, by funneling bags of money into American companies in the form of subsidies, tax breaks, and outright cash."

Bauer was shaking his head. "Aximerva would surely benefit, but you're opposed. Why?"

Preston scoffed. "'Cuz what it amounts to is pork for votes, based on somethin' that the legislators know always rings true with voters, and that is American nationalism. They'll tell you that you can't buy a car because of the chip shortage. They'll tell you that you can't buy a TV 'cuz of the chip shortage. That prices go up 'cuz of the chip shortage. And of course, they've got a villain."

"And who is the villain?"

Preston made no effort to disguise his scorn. "The real villain is the lack of courage and investment by American companies, in their never-ending pursuit of quarterly results for Wall Street. You know, semiconductors made in the USA used to be almost forty percent of the worldwide semiconductor market—but that was back in the 1990s. Today, thirty years later, the US produces maybe twelve percent, and you know why? It's cheaper to get chips from China and Taiwan. So that's where we get 'em. The real villain is our insatiable greed for inexpensive consumer products. But that ain't the villain they want you to focus on."

Bauer, having of course prepped for the interview, feigned shock. "Well, who is that?"

"China and Taiwan, of course," Preston exclaimed. "The EPIC bill proposes to pump two-hundred-and-eighty *billion* dollars into domestic production. On the face of it, it sounds pretty simple. Dig down a little, though." He paused. "Everyone thinks of China as an all-powerful country, bent on world and economic domination. But consider this: America, for example, uses about twenty million barrels of oil each and every day. We produce most of that oil ourselves. China, on the other hand, uses fifteen million barrels each day, but they can only produce a fraction of that consumption. They import ten, maybe eleven million barrels every day."

Bauer shrugged. "We're not talking about oil, though. We're talking about advanced semiconductors."

"My point," Preston explained, "is that China ain't as strong as it appears from the outside. Their need to import energy is a good example. But they can offset that deficit because they've got the advantage of inexpensive labor and a docile, obedient workforce. But that's about it. China is not infallible."

"I see."

Bauer tried to interrupt his guest's monologue, but Preston continued apace. "And you know what, Cleveland? We can beat that with the right investments, here at home, by thoughtful people who understand that government pork is merely moving money from the taxpayer to the government and then back again—it's a shell game. It ain't a free market, driven by capitalism. Instead, it's a step toward socialism, and you gotta wonder how you wean companies off those government subsidies once they become addicted to them."

This time, Bauer was more aggressive, and the host managed to insert a question. "You mentioned free markets and capitalism, but isn't that the structure that led to this situation?"

"No, no, not exactly," Preston argued. "It takes investment, it takes courage to battle the Wall Street analysts who want instant results, and it takes patience. The resources are there—last year, in 2021, Intel posted net income of about twenty *billion* dollars. They can't figure out how to carve out the resources to build a twelve-billion-dollar factory?" The Texan snorted in obvious derision. "Aximerva doesn't have to report to Wall Street, and I've figured out how to do this on my own. And there's no reason—no reason whatsoever—for this EPIC act." He shook his reddened face and made sure to speak loud enough for the lapel mic to amplify the words that had become his catchphrase, "It's pork for votes."

Bauer clicked his tongue and put his elbows on his knees, appearing earnest and thoughtful. "But, Virgil, what's your solution?"

Preston grinned broadly and sat back into the off-white upholstered chair, signaling his confidence. "Aximerva is on the cusp of building an advanced semiconductor plant on the Texas-Mexico border. I'm making that twelve-billion-dollar investment we just talked about—without government hand-outs."

Ever the experienced TV showman, Preston leaned forward to make his follow-up points. "You know, labor rates in Mexico are competitive with labor rates in China, and my building site offers reasonable construction costs—and a footprint that is virtually immune to foreign influence. It is a secured supply chain. I have obtained the funding, and I have the support of the local politicians and residents." Preston winked at the red light above the appropriate camera lens. "Aximerva is ready to rock and roll."

"It's very exciting," Bauer agreed pleasantly. "Your conviction, your enthusiasm, and your efforts are readily apparent. Considering that, your opposition to the EPIC act does make a lot of sense."

"I don't need it. You don't need it. The American taxpayer don't need it," Preston grumbled loudly. "Hmph. The only folks who need it are the folks who want the votes—and I'm not gonna shy away from being specific. The person with the most to gain is none other than the sponsor of the bill, Senator Merritt Coate."

"Yes," Bauer purred smoothly, "it's become apparent that the Senator and you, Virgil, don't see eye-to-eye on this."

"I'll say it again, and I'll say it until pigs fly. Pork for votes. EPIC pork for Coate votes." Preston shook his head vigorously. "Cleveland, earlier you said that I had strong opposition to Coate and his pork. You're wrong; that word ain't strong enough. The word I'd pick is *vehement*. I got vehement opposition to EPIC." He spoke the word slowly. *Vee. Hem. Ent.*

"Your position does resonate with voters and politicians alike, Virgil. There's talk of delaying the vote, which is scheduled only twelve days from today."

Preston was nodding forcefully. "The public, the legislators—they need more time to understand what Coate is proposing. They'll see through the patriotic messaging, they'll understand that the timing of Coate's vote is just before a midterm election, and they'll realize that this is nothin' more than a boondoggle. You pump more government cash into the economy, inflation goes up, the taxpayer is on the hook—and to what end? Where does it end? And at the same time, Aximerva has a solution, the old-fashioned way, where we're gonna make these products ourselves. We're gonna profit from them, fer sure. But we don't need pork!"

Bauer inclined his head ever so slightly; in his earpiece, he could hear his producer's voice calling time on the interview. "It sure sounds like that postponing the EPIC vote would be a reasonable step."

"I'm a reasonable man," Preston drawled. "Senator Coate—well, he's an ambitious man, bent on his own self-promotion." He shrugged. "The voters should have an opportunity to see that for themselves."

Bauer plastered a smile on his face. "Thank you for being with us today, and for being so candid."

"It's mah pleasure, Cleveland," Preston concluded politely. "Mah thanks to you."

Bauer turned away from Preston and addressed a camera directly. "We're with Virgil Preston, CEO of Aximerva, and with the EPIC act due for a vote and passage by Congress in less than two weeks, on the third of November, it's clear that the standoff between Virgil Preston and Senator Merritt Coate continues with no end in sight—and with little chance of compromise or resolution."

The set lights dimmed, and Preston and Bauer shook hands in a hasty goodbye as assistants thronged to clear microphones and makeup.

In short order, Preston stepped outside the Manhattan newscasting studio, where he found his chauffeur-driven, black Lincoln town car idling curbside. Not a man to stand on pretentiousness, Preston opened the right rear door himself and settled into the roomy backseat. With a sigh that became a yawn, Preston released his neck muscles as his head dropped onto the plump headrest as he idly fingered the USB flash drive, garishly emblazoned with the name of a big-box electronics chain, that he protectively kept in his possession for two days, stashed on the Lincoln's rear seat center console only during his appearance on the Sunday morning television program.

Making a decision, Preston picked up the drive daintily, and he began flipping it dexterously with his fingers like it was a casino chip. "I'm runnin' outta time," he whispered under his breath as the Lincoln accelerated into the New York traffic on 6th Avenue. "I know what this thing contains, and I'm damn well screwed. I gotta talk to Bart Williams."

# MONDAY
# OCTOBER 24, 2022

*TEN DAYS* BEFORE THE VOTE

# CHAPTER

## *MORNING — BOSTON*

**IT'S ABOUT A** two-hour drive from Bristol, Rhode Island to the FBI Field Office in Chelsea, Massachusetts, but so that I could be fresh for a 9:00 A.M., Monday morning meeting with the Special Agent in Charge, I departed my sister's home yesterday, on Sunday, and I returned to my little condo, also located in Chelsea less than a mile from the Field Office.

Leaving Bristol on a quiet, sunny Sunday was a good move, I think. I was eager to get Appleton's sign-off on my proposed trip to the Azores, and my mood yesterday wasn't quite jubilant, but it was positive.

"Out and back," I promised Appleton in an email that I'd sent on Sunday, disregarding her instruction for me to bring her my proposed itinerary, breaking the rules again, as usual. My logic was that I'd put the data in front of her before our meeting so that she'd have time to digest it. After all, my travel plans were simple and brief in my email note. "Flight from Boston Logan to the Azores on Wednesday, spend one night, and return on Thursday."

Appleton, however, never replied, and as the day wore on, and as I checked and rechecked my email at home in Chelsea last night, I got more and more unpleasant.

*She's changed her mind,* I decided. *She's ghosting me.*

Then, of course, I made up a set of facts to make it worse.

*She never intended to approve my trip. She was just toying with the idea.*

I capped off my anxiety by blaming myself.

*I should have followed her orders. I should not have sent the email. That's why she's going to reverse course and deny her approval. She's gonna punish me for my insolence.*

Monday dawned as a gray and drizzly October fall day, the weather as reflective as my persona as I swiped my ID card and entered the Chelsea building, a 286,000 square foot, concrete-and-glass edifice to the American taxpayer. Appleton's office was on the top floor of the building, befitting her status as the Special Agent in Charge, and I decided to hike the stairs, foregoing the elevator in the seemingly never-ending quest to keep weight out of my waistline.

I didn't consider that the time it would take to climb eight floors would give me an opportunity to stew over *Almaz,* which turned my thoughts to Anastasia Volkov.

Back when I met her, in 2017, I didn't consider myself to be in her league. Me being a bit overweight and being insecure about my looks, I remained in awe of her.

Enter: seven deadly sins number one, lust.

Then Volkov tried to murder me. That was a buzzkill.

That, of course, triggered a second sin: wrath. For obvious reasons, I was angry at her when she reentered my life. Her goal, I realized too late, was redemption. But I was too defensive, too stubborn, and I think that may in fact have pushed her closer to Miles Lockwood. When Lockwood and Volkov began dating—soon sleeping with each other—I was jealous.

Deadly sin number three: envy.

And then, she drowned. Lockwood, Macallister, the crew—all of them, because I was bent on solving a case on my own, and I never objected to them leaving. If only they'd stayed with me, for a few days, they'd be alive. I could have forced that outcome; Appleton would have supported my logic, and Macallister would have backed down.

I'm really racking up the sins when you add in pride.

*Four out of the seven deadly sins*, I thought morosely, stepping into the executive suite on the eighth floor and selecting a chair at the center of the twelve-seat table within Appleton's empty, glass-walled, private conference room.

*The very least that I can do is to grieve on that beach—the closest I'll be able to get to the site of the wreck. And now, Appleton is going to dash that dream.*

With a whoosh, the glass door swished open, and the SAC entered with her usual grace, gliding across the carpet. Dressed in a tasteful, lavender purple pantsuit, the outfit probably selected as a contrast to the gloomy gray outside, Appleton perched in the chair at the head of the table.

"Move down here, Porter," she ordered, pointing at the chair immediately to her left. "This is ridiculous to have you so far away."

I complied, of course, moving two seats over and muttering, "Sure, sure."

I fingered the polished mahogany surface of the table. No veneers up here on the executive level.

Appleton cleared her throat. "Let's get started. I read your itinerary, but I'd like to delve further, please. What's the real purpose of this expedition?"

"In a word, closure," I said, hoping that leading with simplicity would ensure success.

"Hmph," Appleton grumbled. "Some might call it a waste of time. But I know your history with the people who lost their lives on *Almaz*. I know it's something you need to do." Her voice was professional but kind.

Modulating the sympathy out of her tone, she added decisively, "So go. But wrap it up in the two days that you proposed on your itinerary. Because when you get back, we've got work to do. We have a significant new matter to pursue, nothing like the run-of-the-mill cases that I've assigned to keep you busy while you mourned."

Her directness took me aback. *I didn't realize that she'd been protecting me for eighteen months.*

Appleton continued speaking, "You, Porter, have been specifically selected for this case. The paperwork with your name on it is in process."

"Really? What can you tell me about it?" I couldn't help myself. In a way, I dreaded going overseas, because I knew this would be the end. I'd be forced to put my despair in a box in the back of my mind—but at the same time, I was also excited and intrigued by her tease of a new case.

*Conflicted*, I guess.

Jennifer Appleton caught my eye and stated, "We will continue this discussion tomorrow. Meet me at my house in Salem on Tuesday evening."

"Okay," I said with some hesitation. "Why then? Why not now?"

Appleton replied in a matter-of-fact tone. "I have a full schedule today. Indeed, that schedule is even more chaotic than usual because, Porter, you need to know that as of 5:00 P.M. Friday, at the end of this week, I will be stepping aside as the Special Agent in Charge of the Boston Division Field Office. And shortly thereafter, you will step aside with me."

# CHAPTER 10

## *EVENING — JERSEY CITY, NEW JERSEY*

**"I'M JUST TAKING** *a Greyhound on the Hudson River Line."*

A leathery-skinned, pockmarked, mustachioed man, in his forties or fifties, held up both hands and waited expectantly until a cymbal trilled.

The man's hands dropped. He fingered imaginary black and white keys, air-playing the iconic piano riff of Billy Joel's hit song as it swelled to a crescendo while he sang along to the last notes of the ballad.

*"'Cause I'm in a . . . New York state of mind."*

Rocco Barbutero grinned lopsidedly, exposing coffee-stained, crooked teeth, as he enjoyed the fade-out of the melody—until his phone rang with an obnoxious clang.

"Fuck is that?" He scowled; his *Piano Man*-inspired reverie interrupted. Glancing at the tiny outward-facing screen of the dated Nokia flip-phone device, he muttered, "Shit."

Snapping the device open, he barked, "Yeah, hello Mizz Isaac."

"Good evening, Rocco," Hanna Mo'Nique Isaac purred. "I hope I'm not interrupting anything."

"Nah. I'm good. Just havin' a sandwich." Barbutero snatched up the half-eaten bacon sandwich that awaited him; his go-to, British-inspired, simple pairing of four strips of lightly crisped bacon squeezed between two slices of buttered toast.

He took a small bite as Isaac asked, "It's late for supper, no?"

Chewing, Barbutero managed a mumbled reply. "Yeah, kinda. Still, I gotta go through my orders for tomorrow." Barbutero scanned the dimly lit space, a cavernous warehouse in Jersey City about four miles west of Lower Manhattan. Five box trucks sat under a smattering of bare bulbs, backed into interior loading dock bays within the confines of the high-ceilinged warehouse. The cabs of the trucks were painted a glossy white and were polished to perfection, as were the wheels—gleaming silver and free of road grime and brake dust. All five vehicles featured the recognizable bulge of a refrigeration unit sprouting from the tops of the cargo boxes, which were lettered in gold leaf on each side:

```
Jersey City Provisions
Fine Foods and Prime Beef since 2007
```

"I'm calling to request your services for tomorrow," Isaac said, leaving no room for disagreement in her tone.

"Hang on." Barbutero returned the sandwich to a chipped porcelain plate on his cheap metal desk, placed on a small, raised platform opposite the truck bays, which faced a giant wall of glinting stainless steel doors that led to a series of walk-in refrigerators and freezers.

Grumbling as he pawed through two pages on a clipboard, Barbutero said, "Yeah, I can help you out. Tomorrow is a Tuesday. It won't be too busy. Not like the end of the week, ya know. Where?"

"The usual. Bar Virtuosismo."

"Ah, fuck."

Isaac tittered. "I know, Rocco, you're not a fan of the chef. However, I'm certain you can handle him."

"He's not due for a delivery 'til Thursday."

Isaac sighed loudly, to make it clear that she would not accept an excuse. "Move up the delivery to tomorrow, please. You know the routine."

"It's short notice."

"I'll double my usual fee."

"Yeah, all right," Barbutero grunted. "How many, um, ah, guests?"

"One. His name is Virgil Preston."

Barbutero's bushy eyebrows raised. "Okay. I'll make it work."

"Thank you, Rocco," Isaac sang, and she terminated the call.

Barbutero snapped the flip phone closed and leaned back in the flimsy, vinyl-covered office chair, a relic of the fifties, probably. It creaked as he spun lazily, head back, eyes closed.

After a moment of contemplation, he sat forward at the desk and scribbled a notation on the clipboard, ensuring that his schedule for provisions deliveries to the better eateries in Manhattan was precisely coordinated—and accommodated the slight alteration that he'd just agreed to.

Then, the former butcher picked up his Nokia, scrolled through his contacts, selected one, and pressed the green dial button.

# TUESDAY
# OCTOBER 25, 2022

**NINE DAYS** *BEFORE THE VOTE*

# CHAPTER

## *LATE MORNING — NEW YORK CITY*

**WEARING A LIGHT BROWN,** camel-colored suit, Virgil Preston paced the gray carpet of his 21st-floor suite at The Pierre, a five-star hotel on Fifth Avenue overlooking the southern end of New York City's Central Park. The view from the private outdoor terrace was incomparable; the City skyline wrapped the green space of the park beyond a tall, black iron railing, but Preston was tired of the urban noise of incessant honking and intermittent sirens. Instead, he chose to remain indoors in the suite's sitting room.

The CEO of Aximerva glanced at the glass coffee table that was the centerpiece of the sitting room. Visible through the glass was a bland cardboard box, opened hastily, with bits of white foam packing material scattered on the carpet. Above, on the shiny surface of the table, an entry-level Dell laptop sat open. Sprouting from one side of the computer was a USB flash drive, garishly emblazoned with the name of a big-box electronics store.

Following his instructions from Isaac, Preston had reluctantly purchased the computer the day after their discussion on her rooftop terrace in the West Village. He hadn't even bothered to unpack the computer's charging cord, only using the machine once on Saturday to review the contents of the drive, and then once again this morning.

Bending to the table, Preston yanked the USB stick from the machine unceremoniously. Examining it scornfully, he scowled before dropping it into his right-front pants pocket.

"Sonuvabitch," he grumbled as he sank into the suite's overscale, chocolate brown, tufted leather Chesterfield sofa. Reaching inside his suit coat pocket, he withdrew his iPhone. Scrolling through the messaging app, he found the most recent text from Attorney General Bart Williams, and Preston composed the latest entry in the thread:

```
I'm meeting Isaac for lunch today. I'm
afraid I'm out of options.
```

Stewing, Preston waited for a reply, eventually standing to begin retracing his pacing path, from the French doors that led to the terrace, past the Chesterfield, past the two white club chairs with their contemporary, exposed tubular steel frames, and back. The carpet was mottled with the pointed-toe, square-heel footstep patterns made by his dark brown cowboy boots.

Preston lost count of his pacing circuits by the time his device signaled a reply.

```
You need to hold out longer. You're the
only voice that can stop EPIC. Or at least
pause it.
```

Reading the message, Preston snarled to himself, "Easy for him to say."

He tapped out a reply:

```
I can't. The lenders are threatening to
pull the loan approval because of EPIC.
They're not wrong. I will be underwater as
soon as it passes since I've clearly stated
that I won't accept any EPIC subsidy.
```

Williams' reply came quickly.

```
You've got to protect Aximerva.
```

Preston sighed and typed:

```
    I'll see what I can do, but I am not
    hopeful. Can you schedule a call at 2pm?
```

The device chimed with a thumbs-up emoji from the Attorney General.

Shoving the phone back into his inside breast pocket, Preston strode into the suite's bedroom, a sunny and bright corner room with high ceilings and two windows flanked by massive, thick, heavy drapes. He grabbed his buff-colored cowboy hat off the unmade bed and took one last look at the king-sized bed's headboard, upholstered in an orangey-looking fabric. "Fruity color," he mumbled. "What is it? They'd probably call it tangerine, but, dammit, it's orange."

Preston fled the suite, relieved at last to be one step closer to the NetJets flight that would take him from nearby Westchester Airport back home to Texas. His luggage had been retrieved by a bellman earlier, and outside at the curb, he knew he'd find the waiting Lincoln town car.

One more obligation—lunch with Hanna Mo'Nique Isaac—and Preston figured that he could finally disappear from the chaos, noise, soot, and smells of bustling New York City.

# CHAPTER 12



**IN A BASEMENT** restaurant within Manhattan's SoHo neighborhood, Virgil Preston pushed his plate of pasta Bolognese toward the center of the crisp, starched, white tablecloth in disdain, wiping his tanned, weatherworn chin with a blood-red napkin. "Y'all won't get away with this," he grumbled in a gravelly, Texan drawl. "And what is this excuse of a meal?"

His impeccably dressed lunch companion laughed. "This establishment, I'll have you know, is the *it* spot in New York at the moment. It's called Bar Virtuosismo. Genuine Italian recipes infused with a Californian flare."

"They never heard of a steak, huh?"

Hanna Mo'Nique Isaac's enthusiastic tone didn't wane the slightest. "Farm-to-fork and all organic. And the décor?" She waved an arm lazily about. "Understated but exquisite. Look around. This place is *so* European in style, but it's still so New York—a SoHo basement bistro with high windows and a tin ceiling—and yet the artwork—contemporary and just damn good." She sighed with genuine contentment. "It's all divine. It's been open only for a short while, but dare I say that when the media gets wind of this place, Chef Isola will go from nobody to celebrity overnight."

Preston slouched in his chair, tugging at his camel-brown suit coat. He sighed audibly, unimpressed. "I don't care," he complained. "And I don't care for what amounts to extortion."

"Call it what you want, Virgil." She poked a fork at her kale and beet salad absently, before dropping the fork onto the plate with a clatter. Reaching to the vacant chair next to her, Isaac lifted the sheaf of papers that sat upon it. Placing the stack on the table, she daintily sorted it into three separate, smaller, half-inch-thick piles that had been secured with bulky, black binder clips. "It's a simple purchase and sale agreement. It's the same document you refused to sign on Friday," she explained. "Your signature goes on the last page. Three originals. One for you, one for me, and one for future duplication."

Preston pulled a gold-plated pen from the inside breast pocket of his suit coat. "I don't need to take a copy. Just wire the money."

Isaac watched Preston as he scrawled his signature on the first copy. The instant the pen lifted from the paper, she made a show of tapping at her smartphone before announcing, "The transfer has been initiated." Rotating the device so that the screen was clearly visible to Preston, she added, "See for yourself."

He grunted. "Yeah, okay." Preston signed the second copy and warned, "Listen, Hanna, you got one over me—but let me caution you this: you and your Senator husband may be powerful folk, but you ain't the law. And you ain't above the law."

As he signed the final, third document set, Preston scoffed, "You're buying me off—blackmailin' me—so that your husband's bill gets passed. I got other plans for that bill. That—uh, whaddya call it?—that steaming pile of shit."

Preston shoved his chair back and stood to his full, six-foot-three-inch height, reaching to the chair to his right and retrieving the buff-colored cowboy hat that he had graciously doffed when he sat down at the table, forty minutes earlier.

"Virgil, don't threaten me—or my husband," Isaac hissed through clenched teeth.

Ever the Southern gentleman, using his two fingers on his right hand, Preston courteously tipped his hat at Isaac. "Ma'am," he said politely.

Spinning on a heel of a shiny, brown leather boot, Preston strode toward the door that led to the bar area of the bistro restaurant, which also served as a lobby or foyer to the main stair up to the street level. His stomach growled as he thought, *That pretentious lady booked the whole damn place so she could work me over in private. The hell with that.*

In his wake, behind him, Isaac nodded to the waiter who hovered discretely in a corner. His attention was immediate, and she pointed at the double swinging doors to the kitchen.

The waiter stepped forward, cleared his throat, and called, "Sir? Sir!"

Preston paused mid-stride and half-turned to face the voice. He reached into the left front pocket of his camel brown slacks and withdrew a bulging money clip. "Shee-it, really? I figured she'd pick up the tab," he growled, pointedly ignoring Isaac as he addressed the waiter, a leathery-skinned, pockmarked, mustachioed man, in his forties or fifties.

The waiter held up a hand. "No, no. Not like that." He grinned lopsidedly, exposing coffee-stained, crooked teeth. "It's just that they're, ah, doin' construction work on the street out front. It's a mess. You're better off using the back stairs. Right this way, sir, through the kitchen."

"Alright," Preston replied. As the waiter pushed one of the swing doors open, Preston sniffed and said amicably, "I smell bacon. You got any proper food back there? Like maybe a steak sandwich?"

"Of course, sir. I used to be a butcher. I'm good with a knife."

"You can rustle somethin' up for me?" Preston's voice sounded a cheerful, hopeful note.

"Yessir," the waiter confirmed.

As the duo slipped into the kitchen, Isaac rose from her seat and adjusted her pearl gray blazer before picking up a gris perle, ostrich leather Hermès handbag with gold hardware. Slipping the strap of the bag into the crook of her arm, she headed for the bar, seemingly oblivious to a loud crash that suddenly sounded from the kitchen.

The forty-eight-year-old woman climbed the main stair of the bistro to the quiet street above, where a sole vehicle idled. A black-clad chauffeur opened the right rear door of the black Cadillac Escalade, and Hanna Mo'Nique Isaac disappeared into the luxury vehicle.

# CHAPTER 13



**I DIDN'T WANT** to jeopardize my planned trip to the Azores, so when yesterday morning's meeting with Jennifer Appleton concluded, I paid strict attention to the orders that she issued in a sober, stern voice, "Meet me at my house in Salem on Tuesday evening."

I'd been to Appleton's home several times, and I knew what to expect when I arrived after dark on this Tuesday evening: a pristine, immaculately restored white Colonial home in historic Salem, about fifteen miles north of Boston. Inside, I'd find tasteful décor and furnishings with sort of a contemporary vibe, a modern kitchen, and, hidden below the house in a subterranean basement bunker, a fully operational command center. Appleton received me, as usual, in her living room, pointing to one of the impeccably white club chairs that sat side by side.

In the course of pursuing a previous case, I agreed to falsify my employment papers from the Bureau to create a deep cover for myself, so as I settled into the chair, I began, "You said yesterday morning that you were 'stepping aside.' This bit again? Sure, why not!" I emphasized my final words with an exaggerated wink—wrongly assuming that Appleton was employing the same charade.

My wink and factiousness turned out to be rather inappropriate. Appleton's facial expression didn't change the slightest. "On the contrary, Porter, what I have in mind is significant. And by now, you should know me well enough to recognize that I select my words carefully."

Suitably chastised, I admitted, "Yeah, it's a very specific phrase. 'Stepping aside.' Why the need for circumlocution?"

Appleton smiled thinly. "Quite a vocab word there, Porter." The former SAC lowered herself into the chair opposing mine and explained, "I've secured a new assignment. The Department of Justice has engaged me as an independent investigator."

She paused and shifted her body in the chair slightly, signaling a carefully worded lecture. "As you know, Porter, the FBI is but one of the many organizations that report to the DOJ. The Drug Enforcement Administration, the US Marshalls, the Bureau of Prisons, the Bureau of Alcohol, Tobacco, Firearms, and Explosives—those are all examples of agencies within the DOJ structure. Then, of course, the Department of Justice has its litigation side. Antitrust, civil rights, the Solicitor General. That's not a complete list, and even in addition to those many sub-organizations, there are smaller branches within the DOJ, including something called the National Security Division. Ever heard of it?"

"No, ma'am," I admitted. The organization chart of the US government apparatus is, to put it kindly, complex. There are org charts buried within other org charts, many with overlapping responsibilities, some which are, in my opinion, completely redundant. There is probably a Department of Redundancy Department somewhere in that structure. Who would ever know?

Appleton didn't seem to notice that I was distracted as she continued, "My newly formed investigative task force of the DOJ will report to the Operations Section of the Office of Intelligence within the National Security Division. At least, that's how it will appear, if it's ever noticed in the Federal Register amongst millions of other entries. However, I will report directly to the Attorney General. And I am seeking individuals to build out my team."

Grinning, Appleton added quickly enough to forestall any questions from me, "Porter, my new team will be referred to as the Department of

Justice Q-Group. Would you care to discuss a position?"

I thought, *This was no longer a farcical cover story discussion.*

Appleton was pitching a real scenario that would compromise my status as an agent with the FBI. I'd trained hard, and worked even harder, for my badge; it was a years-long accomplishment.

"Q-Group? That sounds like something out of a movie," I said, slightly dodging Appleton's direct question.

Appleton grinned even more widely. "I thought you'd appreciate it, as it's sort of a play on Q-branch, the original name of the quartermaster's division in the Bond books. However, I selected the letter Q for a completely different reason. It's a reference to the first letter of the Latin phrase, *quis custodiet ipsos custodes*."

I cocked my head sideways. "I've heard that before. It means, *who watches the watchers.*"

"Well done, Porter," Appleton offered, wiping the smile off her face in acknowledgment, perhaps, of my scholarliness. She clarified, "The literal translation of the words, penned by the Roman poet Juvenal, is *who will guard the guards themselves*. I think it's an appropriate description of the task assigned to us by the Attorney General, as we will be investigating, often deep in the background, the thorny issues that tend to arise at the highest levels of power."

As intrigued as I was, I hedged. "This is all very sudden. Can I get some more context? And then have some time to think about it?"

Appleton nodded. "That's a reasonable request. You'll have two or three days. As I'm sure you recall, you're flying out of town tomorrow."

"Yeah, I remember," I confirmed, somewhat sarcastically.

"Here's the deal that I struck with the AG," Appleton continued. "It's been casually in the works for a while, as it was something we'd been exploring since last March, for well over a year. However, at the AG's request, it became very urgent just days ago. He actually flew up from Washington, at a moment's notice, on Friday. I met with him after Volkov's service, and among other things, he specifically requested your participation."

"I'm flattered."

"You're a good fit," she said sincerely. "You see, the AG occasionally requires this type of independent investigatory work. It's not at all temporary. To protect my employment, the AG and I have agreed to an initial five-year term for the Q-Group task force operation. Naturally, there are ways to extend the assignment. There are also ways to end it, but to protect me from, say, a future AG, it will require an order from the White House to terminate the agreement."

I whistled softly. "That's high-level stuff."

"Yes," she agreed. "We will operate outside the confines of the usual bureaucracy, reporting to the Attorney General only—unless there is a case whereby the AG should be recused, in which case we will report only to the president."

I raised my eyebrows. "You've used the word *we* a few times," I noted.

The former SAC smiled. "I fully expect you'll accept."

In response, I offered a compromise. "Can I say that I accept in principle but reserve a final decision based on a bit more detail? Honestly, I'm not sure I am ready to just give up being an agent of the FBI."

"Yes. Yes, that works. You've accepted in principle. Noted." Appleton nodded ceremoniously before continuing, "You've also raised a good point. You're not giving up anything. We will retain the powers of an FBI agent. Badge, gun, the ability to arrest, and the status of the position. But much like the FBI serves as the protective detail for the Attorney General, we will operate in parallel with the Bureau and with Justice."

"Like in our own sandbox," I suggested.

Appleton scoffed. "Only if that sandbox towers above the other sandboxes. I see us more standing atop our own pillar, as part of the law enforcement community, but with a specific mandate to investigate issues of critical national importance to the Attorney General."

"Is this legal? I mean, sounds to me like the AG is stepping around the mandate of the FBI while he's also using his position to directly benefit his needs. Aren't there rules against that sort of fiat without oversight?"

"Yes, there is precedent against this type of structure. I'm not going to say it's illegal. I wouldn't have accepted if that was the case. But one might say it's exigent and therefore sanctioned by other standards." Appleton smirked. "I'm surprised you're expressing these reservations, Porter. Typically, you have no hesitation dodging the bureaucracy."

"You got me there," I replied, laughing lightly. "Can you tell me about the case that caused you to accept the position and the structure?"

Appleton closed her eyes for an instant before saying, "The background of the case is in the public domain. It's the intricacy of the case that I cannot disclose to you until we have a formal agreement. I'll be busy wrapping up my obligations in Boston for the remainder of this week, so let's meet on Saturday, a day after you return from the Azores. We'll get right into the weeds then, because we're on a tight schedule. How's that sound?"

"Sounds good," I replied.

Appleton, of course, couldn't know that she only elevated my anxiety when she eyed me directly, her stare reinforcing her message. "I can disclose that you will be dealing with people in the highest levels of government and business. They can be dangerous, they can be wily, and they are well-informed. I hope you're up to it. Because, in your current state of mind, you're not."

# CHAPTER 14



**HIS LATEX-GLOVED HANDS** carefully clasped behind his back, FBI Special Agent Danny Peck leaned forward to examine a faint, reddish stain on a maple butcher block. Straightening, he shrugged and glanced sideways and downwards at a technician suited in a white coverall.

Behind the pair, an Italian-accented voice complained loudly, "Are you finished? I have to prep the Tuesday night dinner service."

Peck grumbled a non-committal response to the stocky, pasty-faced, white-aproned chef. "Yeah. No. Look, settle down, Chef Isola. Gimme the time I need." The Special Agent poked at the big cutting board, a giant block of wood standing on four substantial stainless steel legs, as he turned his attention to the tech. "No way we're getting this thing outta here without help."

"Not up those stairs," the technician replied. "And not to be uncooperative, furniture moving isn't part of my job description."

Peck smiled slightly at the smaller woman, thinking, *Nor would she be much help lifting*, but he didn't verbalize his thoughts, instead addressing the chef, "Chef Isola, I'm gonna call this in, and then maybe you can have your kitchen back. Got it?"

Looking at the pale, five-foot-nine, grim-faced, balding agent with a badge prominently clipped to the left lapel of his brown checked sports coat, the chef understood it was a rhetorical question, and he exhaled with exasperation, turning his palms upward. "Okay, okay."

Peck addressed the technician. "You want to finish documenting the scene?"

Knowing that this, too, was rhetorical, the technician nodded.

The agent pulled a smartphone from the inside breast pocket of his sports coat and jabbed at the screen as he wound his way through the kitchen to the stair to the street, taking a better look around the commercial kitchen. Reaching the steps, he paused and rotated to face the kitchen, and his side of the conversation was audible to both the tech and the chef.

"Yeah. Hey. I'm at the place. Bar Virtuosismo. Some fancy basement bistro in SoHo that the finance bros like."

Beat.

"Right. Probably fifty bucks for an entrée."

Snort.

"Anyway, the place is empty. No sign of this Virgil Preston."

Pacing back toward the technician and the chef, Peck's brow furrowed as he listened for a moment and then said, "Lemme run through the timeline with you, boss. I got it written down." With his free, phone-less hand, he pulled a small notepad from his coat's outside pocket. Laying the pad on a stainless-steel prep table, and with the tech looking over his shoulder, Peck began, "Okay, Preston lunched here at noon, but then he missed a conference call with the Attorney General scheduled at two. The AG's office tried to contact Preston directly and via his office with no success. I've been here since about four and forensics arrived about an hour later."

Nodding at the forensics technician, Peck concluded, "It's now 6:00 P.M., and my suspicions have been confirmed. We might not be looking for a missing person. There could be foul play here." He placed his phone on the shiny table next to his notepad and tapped the speakerphone icon. "I'm putting on the chef. His name is Isola. Chef, you're gonna be talkin' to the Special Agent in Charge of the FBI's New York Field office, so don't make shit up."

He pointed at the chef and ordered, "Tell 'em what you told me."

Isola adjusted his toque. "Ah, let's see. We were booked for a private lunch and—"

"With whom?" The voice from the speaker was female, clipped, and insistent. "This is FBI Special Agent in Charge Jacinda Burns, by the way. And I already know who your guest was, but I want to understand every detail. Don't leave anything out. Okay?"

The chef continued in a monotone, "I usually open for dinner service only, but I sometimes make exceptions. For this guest, I always accommodate, because it's Hanna Mo'Nique Isaac. I don't say no to her."

"Has she done this before? You're the owner of this place, right?"

"*Sì. Sì.* I've hosted four or five private lunches for *Signora* Isaac. She pays well, she brings her own waiter for privacy, and all I have to do is prepare a meal."

Peck held up a hand. "I'm gonna need names and dates for those lunches."

"Whoa," Burns commanded over the phone. "Not only that, but also a name for this waiter. You allow someone to work in your place that you don't know?"

Isola's pale face flushed as he stuttered, "No, no, no. I—I—yes. *Signora* Isaac insists. She has her man serve the table. I think he's—he's—he's—"

"He's what?" Peck demanded.

Shrugging, the chef replied, "A body double. No, no, no! A bodyguard. I think her private waiter is also her bodyguard."

"Okay." Burns sighed, her exasperation evident even through the phone's speaker. "Tell me about Isaac's lunch companion."

"He was a big, tall man with a Southern accent. I didn't ask his name, and I only saw him when the doors to the kitchen were open."

"Let's move on. Tell 'em about the delivery," Peck ordered.

The chef scowled. "There's nothing to tell. I plated the lunch dishes, and the waiter served them. I made something for myself, and then I got a call from a supplier that they had my delivery. I went upstairs to the truck on the street to inspect it."

Peck asked, "That's what you normally do?"

"Of course. I want to make sure I'm getting the best quality and a complete order before I let the delivery guys lug it down the stairs."

"That's also normal?"

"*Sì*. It's a good company. They take care of me." The chef scratched his chin. "I went up to the street and spent a few minutes in the truck. It was *buono*, so I signed for the order. The men brought it down and then offered to help carry out the trash."

Peck pointed at the swinging door to the dining room. "And by then, the lunch was over. The patrons had left?"

"*Sì*."

"Where was the waiter?"

The chef grunted. "The meal was over, so he was done. He left when the delivery guys left. I got the dishes off the table and began cleaning up. That's when I saw the stain on the block and noticed the missing knife."

The phone crackled. "You saw a new stain in your kitchen, and a knife was missing—but you didn't call the police. Why not?"

Isola rolled his eyes to the ceiling. "I—I—I don't know. It's a knife. I thought at first it was misplaced. And my staff was due to come in at four to prepare the dinner service. I thought I'd ask them, then. But then this man—*Signore* Agent Peck—arrived, and he told my staff to wait outside. They're probably still up there, freezing on the street."

Peck leaned toward the phone. "I'm gonna need a truck and some movers. Chef claims that he didn't use the cutting block to prep for tonight's dinner service, and tech thinks the stain is blood."

A deep male voice rumbled from the small device. "This is Attorney General Bart Williams, and this is terribly concerning, Agent Peck. You'll get the support you've asked for and more. You're running the scene, and the moment additional personnel gets there, have them canvas the street for cameras. I want a visual of that waiter as soon as possible, and then I want an identity."

Peck nodded, even though the caller couldn't see him. "Yes, sir."

"Good," the voice boomed. "I want images of Preston and Isaac as well. Times, angles, everything. We need to know what's going on, but I'm afraid that we must acknowledge that Preston is now a missing person. Someone of his position doesn't just disappear."

The call screen on the device went blank; the connection had been terminated by the receiver. Peck squinted at the chef and asked, "How much for, um, I dunno, a salad? Like a Caesar?"

The chef's eyes widened, and he replied proudly, "We prepare our Caesar tableside, and my recipe, my version of the original from Tijuana, does not use lemons. I use limes, as it should be." Isola sniffed and added defensively, "It's thirty-eight dollars."

Agent Peck whistled. "Well, at those prices, you can probably afford to take the night off. Tell your staff that you're closed for dinner tonight." He turned to the tech and said, "Don't let anyone touch that butcher block. I'm going to lock the doors until reinforcements arrive."

The technician whispered, "That was really the AG on the phone?"

"I guess so. The SAC must have conferenced in the AG." Peck spun in a slow circle, taking in the gleaming commercial kitchen, dressed in stainless and floored with spotless quarry tile. "It's like a hospital operating room in here, but in less than an hour, it's gonna be crawling with investigators." He rapped his gloved knuckles on the butcher block. "And I bet my pension that this is exhibit one."

# CHAPTER 15



*EVENING — SALEM, MASSACHUSETTS*

**INSIDE HER IMPECCABLY** restored, white-painted, Colonial-era home in Salem, Jennifer Appleton sat on a stool in her magazine photo-worthy kitchen, with its stainless-steel appliances and white cabinetry offset by a blue-painted island topped with quartz. She stirred a mug of decaffeinated chamomile tea, her usual pre-bedtime drink as she unwound from the day. As was her custom, she scrolled on an iPad, gaining familiarity with the individuals that the Attorney General had discussed as she began prepping for her new role at the Department of Justice.

Appleton eyed the official online webpage for the United States Senate Committee on Homeland Security and Governmental Affairs. Swiping past an impressive, dramatic photograph of the Capitol building, Appleton paused to examine the portrait photo of the sun-bleached, sandy-haired, tanned face of the committee Chairman, Merritt Coate.

The SAC tapped the "Read Biography" link. Skimming the wordy, self-aggrandizing verbiage, she reached the bottom of the page in short order, and she read aloud, "Merritt and his wife, Hanna Mo'Nique Isaac, reside in Malibu, California."

Swiping to return to the device's home page, Appleton tapped the purple, pink, and orange-hued icon for Instagram, and, in the app's search feature, she typed H-A—and the predictive search function returned Isaac's full name after only two letters, indicating just how popular the investor was.

Tapping on the profile link, Appleton was greeted by the billionaire's unmistakable image.

Forty-eight years old, standing at almost six feet tall, with sweeping, shoulder-length black hair framing her rich, dark brown face, a strong nose and chin, and a fit figure, Isaac posted prolifically, always dressed for the occasion, from athleisure on a coffee run in her hometown of Los Angeles to a ballgown on a Hollywood red carpet. Her posted snapshots ranged from a photo op in an inner-city school to a selfie aboard her Gulfstream jet. Isaac wasn't the slightest bit camera shy for her fifty million followers on the social media app.

Calling up Google, Appleton typed the name into the search box. Isaac's profile and photos filled the iPad's screen, followed by links to countless news articles and videos from shows ranging from the Sunday morning news programs to the weekday gossip gabs.

Appleton tapped on a Forbes link titled "Isaac's Simple Investment Mantra: Don't Buy the Fads."

With a sweep of her forefinger, Appleton scanned the article, a breathy profile about the venture capitalist who preached the benefit of thoughtful investing and thorough research. "Don't just buy the fad," Isaac was quoted. "Buy, grow, sell, repeat. Time the trend. But always hedge with stability and good companies who produce real things."

Her bets ranged from pharma (Isaac bought Moderna and Pfizer in early 2020, just as hints of a pathogen circulated) to consumer products (the investor somehow snagged a chunk of the stock in credit card processor Visa in 2008—which soon became the biggest IPO of that year, rocketing upwards in value). The article estimated that she'd built a net worth in excess of a billion dollars in only fifteen years.

Appleton continued tapping on various sources. Predominantly, Isaac's acolytes praised her financial acumen and her innate ability to read people—and trends. Her critics, a much smaller, less exuberant crowd, pointed out that Isaac had a well-placed source, high in the government who was privy to intelligence not normally available to the run-of-the-mill Wall Streeter or Main Streeter: her Senator husband.

The ring of a phone interrupted Appleton's scrolling. Glancing at the screen, she saw an incoming call from Bart Williams. Lifting the device, she swiped to accept the call and greeted the AG with her customary, "Appleton. Good evening, sir."

The AG's voice boomed from the tiny speaker as he spoke without preamble, "There's been a very concerning development."

# WEDNESDAY
# OCTOBER 26, 2022

**EIGHT DAYS** *BEFORE THE VOTE*

# CHAPTER
# 16



## *MORNING —
## PONTA DELGADA, SÃO MIGUEL ISLAND,
## THE AZORES, PORTUGAL*

**THE DIRECT FLIGHT** aboard an Azores Airlines Airbus A320 from Boston's Logan Airport to the Ponta Delgado International Airport took just under five hours.

The five-hour flight gave me plenty of time to stew further, now with the Almaz enigma compounded by Appleton's almost taunting statement—*"I hope you're up to it. Because, in your current state of mind, you're not."*

Appleton refused to offer clarification. She had said, "Never mind that. A slip of the tongue, nothing more."

*Nonsense*, I thought. The SAC was experienced and precise. She didn't misstate facts, ever.

But I knew that solving that particular mystery would have to be put on hold as the Airbus jerked to a halt on the faded, sun-beaten concrete apron of the single-runway Ponta Delgada International Airport. Looking out the oval window to a bluebird sky as an air stair motored toward the plane, I realized that I was a long way from home.

I grew up in a small town near Providence, Rhode Island, and then went to college in Boston. My first job after graduating from Boston University was at the FBI, working as an Information Management Specialist. And—I still live in Boston.

*So what*, you might be saying. *How is this relevant?*

Courtesy of Appleton's authorization for me to buy a plane ticket, I made it to the Azores—where it is rarely colder than sixty degrees, rarely hotter than eighty degrees, has no snow, and very little traffic; even driving from one end to the other end of São Miguel Island takes only a little more than an hour. In other words, a far cry from Boston, which is snowy and wet in the winter, hot and humid in the summer, and nice like the Azores for a few weeks in the spring and fall.

If this was a vacation, I'd be stoked.

But, of course, it was not. It was anything but a vacation. I saw it more as an investigation, even though I knew it wasn't really that, either.

I considered the finality of my chosen task as I trundled down the airstair and walked toward the low-slung, modernist, glass-and-metal terminal building, listening to the chatter of my fellow passengers—in Portuguese, a language I didn't speak.

Fortunately, at the Sixt Rent-a-Car counter inside the terminal, an agent humored me with excellent English as I signed the paperwork for a car, proffering my Massachusetts driver's license and my personal American Express card—I'd get the credit card points and later, I'd file an expense report, just like any savvy traveler would do if on the company's dime.

There was a considerable pause as the desk agent waited for the transaction to be approved, as she tapped a ballpoint pen on the countertop even as the queue of customers behind me grew more and more impatient.

That delay should have been a signal to me that something was different. Amiss. Amuck.

At that moment, I didn't recognize it as anything but a computer processing glitch, and I'd come to regret that mistake.

# CHAPTER 17



*MIDDAY —*
*NORDESTINHO, SÃO MIGUEL ISLAND,*
*THE AZORES, PORTUGAL*

**JUST UNDER AN HOUR** after departing the airport, I parked my rented Renault Twingo, pulled up on the emergency brake handle, and extricated myself from the compact two-door car.

The green Twingo was certainly a far cry from, say, Appleton's behemoth Tahoe. Instead of a hulking SUV, this island car was a tiny, tinny box on wheels, with a one liter, three-cylinder engine—and like most cars in the Azores, it was equipped with a manual transmission. I confess to stalling once, and mishandling the gearshift three times, reciting to myself, *If you can't find 'em, grind 'em*, and hoping that the fellow drivers wouldn't notice my clumsy shifting. On the positive side of the ledger, traffic in the Azores flows on the right side of the road, like in the United States, so at least I was comfortable with the driving routine as I wound through roundabout after roundabout as I made my way from the populated, southwestern area of the island to the sparse northeastern shoreline, red-tile-roofed houses replaced by verdant hills and a checkerboard of green-and-brown pastures and fields. It was no wonder that São Miguel Island was nicknamed "The Green Island."

After exiting the *Estrada Nacional* (EN) 1-1A, I passed just one other structure—a red-roofed building, a barn from the looks of it, set back at least four or five hundred feet from the gravel road—and I had seen no other vehicles on this rural track by the time I reached my destination: a diminutive chapel: the Ermida de Nossa Senhora do Pranto. *Our Lady of Sorrow*, or, depending on your view, of *Pain*.

Apropos to my journey, perhaps, but from the looks of it, the chapel was anything but sorrowful. It was postcard-perfect: a low-hung, pristine, white stucco building fenestrated with a handful of small windows and a heavy oaken door. The church was appropriately topped with a steeple, but instead of a towering tower, this one was stubby and blocky. Understated. Like the chapel itself.

Immaculately trimmed hedges of purple-blooming hydrangea bordered a serpentine white stucco solid fence that surrounded the little church. The compact compound was set amongst mowed fields with the sapphire blue of the ocean beyond a lush and bushy green bluff.

I took it all in as I stood slack-jawed next to the Twingo.

*Breathtaking.*

There was not a single vehicle or human in sight as I slung my backpack over my shoulders and paced toward the bluff, following a satellite image map that I had downloaded to my iPhone. I walked a dirt path between a fallow field and a low-cut green pasture and aimed for a break in the tree line at the bluff, where I found a shoulder-width trail.

Then it became heavy going as I pushed aside branches, careful to keep my footing on the loose, sandy soil, delicately making my way down a ravine to the edge of the Atlantic, and all the while, fearing not only what I'd find at the bottom but also dreading the climb back up to the fields.

I shouldn't have worried about the former, because once I reached the blackish sand and heavy boulders of the beach, I found nothing.

Nothing but rocks and gently lapping wavelets.

The beach was narrow, if one could even call it a beach. It was more of a rock-strewn shoreline with dark, pebbly sand, peppered with bits of seaweed, the occasional shell, and a few reedy weeds.

According to the map on my device, this was the spot where the raft was found, and as I rotated my body slowly in a circle, I realized that this was about as a lonely spot as one might find. There was literally no sign of human habitation anywhere. It was invisible to the land above the cliff-like bluff, and to the north, the featureless Atlantic stretched to the horizon.

I knelt and caught my breath.

*This is the spot.*

Looking northwards, I tried to visualize the watery grave of *Almaz*. I couldn't bear it; I couldn't bring myself to imagine the sensation of drowning, of gulping seawater and gasping for breath, and of finally giving up.

*What would it feel like?*

Rising, I stumbled, almost in a daze, back toward the bluff, and I found a spot in the rocky face of the cliff that sort of overlooked the location where the raft was discovered. Reaching into my backpack, I withdrew the brick-sized stone that likely confounded the TSA agents in Boston when my belongings were scanned.

Measuring perhaps three inches by six inches, the stone was a mottled gray granite that was quarried near a small village in Vermont called Mount Tabor, and then etched deeply with three lines in a simply serifed font:

```
In Memory
Anastasia Volkov
1986–2021
```

I wedged the stone into the crevice in the cliff, working it in tightly while making sure that the lettering was visible—even though I recognized that few people, if any, would ever see the diminutive memorial to a woman lost at sea.

I sank to my haunches, squatting on the narrow beach.

*This is it. This is all I can do.*

I don't know what I expected—a sign, a thunderclap, an epiphany, or at the very least, a sense of that elusive closure—but all I found, really, was a rocky beach under a foreboding bluff, the stillness of the land offset by the repetitive whoosh wash of the waves lapping against the shoreline.

Standing, I decided that my work was complete. I stepped back from the almost-sheer face of the bluff and twisted to face the ocean. Catching my breath, I wondered how the tiny waves that I saw could lift a raft some eight feet in diameter and deposit it some seventy-five feet from the water.

I thought, *Storm swell, maybe?*

Pulling my phone out, I scrolled until I found the photos of the area that were taken by a man named Santiago Botelho, the local farmer who discovered the raft, and I reconfirmed that I was in the correct location. Turning my vision to the ocean, I squinted, trying to focus on a distant vessel that had appeared on the horizon. *I'd surely be invisible from that boat.*

Blinking in the bright sun, I refocused on the phone and glanced at the time display. Botelho would be meeting me at the church in an hour, and I retraced my steps, laboriously climbing the bluff, thinking all the while, *If I wanted to disappear, I couldn't pick a better place.*

# CHAPTER
# 18

**WHEN I IMAGINED** Santiago Botelho, the man who discovered the raft, I painted a mental picture of an overalls-wearing, straw-hatted, white-haired farmer.

As usual, the false assurances that you give yourself with uneducated, stereotypical speculation proved me wrong.

A shiny, electric blue Ford Fiesta RS, a so-called "hot hatch" equipped with a giant rear spoiler, was parked next to my basic Twingo rental. The man leaning on the Ford stepped toward me, his lightweight, white linen, button-down shirt entirely unbuttoned, presumably to show off his cut six-pack abs, and his black jeans were impossibly skinny. He sported a bit of a goatee beard, and not a fleck of gray hair was evident in his dark hair. "Mister Porter," he called, white teeth flashing against tanned, tawny skin, "I'm Santiago!"

I grinned but asked, "How'd you know I was Ben Porter?"

Botelho laughed. "No one else here today at the chapel. So. You must be him. Yes?" His slightly Portuguese-accented English was perfect.

"Of course," I replied, sucking my gut in, trying not to breathe heavily after my climb from the shoreline. "Thank you for meeting me."

"No, no, no, *senhor*, thank you. It is my pleasure. And the woman who called me? She was *muita* insistent. Very much so!"

I knew Botelho was referring to Appleton, who had arranged the meeting and made the calls herself after explaining to me that it would look odd to the agents and the bureaucrats that I was interviewing a witness to an investigation that wasn't my own. Therefore, she handled it quietly in the background.

"Yes, yes," I replied to Botelho, "that would have been my boss. Insistent for certain."

Botelho brushed his shirttails back and planted his hands on his hips, flashing a shiny black belt and a large, rectangular belt buckle that was framed with small, colorful, glittering gems. "What can I do for you, Mister Porter?"

"Remote spot here," I offered as a lead-in to my question. "Do you work here?"

"Oh, *sim*, yes. I tend the fields. My family's farm." He pointed at the barely visible red barn. "All this land is ours," he added, sweeping his arm in a vaguely circular motion.

"Well, you know I'm here about the raft," I said. "What brought you down to the shoreline that day?"

"Ah, it's good exercise, as you see," he grinned, pointing at my sweat-soaked dark blue t-shirt. "But too, on some days, I like to be near the water." Botelho talked with his hands, and this time, he swept his hand toward the sea. "Perhaps I should have been a fisherman, not a farmer."

"It's quite a climb," I agreed. "Do you go down there often? Every day?"

"No, no, not really. No time for that. Maybe once a week. Maybe less. And, you know, it makes it more special."

The immediate conclusion that I reached was that his statement supported my budding thesis: if he didn't go to the shoreline that frequently, the raft could have sat, unnoticed, invisible, for days. I prodded, "Did the investigator that spoke to you last April ask that question?"

The farmer shrugged and huffed, "I don't remember. I don't think so." He scratched his goatee and continued, "I remember finding the raft. I poked my head under the canopy to see if there was someone inside, which, no, there was not. I called the GNR right away."

"The GNR?"

"The, ah, *Guarda Nacional Republicana*. Or as you say, the National Republican Guard. They are responsible for the maritime patrol. See, I should have been a fisherman!"

I smiled blandly before asking, "And then what? Did you move the raft? Drag it up the beach?"

"Oh, no, no. Like I said, I didn't touch it. I took lots of photos with my phone." For emphasis, he pulled a black, encased iPhone from his back pocket; clearly, the device was too bulky to squeeze into the front pockets of his skinny jeans. "Do you want to see?"

"No," I grinned, "I've seen all the photos already. You were very thorough." Wiping the smile from my face, I held up a palm and asked, in a serious tone, "One question—the day you found the raft, did you also look around for anything else?"

"Oh, no, no, no. Like I said, I saw the raft right away once I got to the beach, and that's when I called the GNR. I waited for them to show up."

"It could have been there for days."

My comment was meant to be a statement, but Botelho took it as a question. "Oh, sure, sure, sure." He twisted his phone to look at the face of it as he tapped the screen with a thumb. "Oh, *merda*, I gotta go. Anything else, Mister Porter?"

"No, no, no," I replied, unconsciously mimicking his repetition. "This has been helpful. And I've got your mobile if I've got any more questions. Is it okay if I call?"

"Of course! Of course!" Botelho grinned widely before spinning toward his Fiesta. He jumped into the little sports car, started the motor, and gunned the gas. Gravel spat from the tires as he sped down the road toward the barn, the engine revving much higher than necessary as he held the gear shifts for maximum acceleration.

The blue Ford blasted past the barn and continued toward the main road. I shrugged and tried to dust off my now dirty shirt even as I shook my head, muttering out loud, "It's a basic question: 'how frequent were your visits to the beach, sir?' And yet, not asked."

I pulled out my phone to dial Appleton but paused. It was getting late in the day, and I wanted to find my hotel before dark, so I hopped into the Twingo. Its suspension wheezed slightly as I put my weight in the driver's seat, and when I started the motor, I knew that it would be futile to attempt to replicate Botelho's burnout. Instead, I placed my phone on my right knee and drove sedately to the main road.

As I swiped for Appleton's contact card with my right hand, I paused for a gearshift as I passed the red barn. A black Nissan Juke with beady round headlights was parked in the shade of the structure, and I as drove by, it began to move, following me to the main road.

I turned right, and in short order, the black car did the same.

I put my phone on the passenger seat; I'd call Appleton later, recalling that the Nissan had not been parked at the barn when I pulled up the remote lane to the chapel.

*Was it pursuing me?*

I pushed on the gas pedal, wondering if the black car would match my increasing speed—and it did.

I had acquired a tail.

# CHAPTER

# 19

**I DID MY** NAT course—New Agent Training—at Quantico almost three years ago, graduating from the Academy in November 2018. Since then, I'd put much of my training to real-world tests.

But not, unfortunately, surveillance detection.

With the black Nissan hanging well back, but remaining visible in my rear-view mirror, I mentally ran through the three tests of situational awareness. First, was I being followed over a distance traveled? So far, yes. Second, how about for a length of time traveled? Again, yes. And third, when I change direction, does my follower follow?

*Yep.*

But—I considered—I'm heading toward the main commercial center of Ponta Delgada, at the end of a workday, traveling west into the setting sun.

*You're being paranoid*, I chastised myself. *It's nothing but a farm worker who coincidentally left at the same time as me.*

Except—*They weren't parked at the barn when I arrived at the chapel*, I recalled.

Turning south near Riberia Seca from *Estrada Regional* 3-1, the black Nissan shadowed me as I navigated the roundabout. The next directional test would arrive less than five miles later when I would wind my way on the cloverleaf interchange to pick up the southern loop of EN1-1A that led to Ponta Delgada.

*Test the theory*, I advised myself, and instead of following the exit toward Ponta Delgada, to the west, I headed east. Once again, the Nissan trailed my Renault.

It was not a blatant tail, which to me, made it more suspicious. The Nissan was piloted expertly, in my opinion, always three to six cars back, occasionally dropping speed and then catching up. If I hadn't kept focused on those beady headlights—or if it was a car that didn't have such a distinct front end—I might have missed it.

As the unplanned convoy approached the town of Aqua De Pau, I slid into the left lane of the *Estrada* and accelerated. Then, at the last possible moment, I exited sharply to a blare of a horn from a lorry. Reaching the terminus of the exit ramp, I made an illegal left, crossing the striped median to pick up the entrance ramp to the westbound Estrada.

Sure enough, as soon as I'd settled into the flow of traffic, I caught sight of that beady snout, seven cars back.

That the Nissan duplicated my extreme, sudden, one-hundred-and-eighty-degree directional change was an obvious tell and satisfied the third situational awareness test.

*Not good*, I thought with increasing trepidation. *Who the hell would be following me here? Who even knows I'm on São Miguel Island?*

Appleton's warning blared in my brain, and I heard her voice saying, *"I can disclose that you will be dealing with people in the highest levels of government and business. They can be dangerous, they can be wily, and they are well-informed. I hope you're up to it. Because, in your current state of mind, you're not."*

Decision time.

*She is wrong. I am up for it.*

I pushed the accelerator pedal, and the Twingo whined in protest. I was due to check in at my hotel, the VIP Executive Azores Hotel, and the exit from the *Estrada National* was three short miles ahead. There, at the exit, I'd find a fork in my path.

*Do I just continue driving and loop aimlessly all the way 'round the island? Or do I exit?*

I made my call, and I ignored the courtesy of the right turn signal as I swerved sharply, at the last possible second, off the highway and onto the exit ramp.

The Nissan followed.

I inhaled deeply and realized I was sweating. *I'm being followed. I'm unarmed. I'm in an unfamiliar city. I don't speak the language.*

Exhaling, I considered my two options.

One, I could try and run an SDR—a surveillance detection route. But two problems with that: first, those routes are typically preplanned in advance to flush out surveillance, and second, *I'm not a black-book operative. I'm no Scot Harvath or James Reece.*

My second option, therefore, was to face my foe. I reminded myself, I might not be one of those Tier One operators. But I am an agent of the United States federal government.

Passing one last roundabout, the curved façade of the seven-story modernist hotel loomed above me, and I turned right to the rear-located main entry.

Tapping the brakes, I slowed to a crawl, and I watched as the Nissan pulled abreast of the turn I had just made. I couldn't see inside the black car; the dim dusk light did not illuminate the interior. I could see the car hesitate, and perhaps I even saw the front wheels twitch as they may have turned a bit in a canceled effort to turn into the lane behind me— but instead the Nissan accelerated and did not follow. I lost sight of the black car as it sped away into the darkening dusk and the Ponta Delgada evening traffic.

Reluctantly remembering the hotel's website, featuring the facility's two restaurants, the indoor and outdoor pool, and the opulent lounge space, I realized that I erred. I might be temporarily in the clear, except that I had just telegraphed the location of my planned accommodations to my stalker in the black Nissan.

Pressing the gas pedal and shifting as I passed the portico, I decided that I would not be checking into the VIP Executive Hotel. It was time to find alternate lodging.

And that assessment turned out to be another mistake.

# CHAPTER 20

**THERE WAS NO QUESTION** in my mind that the black Nissan was tailing me, so I figured my first priority was to scrub my presence in Ponta Delgada. Instead of looking for a different hotel, I headed to the airport to return my rented Renault Twingo.

At the rental car counter, I picked up a stack of lodging brochures and shuffled through, eventually pulling a trifold from somewhere in the middle of the pile. Angling to the currency counter, I traded American dollars for Euros. Turning my phone off, I ventured to the curbside, hailed a taxi, and directed the driver to the Hotel São Miguel.

It seemed ideal as a crash pad; a tiny, two-star place nestled in the heart of Ponta Delgada on a narrow one-lane street. I paid with cash, and I was directed to a third-floor walk-up room with a small balcony and a perfectly suitable bed.

But I didn't sleep much, instead chasing the same question around and around in my head: *Who would be surveilling me in the Azores? And why?*

My trip was on the down-low, though not perfectly clandestine. Appleton obtained my air ticket through the Bureau; that alone would leave a trail. The rental car was in my name and on my personal credit card, as was the pre-booked hotel reservation. Appleton arranged the meeting with Botelho, and that was certainly another touchpoint for someone to track me.

Therefore, my presence on the island was no secret, and I continued to circle back to the "why" part of my question, but to no avail.

As the sun rose to my bloodshot, sleepless eyes, I gathered my few possessions into my backpack and slipped out of the hotel, leaving my key on the counter with a bored clerk. Finding a coffee shop only a few hundred feet down the lane from the hotel, I whiled away an hour or two, bored out of my mind, desperate to power on my phone but resorting to drinking several cups of strong, black coffee while looking at the pictures in a printed newspaper. Naturally, I couldn't read the articles—they were of course written in Portuguese.

Again paying with cash, I finally departed the café and began walking aimlessly toward the harbor. My flight home was booked for 6:00 P.M.; I had a day to kill.

Or, perhaps, I had a day to stay alive.

*Stop it, Ben*, I chastised myself. *No one is trying to kill you.*

Even as I admired the waterfront and tried to enjoy a cloudless, cool day as the clock ticked painfully slowly, I couldn't help but feel that I was being watched. A sixth sense, you know; you get that tingle on the back of your neck and a premonition that something bad is about to happen.

Only—nothing did happen.

*It's the coffee, Ben. Your nerves are shot because of the caffeine.*

I found a hole-in-the-wall restaurant near the harbor and, famished, ordered a burger, only to be informed that the kitchen didn't have any meat. I settled for a fish sandwich for lunch. Bought a beer, too, and then another. Anything to calm my hyperactive mind.

I walked it off, literally, by hoofing it to the airport. It was actually quite a nice stroll; less than an hour, and I finally powered my phone back on in order to check in for my flight, with plenty of time to spare.

Boarding the Airbus for the direct flight back to Logan—which, because of the east-to-west route and the time change, would take off at 6:00 P.M. local time and then land at 7:50 P.M. local time in Boston—I collapsed into my seat, exhausted from playing the spy games.

As the jet's engines spooled up and the airstair backed away from the Airbus, I reached to power down my phone for the flight, realizing that the battery charge was almost in the red zone at 21%. That's a thing, really—like range anxiety in an electric car, there's phone battery anxiety, too. I'd never be able to drive a Tesla. Besides, I figured that I would sleep for the next five hours.

I took one last glance at the screen of my device as I prepared to squeeze the buttons to shut it down—and it dinged with a text message notification from a sender with a blocked number.

Immediately, the concept of getting some rest proved impossible as I read the words:

```
i'll get you eventually
```

# THURSDAY
# OCTOBER 27, 2022

**SEVEN DAYS** *BEFORE THE VOTE*

# CHAPTER
# 21



**I SHIVERED** as I stepped to the curb at Boston's Logan International Airport, trying to convince myself that it was the unseasonably cool air, especially after the warmth in the Azores, that caused my muscles to involuntarily react, and not the aggressive words of the text that I'd received.

Were those words a threat?

"I'll get you eventually"

Four words. Five, really, if you count the contraction as "I will." No period. That missing punctuation mark, at least in my assessment, left the statement as open-ended and vague as the final word.

And, again in my opinion, made it all the more intimidating.

Confirming that the red Honda Pilot with Massachusetts plates matched my Uber reservation, I climbed into the car and exchanged pleasantries with the heavyset, dark-haired driver. "Patrice? I'm Ben."

She glanced at the smartphone that rested in a windshield-mounted suction cup apparatus. "Right. Hey, Ben. This place in Chelsea?" She pointed at the device.

I squinted and confirmed that the Uber app, to no surprise, showed the address of my little townhouse in Chelsea, a short twelve-minute drive from the airport. "Yeah, that's it," I confirmed, and as the Honda accelerated smoothly, I returned my attention to my phone, reexamining the words from that anonymous text message.

I needed a second opinion, and since I didn't check in with Appleton after meeting with Botelho, I also figured the SAC deserved an update. I tapped out a message, using complete sentences that were more befitting an email than a casual text:

```
    Hello, SAC Appleton. I'm back. We talked
    about meeting Saturday; can we move that
    up to tomorrow? Thank you.
```

The response was lightning quick, and it wasn't a text, it was a ring. Appleton must have dialed me immediately, and I answered, "Um, hello?"

"Porter, I've come to expect the unexpected with you," the SAC said coldly. "But I would have at least expected a call during your trip."

"Apologies, ma'am," I stuttered. "I was, um, met with a, um, situation. I decided to keep my phone off."

There was a pause before Appleton asked, "What kind of situation?"

I inhaled to buy time and choose words that would be innocent enough for my Uber driver. "I checked out the site and met with our, um, friend, and I discovered an inconsistency, if you will. Then I was tailed by an unknown. I, ah, can't really go into the details right now," I explained. "I'm in an Uber. That's why I wanted to see if we can meet tomorrow. I'll give you the full rundown."

"You're in an Uber?"

"Um, yeah."

Appleton grunted. "Huh. That's actually good. I'm at home. Give the driver my address in Salem and come here."

"Now? To your house?"

"Yes, Porter," she said, with a note of exasperation in her voice. "Now," she demanded, leaving no room for interpretation or discussion.

"Ah, yes ma'am. Ah, see you in about, um, forty-five minutes."

I waited for her reply; the phone was silent. Checking the screen, I realized that the SAC had ended the call. After changing the destination address with my Uber driver Patrice, I sat back and prepared myself, figuring that the SAC would call me on the carpet (perfectly white, of course, to match the perfectly white club chair that she'd be perched in), and she'd chew me out for being incommunicado.

At least, I thought I knew what to expect, but as I'd been doing lately, my preconceptions would turn out to be wholly incorrect.

# CHAPTER

# 22



**AS THE UBER CAR** glided away, with a five-star rating and generous tip for driver Patrice, I mounted the steps to Appleton's front door at her center hall Colonial in Salem. With my backpack still slung over my shoulder and wishing for a heavier coat, I idly watched as a single car drove past slowly, clearly observing the conservative speed limit on this quiet, residential road as I waited for Appleton to respond to the doorbell.

At last, I heard the deadbolt snick, and the door swung open on silent, greased hinges. As was her custom, the SAC was neatly attired, in slim black pants, a mauve cardigan, and comfy-looking slippers. Or moccasins. Or whatever—but she interrupted my appraisal of her outfit by announcing, "He's here."

I paused for a moment on the stoop, considered the SAC's words, and wondered, *Who is she talking to?*

A booming, deep voice that seemed familiar to me sounded from inside, "It's about time. Let's get going."

Appleton chuckled and called over her shoulder, "Oh, relax. He just got off a plane." Turning her attention back to me, she offered, "Porter. Come in. Oh, and those shoes? Can you take them off?"

I recalled that Appleton's home was always perfectly clean, so naturally, I'd already begun to do just that, slipping off the sneakers that I'd been wearing for days; soles caked with Azores dirt and scuffed on cobblestones and aircraft carpeting alike. And I knew that voice, too, and I finally placed it the instant I was escorted to Appleton's living room, where I was suddenly face-to-face with the Attorney General of the United States, Bart Williams.

I stammered out a greeting. "I—I'm, uh, hello, Attorney General Williams." I'd worked with, and met, Williams on a couple of prior occasions, so I added, "A pleasure to see you, sir. And a surprise."

The AG nodded curtly. "Agent Porter."

Typically, the AG would be attired in a dark-colored business suit—navy blue, charcoal gray, or deep chocolate brown—but this evening, he was dressed down, standing in Appleton's living room wearing blue jeans, a light blue button-down shirt, and a gray quarter-zip sweater. Of course, given the mandate of the homeowner, the AG was shoeless, but he sported light gray socks.

I concluded that whatever discussion was taking place was off the books, but given that my previous assumptions were not materializing, I thought I'd better stop making guesses and wait to be addressed as both Appleton and Williams lowered themselves into white club chairs, clearly taking the seats they had occupied before my arrival. The AG reclined and crossed his left leg over his right. I noted, to my surprise, that his left sock had a small hole in it.

After a moment of awkward silence, Appleton chided, "Porter. Your report?"

I looked at Appleton warily. "Uh, ma'am, has the AG been read in on my trip?"

"Of course," the SAC replied. "What is this inconsistency you referenced on the phone?"

Tearing my eyes from the hole in the AG's sock, I remained standing, and I blurted, "The witness who discovered the raft admitted that his expeditions to the beach were infrequent. That question wasn't asked by our investigators. It's an oversight, and it creates a gap in the timeline. That raft could have sat on the beach for days." I bit my lip and asked, "Is it possible that the raft wasn't empty?"

"No," Appleton replied firmly. "Recall the Bureau's investigation of the *Almaz* matter. We liaised with the National Security Agency, and the NSA had cooperation from the Central Intelligence Agency, Interpol, and the Portuguese SEF—the *Serviço de Estrangeiros e Fronteiras*, or the Foreigners and Border Service. The search that the NSA conducted focused on Lockwood and Volkov, using facial recognition and other tools, at airports and transportation hubs in the Azores and mainland Portugal. Those two individuals were not located anywhere. If one or both survived, surely, they would have appeared for an instant on the surveillance networks in the year-and-a-half since the wreck."

Appleton squinted at me and, before I had a chance to respond, she scolded, "But you know all that because you've read the report. Nevertheless, that doesn't explain why you didn't inform me of this theory when you developed it."

"Yes, ma'am, I apologize. And I agree, the *Almaz* investigation was definitive." I sighed, because I'd gone to the site, placed my memorial stone, and as I'd promised to myself, it was time to put *Almaz* behind me. Straightening, I spoke clearly, "Before I departed, you warned me that the Q-Group assignment would pit us against high-level, well-informed people. You used the words dangerous and wily."

I paused to offer Appleton a chance to either object or confirm, and she chose the latter. "Yes, Porter, I recall that discussion. Go on."

"I also mentioned on the phone, earlier, that a situation came up, and I deemed it prudent to go off-grid as best as I could, under the circumstances. You see, after I met with the witness, Mister Botelho, I was tailed, all the way across the island and back into Ponta Delgada."

The AG uncrossed his legs, planted his feet on the white carpet, and leaned forward with his elbows on his knees. "How do you know you were followed and that it wasn't a fluke?"

I set my backpack on the floor and then stood straight up. "Time, distance, and direction," I recited. Folding my hands primly at my belt buckle, I told my small audience the rest of the story and concluded, "I would have considered my evasion tactics to be successful until I received a text message from a blocked number."

Pulling up the message on my phone, I handed the device to Appleton, who in turn angled the screen so that both she and the AG could read the short note.

Appleton read the words out loud. "I'll get you eventually."

The duo shared an odd glance at each other, and then both spoke in unison. "Barbutero?"

The AG directed his voice at Appleton. "How is it possible that they are ahead of us?"

"I don't know, of course," she replied. "Porter's trip to the Azores was not a locked-down secret; it was framed as a final fact-finding verification mission as an addendum to the *Almaz* investigation. I recorded the time as corroboration of witness statements." The SAC groaned. "There were people in the know within my office. What about in yours?"

"I'm afraid you're correct. We've been setting up the protocols and logistics for the Q-Group. Porter's name is listed on the documents."

"We are compromised," Appleton suggested.

"Yes," the AG murmured. "And the wording of the message," the AG mused, "was taunting. Direct. Barbutero has the chutzpah to reach out with a threat."

"It fits the profile," Appleton agreed.

Feeling way out of the loop, I demanded, "Who are we talking about? Who is this B—Barb—this barber guy?"

The AG ignored me and addressed Appleton. "Play it out. We know they're connected, and it's plausible that he tailed Porter. They've got that kind of reach. They've got access to private transportation."

"Unfortunately, it's only conjecture that Barbutero tailed Porter," Appleton grumbled. "And if he did, why?"

"I have no idea who you're talking about," I complained.

Williams exhaled with a huff and pointed at a sofa opposite the club chair grouping, commanding, "Sit."

I sat carefully and placed my hands palms down on my knees, like a scolded schoolboy. "Yessir." Sitting back on the sofa and crossing one leg over the other, I probed, "Compromised? By the barber—barbarian—I dunno what his name is. *That* guy. Earlier, you asked if, um, *they* were ahead. Who are *they*?"

In response, Williams rubbed his chin as he asked slowly, "Before I explain our suspicions about the man named Barbutero, and why he may have tailed you to the Azores, I have a question for you, Porter. What do you know of a woman named Hanna Mo'Nique Isaac?"

# CHAPTER 23



**NO LONGER** in New York City, Hanna Mo'Nique Isaac reclined on a cushion-topped metal chaise lounge by the hot tub that was recessed into the wide planks of the lower deck at her Malibu home. On the vacant chaise to her right was a half-full glass of rosé wine; condensation dripped from the wine glass onto the small, round, teak table between the lounge chairs. A balmy, light, westerly breeze tickled Isaac's hair as the remaining glow on the far Pacific Ocean horizon dimmed past sunset. She wiggled her bare toes and sighed with exasperation.

This was normally Isaac's favorite spot. The upper balconies were encircled by glass rails that blocked the wafts of wind and diluted the sandy smells of the wide beach, unlike this open-air, unenclosed lower deck. It would have been a perfect, Southern California evening—except for the iPhone in Isaac's left hand and for a single, white AirPod in her left ear. Isaac hissed a two-word question, her mouth aimed at the water, but her voice was picked up by the sensitive microphone in the AirPod: "Who's there?"

Isaac's expression dimmed as she nodded along to the reply. She reached for the wine glass, but mid-lift to her lips, she paused and asked skeptically, "You don't know who the third guy is? He showed up at the Boston FBI Special Agent in Charge's personal residence in an Uber?"

Managing only a quick sip during the curt reply, Isaac licked her lips and demanded, "I hope you were smart enough to snap a photo."

Isaac smiled as she listened to a brief response before ordering, "Good. Text me the picture when we hang up. I don't care if it's grainy. But—hang on. Let me check something."

Isaac drained her wine glass and stood, retreating into the modern, three-level home set below the Malibu cliffs that she'd purchased only months before, paying eighty-five million dollars. It was a reasonable price for 195 feet of beach frontage, privacy, and invisibility, and the investment in the home represented only a fraction of her wealth.

Reaching a table inside the nine-foot-tall sliding doors that retracted invisibly into pockets on the exterior wall of the home such that the water view was unencumbered by any visual obstruction, Isaac flipped up the screen of a MacBook Air laptop computer and swept her fingers over the sleek trackpad. Finally finding what she was looking for, she spoke again, the AirPod transmitting her words, "Okay. Don't interrupt whatever is going on at the SAC's house. Williams has a ticket for the 5:05 Acela high-speed train from Boston to Washington. Get on that train and do your thing there."

The investor terminated the call with a swipe and, AirPod still nestled in her ear, she scrolled through her iPhone's screen until she located the correct contact. Quickly composing a two-word text message, she attached the grainy image of a somewhat stocky, slightly overweight man with a backpack, standing on the stoop of a pristine, white, Colonial-era home, and she tapped the "Send" icon.

The reply to her texted two-word question, "Who's this," was almost instantaneous:

    FBI Special Agent Ben Porter

"Shit," Isaac whispered. Swiping back to the "Recent Calls" menu, she tapped the topmost number, and after a moment, she said, "Rocco. We've got a complication."

# FRIDAY
# OCTOBER 28, 2022

**SIX DAYS** *BEFORE THE VOTE*

## *MIDNIGHT — SALEM, MASSACHUSETTS*

**A TRADITIONALLY CARVED,** polished mahogany grandfather clock in a corner of Appleton's living room sounded softly, its four quarter bells first chiming out the chords of the "Westminster Quarters" melody, followed by a single bell tolling twelve times.

"Midnight," Appleton said quietly. "Long day."

"Indeed," murmured Bart Williams. "You don't silence your clock at night?"

Appleton shook her head. "No. The clock is quiet enough that I can't hear it upstairs. But I love having the sounds every fifteen minutes downstairs."

"Hmm. Hadn't noticed them, before," the AG said, even as his phone chimed with a series of notification sounds. Silently, he examined the screen before turning his attention back to me. "Well, then, Porter, you haven't answered my question. What do you know of a woman named Hanna Mo'Nique Isaac?"

The chiming clock had given me a moment to think—because I thought the answer was self-evident. "Well, sir," I replied, directing my gaze at the AG, "Who doesn't know of Isaac? The Instagram famous, billionaire investor married to Senator Coate. A mixed-race, childless power couple. Both born of below-average means; Coate in the Kansas heartland, and Isaac in the low-income Watts neighborhood in Los Angeles. Their story is literally the American dream. Like, *everyone* knows who they are!" I scratched my chin. "You know, Coate was at Macallister's service. In Boston."

"I know. I was there, too." Attorney General Williams nodded solemnly before offering, "Then it comes as no surprise to you that critics of Isaac point out that the investments made by Senator's wife seem to slightly predate political announcements by Coate."

"Yes, I've heard or read that, somewhere," I said. "But—hang on. Why would Isaac's investments be scrutinized when it's her spouse holding office?"

"Well, because of that," the AG explained. "Spouses are required to disclose their trades and investments."

Appleton stepped in. "Congressional stock trading is monitored carefully by a number of different watchdogs.  However, there's never been an instance where it has been blatantly obvious that Isaac benefited from insider information. Instead, there are allegations, but in reality, Isaac's image, together with Coate's political popularity, those claims don't amount to any real negative press. Both are so charismatic, it's just assumed that they are both smart, savvy investors, just as they are both smart, savvy political and social operators."

I harumphed. "Why do I get the feeling that you have suspicions that this is not the case?"

The AG explained, "The Department of Justice is concerned about the impropriety of conduct by the Coate / Isaac couple. Indeed, that is one of the mandates of my office." He paused and eyed me quizzically. "Porter, do you remember what you said when we last met in person, last March? You quoted British historian Lord Acton."

I brightened. "Yes, sir. Acton wrote, 'Power tends to corrupt; absolute power corrupts absolutely.'"

"Precisely," Williams replied. "Consider the political power that Coate has accumulated, all while Isaac masses monetary power. Could it be that they have come to believe that they are immune from scrutiny? That they are above the law?"

"It seems that way," I concurred.

The Attorney General continued with thoughtful caution evident in his voice. "And yet, this is not something that we can investigate publicly. For example, I can't task a regular FBI squad to shadow this couple and dig through their trash or raid their several homes. First, I don't have a warrant. Second, if I manage to obtain said warrant, it's going to be flimsy. And finally, if I authorize an investigation, how's that going to look? What are the external optics?"

"It's gonna look like a vengeful witch hunt against a presumptive presidential candidate," I suggested.

"Exactly."

The Attorney General was nodding his head as I asked my question, and he elaborated, "That's why I'm here." He raised his right arm and made a circling motion. "But what's not here?"

I'd been wondering about that, especially considering Appleton's pending departure from the Boston field office. "You've got no aides with you, and more to the point, I don't see your security team. Your protective detail."

"Quick study. Bravo," the AG said complimentarily. "I'm here incognito. I traveled here by train, without bodyguards, and with a slight disguise. Appleton and I have had a great deal to discuss, and this location seemed apropos, especially since tomorrow will be her last day in the field office. Anyway, I will be returning to Washington on the first train out this morning, in a few hours. Now, the question is: are you coming with me?"

I stammered, "Excuse me?"

"Appleton has already outlined her Q-Group to you, so let me get straight to the point. Are you in?"

The Attorney General didn't offer any further explanation. Instead, and despite his phone dinging with yet another notification sound, he kept his attention on me as he sat back in his chair, recrossed his legs for the umpteenth time, and waited.

I wished I had my team, still. Macallister, Lockwood, Volkov. But—I reminded myself, *Time to move on. Besides, I still have Appleton on my side.*

As I stared at the hole in the AG's sock, I puffed out my cheeks and exhaled slowly, mostly to buy a tiny bit more time. I knew that I was on the cusp of making a decision that would quite literally start a new chapter in my life.

"I'm in," I stated.

The AG's expression was decidedly more somber. "That's good news. I believe that you, Appleton, and you, Porter, will continue to be a formidable team. But your upcoming task will be daunting so, now, let me explain what you're *really* up against."

# CHAPTER 25

**AS APPLETON PREPARED** a pot of coffee, I pulled out my phone and checked the time—1:20 A.M.—and even though the AG was tapping at his device, I dared to interrupt him. "What time is the train to Washington?"

Without looking up at me, the AG grunted, "Five oh five." He examined his device and announced, "I need to use the restroom, and I need to make a call. Excuse me."

The AG stood and headed toward the privacy of a powder room, leaving me momentarily alone, literally twiddling my thumbs while watching the minutes tick by.

*Twiddling. There's a word you don't hear much anymore,* I mused.

Eventually, the AG returned as Appleton glided into the living room bearing a tray with three steaming mugs and a variety of coffee accouterments. Setting the tray down on a coffee table—for once, being used for its named purpose—she offered, "Porter, I'm driving the AG to Boston South Station. We'll leave a little early, so you have time to run by your place to get anything you require."

That did not excite me for two reasons: first, hours ago, I'd deplaned from a long trip to the Azores, and two, I did not relish the opportunity to show my tiny townhouse to the world's most powerful attorney and my boss. I pled, "Are you sure I can't just meet you in Washington later?"

The AG lifted a mug to his lips and slurped. With an almost dainty motion, he raised a cloth napkin to his mouth and wiped an invisible drop of coffee away. "I'm sure of that. We'll be on the five oh five Acela." He reached for the mug and took a second sip before elaborating, "We'll dispense with the formalities of paperwork and non-disclosure agreements for now. I know your file and your reputation, Porter, and I know I can trust you. But—suffice it to say, this is off-record."

"Understood," I agreed, drinking greedily from my coffee mug. It was delicious; a medium roast which I thought was far more palatable than the rich, heavy Portuguese blend I'd drank some three thousand miles to the east less than twenty-four hours ago. *To each his own coffee,* I thought, as Williams recrossed his legs, exposing the hole in his sock and preparing me for an attorney's briefing. *Here we go, again.*

"You've heard of the chip shortage, I presume," the AG rumbled. "Semiconductors. They're in basically every electronic device, from appliances to cars. The Covid pandemic disrupted supply chains in 2020, and semiconductor manufacturers were not immune, leading to a scarcity of chips. It's basic supply and demand: not enough supply, and prices rise creating an inflationary cycle that reverberates into other sectors. Inflation is at extreme levels, interest rates are rising, and we're facing a recession."

"Understood," I repeated. "But macroeconomic forecasting is not my specialty. Chasing bad guys is more to my liking, so where does our suspect come in?"

"This is where there are issues of collusion," Williams outlined. "Senator Merritt Coate authored and is now stumping a bill to subsidize and develop the semiconductor industry here in the States. It's called 'An Act to Enhance Production of Integrated Circuits,' which, like many of these showcase pieces of legislation, is deliberately named so it can be referred to with a catchy, media-friendly acronym."

"Yeah," I responded, quickly consolidating the letters in my head. "I've heard Coate refer to his bill on television as the EPIC act."

"That's the one," the AG confirmed. "He's offering a message of domestic jobs and materials that he argues will make the United States less reliant on overseas supply from places like Taiwan."

I shrugged. "Seems like good policy. Seems like a logical bet for Isaac, too; she cannot be alone in that evaluation. Frankly, it seems pretty boring to me."

"That is a fair assessment," admitted the Attorney General. "But that's what this all appears to be on the surface. Deeper down, it's much, much more, ah, calamitous. Coate has faced significant opposition from one company in particular, which is helmed by a colorful and popular self-made Texas businessman named Virgil Preston."

Appleton picked up the narrative. "That company is named Aximerva. It's based in Austin, Texas, and it's proposing to build twelve billion dollars worth of advanced semiconductor manufacturing space in Texas and across the southern border in Mexico. The company represents a threat to the established players and does not seem to want or need Congressional subsidy."

This big business stuff was beyond me, and I shrugged once more. "That, too, seems like a pretty good thing. Locally national production, some foreign production but without an overseas transit. No taxpayer dollars. I'm not an economist, but like I said, that seems like a good deal."

The AG snuffled humorlessly. "Would you think it is a good deal for Isaac to arrange for a murder to protect her husband's interests?"

My eyebrows raised involuntarily as I repeated, "A murder?"

"Indeed," boomed Williams. "Virgil Preston, the founder and chief executive officer, was murdered four days ago, on Tuesday, October 25. Actually, we can't conclude murder, as we haven't located the body, but that is the day he disappeared under suspicious circumstances— immediately following a private lunch and a steak sandwich with none other than Hanna Mo'Nique Isaac. Preston has gone off the grid—he abandoned his luggage in a car service Lincoln, and he missed a reserved NetJets flight back to Texas. Both actions are incredibly uncharacteristic of him. He's a very fine man. Self-made, doesn't drink, doesn't smoke, donates to charity. He's a model citizen."

I asked, "You suspect foul play, because he vanished?"

"Exactly. We have supporting evidence. We have a suspect, the man we discussed before—the man who quite possibly tailed you in the Azores. His name, again, is Rocco Barbutero. We have established a connection between Barbutero and Isaac, and we strongly believe that she is behind the hit."

"This sounds like an investigation for the FBI," I noted.

"Oh, that's already happening," the AG confirmed. "The Bureau's New York Field Office is investigating Preston as a missing person case. We are not releasing either our data on Barbutero's relationship with Isaac or any crime scene details, for all the reasons that I've discussed and for reasons that you'll soon understand. Furthermore, given the fact Barbutero vanished from our domestic surveillance nets during the same time that you were tailed in the Azores, it's logical to conclude that the secrecy of our investigation may be compromised. And that's why you're coming to DC with me. You're going to follow the trail."

The AG stood, stretching his legs. "We'd better be headed for the train soon." From his standing perch, he looked down at me. "If we go public with that connection to Isaac, the case will become mired in the Twitterverse, and it will become fodder for the talking heads on television. Because this thing is a political football." He shook his head and scoffed, "No, it's a political hot potato. Imagine the story on every website, broadcast, and newspaper." The AG held up his hands and air-quoted as he improvised a headline, "The FBI Accuses Hanna Isaac of Foul Play Just a Week Before the Vote on Her Husband's EPIC Act."

"I can see how that's less than ideal," I commented.

Appleton followed the AG's lead and also rose from her seat. "Let's continue this discussion in the car. We've got to get going."

I followed the AG outside, after reshoeing, of course, and Appleton locked her front door behind us. The lights of Appleton's black Bureau-issued Chevrolet Tahoe flashed as she turned from her front door, tapping her key fob to unlock the car. The AG took, probably as was his custom, the left rear bucket seat in the Tahoe, so I climbed into the shotgun seat. Buckling my seat belt, I had to admit to myself that I was a tiny bit disappointed. *Sure, it's a tricky case. But a train ride with the Attorney General? No yachts, helicopters, or international intrigue . . .*

That sentiment lasted as long as it took Appleton to back the Tahoe out of her driveway, and as she shifted the vehicle into *Drive*, the rear window exploded with a *bang* into a zillion shards of tinted, tempered glass.

# CHAPTER 26



Jennifer Appleton didn't need to shout that warning, to me, at least. Rear windows don't just shatter for no reason. I'd slumped down in the passenger seat in the Tahoe mostly out of reflex to the noise of the glass breaking, but also due to the force of acceleration as Appleton mashed the accelerator pedal of the big SUV.

I peeked into the back. *Good instincts and quick reflexes*, I thought with admiration. The AG was hunched into what I can only describe as the "crash position"—what they used to tell you on airplanes: head between the knees, with hands cupped under the thighs.

"Sir! Mister Williams," I blurted. "Are you okay?"

I could see his shoulders tense as the Tahoe jerked left, tires squealing, still accelerating, and I caught a glimpse of headlights in the void where the back window used to be.

The AG's head angled up slightly. "Yes, yes, I'm fine."

"*Brace!*" Appleton yelled.

The AG's head dipped down again, and I barely had time to jerk my body forward to the relative security of the shotgun seat before the SUV twisted to the right just as I heard the report of a gun.

Appleton, as usual, was unperturbed; while she was slightly huddled in the driver's seat, keeping her skull below the headrest, I imagined that she knew that the flimsy seat offered no protection from a gunshot. Only the metal skin of the Tahoe afforded a modicum of safety as it swerved into another gut-wrenching turn. What she really wanted, I knew, was speed. And distance. And—four-wheel drive?

The Tahoe lurched as it hit a curb at speed, and I realized that we were no longer on a road. The scene outside, from what I could tell, was only grass and dirt.

Trained, like me, at Quantico, Appleton used every pony under the hood to make escape from our unwelcome tail. It also became clear to me that she used her local knowledge, too, even as she fiddled with a switch to the left of the steering wheel.

"Got eyes on 'em, Porter?" she asked, her voice just loud enough to be heard over the roar of the engine, but not loud enough that she was screaming. She was dealing with the crisis by reflecting calmness, belied by her aggressive driving that shook the Tahoe in unimaginable ways.

I followed suit, purposely raising my head to look astern of the speeding Tahoe. The lateness of the hour certainly made Appleton's evasive maneuvers feasible, and it made my task easy: I didn't have to pick out anything but lights or, possibly, a light-less pursuing vehicle. "Nothing," I stated matter-of-factly. "Either you've outrun them, or they gave up." I twisted my head to look out the windshield. "Where are we, anyway?"

Somehow, Appleton traded the side streets of Salem for a forest. Instead of shattering glass, now I heard the dual noises of elongated shrieks as tree branches dragged grooves into the Tahoe's painted flanks and pounding thuds as the suspension absorbed, as best it could, the uneven dirt below the wheels. But I could see very little except for the scraggly, uneven shapes of trees in various states of leaflessness.

Despite the darkness, Appleton piloted the SUV with purpose, following an invisible path. The Tahoe had slowed significantly as the foliage grew denser, and after another sixty seconds of rustling, screeching, and thumping, we stopped.

In utter darkness—the only illumination from the glowing dashboard, and I muttered, "Lights?"

"Where?" Appleton demanded.

"No, no," I stuttered. "You've lost them. But—our lights. Your lights. How did you know where you were going?"

Appleton chuckled quietly. "I know the area. I turned off the headlights, and I've got a defeat switch for the running lamps and the brake lights." She turned and spoke over her right shoulder. "Bart? You alright?"

I don't think I'd ever heard anyone address the Attorney General by his first name, but he seemed unfazed by the familiarity or by the commotion as he replied in an even voice, "Yes, perfectly fine. Well done there. Very good driving."

*You don't say*, I thought, before adding out loud, "Yeah, nice work losing them. But, um, who's them? What the hell was that?"

"Like I explained, Mister Porter," the AG rumbled, "calamitous."

"I gotta say, sir, with no disrespect meant, that's a strange choice of word. You used it before."

"Indeed," he replied. "Dire, or frightening, or alarming—those words don't seem to reach the level of calamitous. For that is what we are dealing with here."

"I'm beginning to see that," I agreed. "Especially because neither of you seems particularly surprised that we've been shot at and chased."

Appleton was nodding. "Yup. Frankly, they've done us a favor. This little episode confirms our suspicions. I'm a target, the AG is a target, and now you, Porter, are one too. That's assuming, of course, that my house was under surveillance and that they ID'd you. Not much of a stretch, though, to reach that conclusion."

I raised my hand slightly as if I was in a classroom asking a question. "They?"

"Isaac, Coate, and whomever they've got with them. Possibly Barbutero. Their resources are vast."

"Wait, what?" I exclaimed. "How do you possibly know this is related to Isaac and Coate?"

"That's going to be your task," the AG intoned from the back seat. "We'd better get going. I want to make the five-oh-five Acela."

"Yeah," agreed Appleton, as she released the brakes. The Tahoe lurched forward as she explained, "We'll skip Porter's place; he can acquire what he needs in Washington. I'll drop you off at the station, and then I'll return this car to the Bureau. I'll say it was vandalized."

The AG affirmed the plan with a grunted, "Good." As the Tahoe burst out of the wooded area and onto the dirt infield of a baseball diamond, he added, "Appleton, you've got your backup vehicle, and Porter and I will be safe in the anonymity of the train."

I'd soon learn he would be wrong about that, too, as the mistakes kept piling on.

# CHAPTER
# 27



*EARLY MORNING — BOSTON SOUTH STATION*

**THEY, WHOMEVER THEY** might be, call it "oh dark thirty." Accurate, because the skies above Boston were pitch black just before 5:05 A.M. when the Acela 2151 train was scheduled to depart out of South Station.

Appleton dropped the Attorney General and me off at the apex of the semi-circular, pinkish-brown granite façade of what was once, in 1899, the world's largest train station. The sidewalks were as dull as the sky. The station opened officially at 5:00 A.M., and given the early hour, it was quiet and sparsely populated.

Dark and devoid of people was an ideal combination, given the appearance of Appleton's Tahoe—missing rear window and long, jagged scratches running along its sides, punctuated by a handful of dents. At least there were no bullet holes.

The AG and I walked briskly through the center door of the station; five stories above, a twelve-foot diameter clock reminded us that our train to Washington, DC would depart in mere minutes. Despite the rush, the AG whispered conspiratorially, "You know, Porter, that was a warning. If someone wanted to take us out, they could have done so with clean shots when we stood on Appleton's doorstep."

"Yessir," I agreed, "that had occurred to me as well. They also gave up the chase much too quickly, in my view."

We reached the train, its exterior silver with swooping blue accents. The AG marched to the first car behind the aerodynamically, slope-fronted engine. "Good point," Williams affirmed as he stepped aboard holding two sheets of paper. He handed me one, saying, "Reserved seats on this train, so take what you're assigned. The empty seats will probably fill in down the line. You're in 13A. I'm 4F."

"We're not sitting together?"

"No," he replied softly. "Appleton and I booked your ticket after mine. Enjoy the ride. And get some rest. We have much to discuss when we get to Washington at . . ." His voice trailed off as he consulted the piece of paper that remained in his hand, and he announced, "11:54. Just before noon."

As he settled into the blue leather seat, he concluded the pre-trip briefing. "I like these seats—the ones that only face forward and are alone. No seat companion. You'll enjoy the same." He winked and then turned away from me to push his small, soft-sided mahogany-colored satchel into the gap between his feet and the side of the train.

I'd never been aboard an Acela train before, much less in a first-class car. It was nice. A wide aisle separated a line of single seats on the right side of the car from the double seats on the left side. Most of the seats faced the front of the train, save for a handful that presided over small conference tables and therefore aimed rearward. The arrangement switched halfway down the car, such that I found my single seat on the left side.

I stowed my backpack—at the moment, my sole possession, now stuffed with dirty laundry leftover from the Azores trip—and I plopped into seat 13A, glancing at my phone. Battery at 38%. You know how I feel about that, so you've already guessed that I turned the phone off, and then decided to turn myself off, closing my eyes and ignoring the soft shuffles at my right shoulder as a handful of fellow travelers found their seats, sporadically filling maybe ten of the seats in the forty-five-seat cabin. Only two passengers—bored and tired-looking, business-suit-clad men presumably traveling together—were seated in the forward section, near the AG, with five or so people taking random seats near me, all apparently, like me, traveling solo. There was no conversation, which I didn't mind one bit.

I dozed off, sleeping through stops at Boston's Back Bay and in Westwood, Massachusetts, before being jolted awake shortly before 5:40 A.M. as the train made its third scheduled stop in Providence, Rhode Island. The pause was brief, and the Acela gained speed as it headed southward into the dark, pre-dawn New England morning.

My nap was short. Too short, perhaps, because as the train rocked through my birth state, the only sounds being the regular clack-clack of the track seams under the wheels against the white-noise rush of the air turbulence that the train made, I found myself thinking about the few facts that I knew about the only high-speed train in America that could travel at 150 miles per hour.

Limited by track design and curves meant for slower trains, the Acela was only momentarily a high-speed train until it reached Pennsylvania. Here in New England, the train would hit its advertised speed in only a handful of places, each only for minutes, and its average speed wouldn't even reach 70 miles per hour. On the nearby I-95 highway, which loosely paralleled the Northeast Corridor tracks, cars might risk speeding tickets but could travel faster.

But those cars don't tilt, which was one of the standout features of the Acela that made it workable on the aging Northeast Corridor tracks. To counteract the effects of centrifugal force, the Acela cars lean into turns by a few degrees, making the ride more comfortable for passengers.

Except, perhaps, for me, because I was wide-eyed as the train shot, near its top speed of 150 miles per hour, past the Kingston, Rhode Island station, about twenty-five miles south of Providence. My brain, consumed with useless but important information about the train line, refused to rest.

And, with that, my string of mistakes came to an end.

# CHAPTER
## 28



**THE INTERLOPER** in the first-class car of the Acela train was immediately obvious to me.

Now, I know, I'm not supposed to profile.

But when a short, fireplug of a figure wearing a black balaclava, black pants, and a black sweatshirt tiptoed past 13A holding a black pistol with a stubby black suppressor screwed to the muzzle, yeah, I took notice.

Unfortunately, I was unarmed myself. I blinked my eyes to clear the post-nap fuzz and remembered that only hours ago, I deplaned from an international flight, hopped into an Uber, and then been waylaid at Appleton's house. I literally had nothing in my hands except a powered-off phone.

The interloper reached the jog in the aisle at row nine, where the one-by-two seat arrangement swapped sides. Just ahead, I could see the Attorney General's closely cropped, curly gray-and-black hair, head resting to the right side of his seat, toward the window.

I did the only thing I could do as the interloper reached 4F and raised the pistol. I sprang from my seat and ran forward in the car, timing my paces to the gentle rocking of the train car. One step, a bound, a swerve at the jog in the aisle, and one more leap—and I was abreast of row seven, twisting my body slightly to the right even as the interloper casually raised the suppressed pistol above the AG's seatback.

I was too late.

*Phop.*

But I was close. *So* close. Maybe an instant after the gun fired, or maybe just as the trigger was depressed, my right shoulder smacked at full force between the interloper's shoulder blades, and the pistol hand was aimed upwards as the body fell forward, stunned by the unseen and unexpected impact of my momentum.

The report from a suppressed pistol is audible, but to a non-trained ear, this particular sound might have been difficult to distinguish against the whoosh of air outside and the relentless clack-clack of the train wheels.

Naturally, I didn't examine the scene for the bullet impact—I was too busy trying to find a way to keep that pistol hand from aiming the gun at me. The interloper grunted, hitting the floor with a thud, and I toppled, too, twisting my body now to force my chest into a writhing back. With both hands, I grabbed the interloper's pistol hand and slammed it twice on the short-pile carpet of the cabin aisle floor.

The pistol was in plain sight as the interloper squirmed—and out of the corner of my left eye, I saw a business-suited man launch himself at me.

*Thunk!*

"Oof," I gasped, as the weight of the guy crashed onto me, crushing my body into the interloper's burly frame. I drew in a short breath and sensed a whiff of—bacon?

The business-suit man pushed the pistol out of reach—using his knuckles, I noted, even as we both chorused, to my surprise, a staccato in between breaths, "F! B! I!"

*What?*

It suddenly dawned on me—the only permanent, personal protective mission maintained by the FBI was for the United States Attorney General. Those two guys seated together up front weren't businessmen.

They were undercover Special Agents assigned to Bart Williams for this train ride.

But there was nothing I could do, as now the second man joined the first, and my face was smushed into the interloper's back. I could sense that the interloper was male—he was wide in the waist and fleshy on his back, with substantial flab noticeable even through the sweatshirt. It was the smell, though, that ID'd his gender to me—musky, faint coffee notes, and those hints of bacon.

No woman smells like bacon. At least, none that I've ever met.

To my right, Williams rose and daintily shoved the gun further out of reach with a sock-clad foot.

*That's the one with the hole in it*, I mused, pointlessly.

"The situation is under control," the AG said calmly, addressing nobody specifically but clearly intending to reassure the passengers seated toward the rear of the car. He leaned down to the pile of us on the floor and put a hand on my shoulder. "This one is with me, gents. Some breathing room, please."

The two undercover agents efficiently unwound the melee even as they ensured that the perp didn't have a chance to move. One of the agents darted in the direction of the first-class cabin attendant, a high-cheeked, formerly cheerful but now dour-faced Black woman, with long, curly, black hair, dressed in a white shirt and dark-colored vest, who stood rock-still against the forward cabin wall, immobile. Her expression morphed from fear to stoicism as the agent whispered something in her ear, perhaps reassuring her that the commotion was done.

All in, maybe ninety seconds had passed since the interloper snuck into the first-class car.

With the pressure off my body and now with the confidence of knowing that I had not only an ally but also that the weapon was out of reach, I stole a glance up, to the headliner of the overhead luggage rack. There was one, small, black hole marring the white vinyl surface, above 5F—one seat behind the AG.

I hauled myself to my knees and looked rearwards. The few passengers seated toward the back of the car who were still awake watched with curiosity, but I figured they were too far back in the cabin to have heard the gunshot, muffled as it would have been by the rush of air outside the speeding train and the rhythmic clunk of the wheel carriages passing over seams in the track. All they saw was a fight, and as odd as that was, none of them seemed terribly fascinated by the altercation.

I turned my attention to the man at my side and whispered, "I'm Special Agent Ben Porter. Boston Division."

He nodded. "Dale Morris. DC office." He scratched his chin and admitted, "Um, well, ah, well done. Didn't see that coming. Obviously."

"Yeah, sure. I guess I had the benefit of time and seeing his approach as he passed me. I guess our new friend here supposed the AG would be on the train alone." I looked down at the prone man on the floor. "Mind if we see who we've got here?"

Morris cracked a slight grin. "Sure. Be my guest."

I yanked off the interloper's balaclava, just like they do in the movies. It was actually pretty satisfying, and I revealed the attacker—a leathery-skinned, pockmarked, mustachioed man, in his forties or fifties, I'd estimate, with coffee-stained, crooked teeth.

At my shoulder, Bart Williams gasped in surprise as he examined the man's face.

I had a feeling that our trip to Washington was going to take substantially longer than expected, but apparently, the AG had other plans.

# CHAPTER

# 29

**THE ATTORNEY GENERAL ROSE** to his full height, addressing the cabin attendant and the passengers in the train car. "I'm Special Agent Ben Porter. Federal Bureau of Investigation, Boston Division."

I gaped at the Attorney General. *The AG is impersonating me?*

Before I could object or question his motives, the AG went on, "The situation is under control. I will connect with my colleagues, who will board the train at the next stop in New Haven and who will remove the perpetrator. We'll keep any delay and inconvenience to you at a bare minimum."

*I wish I talked like that*, I thought. *Commanding, clipped baritone. No room for negotiation or misunderstanding.*

The AG squinted at me. The awkward stare between the real Ben Porter and the copycat lasted only a moment before the AG boomed, "Thank you for your attention. Apologies for the commotion."

He turned to Morris and me. "Escort this man to the forward-most seat in the car and sit with him there. I'm calling Appleton so that we can be met at the next stop."

"We're going to taint the crime scene?" The incredulity in my voice had to be obvious to the highest attorney in the land. The mere idea of rearranging the scene would cause heartburn for a prosecuting attorney, and I couldn't believe that the Attorney General himself would condone that action, adding to the fact that he'd already used a false identity to communicate, quite publicly, with civilians and the attendant on the train.

My concerns were addressed indirectly as Williams knelt on the carpeted floor of the swaying first-class train car. He motioned to the other agent to return to join us, and as he approached, he waved Morris and me down to his level. Our heads met inches above the side-turned face of our perp, and Williams hissed angrily, "Well, well, well, Mister Barbutero. We've been looking for you."

"Barbutero? This is the guy you talked about?" The disbelief remained in my tone.

Williams nodded at me but spoke to the man on the floor with venom dripping from each word. "I am shocked but somehow not surprised. So, tell me. Are you going to cooperate? Let's not make more of a scene. You're a professional, right?"

I saw the corner of the man's mouth wrinkle into the hint of a grin, and he whispered, "Yeah, okay, Bart."

*Ah, what?* I couldn't believe my ears. *Balaclava guy was not only the suspect that Appleton and the Attorney General had fingered in the Preston case but also as my tail in the Azores—and the AG was also on a first-name basis with the perp?*

Williams was unfazed. He looked over to me one last time and said reassuringly, "Mister Barbutero will behave. After all, now he's outnumbered, and we've got his weapon."

The AG rose and settled back into seat 4F. I pulled the man named Barbutero to his feet. With my right hand on his back, he shuffled forward and sank into the vacant seat at the very front of the car, 1F.

Morris and I hovered over him, awkwardly leaning on the forward cabin wall. Morris's partner returned to his seat discretely and pulled out a phone to make a call. I nudged Morris and whispered, "What's your partner up to?"

"Probably calling this in. We have two other agents at the back of the car keeping an eye on the other passengers. Not sure how our perp made it past them, but they'll definitely be on the receiving end of a third-degree debrief."

"Are there any actual passengers in this car?"

Morris shrugged. "Three or four, maybe, for now. The train will fill up when we get to New York. We can't buy all the tickets and remain low profile, you know."

I grunted a non-committal reply, thinking, *Seems like lax security to me.* With my eyes above the rows of seat backs, I watched as the AG held a smartphone to his ear. He caught my eye and mouthed three distinct syllables, which I inferred meant Appleton.

Scanning the rear of the car, I was perturbed by the security arrangement. *Two protective agents at the rear, two in front. Flanking the AG, essentially. That's good protocol. Yet the interloper sauntered right by the rear guard, and then the rear guard didn't even engage in the take-down.*

And the lack of interest in the confrontation from the passengers in the cabin bothered me. No phones were being held to take video, and there wasn't a sense of panic or even distress.

*This is all very surreal*, I thought. *None of it makes sense.*

But there was nothing I could do about my unease, and soon enough, the skies lightened outside, and the train slowed to a gentle stop at New Haven's Union Station.

Four men wearing dark blue windbreakers emblazoned with "FBI" on their backs in yellow letters boarded the car. The AG rose and strode forward, demanding, "Who's in charge?"

"I am," said a tall Black man who also wore an FBI-issued baseball cap. "Agent Hurst. SAC Appleton gave us our instructions."

The AG asked, for confirmation, presumably, "Which were what?"

"We're to take your man into custody and hold him for her questioning. She's driving down from Boston. It's, ah, a little past seven in the morning. She said she'd be here around eleven thirty. No later than noon." Agent Hurst nodded toward Barbutero. "He'll be isolated until she arrives, per her orders."

"Very well," Williams agreed. "Carry on."

As the agents escorted the interloper off the train, Williams took his seat, two passengers from the rear of the train disembarked, five boarded, and I returned to 13A. The remainder of the journey to Washington was uneventful, and the train pulled into Union Station only five minutes behind schedule at 11:59 A.M.

I made a mental note to Google "Why are so many train stations called Union Station" as I followed the Attorney General, now flanked by his four protective agents, onto the platform and then to the vast, central hall with its arched ceiling. Exiting to the sidewalk, we were met with humid air and two waiting black Suburbans with deeply tinted windows. The agents from the rear of the train carved off to the rear-most Suburban, and Williams, Morris, the other forward agent, and I clambered aboard the first SUV.

I had plenty of questions for the AG—but they would wait, for his phone rang. He smiled and looked at me. "It's Appleton." Swiping the device to accept the call, he forwent a greeting, instead asking, "Well, that was quite a coincidence, though I don't believe in coincidences. How is Mister Barbutero?"

His expression clouded, and his jaw drooped as he listened to Appleton's reply. Finally, he said, wheezing out the words in exasperation, "I'll brief Porter, and we'll call you back from the office."

Williams jabbed at the screen. The normally unflappable AG was agitated as the Suburban accelerated into traffic. "Barbutero is gone. How did *that* happen?"

# CHAPTER 30



**SITTING IN** the left rear seat of the Suburban, normally I'd have an outstanding view—passing the dome of the US Capitol building visible the length of Lower Senate Park, then admiring the Washington Mall, bordered by museums, stretching down Constitution Avenue, during the nine-minute drive from Union Station to the Attorney General's office.

Instead, I focused my attention on the AG himself, peppering him with questions as soon as he disconnected from the call with Appleton. "How do you know this guy? And whaddya mean that he's gone? Who was it that met him at the train? Those were FBI agents, right? And—"

Williams held up a hand. "Stop." He sighed. "One at a time. There's a lot to unpack, and I will get you up to speed quickly. However, the focus must be on Barbutero."

I shook my head. "No. Totally disagree. That's out of our hands. That's on Appleton, right?"

It was Williams's turn to object. "No. Remember, Appleton is no longer in her seat. Her hands are tied."

I couldn't believe that I was going to continue to argue with the highest-ranking lawyer in the land, but, true to form, I did. "No. Wrong.

She said that her effective date to step aside was five o'clock this afternoon. As of this moment now, she's still the Special Agent in Charge."

"It's irrelevant. She's a lame duck. She should be packing up her office."

"She's not in Boston. Agent Hurst said she was driving to New Haven. To meet your man Barbutero."

The AG scoffed, "My man?"

"Yeah," I retorted, "your man, who is on a first-name basis with you, Bart."

He scowled but remained silent as the SUV carved a right opposite the Smithsonian National Museum of Natural History onto 10th Street NW. This was the first block of the so-called seventy-acre Federal Triangle, occupied by ten government buildings starting with the Robert F. Kennedy Department of Justice building, a seven-story, 1.2 million square foot building clad in Indiana limestone. I knew the area reasonably well; only a block north, across Pennsylvania Avenue, was the FBI's headquarters inside the J. Edgar Hoover Building.

Up front in the Suburban's shotgun seat, the nameless agent from the train raised a radio to his lips and whispered something as the car decelerated and then slewed right again, slowing to a crawl. Twisting my neck, I managed to look up through the windshield to read the words carved into the imposing, limestone lintel above the vehicular entry to the interior courtyard of the massive building:

```
      Justice is the great interest of man on
      Earth. Wherever her temple stands, there
          is a foundation for social security,
        general happiness, and the improvement
                and progress of our race.
```

A gate lifted and the Suburban rumbled across a cobblestone apron into the courtyard as the AG smiled thinly. "You know, Porter, you might be advised to hold your tongue once in a while. But I cannot deny that you were correct. I *do* know Barbutero. He was an informant at one time."

"Maybe he changed teams," I suggested. "In my admittedly limited experience, informants are informants because they are adept at lying. You can never really trust them."

"Perhaps." Before the car stopped, the shotgun rider had his door open, and he jumped to the cobblestone-paved courtyard to open the rear door for the Attorney General.

The AG shot a glance in my direction. "Follow me and cease speaking until we're in a secure location," he ordered.

I tailed Williams to a stair where a guard pointed at me as he held up a hand to halt the AG. With a tone of both familiarity and respect, the guard said, "Excuse me, sir, but I need identification from your guest."

"Not this time," the AG replied. "Mark him down as a John Doe, on my personal authority."

The guard nodded and made a notation on a tablet computer as the AG brushed by with me in tow. As soon as we were out of earshot, I whispered, "What's that about? Why no ID?"

"This will be the last time you're in this building. I'm going to introduce you to a few people, and then you're on your own. We've got a place for you to work from, but this is happening faster than expected, so today you're here incognito."

At the top of a wide, ornate stair, the AG turned down an equally wide, marble-floored corridor, flanked with carefully lit statues and paintings. The atmosphere was more museum than office until the AG twisted to his left and pulled open a thick, polished mahogany door to reveal a small conference room.

At his heel, I couldn't see much until he pulled out the chair at the head of an oval, oak table and sank into the brown leather. Three faces stared back at me—two men and one woman.

I sighed happily. Finally, my outlook brightened, for sitting before me was the captivating Sara Lin.

# CHAPTER
# 31

**"INTRODUCTIONS, FIRST,"** Bart Williams boomed, his voice modulated by thick, blue carpet and by heavy, navy drapes that covered the room's one window. "To my left is Joshua Toonin. To his left, Jaylen Kinnar-Hering. To his left, Sara Lin. Sit."

I nodded quickly at the two men, the first a pale, white-skinned, scrawny guy with a mostly bald head, narrow eyeglasses, and a darkish tie knotted tightly at his neck, his Adam's apple bulging prominently above the knot. The second man spoke softly, "That's Kinnar hyphen Hering if you please." His white teeth flashed against brown skin as he rubbed a closely cropped black goatee.

"A pleasure to meet you both," I replied breezily and superficially. I was drawn toward Lin, who rose from her seat and offered a hand. I allowed myself a brief moment of reflection as I shook her hand formally; in this situation, an embrace would probably have crossed some line of etiquette.

I knew Sara Lin, of course. We'd last seen each other over a lengthy dinner the previous March, some eighteen months ago, where I enjoyed the opportunity to stare at her face: flawless light brown skin and soft, dark eyes framed by subtly wavy hair. I soaked in her words as she breathed, "It's good to see you again, Ben. I've missed you. And I must admit, I was so happy to hear that you would be joining this team."

*Oh, that voice,* I thought. A touch of a Japanese accent combined with a little Northeast US privileged lockjaw interspersed with a Southern California drawl, all thanks to a childhood in Japan, then boarding school, college, and law school in the States at A-list institutions: Hotchkiss, Stanford, and Columbia.

"I remembered that you two worked together previously," the AG rumbled, interrupting my reverie, "and as such, I'm sure you will collaborate productively again. Let's get to work. Have a seat, Porter."

Naturally, I selected the leather chair next to Lin.

Williams continued, "Let's pick up where we left off, in the car, with Rocco Barbutero. Twenty years ago, Barbutero got his start as a butcher. He built himself a small business selling meats and provisions to New York restaurants, but his appetite—no pun intended—wasn't satiated, and he delved into more, ah, lucrative deals."

I held up a hand. "What sort of deals?"

"Protection rackets, bribes, insider info. Barbutero is charismatic. He's entertaining. In fact, he's an accomplished pianist, and he's got a very good voice. Imagine the meat delivery guy tickling the ivories and belting out Billy Joel covers—with that talent, Barbutero assembled a network of spies—waiters, chefs, maître 'ds, delivery men, busboys, and that set him up to go into the business of trading intel."

The AG leaned toward me. "You see, Porter, a lot of business happens in restaurants, especially in those days of the three-martini lunch or the late-night dinner. Barbutero made it his business to know everyone else's business, and he was charming while also being fearless. His luck ran out, ultimately, when he ran afoul of a Jersey mobster, and to save his own ass, Barbutero turned State's witness. He helped crack that case in exchange for a supervised release and no jail time. Guess who was the New York District Attorney at the time?"

I'd noticed that the AG's inflections reverted to the slang of the streets rather than the polish of his elite office, and it wasn't much of a guess to venture, "You, sir?"

"Exactly. Since then, he's been a fount of good intel, and he owes me some favors. I figured he was as loyal as they came, and so when he pinged me with information about Isaac's wealth, residences, and travel arrangements, I began to have suspicions of insider trading. But, not really insider trading as it's known on Wall Street. A different breed, whereby the inside info is from politics. From the government."

"From Coate," I concluded.

"Exactly," the AG affirmed. "As I explained in Salem, Isaac's record is timed almost perfectly to predate significant government actions. She's profiting off the pillow talk. This, in my mind, is a gross dereliction of duty by Coate. Though I cannot prove it, the circumstances would indicate that he is breaching the confidentiality of Congressional work."

That got my attention. "Isn't that borderline treason?"

"Indeed," boomed the AG in his usual baritone. "It's one of the many reasons I believe that Senator Coate is not fit for public office."

"Okay," I offered agreeably, "so in a manner of approaching that sideways, your attention has been focused on Isaac and her transactions."

Joshua Toonin spoke for the first time, speaking in a nasal voice, "Pfizer. Visa. We've got a whole file of Isaac's investments."

"However, she's done nothing illegal," Lin said quietly. "It doesn't look good, but there's no specific law against it. And, given the rising popularity of Coate, not to mention Isaac's own carefully burnished public image, no one seems to mind. Not the media nor the voters."

"We've been over this ground before," I complained to the AG. "Let's get to the point. How does Barbutero get involved with Isaac?"

"Good question," Williams said complimentarily. "Barbutero's delivery business was hamstrung by the restaurant closures during the pandemic, and he began offering provisions to wealthy New Yorkers— including Isaac. Got to know her quite well."

"I thought Isaac was from California," I queried.

"Yes, that's her primary residence. She recently bought a mansion in Malibu. However, New York is the financial capital of the world. Her office is in New York, and she maintains a home in the City. Besides, with her Gulfstream jet, it's no trouble to trot back and forth."

"Right. And we know that Isaac, Preston, and Barbutero are all in New York on Tuesday, October 25th, at the bistro."

Exactly," the AG said. "She had been courting a deal, Preston told me, to buy Aximerva in order to silence Preston's opposition to the EPIC bill. I've got this firsthand from Preston, and his position never wavered. It was a hard no."

"Okay," I nodded. "I know all this. Isaac has lunch with him, and Preston disappears. The FBI pieced together surveillance footage, and we have Preston and Isaac entering the building, at separate times, but only Isaac exits. On a side street, we have images of Barbutero, and the FBI has been looking for him, but he vanished."

"Consider the timing," the AG noted. "Barbutero missing from our usual surveillance nets matches the dates that you were overseas, in the Azores. As we've theorized, perhaps he flew there on Isaac's Gulfstream. Then, you return to Boston, someone shoots at Appleton's vehicle with us in it, and hours later, Barbutero turns up on the train with a gun."

I shrugged. "That's circumstantial, but it's a plausible theory, I suppose." I paused, reflecting and then countering, "But you dropped the line on Barbutero. How does he disappear in New Haven while in FBI custody?" I air-quoted "disappear" as I stared at the AG.

The AG looked at the table before responding. "Don't forget that Coate runs the Senate Homeland Security committee, which oversees national intelligence and the FBI. He's got connections in the Bureau. He could be involved, pulling the strings from afar. That's another reason to get Appleton and you involved. Keep some of this thing off the FBI books."

"That didn't occur to you before you let Barbutero off the train with a couple of Special Agents that you didn't check out in advance? Especially given the circumstances?" I enjoyed the gaping mouths of Toonin and Kinnar-Hering as I chided their boss.

The AG took the critique in stride. "That's why you're here, Porter. I won't make that mistake again." He offered a very brief, somewhat sheepish smile, before getting back to business. "I've got to get to my office. Toonin will brief you on the logistics and will get you the location of your new office. You'll have to find accommodations. You'll be reimbursed for all expenses, of course, including clothing and meals."

"Fine," I agreed.

"Good," the AG said as he stood. "Get started."

I rose as well. As the AG pushed the heavy door open and departed, I asked Toonin, "Where's this office? I'm getting to work tomorrow."

Toonin's face went even paler as he stuttered, "To-to-tomorrow? It's Saturday."

Lin quickly brushed off the objection. "You guys don't worry. I'll start with Ben tomorrow. We'll see you at the office at 9:00 A.M. sharp on Monday." She turned to face me. "Maybe Ben and I get it on tonight. Dinner?"

I grinned my enthusiastic agreement, thinking, *Things are looking up.*

That euphoria would last for only the weekend. . . but it would be a helluva weekend.

# SATURDAY
# OCTOBER 29, 2022

**FIVE DAYS** *BEFORE THE VOTE*

# CHAPTER
# 32



**I WOKE WITH** a start—to a faint scent of hibiscus and to an unfamiliar pressure at my side—until it all came back to me. The pressure and that lovely, captivating smell were that of Sara Lin, nestled beside me.

Staring at a white-painted ceiling, I revisited the night.

We'd left Main Justice, as the Kennedy building was known by its occupants, and strolled at a leisurely pace in a westward direction, paralleling the Washington Mall, passing between the White House and the Washington Monument, and eventually carving northwest on Virginia Avenue. It was forty-five minutes of bliss by the time we reached Lin's townhouse in the Foggy Bottom area of The District.

And—quite a pad it was. The right-side unit within a two-unit, two-story painted brick building, each half had a distinctive color scheme. Lin's cheery aquiline blue front door led into an open plan first floor, with bright, modern furnishings and playful décor. Outside the front door, two whimsical, wire-framed armchairs looked over the sidewalk from a raised brick terrace, and in back, I found a cedar-walled enclosed patio, lit with dainty fairy lights.

I'd whistled. "Quite a place for a Department of Justice attorney." I meant it to sound complimentary, but I was immediately afraid that it came out judgey.

Lin giggled cheerfully. "You'd think I'm skimming bribes, right?" She grinned at me, locking eyes. "Nah. Helps to have rich parents. This place is in their name. I just get to live here."

"You're always so transparent," I said with admiration. "No pretense."

"Never. Just not worth it." She smiled again, and I felt a rush of warmth in my body—until she broke the tension. "But don't worry about my parents. They're home in Japan. In fact, they've never been here. I'm just a caretaker for their million-dollar investment in Washington real estate." She batted her eyelashes. "So, we've got the place all to ourselves."

"Well, it's a super nice setup," I gushed—as she pulled me close and kissed me under the twinkle of the fairy lights, the warm, late fall Washington breeze caressing our skin.

We eventually walked to a restaurant for dinner, and then we returned to the Foggy Bottom townhouse to collapse into Lin's bed.

Saturday morning passed peacefully—a walk to a café for coffee and breakfast, then a stroll eastward to Georgetown so that I could purchase clothes to augment the limited wardrobe in my Azores backpack. I rang up well over two thousand dollars worth of garb—both casual and business attire—onto my American Express card. I'm not much of a clothes horse, so the expenditure felt gauche, almost excessive—but I didn't see that I had much choice. My usual Bureau outfits of suits and ties were back in Chelsea, and here in Washington, I knew that I needed to dress smart if I wanted to look smart.

Shopping mission accomplished, Lin suggested, "Let's head to our office," and as we set off on the twenty-or-so minute walk from Georgetown back toward Foggy Bottom, my phone rang.

It was Appleton, and she got straight to the point. "Porter. We've made progress."

"That's great," I replied, flashing Lin a thumbs-up. She, of course, was fully briefed on the episode on the Acela.

"Not really," Appleton groaned. "The agents who met the train to remove Barbutero—they are all stand-up guys with squeaky-clean records. In particular, Agent Hurst is one of the most well-regarded men in the New Haven Field Office."

"How are you getting this intel? Wasn't yesterday your last day as SAC?"

Appleton chuckled humorlessly. "Unfortunate timing. It would help if I was still in that seat with access. However, I'm owed plenty of favors. And I talked to Hurst on Friday while I was still the Boston SAC."

"You trust him?"

She sighed. "At this point, I'm not sure who to trust. But, yeah, he's got a clean record. And he tells me that his team was met by a second FBI team outside the New Haven station. They showed him written orders that they were to take Barbutero into their custody. And—get this—Hurst said that the orders came from the Hoover building."

I wagered, "It was an inside job, then."

"Looks that way," Appleton agreed. "Somebody at the Bureau in Washington got wind of this."

"It's all still inside the Bureau, then," I observed. "Do you think you can track down Barbutero's location?"

"I'm working on it. Hurst got the name of the lead agent who intercepted Barbutero—her name is Mariana O'Toole. I'm running down her jacket but since she's not inside my former Boston field office, it will take a little longer to establish who she is, who she reports to, and where she is. But I'll find her, and then I will find Barbutero." She paused and added in a cautionary tone, "But there's more."

Appleton's tone caused the hairs on the back of my neck to shiver. "Yeah? What's that?"

"Hurst told me that he didn't get a copy of the orders from that second team, but he looked at them very carefully to ensure that they were legit—because there was a moment of confusion when Hurst authorized the transfer of custody to this Agent O'Toole. There were two names on the custody order: Rocco Barbutero and Ben Porter."

# CHAPTER
## 33

**AS WE WALKED** eastward on Pennsylvania Avenue, crossing Rock Creek, and leaving Georgetown behind as we entered Washington's West End area, Lin and I dissected Appleton's intel.

"I heard you say to Appleton that it was an inside job," Lin observed. "Gotta be. The FBI runs the AG's protective detail out of the Hoover building. Those agents report back to Washington."

"Right," I agreed. "I can't prove it, but I can easily conclude that the agent who was on the phone aboard the train called it into headquarters while the AG was calling Appleton. Appleton dispatched a team from New Haven, and Washington did the same."

"I think it's just a turf mix-up, Ben," Lin suggested.

I shrugged. "Makes sense, I guess. But why was my name on their list?"

"Simple. You said that the AG impersonated you and used your name."

"Yeah, that makes sense, too," I agreed. Inwardly, though, I was reluctant to reach such a quick conclusion. My name listed alongside Barbutero's just didn't add up.

I kept that to myself, though, and added, "Anyway, I guess the good news is that Barbutero is in Bureau custody. He didn't just disappear. And, hopefully, Appleton's contacts will quickly let us know who has him—and where—so we can talk to him."

Lin asked, "What's her plan?"

"She's staying local in the northeast until she tracks him down." I looked at Lin and stated, "She'll find him. Appleton is very good. But," I added, as I looked around at an unfamiliar Washington street, "where are we? And where are you taking me?"

I glanced over at Sara Lin, her wavy hair pushed alluringly behind one ear as she looked over at me. "Almost there. See that statue," she said, pointing at the bronze figure of a man astride a galloping horse, set atop a marble pediment at the center of a circular park at the busy intersection of K Street, Pennsylvania Avenue, 23rd Street, and New Hampshire Avenue, "that's the George Washington Equestrian statue. We're going up New Hampshire Avenue."

Lin halted us on a sidewalk just northeast of the statue. She pointed at a five-story, red-brick-clad, long building fenestrated with black-edged, arched-top windows. At one corner was a circular mass—a turret, almost—and Lin aimed a forefinger at the windowpanes set at the top. "There it is. Let's go up."

Tapping a ten-digit code on a keypad, we entered at a non-descript side door, which opened to a bare elevator vestibule with only one other door in sight. "That's the fire stair, and you cannot open the doors from the outside. It's emergency egress only," Lin explained. "There's only one way up to the fifth floor, and that's an elevator with an independent power supply. We'll ride the lift."

Inside the elevator car, there was another keypad—and only two buttons, marked *1* and *5*. After she punched in a code, the *5* button lit, and Lin pressed it gently. The elevator whirred quietly and rose.

With a ding, the elevator stopped, and the wood-veneered carriage door slid open to reveal a foyer, tastefully decorated with modern furnishings: a sleek reception-like desk, sofa, two club chairs, and a series of closed, maple-colored doors. "Follow me," Lin ordered, and I tailed her to the leftmost of the maple doors to find yet another keypad.

"How many codes do I have to remember?"

"Just three. The outside entry, the elevator, and then the interior office doors. We will change them periodically, and we shouldn't share the codes," Lin replied as she clicked the door open. "This door leads to your office. After the tour, I'll show you how to change the code. Get in the habit of changing it daily, and you'll know that the contents of your own space are secure and accessible only to you."

The room inside was clearly at the top of the turret that I'd seen from the sidewalk. Circular in shape, there were no right angles except at the entry door. Lin narrated the tour. "This is it! Your office. It's got a very nice seating area for four." She pointed at a tidy grouping of four barrel-shaped chairs, and then she swept her hand sideways and said, "And over here, you've got a credenza and a desk. Aeron chair for you and two chairs opposite your desk for visitors. Do you like the desk?"

I eyed the sleek, glass slab that balanced atop thick, black iron legs. "Nice. Very clean." The décor matched the vibe—unlike the exterior, which was Washington Gothic, the interior of the fifth-floor private suite was almost Scandinavian. It oozed a new money style. And, unlike the field office back home in Boston, I'd be settling into the real deal—no imitation Aeron chairs here. Whoever set this place up spared no expense.

I narrowed my gaze at the items on the surface of the desk: an iPhone, an Apple laptop computer, and a writing pad. What I didn't see, and kinda hoped for, was a Glock Model 22 pistol—I had locked my service weapon inside a gun safe, the morning of my flight to the Azores, before leaving my Massachusetts home, and I felt uncomfortably unarmed. I'd have to figure out that later.

Lin paced over to the windows that looked down to New Hampshire Avenue as I asked, "Am I to understand that you're working from here, too? Not from Main Justice?"

"Correct," she replied as she continued to gaze from the turret windows, her back toward me. "With Josh and Jaylen, also. We can accommodate more people if we need to."

"We will," I suggested. "Appleton, obviously. Eventually." In my head, I also thought, *I'd like to have the rest of my team here, too*, but I knew that sort of thinking was unproductive.

"Definitely Appleton. When she arrives, arrange to meet her outside so you don't send the access codes via unencrypted text message," Lin cautioned, finally turning from the New Hampshire Avenue view to face me. "Listen, get yourself set up and comfortable. I'm gonna duck into my office and confirm the meeting that we have tomorrow."

She paced to my office doorway and as she reached the jamb, I asked, "What meeting?"

Lin smiled wickedly. "I figured that you might as well get to know the players face-to-face. These Washington relationships, if I even dare call them that, are circular. One day, someone is your mortal enemy. The next day, that same someone is your bestie."

"I don't follow," I confessed.

"Tomorrow at noon, you're gonna meet the man in the middle of it all, just as soon as the usual Sunday morning talk show circuit concludes. You'd better do your homework and prepare your questions." She walked out of the office.

Annoyed by her coyness, I called angrily, "For who?"

I heard Lin's tinkling laugh from the foyer outside. She was clearly enjoying the suspense. Finally, she stuck her head around the edge of the door jamb and grinned, saying, "The man himself. Senator Merritt Coate."

# CHAPTER
# 34



**HER STYLIST PREPPED** the outfit with the season and the locale in mind, and so when Hanna Mo'Nique Isaac stepped from a black Cadillac Escalade to the wide sidewalk of Elm Street in New Haven, Connecticut, she embodied an almost-perfect match to her surroundings. Her overcoat was a shade of golden yellow, mimicking the fall leaves of the ubiquitous elm trees, her boots were a deep brown as if they stood in as tree trunks, and her Chanel handbag was a subdued burnt orange. She was Instagram worthy, but no photographers were in sight as she swept past a low, white, picket fence and approached the Kelly-green front door of a quaint-looking, white-clapboard, two-story house, dotted with coordinating Kelly-green shutters flanking its symmetrically arranged, six-over-six, double hung windows.

A small sign to the right of the door bore two words in a tasteful font: "Members Only."

Ignoring the warning, Isaac pulled the heavy door open and disappeared inside. As an invited guest, she had every right to enter, and just past the threshold and in a high-ceilinged foyer with shiny wood floors and a grouping of dowdy wingback chairs upholstered in a busy floral pattern, she was met by a short-statured, pale-skinned, red-cheeked, red-headed woman wearing a conservative Kelly-green pantsuit. The woman spoke in a high-pitched voice and addressed Isaac, "Good afternoon, ma'am. I'm Special Agent Mariana O'Toole. We last spoke on the phone yesterday."

Isaac bowed her head politely. "Of course. A pleasure to finally meet in person, Agent O'Toole. I've so enjoyed our many telephone calls. And I love the color you're wearing—it's quite apropos for the location."

The agent stuttered, "I—I'm not sure what you mean, ma'am."

Patting her on the shoulder and noting a bit of padding meant to enhance the smaller woman's shoulders, Isaac smiled. "The front door of this place matches your suit, and that color brings out your eyes. It's very lovely." She paused as the agent beamed at the compliment, especially since it came from a fashion icon with fifty million followers on Instagram. Isaac allowed her innate charm to sink in for a moment before continuing, "By the way, why are we meeting here? The FBI Field Office is only a half-mile away."

Still glowing, O'Toole replied, "Too many eyes and ears at the office, not only on our witness but, frankly, on you. I thought it best to have our discussion here, at the Elm Tree Club. It's a private place unassociated with the Bureau, and on occasion, the lower-level drawing room is useful because it is secluded."

"Wonderful. Lead the way."

The two ladies wound their way down a narrow stair, Isaac trailing the Special Agent but towering over her by at least a head. The investor ducked slightly to clear the beam that crossed the lowest step as she eyed the ceiling warily. It was no more than six-and-a-half feet high, and it was crossed by dark, heavy, hand-hewn, axed beams. The shorter agent darted further ahead to open a wooden door. "Right here, ma'am."

The light inside the drawing room was dim, the space lit only by two table lamps and a single, small, three-paned sash that was set in a stone-encircled window well. The dark beams continued in this area, too, and the floor was a bumpy concrete, covered with a richly patterned Oriental rug. A grouping of a brown leather sofa flanked by two orange and brown wingbacks faced the stone surround and ornate wooden mantle of an unlit fireplace.

The sole occupant of the room, a leathery-skinned, pockmarked, mustachioed man, in his forties or fifties, stood from the right-side wingback as the two women entered, his eyes slightly below the level of O'Toole's gaze. He grinned lopsidedly, exposing coffee-stained, crooked teeth. "Hello, Hanna."

Isaac did not return the smile as she addressed the man flatly with only one word. "Rocco."

He smirked. "Oh, please. What's with the cold shoulder?" Turning to the smaller woman, he added, "Maybe you'll be a little nicer, Agent O'Toole?"

O'Toole settled into the left-side wingback and waved at the more expansive, somewhat nicer-looking sofa. "Ma'am, please, have a seat." As Isaac sank into the leather and crossed her legs, O'Toole addressed the man who had resumed his seat in the opposite wingback. "Mister Barbutero, I don't believe that niceties have anything to do with our discussion this afternoon."

Barbutero repeated himself in a mocking tone. "Oh, please. You folks need to simmer down. Everything is a crisis to you. I assure you, it's not."

Isaac leaned forward. "Except, it is. We are in crisis mode. I flew all the way across the country at a moment's notice because of your failure. You failed on the train. You're lucky that the contingencies kicked in, and O'Toole got word to remove you from the situation. You're lucky that O'Toole happened to be driving from Boston to DC after that botched operation. You're lucky that she managed to get orders signed and printed by the time that train reached the stop here in New Haven. You're—"

"I get it, I get it, I get it," Barbutero protested as he leaned his body toward the sofa. "It coulda gone better. It coulda gone to plan. I woulda given the AG the message. He woulda backed off."

Isaac grimaced. "But, Rocco, that's not what happened. Not only did you fail to send that message, but you were also exposed in the process. Because of that, this whole thing could unravel. The AG didn't get to where he is by blithely ignoring matters like this. He's stubborn and determined, and now he has a thread to pull on."

Barbutero shrugged. "Yeah, so what? He ID'd me. And, yeah, he'll link me back with you. But whaddya worried about? That was bound to happen."

"Except that drastically compromises us," Isaac snarled.

Barbutero chuckled softly. "Still not a crisis. Nor has the timeline altered one tiny second, ya know. Trust me—he got a message. He knows you're onto him." Barbutero pointed a stubby finger at Isaac and hissed, "We ain't playing some parlor game here. Fuckups are bound to happen when the stakes are so high. Get over it. You're supposed to be a pro at this. So—act like a pro and move on."

Isaac sighed, her expression softening as she nodded her agreement with Barbutero. "Bart Williams's time has come, that's for certain. The man is rotten to the core. His personal agendas and vendettas must be stopped."

Barbutero squirmed in the wingback. "Yeah. Agreed. Hey, O'Toole, can I smoke in here?"

"No," the agent grunted, before asking Isaac, "You're certain that the political attempts have been exhausted?"

Isaac rolled her eyes. "If my husband can't get it done, no one can. That's why we've been backed into this corner. We thought that if Virgil Preston's support of the AG suddenly evaporated, the AG would cave. He'd see the writing on the wall. He'd get the message that his vendetta is going to be exposed."

"On the train, I gotta admit he was a very cool customer," Barbutero observed. "He was unfazed."

"His power has gone to his head," Isaac said. "He thinks he's above it all. He thinks that by teaming up with Preston, he can sink my husband's bill. The EPIC act doesn't pass, my husband is humiliated, and his political capital is trashed. Meanwhile, Williams begins to use the justice system to bulk up what he supports and tear down what he opposes. He uses the FBI as his own personal army. Hell, I heard he's starting his own proprietary investigation office."

"That's what concerns me, and it's why I'm cooperating with you," O'Toole interjected. "That intel is also being circulated in the Bureau headquarters in DC, and if that's really what he's planning, Williams will violate more laws than I can count. Watercooler gossip has it that the Boston SAC stepped aside so that she could work directly for the AG."

"Yes," Isaac muttered. "Jennifer Appleton. I'm familiar with her."

O'Toole continued, "And then there's this Ben Porter. It's too bad that he didn't get off the train with Barbutero. We assumed—incorrectly, obviously—that he would disembark in New Haven. After all, we know that the AG used Porter's name when he addressed the passengers in the train car. I would have liked to have Porter at this meeting."

"Tell me what you know about him," Isaac commanded.

"He's the golden boy of the Boston office. As an Information Management Specialist, he stopped a terror attack. Then he led the Eleanor Thornton case and ultimately took down an international threat. Most recently, he exposed a government operation. All very hush-hush. In sum, he's a very good investigator, and he's got this vibe that he's unassuming, so he's underestimated."

Isaac shook her head morosely. "Now he's linked to the AG?"

"Seems that way," O'Toole confirmed. "We know from the files that the AG and Porter have interacted on cases. Then Barbutero spotted Porter at Appleton's residence."

Barbutero smirked. "Guess that threw a wrinkle into the plan."

"What is this, amateur hour, Rocco? You're awfully cavalier." The scorn was evident in Isaac's voice.

The hitman scowled, and his expression darkened dramatically. Narrowing his eyes, he snarled, "Listen, Hanna, what you judge as, what was it—cavalier? That's because I take risks—so you don't have to. That's why you hired me, right? Don't want to mess up that fancy manicure of yours, do you?" Barbutero raised a hand and rubbed his temples as the color faded from his pockmarked cheeks. "I'll admit this has not been my finest hour. However, I assure you, we ain't even close to the finish line yet, and bad shit is bound to go down. I gotta take the misses and the fuck-ups without getting buried by them. *Capishe?*"

As Barbutero met Isaac's gaze, she understood that his sideways apology was the best she'd get, and wise to the ways of manipulation, she modulated her tone to resemble kindness and curiosity as she offered her own olive branch. "Of all people, you know the AG the best. Your intel on this is key. You used to spy for him, for crying out loud. What's his next move?"

The fireplug of a man shrugged a second time. "Used to work for him, yeah. It was productive until it wasn't. Until the AG wanted to use my intel, my connections, for his gain. Then I knew it was time to find an alternative source of employment. I fed him bullshit and kept him in the dark, like a mushroom." He laughed softly, but then looked at his feet and added, "But I've been exposed, so obviously I'm compromised."

O'Toole scowled. "Dare I say, you're useless, Barbutero. You're in hiding from now forward." She addressed Isaac. "However, I'd like to suggest you consider my workaround."

Isaac rearranged herself on the leather sofa, uncrossing then recrossing her legs. She absently fiddled with one of her boots, caressing the material. "Ah, yes, yes, I agree completely. That was a good concept, O'Toole. We need to get in front of this Ben Porter. He's our inroad to whatever the AG is up to."

Barbutero grimaced. "You want me to go to DC and, um, introduce myself? I can be quite charming, ya know."

Isaac smiled wickedly at the mustachioed man. "I'm ahead of you. You see, Rocco, this is why I pull the levers. As soon as the very capable O'Toole gave the rundown of what happened on the train, I managed to arrange a meeting with Mister Porter."

"Impressive," Barbutero gushed. "When and where?"

"Tomorrow, in Washington. But not with me, or with you—that would be reckless." Isaac laughed. "We need Porter on our side, for the sake of the nation, and there is no one in the world who can be as convincing as my husband."

As O'Toole and Barbutero nodded in unison, Isaac concluded confidently. "Merritt will speak with Porter, and I'm quite sure that after that conversation, Porter will come around. And if not, I already have a backup plan that will ensure his cooperation."

# SUNDAY
# OCTOBER 30, 2022

**FOUR DAYS** *BEFORE THE VOTE*

# CHAPTER
# 35



**AT HALF-PAST TWELVE** on a hazy, warm, Washington weekend afternoon, I was ensconced in one of the four boucle fabric upholstered barrel chairs that clustered around a low, glossy white, tulip base, oval-shaped coffee table. I'd quickly acclimated to my swank new office inside a fifth-floor turret overlooking New Hampshire Avenue, spending most of yesterday afternoon hunched over a laptop computer while working out a background profile of Senator Merritt Coate. My work carried into the evening, paused overnight for another blissful stay at Sara Lin's townhouse, and I picked up the research again this morning.

I wrapped up just an hour ago, and I felt thoroughly prepared but the Senator was a half-hour late, and I was beginning to assume that I'd been blown off when my phone chimed with a text from Lin, who'd been waiting for our guest on the sidewalk below.

On our way up. You ready?

Pressing and holding the text bubble on my iPhone, I signaled my reply with a thumbs-up tapback, wondering whether Android devices offered the same instant value judgments—a thumbs-up or thumbs-down, a heart, and a few other options—that were available to IOS users. Indeed, I'd often speculated that Apple should offer a middle-finger tapback. There were times that would be singularly handy (no pun intended)—*If not a tad inappropriate*, I thought.

Setting aside my tremendous idea that would contribute greatly to the text messaging universe, I stood and paced to the windows that encircled my turret lair. Looking down, I could make out two black Suburbans pulled to the curb, and I wondered if the Senator would be accompanied by aides.

Fidgeting with my hands, I decided to wait for the Senator at the doorway, and soon enough, the elevator door slid ajar to reveal Lin and, towering over her, the six-foot-two-inch, tanned, sun-bleached and sandy-haired Merritt Coate. He strode from the maw of the elevator cabin and extended his right hand, calling out in his folksy drawl, "The one and only Ben Porter. It's quite an honor, you know, to meet the legend."

I surreptitiously wiped my right hand behind my back to dry a sweaty palm before grasping the Senator's outstretched paw. "It's a pleasure to meet you, Senator. But I'm not so sure about the legend part."

"It's Merritt, Ben. I've got no use for titles, especially in this company. I'm cleared Top Secret, so I know quite a bit about your work in the field. You've accomplished a great deal, Ben, and I know I speak for a grateful nation when I acknowledge our gratitude for your service."

*Typical politician*, I thought. *Laying it on thick.*

But, as much as I wanted to dislike the man that the Attorney General claimed was undermining the nation, I was awed by his charisma. His blue eyes flashed brightly, and his grin appeared sincere.

I shook it off. *This is an interview, Ben*, I chastised myself. *Focus.*

"Sir, I, uh, I think I'm gonna stick with Senator, if that's okay. Just a thing I have, I guess, for my superiors." I waved my hand toward my office. "Please, join me in there. Let's sit. Can I get you anything? Coffee? Water?"

"Nah, Ben, I'm all set," Coate said, shrugging off his navy-blue suit coat and dragging a white handkerchief across his cheeks. "That darn makeup. They plaster it on, you know, for the Sunday morning TV shows. I washed it off, but man, it seems to stick something fierce." The Senator tossed his jacket onto one of my barrel chairs and sank down with a sigh. "This is more my speed, ya know, than preening for those TV cameras."

Lin perched to his left, and I took the chair opposite Coate. "Well, thank you for joining us after doing those shows, sir. I'm sure you'd prefer an afternoon off."

The Senator grinned again. "As long as you get me outta here by, say, 1:30, I can catch the end of the Steelers-Eagles game."

I narrowed my eyes. "I thought you were a Kansas City Chiefs fan, sir. Born and raised in Lansing, Kansas, right?"

"You've done your homework, eh, Ben? Sure enough, the Chiefs are my football team. But the Philadelphia Eagles look pretty strong this year, so I gotta keep an eye on the competition. Besides, the Chiefs have a bye this week, which gives me a chance to watch some other teams."

"Well, I won't keep you long, Senator. Just a few questions."

"Shoot, Ben. Lemme at 'em."

I decided previously to forego notes, as I wanted the interview to appear spontaneous. The first question, though, was an easy one to remember, because it would set the tone. "Can you educate me? I don't know much about politics or business. I—"

"Now, Ben, I don't buy that for a second," Coate gushed. "I know from your record that you've got a helluva noggin." Grinning, he tapped his head for emphasis.

"I appreciate that, sir. Pretend, then, that I'm not that guy. That I'm just a voter, wondering what the EPIC bill means to me."

Coate leaned forward earnestly. "You've heard the phrase, a rising tide lifts all boats, right? That's what my bill aims to do. It doesn't just benefit the folks who manufacture semiconductors. It puts those people, those jobs, within our borders, making us less reliant on foreign sources while localizing a domestic supply chain."

I could see he was back in television interview mode, clearly reciting the sales pitch that had become second nature to him. Coate continued, "Look around at the blank spaces. The empty car dealer lots, because they can't get semiconductors and build vehicles. Backlogs and backorders up and down the supply chain for computers, circuit boards, and even household appliances like televisions and even refrigerators. They all use chips. And we don't control that supply. We've fallen so far behind, and it's time to put American manufacturers back in the driver's seat."

The Senator's expression was grim and focused—but he exuded confidence. It was the same charisma that my sister Grace and I saw on the TV in her living room only days ago. Coate's passion and utter commitment to the bill that he'd authored was obviously genuine—especially in person.

*Shake out of it, Ben,* I thought, admitting to myself that I'd been wowed by the celebrity Senator sitting across from me.

Refocusing on the interview, I said, "The bill seems to be very popular. It comes up for a final vote in just a few days, and from what I've heard, it's gonna pass with bipartisan support."

Coate grinned. "I've spent over a year workin' on this. A version of EPIC sailed through the House and then passed the Senate. We've got to dot the I's and cross the T's on the final, compromise bill, but we're close. And do you know why, Ben? 'Cuz it makes sense. It's clear. It's not saddled with earmarks addin' on pork. Not that there's anything wrong with pork—if you're eatin' it. Know what I mean?" He chuckled at his joke.

I noticed that Coate's tone became more down-home Kansas than polished Californian. He knew how to lay it on as if he was a regular guy. One of the boys. He was pulling me into his orbit, his aura, just as he'd done so successfully with not only voters but also with his fellow politicians.

It was time to reset the tone, and I started to dig. "Sara told me that she explained the background to you. That we're tasked by the Attorney General to investigate, among other things, the disappearance of Virgil Preston, the CEO of Aximerva. And Aximerva, as one of the largest US manufacturers of semiconductors would seem to gain a lot from the EPIC act—and yet the company's CEO was adamantly opposed to your bill. Why?"

Coate leaned back and looked up at the ceiling for a moment before asking, "This office is secure, correct? We're not being recorded, right? I mean, you could lie and tell me no, but then, because I've asked, you can't play the tape."

"Yes and no, sir. Yes, it is secure and, no, there are no recording devices present," I replied, carefully making eye contact with the Senator.

"Just checking," Coate said with a wink. "Look, lemme explain. Aximerva was doing this lone wolf thing, insisting on building a new plant on their own. As a layperson, Ben, you might say that's the right thing to do, naturally, but you gotta think bigger. It's counterintuitive, but if we're gonna fix the semiconductor industry here in the States, we gotta do it together. We can't have one company as a maverick. We need cooperation."

I recalled my research and queried, "But doesn't that smack of a government-subsidized monopoly? Where's free enterprise and capitalism fit in?"

"Oh, they fit, for sure. But how does it work, at least initially, if you've got this one outlier, Aximerva? We're gonna be trying to give firms an equal chance, an equal footing, but Virgil Preston wanted none of it. He wanted control, opportunity, and frankly, the advantage that goes to the first mover, all to the benefit of Aximerva only. He had no interest in cooperation for the long-term benefit of the United States. He wasn't patient nor was he open-minded. His attitude was, hey, to the hell with the rest of 'em."

I prodded, "You knew him, right? Preston? You'd met with him?"

The Senator clicked his tongue and frowned. "Ah, Virgil. 'Course I knew him. He was a good man. A fine businessman. And I say that without reservation, even though we didn't see eye-to-eye on his recent expansion plans." He pursed his lips and exhaled. "I think my wife was one of the last people to see him. She had lunch with him, ya know, the day he disappeared."

"Yes, I'm aware of that," I confirmed. "Did Preston deserve to, um, disappear for holding onto his position? Opposing your bill?"

Coate started in his seat. "Whoa, whoa. Hang on there, Ben."

Lin raised her hand slightly, perhaps as a warning to me, but I barreled on from my barrel chair. "Here's the situation, sir. I'm no macroeconomist, so I can't speak to the effectiveness of the semiconductor bill. I can't opine on manufacturing or subsidies. I can, however, wonder how it came to be that Preston—the last, powerful opponent to your EPIC act—disappeared immediately following a meeting with your wife."

Coate shot to his feet and shouted, "How dare you?"

*Whoops*, I thought. *Maybe I jumped on that too quickly.*

The Senator grabbed his jacket and snarled to Lin, "You told me this fella was worth talkin' to."

As he strode to the door, Lin spoke for the first time in the meeting. "Senator, please. I assure you; Ben is worth it. You've got to give him a chance."

"Forget it," Coate snarled. "How do I get outta here?"

Lin's glare shot daggers at me as she hissed angrily, "Are you kidding, Porter? What were you thinking?" She dashed after the Senator, calling, "Sir! Wait! Please."

I exhaled. This was supposed to be the meeting when I established a rapport with Coate. At the Bureau, we interview, we don't interrogate. And with my direct question and veiled accusation, I crossed that line.

*Maybe I'm not cut out for Washington*, I thought with embarrassment. *Now what?*

Fortunately, Lin would solve that problem for me, and I'd realize that her talent for persuasion was incomparable.

# CHAPTER
# 36

**THERE WAS A RUSTLE** outside my office door which I assumed was Coate boarding the elevator in a huff, but I was wrong—it was, instead, Coate shoving his way past Lin as he pushed back inside my turret.

The Senator wagged a finger at me. "Ben, you're lucky that you're working with Sara, here. She's smart. She's level-headed. She's pleasant. You could learn a lot from her, Ben."

"Yessir," I said, rising from the barrel chair. I bowed my head, "Actually, sir, I was just thinking that. She is accustomed to The District. I'm not quite as polished."

"Nonsense," the Senator scoffed. "Nothing to do with polish or Washington. Mind your tone, fella, and be more polite. You get a lot more with honey than with vinegar."

"Lesson learned, sir," I replied contritely as Lin and the Senator lowered themselves into the chairs they occupied earlier. This time, however, instead of casually flinging his coat onto the neighboring chair, Coate carefully folded it before draping the cloth over the back of the barrel. As he completed the task, I offered, "I apologize, sir."

"Sure thing, Ben." He sniffed. "Look, here's the deal. Here's what Sara explained to me, outside. I know you're both tight with the AG. I get that. But Bart Williams has got a hard-on for me and my wife and—"

He stopped suddenly, raising his eyebrows, and quickly apologized to Lin. "Shoot. Sorry about the language, Sara." He grinned sheepishly. "I gotta remember to clean up my act. That kind of talk is not presidential, if you know what I mean."

"No worries, sir," Lin said pleasantly.

Coate cleared his throat and crossed his legs. "What I meant to say was that Bart Williams has traditionally been less than impressed with my wife. He's become somewhat of a broken record—and yes, I know I'm dating myself with that phrase." The Senator chuckled. "Lemme try some more modern slang. These days, they'd say that my wife is sus. Suspect. Her gains in the markets and in her investments are well-timed, for sure, but she's got a very good track record."

"I'm not sure I follow, sir," I confessed.

The Senator pursed his lips and looked away for a moment. "Take her investment in Pfizer. She did very well. But, did she have inside intel, as Bart Williams would like you to believe?" He snorted. "Any damn fool could see what was coming—not specifically a virus, or a vaccine, but turbulence. Uncertainty. The markets move as a herd, and when the herd gets spooked, it bolts. If the herd is happy, it races together, toward the kill. But here's the trick, Ben—ultimately it doesn't matter." He squinted at me and concluded, "Hanna tracks the herd. She senses the direction the herd is gonna take, and she acts accordingly. She's very good at reading emotions. Frankly, so am I. We're cut from the same cloth."

I shrugged and said, hoping to sound non-committal, "Makes sense, I guess. However, I do believe that the Attorney General is not working off assumptions. He has data, no?"

Coate chuckled. "Probably, yes. But—that's the trouble with data, though, isn't it? You can manipulate it to reach a variety of conclusions."

Using my best obsequious tone, I asked, "You're saying that the AG is manufacturing a case?"

"Right on, Ben," Coate confirmed, but his enthusiastic voice didn't match his grim face. "I have to wonder if Bart has political aspirations of his own. And you know that nothing gets votes more than someone who looks squeaky clean in the face of a scandal. Makes you wonder, doesn't it?"

It did, but I wasn't ready to capitulate. "With all due respect, Senator, isn't that your end game, too? Play both sides and get the votes?"

Coate burst into laughter, a genuinely hearty guffaw. "Of course! Right on again, Ben!" He took a series of deep breaths, enjoying his moment, before adding evenly, "However, Ben, I'm in it for the long haul. I've been at this for years, working on behalf of not just California, not just my birth state of Kansas, smack dab in the heart of this wonderful union of states, but for all of the American people. This latest effort—my EPIC act—is just one play as we matriculate the ball down the field on behalf of our great nation."

I blinked. Once, twice, and then a third time. "What?"

Coate clenched a fist and repeated, "Our great nation!"

"No, no, no. The part before. You're doing what? Down the field?"

Coate laughed again, grinning widely. "That's a terrific phrase, isn't it? Credit to Kansas City Chiefs Coach Hank Stram, when the Chiefs won Super Bowl IV, back in 1970. Stram was mic'd up. One of the first, if not *the* first, occasions that a coach was recorded on the sidelines, and Stram dropped that very memorable line." The Senator shrugged and attempted to sound modest. "I personally think it's a great analogy for what I do in my job. It's a lotta work, you know, but we all gotta work together as a team to move the ball toward the goal."

Lin cocked her head and said cheerily, "I believe it's a metaphor, not an analogy, sir."

Coate snorted. "Whatever."

I closed my eyes for a second, breathing lightly through my nose. *Coate is charming*, I thought. *And he's right. I can't just take the AG at face value. After all, I've done nothing to independently verify his claims against Isaac. I'm merely taking his word for it.*

I smiled as I reopened my eyes to meet Coate's stare. "One more question, sir. Say you're correct. Say the AG is creating a case. Aren't you concerned that I'll report this discussion back to him? What does he say to that?"

"I got nothing to hide, Ben," Coate said firmly. "Look, like I said earlier, I am read in on your background and on the cases you've solved. Quite adeptly, I might add. I want you to do your own investigation, and that's why I agreed to meet as soon as Sara suggested it. Transparency is key. And to that end, may I ask you a question?"

"Um, sure," I agreed.

"Has Bart Williams been transparent? Or has he obfuscated in the name of secrecy?"

I licked my lips. *The Senator can read my mind. I literally just thought that.*

Buying time, I scratched my right ear and mumbled, "I'd prefer not to answer that specifically, but, yes, I will concede you have a point."

"Hmmph," the Senator grunted. "Looks like you got some work to do." He stood and glanced at his watch. "One thirty on the dot. We good, Ben?"

I rose and nodded. "Yessir. Thank you, sir."

We shook hands, and this time Coate patted me on the shoulder in a friendly manner. "We got off on the wrong foot earlier, Ben. I'm glad I stuck around, though. Sara was correct, as usual. You're a good man."

I repeated, "Thank you, sir."

Coate made for the door but paused to turn back and address me one final time. "Last thing, Ben. You wanna talk to Hanna, you just let me know. Sara's got my private line. I'll be happy to set that up."

"I think that would be very productive, sir, and I'd like to take you up on that offer, right now. I don't need to think about it. If you'd be kind enough to make the arrangements, I will obviously make myself available whenever it's convenient for her."

The Senator from California winked. "Good call, Ben. You're a quick study. You understand how helpful a face-to-face will be." He nodded and pledged, "I'm on it."

Lin escorted Coate to the elevator, leaving me to pace my office, passing one window after another as I circled the fifth-floor turret. Reaching the grouping of the four barrel chairs, I realized I returned to where I'd started—*Much like this case*, I thought.

*We're going in a circle. First the AG pins Isaac and Coate. Now Coate points a finger at the AG. Who am I after?*

Thinking back to my previous cases, a solution hit me at once.

# CHAPTER

## 37

**IN MY FIFTH-FLOOR TURRET,** I quickly packed what I required in a small, brown, leather briefcase that I'd bought yesterday in Georgetown. Laptop, charger, and notepad, and I shoved my phone in my pocket.

As I shut off the lights and locked my office door behind me, Lin exited the elevator and demanded, "Where are you headed? You weren't gonna wait for me?" Her voice was plaintive.

"Ah, we've only got one elevator. And you were on it. That's why I'm waiting at the door."

She giggled as she reboarded the elevator carriage. "Good point." Her expression hardened, and she asked seriously, "What did you think of Merritt Coate?"

Stepping inside the carriage, I spun one hundred and eighty degrees, instinctively, as we all do for some reason, to face the door. I admitted, "I was impressed. He's far more down to earth than I expected." I paused and studied Lin's face. "Here's what I don't understand. You clearly know him. You've got a direct line. How is it that the Attorney General doesn't know that? Or does he?"

"Oh, he knows, of course. That's why he assigned me to this investigation. Remember what I said earlier? Everything in Washington is circular. You make connections, and then you use them."

"Interesting choice of word," I replied as the elevator reached the ground level, and the door slid open. "Circular. Like what we're doing."

Lin grunted. "Huh? What's your plan, anyway?"

"Problem-solving. And the first problem is that I'm hungry for some comfort food and thirsty for a beer."

"I know just the place," Lin announced.

I followed Lin for ten minutes as we made our way to the heart of Foggy Bottom, where she carved into a place named Tonic, a two-story restaurant located in the historic Quigley pharmacy building. With the lunch rush over, we were fortunate to have an end of the bar to ourselves, and I pulled the notepad from my satchel as Lin flagged the bartender and whispered an order.

I squinted at her. "I didn't hear that. What are we having?"

She grinned. "How are we problem-solving?"

I was drawing a circle on a blank sheet of paper, and I divided it into four quadrants. Narrating to Lin, I wrote in the northeast pie and said, "Barbutero. He's the guy from the train." Then I drew an arrow to the southeast pie and said, "Williams. The AG decides to run an off-the-books investigation on a presumptive presidential candidate. With me so far?"

"Yep," Lin confirmed.

"From Williams, we draw an arrow to here. The southwest quadrant." I wrote Coate in that area and then drew a fourth arrow upward to the northwest quadrant. "And here we have Isaac. Who, according to the AG, is profiting off her husband's inside intel, and who, again according to the AG and Coate himself, was placed with Virgil Preston." I drew a fifth and final arrow from Isaac's name to Barbutero's name and concluded, "The AG said that Barbutero was spotted outside the place where Isaac and Preston met."

I set the pen down as the bartender delivered a pair of pint glasses, each filled with golden lager and topped with a thin layer of white, foamy bubbles. Taking a moment to enjoy the taste of the beer, I tapped the pen on the pad, licked my lips, and said, "Circular. Next step is Isaac. Can you call the Senator and confirm that as soon as possible? And in the meantime, Appleton is tracking down Barbutero, and then we go talk to him."

Lin pulled out her phone and composed a short text message. Tapping the device one last time with finality as she pressed the send icon, she looked over at me and asked, "What's the end game?"

I rolled my eyes. "Someone is not telling the truth. We gotta figure out who that is. Could be Coate. Could be Williams."

She nodded. "I was beginning to worry about that. Coate is convincing. The AG is, frankly, not. He's blustering." She sighed. "It's quite obvious, now, isn't it?"

"I'm afraid so," I replied dully. "It's possible that we—you, me, and Appleton—are all being played by the AG in pursuit of his own goals, whatever they may be."

"Well, not all is lost," Lin chirped.

"You sound way too cheerful," I muttered.

"We'll figure it out. In the meantime—eat." The bartender delivered a platter heaped with tater tots, surrounded by small dishes of sauces. "House specialty. You'll love 'em."

As I sampled a deliciously deep-fried, airy, and crunchy tot, she patted my arm and grinned, angling her phone in my direction. "Coate responded. Isaac is in the New York area, she will be in Washington late tonight, and she's coming to see us at the office at nine in the morning."

"That was fast," I mumbled through a mouthful of potato.

"I'm beginning to see the AG as cagey while Coate is responsive. I think we're onto something, Ben."

I washed down the tots with a healthy gulp of lager, nodding at Lin, but thinking, *I am definitely being played. But by who?*

No—sorry—*But by whom?*

# MONDAY
# OCTOBER 31, 2022

**THREE DAYS** *BEFORE THE VOTE*

# CHAPTER 38



**MY SISTER GRACE** *would be sooooo jealous*, I thought at nine in the morning sharp when Hanna Mo'Nique Isaac, her stately and assured demeanor instantly commanding the space, swept from the maw of the fifth-floor elevator and entered my now familiar office on New Hampshire Avenue.

Granted, the only occupant of the room to command was me. Lin and I agreed that we would ask the associates assigned by the AG to help us, the thus-far useless pair of Toonin and Kinnar-Hering, to remain at Main Justice. Their presence would only require an explanation and create a distraction.

I needed no distraction, as focused as I was to meet the famous investor. But as awed as I was by the sight of Isaac in person, I was then floored, as the familiar silhouette of Merritt Coate emerged from the elevator car.

*Both of them?*

Lin emerged from the Senator's shadow and was quicker on the take than I. She announced cheerily, "Welcome, Senator Coate and Madam Isaac. Thank you for allowing us the time."

*With no security detail for the Senator? Or aides?* I fumbled for words but failed.

Isaac beamed, her white teeth positively shining, framed by full lips with just a hint of gloss. She tossed her wavy black hair as she swept off a muted sandstone-colored overcoat that covered a high-necked, off-white, cashmere-y-looking turtleneck sweater topped with an intricately-patterned tiger motif silk scarf and completed by a tangerine, calf-length leather skirt over knee-high, chocolate brown boots.

*Tangerine?*

I realized I was thinking as if I was composing a breathy Instagram caption, and honestly, I wouldn't be able to explain the difference between tangerine, carrot, or squash. It's orange. Let's move on.

I stuck out my right hand and followed Lin's lead on the salutation. "I'm Ben Porter. It's a pleasure to meet you, Madam Isaac." I turned to the Senator, who was overcoat-less and attired in another natty navy-blue suit with an American flag patterned tie. "Senator. This is a surprise."

Coate grinned and stepped to his spouse's shoulder. "I carved out a hole in my schedule to make the introduction in person. I'm not staying. But I did want to be here to impress on you, Ben, the significance that Hanna and I both place on this meeting."

His tone was warm and genuine, but even so, it was no match for Isaac's melodious voice as she looked me square in the eye and said, "Ben, the pleasure is mine, and it's Hanna. None of that madam nonsense, please." She winked and the right corner of her mouth curled up in a smile. "When Merritt explained the circumstances of this meeting to me, I immediately agreed. When he hinted at your background, Ben, I was suitably impressed." She grasped my arm lightly and leaned closer; I could smell her minty breath. "Don't fret—no national security secrets revealed, naturally. We simply do not cross that line. But Merritt did speak in general terms about your very capable ways."

Isaac faced Coate. "Thank you, darling. I've got it from here." The couple leaned together and air-kissed, sweeping cheeks closely.

"I'll escort you out, sir," Lin offered, and she boarded the elevator with the Senator.

I led Isaac into my office where I motioned to the barrel chair that Coate occupied yesterday afternoon. She draped her overcoat on the adjacent chair and adjusted the scarf at her neck.

"That's an elaborate and quite beautiful pattern on your scarf," I commented, trying to make light conversation with the icon. "Does it represent anything in particular?"

"Oh, thank you so much," she purred. "The pattern and color reflect the year of the Water Tiger which began on the lunar new year of February first. It was given to me by a close friend in China, which of course was the origin country of the silk." She lifted a corner and cooed admiringly, "It's just *so* gorgeous, isn't it?"

Doing my best to remember my manners, I paused and waited until she sat, crossing a brown leather booted leg over the other and smoothing her skirt, before I sank into my own barrel. She eyed me with a look of either curiosity or expectation, and I gulped, rocketing to my feet. "Apologies. Coffee? Tea? Water? I can't offer much in terms of hospitality." I felt foolish for not providing some sort of breakfast-type finger foods.

Isaac laughed, a warm, carefree tinkle. "Oh, dear, no. But thank you all the same. Please, don't stand on such formalities."

Lowering myself back into the barrel, I stammered, "I'm not used to, um, entertaining, um, folks like you."

"Seriously? Because I'm Insta famous?" That laugh again before she continued, "Or because I'm wealthy and married to a VIP?"

"Both, I guess."

She smiled sweetly. "You're originally from Rhode Island." It was a statement, not a question. "The Ocean State. Really lovely—that mix of seaside charm and New England sensibility. And oftentimes, more authentic than my home state of California."

"Well, we have a lotta Dunks, so we got that going for us. Maybe the most per capita in the country."

Isaac cocked her head slightly. "That's not accurate, though one might assume so. I believe that title goes to New York State."

Her tone was studious and took me aback. I stammered, "Oh, I apologize. I just made that up. I have no idea, really."

"I'm just teasing you, Ben. Relax. It's not a test." She cocked her head a second time as she brushed a few strands of hair back. "You know, you just displayed emotional intelligence. You didn't obfuscate or get defensive. You immediately set the record straight." She grinned slightly and added, "Ben, Merritt used the word earnest when he described you to me, earlier. I'll offer the word *authentic*."

"I try," I replied, while trying to sound earnestly authentic.

*How does one exude earnest authenticity?*

Isaac tapped her chin with a manicured finger. "That's the trouble with Washington and politics in general. Authenticity is missing." Isaac pursed her lips, recrossed her legs, and stated, "Let's get to business, shall we? Let's talk about Bart Williams and his vendetta against my husband and me."

Her voice was clear and firm, and I replied in kind, "Sounds good to me. Do you mind if I take notes? Can we wait for Sara to return?"

As if on cue, my office door opened, and Sara Lin appeared to announce, "Senator Coate is on his way back to the Capitol building. Did I miss anything?"

Isaac motioned to one of the empty barrels and invited Lin to sit. "You haven't missed a thing. We've just been getting acquainted." She nodded at me and made a writing motion with her right hand as if she was grasping a pen. "Ben, be my guest and scribe away. I've got nothing to hide."

I quickly rose and grabbed the notepad from my satchel that I'd left on my Aeron chair at the desk. Flipping to a fresh page as I returned to sink into my barrel, I urged Isaac to begin. "I'm ready when you are."

"Oh, I'm ready. It's about time this got aired," Isaac said, almost with a weary voice. "Let's start with the CEO of Aximerva. Let me tell you about *all* of my discussions and meetings with Virgil Preston."

As the wealthy investor spoke, I listened and scribbled . . . one page, then another, and another, with revelations verbalized by Isaac coming as fast as I could write.

# CHAPTER
# 39

**HANNA MO'NIQUE ISAAC PAUSED** her monologue and took a very deep breath, pushing her shoulders backward, as if she was relieved to air a long-kept secret.

Lin, too, exhaled and then spoke for the first time since joining Isaac and me in the fifth-floor turret. "That's a lot. Can I get you anything? Coffee? Water?"

Isaac daintily licked her lips. "Coffee, please. Might you have oat milk?"

"Sure do," Lin sang, and she hustled out of my office in the direction of our little kitchenette.

Meanwhile, I paged through several—five, to be precise—pages of notes, mumbling, "Agent O'Toole. New Haven. Elm Tree Club. Kelly green. The Italian place in New York—"

"It's so divine," Isaac exclaimed. "Ben, we simply must go. My treat, of course."

I nodded agreeably but didn't commit as I resumed, "The Italian place in New York where you lunched with Virgil Preston. Alone." I looked directly at Isaac and requested, "Can you run that by me one more time?"

"Certainly," Isaac replied. She pulled an iPhone from the pocket of the overcoat that she'd placed on the adjacent chair, earlier, and she tapped and swiped at the screen, finally announcing, "It was a Tuesday. October the twenty-fifth. Virgil and I lunched. And—"

Unfortunately, Lin's timing interrupted Isaac, as she returned to my office carrying a platter piled with coffee cups, a full coffee pot, and various smaller containers. She set the platter down on the oval table that sat in the center of the four chair grouping, and she poured. Offering a cup to Isaac, she pointed at one of the smaller containers. "Oat milk, as requested," she said proudly.

Isaac fiddled with her coffee and then sipped daintily. "Ah, that's better. I was getting parched. This is lovely. Thank you."

"You're quite welcome."

True to my usual form, I was getting impatient with the pause, so I asked, in what I hoped was an earnestly authentic tone, "May we continue? You were talking about Preston."

"Oh, of course," Isaac replied after another sip. "I have a great deal of respect for Virgil and Aximerva. Trendsetters, indeed. But he was moving too quickly. You see, if he had waited for the semiconductor bill to become law, he would have competed on the same playing field as our other States-based manufacturers, like Intel. He didn't want to do that. He wanted to get his factory going as a reason to defeat the bill— he could demonstrate that government involvement wasn't necessary. Therefore, if he was successful in killing the bill, not only would he have a head start on production, but he'd also ultimately enjoy a bigger share of US-based production."

I shrugged, mostly to disguise my confusion, but I plowed ahead. "What was the point of your meeting with Preston?"

Isaac touched her coffee cup to her lips once more. "When Preston made it clear that he was going to build his factory, bill or no bill, I proposed a deal to buy Aximerva. It's a private company. I thought my bid was unrefusable. Initially, Preston wanted no part of it, stubborn and prideful as he is."

"That doesn't make sense," I argued. "Am I to understand that if you bought the company, you would have paused Preston's plans for a new plant?"

Isaac nodded. "No, not entirely. I would have paused long enough to ensure that Aximerva was strategically positioned to prosper. It's like this, Ben. Have you ever noticed that there are often multiple gas stations on a single street corner? Or several restaurants right next to each other in a neighborhood? Have you been to a mall with countless shops, some big, some small? Competition is good, Ben. Being first to a market isn't always a recipe for success."

"You're saying that you'd let other US-based semiconductor companies catch up to Aximerva? Wouldn't that, um, hurt your investment?"

"No, not in the least, because I would have availed Aximerva to the advantages offered by the EPIC act," Isaac disclosed. "You see, Preston was planning on leveraging Aximerva to the hilt in order to build his plant. He'd risk it all—but his assumption was that he'd have a massive advantage over his competition, and therefore he'd earn his way out of debt. Then the EPIC bill came along, and Preston freaked out, because, of course, then the competition could afford to catch up, with the EPIC subsidies."

"That does explain why Preston was so opposed to the bill," I said, almost as much to myself as to Isaac. "However, why wouldn't he just take those subsidies, too? Wouldn't that have decreased his need for debt?"

"Good, Ben, very good. Yes, that's one potential outcome. But you're forgetting Preston's pride. To do so would force him to admit he was wrong about EPIC. And he'd made deals with the debt—future profits, a carried interest, special terms, that sort of thing. He may have backed himself into a corner."

This big business stuff was giving me a headache. Maybe it's giving you one, too. To get back on track, I asked, "You offered Preston a deal to sell the company to you, but Preston didn't agree to your terms?"

Isaac's expression clouded for a split second as she answered, "Initially, no. But at our lunch, I finally convinced him that the deal was in his best interests. I was able to make a very compelling offer, which he accepted."

"What? You two did your deal?"

I was stunned. Hanna Mo'Nique Isaac's acquisition of Aximerva would be headline news, and yet—crickets. Nothing.

Isaac cocked her head slightly and confirmed, "Yes. I own Aximerva."

# CHAPTER 40

**I COULD HEAR** the faint sound of a horn honking, five stories below my turret office windows. The silence that hung between Isaac and me, however, soon became awkward. I realized I had to say something, so I tried, "Okay, so you bought Preston's company what, about a week ago? But other than me, not a single person in the world knows this? No regulatory agencies? No media? No one?"

Isaac cocked an eyebrow. "Well, it's a private transaction. It's not an open market stock deal that would have to go before the Securities and Exchange Commission, for example. Even my husband doesn't know yet." She waved a hand. "Play it out, Ben. The deal goes public and—what happens? What does that look like?" Eying me carefully, she concluded, "It looks like I bought him off, and that doesn't look good for Merritt. Therefore, my deal with Preston is that he lays low, and we both agree to keep the transaction confidential until after the vote on EPIC."

*Lays low is a euphemism for dead, maybe*, I thought.

"He lays low, huh? Let's assume that checks out," I said, trying to keep the skepticism out of my voice. I let my gaze wander to the turret windows as I asked, trying to sound casual, "Where does Bart Williams fit in?"

"He wanted to kill my deal to buy Aximerva. Honestly, Ben, I received information that Preston was disclosing my private business to the Attorney General. Preston and the AG were cooperating, and the AG considered my proposed acquisition of Aximerva to be a conflict of interest, as he called it."

I probed, "And you know this how?"

"I don't feel like I'm ready to discuss my sources, Ben."

"Fair enough," I replied. "However, those sources will become a material part of verifying your recollection."

"Let's set that aside for now. What's not recollection or opinion is this: it's obvious that because my husband proposed the semiconductor bill, I'd benefit. But the fact is that Williams is a petty-minded attorney with a big appetite for power. If he stopped my deal, he knew it would not only hurt my reputation, but he also would expose my husband's role—not that we've tried to disguise any of this. Then Williams would use the publicity to raise his profile. Maybe even run for president, or at least for a Senate seat as a stepping stone to the Oval Office."

"The AG shuts you down, puts you in your place, smears your Senator husband, and comes out looking like the white knight who is protecting American industry and national interests," I suggested. "Furthermore, the AG successfully pauses or kills the EPIC bill, it also appears that he's ensuring that the American voter isn't swayed by a big government assistance bill that's passed only days before a midterm election."

Isaac clapped her hands together and smiled broadly. "Precisely."

"Not so fast on the celebration," I said evenly. "Where does Rocco Barbutero fit in?"

"That's easy," she huffed. "But first, let me guess something. I'd bet my house in Malibu that Bart Williams told you that Barbutero was one of his New York City informants, but then he switched sides. Abandoned the AG. Am I close?"

I tried to shrug in a non-committal way, but I couldn't deny that Isaac was correct—and I wanted to hear what she would add. "Much as I'd like a house on the Pacific Ocean, I gotta admit that yes, that's essentially what Williams said."

Isaac nodded. "I'm unsurprised. The real story, however, is that Barbutero started as a butcher, working out of a little shop across the Hudson in Jersey City. He built a nice business supplying restaurants with meats and provisions, and one by one, he nabbed the good ones. Name brand spots—where deals are made. Barbutero ingratiated himself, and you know, when you see who is dining together, you start to learn the networks. He's a smart guy and a spun a web of information on his own."

"Information useful to the justice system, I suppose." I phrased my conclusion as more of a statement than a question.

Isaac confirmed my supposition. "Exactly. But Barbutero's network was in New York, not in Washington. Recall that the AG was once the New York DA. As Williams rose in power and eventually made it to Washington, he used Barbutero as a source less frequently until, ultimately, he ditched Barbutero. Maybe Rocco is bitter that he got left behind, so maybe he's got an ax to grind with the AG."

"How did you connect with Barbutero?"

"I met him during the Covid pandemic. Remember when the restaurants were closed? Barbutero's company started doing home deliveries, and whenever I was planning to be in New York, I'd have him stock my place. He got to know my staff and maintenance people, and we eventually gave him the access codes so he could keep the pantry and freezer chock-full of the best provisions in town. He'd even provide pre-cooked meals for us, and he's a talented cook, too, even if he leans a little too much toward adding bacon to his dishes."

"Well, everyone knows that's cheating," I commented dryly.

"What?"

"Any good chef will tell you that," I continued. "Adding bacon to a dish is cheating. You get flavor without trying too hard. It would be like, say, sex scenes in thriller novels. If the author can't keep your attention with action, intrigue, and the occasional oddball, off-topic riff, and instead resorts to titillation, well, it's not much of a thriller."

"Good point," Isaac agreed, nodding thoughtfully. "But Barbutero couldn't help himself. He loves his bacon, and my husband likes pork, too. We were both well-fed and charmed by Rocco. He's a hustler."

I held out my hands, palms up, and decided to reveal a card or two. "A hustler, huh? He sure gets points for being versatile. Did you know that Barbutero attempted to kill the AG on the Acela train?"

Isaac scowled at me. "That's not what happened."

"You know about it, then?"

"Of course. My sources—the same sources that I referenced before, to be clear—informed me that Williams would be on the Acela, and I sent Barbutero to that train. I asked him to go to the AG and reason with him. None of this is good for anyone. We somehow need to find a compromise."

"Barbutero was armed," I protested. "He shot a hole in the ceiling of the train car."

"Oh, please," Isaac complained in a snide voice. "He was armed for his protection, in case one of the AG's goons tried to intercept him or work him over. When you tackled him, the gun went off. The shot was *your* fault."

I stared at Lin and then at Isaac. "How do you know that?"

"Like I told you earlier, while you were writing your notes, I was with Barbutero yesterday. In New Haven, with Agent O'Toole. Were you not paying attention?"

I flipped to the page that dealt with her meeting with Barbutero at the Elm Tree Club and re-read my handwriting. "You most definitely did not mention the gunshot."

Isaac exhaled through her nose and looked up. "Oh dear, maybe I didn't. It was a detail, and I suppose we didn't talk about it right then." She lowered her head and glared at me. "That doesn't change anything, however. The facts remain the facts."

I put my hands up in the air as if I was surrendering. "Okay, okay. I need to write up the timeline properly and then fill in the holes. I'll do that. But, what about Barbutero in New York? Spotted outside the Italian place—ah, Bar Virtuosismo, right? About the same time, you departed in a black Cadillac Escalade."

Isaac squinted. "What—what does that matter? I had lunch with Preston—a private lunch. As I'd done many times previously, in lunches with other business colleagues, I asked Barbutero to serve the table. To ensure discretion. To ensure that there were no unfamiliar faces listening in. There's nothing more than that. After all, Barbutero's business is a supplier to the restaurant, and while Barbutero has never met the chef personally—because, after all, Barbutero doesn't drive the truck himself to do his deliveries—he's told me he's not a fan of Chef Isola because of a slow payment history." She shrugged. "They're both small businesses, and I know that cash flow can be tough for those little guys. Anyway, business is business, and occasionally it makes for odd bedfellows."

I needed a moment to think. *This all seems so coincidental.* That was not a word used lightly in investigations, and true coincidence is rare. *But it's plausible. Except—*

The words came out of my mouth almost involuntarily, though, in the back of my mind, the question had been there since I'd first sat down with Isaac. All the same, I probably was too direct when I blurted, "So, Hanna, you're saying that you didn't order Barbutero to murder Virgil Preston?"

Isaac shot to her feet, almost toppling the table topped with coffee paraphernalia. "What?!"

I remained in my seat and stated calmly, "That's the AG's conclusion, based on an FBI investigation. Barbutero was involved in the disappearance of Preston, and now that Preston hasn't reappeared, the FBI suspects murder."

"That's the most ridiculous, outrageous thing I've heard in quite some time," Isaac hissed, snatching up her sandstone-colored overcoat and whipping it off the arm of the chair where it had rested.

I remained seated and kept my voice level. "That's a very emotional reaction you just displayed. Why?"

Isaac cocked her head sideways one final time and announced scornfully, "Virgil Preston wasn't murdered. That's beyond preposterous. I texted with him yesterday, and he's very much alive."

# CHAPTER

# 41

**"VIRGIL PRESTON WASN'T MURDERED,"** I repeated dumbly, staring at Hanna Mo'Nique Isaac. "You were in contact with him yesterday? Where?"

Isaac's back was to me as she hurried to the door, and she turned slowly. She spoke with venom in her voice. "I am appalled that you'd insinuate that I was even remotely connected to a murder."

"Okay, so produce Preston," I countered, not willing to back down.

Isaac scowled. "My husband told me you were some crack FBI agent. Apparently, that reputation is sorely undeserved."

"See what you want to see," I argued. Placing my palms out and upwards, I added, "I can only see what I can see. And my intel tells me that Rocco Barbutero and you were the last people to see Preston, which makes you both persons of interest in this matter. I don't know where Preston is, but you do. Seems to me that you have an ironclad way of proving the FBI wrong by directing us to him."

She pulled on the beige—sorry, sandstone—overcoat, and she adjusted the silk scarf so it peeked properly above the coat collar. "If that's the case, why haven't you questioned Barbutero?" She wrinkled her nose and added, mockingly, "As a person of interest."

"I would like to, as well. But I don't know where he is," I confessed.

"However, you've told me that you met with him, in New Haven. Produce him, too."

"There's no need for me to do that," she retorted. "After all, the FBI, or more specifically, Special Agent Mariana O'Toole, remains in contact with Barbutero. Make your demands to your fellow agent."

Isaac's ire was palpable and showed no sign of letting up. She took a step toward me and hissed, "This should demonstrate to you, Mister Porter, in no uncertain terms, just how manipulative Bart Williams can be."

I took a deep breath and stood, unfortunately realizing that Isaac still was able to look down at me from her superior stature. Taking a conciliatory tone, I changed course, admitting, "Look, you're right. There are several, um, inconsistencies, in my data set. But all the same, that's what I do. I try to examine the facts presented to me with an open mind, without bias." I clasped my hands together as if I was praying and concluded, "Please, have a seat. I think we're making significant progress, as bumpy as it's been."

Isaac's expression softened as she moved to the chair. "Hysterics aside, your statement shocked me, Ben. You *really* need to get up to speed."

"I'm not gonna make excuses, but this intel is coming at me pretty fast," I allowed, trying to exhibit humility—or even earnest authenticity. "One of my colleagues is contacting this Special Agent O'Toole. What can you tell me about O'Toole?"

Isaac looked up at the ceiling for a moment, composing thoughts. "O'Toole works out of the Hoover building and focuses on white-collar crime. She's part of the Corporate Fraud division, and I reached out to her in the course of my research on Aximerva."

"Why?"

"Virgil Preston and the Attorney General are tight. I'm not going to say any more than that, other than offering that I was concerned about improprieties."

I suggested, "How about this—my colleagues at the Bureau will convene with O'Toole, and you connect me with Preston. Wouldn't that be the easiest way to clear this up?"

"It should be easy," Isaac agreed, finally sinking back into the chair, but leaving her coat on, perhaps to make a hasty exit. She sighed. "You should definitely talk to O'Toole. You'll see firsthand—if there's one thing that the AG is good at doing, it's making a mess of things, in my opinion."

Following suit and sitting, I realized was beginning to agree with Isaac, though I didn't say so. Instead, I thought, *If Isaac is telling the truth, her private business deals made of free will are of no concern to the FBI.*

That wasn't my call, though. I cautioned, "You realize, of course, that I'm not the ultimate arbiter. But—before I discuss anything with the AG, I'll do my homework with my colleague, who is an independent, intelligent party, in my opinion."

Isaac stiffened. "Who do you propose?"

I grinned. "Not to be petty, but if you're not going to disclose your sources, I'm not ready to disclose my partners."

The investor laughed. "Well, this is Washington, after all. We make deals here. We trade information. A quid pro quo, so to speak."

"Certainly," I said affably. "I will promise this, too. If you put me in touch with Preston, I'll confer with my people, and then you and I regroup. An open dialogue would benefit us all."

Instead of replying, Isaac twisted her body sideways and pulled her iPhone from a pocket in the sandstone overcoat. She tapped at it a few times and then handed the device face-up to me, the screen lit with a contact card. "That's Preston's mobile. Write it down. And feel free to tap the message icon. You're welcome to read the previous texts."

Placing a finger on the screen so it would not resort to sleep mode, I used my free hand to scribble the number on my pad. Then, as instructed, I tapped the message icon. Sure enough, the bottom bubble, iconed with the initials "VP" to the left, was timestamped yesterday, October 30, at 3:31 P.M.:

```
I, too, hope you too continue to hold up
your end of the bargain. And yes, it's
nice. Hitting them straight!
```

"What does this mean—hold up your end? And who is he hitting?" I handed the device back to Isaac.

She glanced briefly at the screen and replied, "Well, first, he's off laying low and playing golf." Looking up at me, she rolled her eyes. "Hitting golf balls, Ben." She smiled thinly and added, "I'd thanked him for remaining quiet, and as per our deal, he's reminding me that the mutual gag order applied to both of us." Returning her gaze to me, she added, "Not that I needed the recap. It's certainly in my best interests."

I scratched my right ear and conceded, "It's not lost on me that you've technically violated that agreement in sharing this information with me, and I assure you, I will keep it in the strictest confidence."

"Very perceptive," she cooed. "I dare say this is how it's supposed to work. A relationship is nothing if it's not built on trust, and trust is earned with transparency and honesty." She tapped at the phone again and handed it once more to me with a new contact card visible on the screen, below a headshot of Isaac herself. "Here's my info for your use, Ben. Write it down, and then please create a new entry with your information. At the very least, we shall be in direct communication."

As I tapped at the device, doing as she directed, I muttered, "You've made the value of that direct transparency quite clear."

Completing the entry, I glanced at Lin. Her face was placid and remained so as I passed Isaac's phone back to the investor and concluded, "Bart Williams has not been as forthright as you."

Isaac's response was a noncommittal, "Hmmm," but nevertheless, her disdain was evident. She offered, "Call that number and speak to Preston. Ask what you want."

She rose to her feet and smoothed her orange—er, tangerine—skirt. Snugging the overcoat, she addressed me directly, "Consider this, though. If Preston receives a text or a call from an unknown number, it's quite likely that he'll ignore it and will decline to respond, or he might block it. Give us both a favor and allow me time to forward your contact info to Preston. In turn, I'll contact you immediately when you're clear to reach out."

"Makes sense," I agreed, rising to my own feet.

"Good," she replied. Turning to Lin, she asked, "Sara, would you kindly escort me out?"

Lin chirped, "Certainly."

Isaac extended a hand to me. "Ben, this has been productive. I can see why you're held in such high regard. Thank you for being so accommodating."

She didn't wait for me to reply as she led Lin to the foyer, a whiff of perfume in her wake.

*Not just a whiff of scent. A whiff of fresh air. Of someone straightforward, with nothing to hide*, I thought, waiting for Lin to return.

I crossed to my desk and sank into the Aeron chair, laying my notepad on the surface before me. Programming my device with the various contact details, I sighed, conflicted. *If I do what Isaac and I agreed I'd do, I'm essentially excluding the AG—my boss—from my investigation. I'm breaking the rules and playing against my team.*

But I knew that I had to do it.

# TUESDAY
# NOVEMBER 1, 2022

**TWO DAYS** *BEFORE THE VOTE*

# CHAPTER
# 42

## *MORNING — FOGGY BOTTOM*

**TRAPPED,** bound by twisting, tight restraints, I couldn't move—and the incessant buzz of an insect cut through the darkness like a spluttering, on-and-off chainsaw being revved.

I opened my mouth to scream and tore at the—

Sheets?

*What the*—and dragged out of sleep, I realized, no, this isn't a nightmare. This is me, the millennial, sleeping with my phone on the bedstand next to me, its screen lit with an incoming call as the device itself vibrated and jiggled and buzzed on the flat surface of the bedside table.

Blinking rapidly to clear the cobwebs, I squinted at the name—

```
Hanna Isaac
```

*Shit.*

I shoved the sheets aside, waking Lin in the process, as I grabbed the device, noting the time display at the top left corner of the screen:

```
7:02 A.M.
```

Slurring out what I hoped was a word-like noise, I managed, "Hello?"

Isaac's mellifluous voice sounded cheerily in my ear. "Good morning, Ben! Hope I'm not getting you too early."

"No—no—no, um, of course not. Just, ah, had to grab my phone from the other room," I fibbed.

"Great," she enthused. "I would have called earlier, but I only saw the text after I just wrapped up my Peloton workout. Virgil is waiting for your call this morning."

"That's terrific," I replied, trying to match her absurd level of morning gusto.

She talked over me as if I hadn't said a word. "And you better call him soon! His text was that he had a tee time at 8:08. That's only, what, an hour from now!"

"But it's dark out," I observed.

Isaac laughed merrily. "He's not in The District, silly man. I paid him a lot of money. He's in Jamaica, nice and warm, and I'm certain that there, right now, it's a bright, sunshiny day." She had sung those words lightly, channeling her inner Bob Marley, and she chirped, "Are you going to call him? You'll want to call him before he tees off."

"Yes! Definitely. I'm on it."

"Excellent! I'm reachable this morning, so let me know how it goes," Isaac requested. "Bye!"

"Um, sure, goodbye," I said, belatedly realizing I was talking to no one. Isaac hadn't waited for a reply before terminating the call.

"What was that all about?"

I faced Lin, who'd modestly pulled a sheet up to her neck, and I scrabbled with an edge of the sheet myself, realizing that I was, um, hanging out. "That was Isaac. She said she'd heard back from Preston, but that I've only got an hour window to call him."

"Amazing," Lin said, drawing out the word. "The AG, the New York Field Office, the agents on site—they all suspect foul play. And yet—"

"Yet he's about to play golf. In Jamaica." I shook my head in disbelief. *We got this so very wrong.*

Lin seemed unperturbed. In fact, I read excitement in her expression, and she confirmed my supposition when she said eagerly,

"We'd better get going. I'll put on some coffee, and you get yourself dressed and organized."

She leaped out of bed and trotted—naked—toward the kitchen, grabbing a t-shirt from a chair near the bedroom door.

I admired the view for a moment and then forced myself back to reality.

*What do I ask a man who is supposed to be dead?*

# CHAPTER
# 43

**AFTER A SIXTY-SECOND** cold shower, I pulled on sweatpants and a t-shirt and padded to the kitchen, far more alert than I'd been when Isaac called five minutes ago.

Lin, dressed only in an oversized t-shirt, was pulling mugs out of a cabinet as the coffee machine wheezed and dripped. Enough of the dark nectar had accumulated in the pot for her to fill one mug, which she handed to me. "Straight up and hot. That'll clear your head."

"Thanks," I mumbled, accepting the mug while pulling my notepad and a pen from the leather satchel that I'd left in the kitchen the night before. I fiddled with the pad, wrestling with a decision: *Do I include Lin on the call? Or do I go solo?*

I pulled my phone from the pocket of my sweatpants and checked the time:

7:27 A.M.

Plenty of time before Preston teed off, but all the same, I didn't want to call as he was—well, I don't know. I don't play golf. I wondered, *What do you do before a round of golf?*

I couldn't answer that, so instead, I did what I do best. I winged it. Wung it? Whatever.

Placing the phone face-up on the little, two-seater kitchen table, I scrolled to the contact card that I'd created yesterday afternoon after Isaac had departed. Confirming that I entered the digits correctly by comparing them to the notes I'd written on my pad, I tapped the number, and the screen changed to show the outgoing call.

It took several seconds to connect, but I was eventually rewarded with a twangy, "Howdy. Who's this?"

"Ah, Mister Preston, my name is Ben Porter. I believe that Hanna—"

"Right-o," the voice interrupted. "Hanna said you'd be callin'. What can I do you for, Mister Porter?" *Mistah Portah.* Preston's heavy Texas accent was evident even through the crackle of a cellular call on speakerphone.

"Um, Ben is fine, sir. I'm a Special Agent of the FBI, as I hope you already know from Hanna's introduction. And I've got you on speaker with my associate, Sara Lin. She's an attorney with the Department of Justice."

"Hello," Lin cheeped.

"A pleasure, I'm certain," Preston drawled.

I peeked quickly at Lin, perched demurely on the stool to my right. She shrugged.

I took that as a sign that she'd completed her introduction, so I said, "Sir, I'll be brief. Hanna told me you're teeing off shortly. I don't want to interfere with your warmup, so—"

"Warm up?" Preston brayed, cackling somewhat. "What, you think this is some sort of calisthenics exercise? I'd warm up a cigar, but it's a little early for a smoke. I'm just sittin' here in mah golf cart, enjoying the, ah, scenery."

"Sounds nice," I replied. "Hanna says you're in Jamaica?"

"Yessiree. I'm at, ah, a resort outside, ummm, Montego Bay. You know, maybe I'll have me a Red Stripe later."

"Well, I won't take much of your time. I'm just verifying some details of an, um, investigation. Can you confirm you were in New York last week? With, um, Hanna?"

"Yup," Preston said. "We had lunch. Hanna and me, we've got a, ah, transaction pending. Workin' out some, uh, business details. That sorta thing."

"And after the lunch, what happened? Whadya have, by the way? Do you remember the name of the restaurant?"

"Ah, the name? Ah, lemme see . . . Bar Virtue, or somethin'. Hanna really likes the place. I had a pretty good steak sandwich. I mean, not a proper Texas sandwich, but good enough."

I scribbled as he spoke, and not wanting the conversation to wane, I rushed to repeat, "And after the lunch, what happened? Where'd you go next?"

"Ah, the waiter, he showed me how to slip out the back door after the meal. Hanna and I didn't want to be seen together, you know, for, um, the obvious reasons." He paused, ever so briefly, before continuing in a slower cadence, "I'm sure you're aware, uh, Agent Porter, of the, uh, upcomin' legislation that, uh, pertains to mah industry?"

"Yes, sir. I've discussed that with both Hanna and her husband."

Preston chuckled. "Ah, really? The Senator himself? You're very well connected."

I glanced at Lin. *She's the connected one.*

"Agent Porter? You still there?"

I realized I'd gone silent, and I blurted, "Yeah, yeah. Right here. So, sir, Mister Preston—picking up there, did you remain in New York? Did you return to Austin?"

"Nah," Preston replied, drawing out the word. "Hanna and I agreed that we'd both, ah, stay below the radar, so to speak. Lay low, ya know? I've been quite enjoying mahself, to be truthful. I thought I'd be bored to tears, but frankly, it's been nice to have a break, ya know."

"I'm sure," I said agreeably. "One last question. When do you plan to return? To reappear?"

"Ah, lemme think. What day is it? They're all blendin' togetha."

"It's Tuesday, sir. The first of November."

"Well, then, how 'bout that? Already Tuesday," Preston muttered. In a brighter tone, he added, "Couple days more, then. After the, ah, the— well, you know?"

"May I be blunt, sir? After the vote on the EPIC bill?"

Preston laughed, quietly at first, perhaps under his breath, and then quite obviously. "Well, ah, Agent Porter, that's a very specific milestone you've referenced there. But I'm not gonna refute you, if ya know what I mean."

"Understood, sir," I replied evenly. "Hanna has emphasized to me the necessity of strict confidentiality, and I am comfortable with that requirement."

"Hmmm. Very good, Agent Porter. Hanna said you were one of the good ones, and I sure feel that way after this little talk. Is there anythin' else?"

"No, sir, I think that covers it. Thanks for taking the time. Hit 'em straight, sir," I concluded pleasantly, hoping that by adding in the golf jargon that I'd gleaned from Hanna Isaac, I made it sound like I was well-versed in the game.

"You betcha," Preston said. "*Adios*, Porter."

The screen on my phone reverted to the usual icons the instant that the call ended, and I looked up at the ceiling. "Well, this complicates things." I dropped my head to the table and blew out my breath with an audible whoosh, making tiny waves on the surface of the brown liquid in my coffee cup. "Now what?"

# CHAPTER 44

**"NOW WHAT?"**

I repeated my question, turning to look at Sara Lin.

She examined me with a squint. "Isn't it obvious, Ben? Do what you've been told to do. What you agreed to do."

I stared at her. "Remind me. What was that?"

"Really?" Her tone was scornful. "You said that you'd call Isaac after you called Preston. Check back in with her."

"Right!" I exclaimed.

Looking down at my pad, filled with scrawled notes that had to be illegible to anyone other than me, I knew it was not that simple. "At some point," I said to Lin, but also to myself, "I need to come clean with the Attorney General. Or at least with Appleton. I can't be going off on my own here. I've learned that lesson one too many times."

"Makes sense," Lin agreed. "But take it step-by-step, I'd suggest."

"Yeah," I whispered, and though my thoughts were all over the place, my hand reached again for my phone, and I called up Isaac's contact card. Without allowing myself another second of second-guessing, I tapped the number and selected the speakerphone audio mode so that I could take notes without holding the phone.

Isaac answered immediately and dove right in. "How did it go, Ben? Did you talk to him?"

"Yes, we had a nice chat," I said non-committedly. "Sounds like he's having a pleasant, um, vacation."

"Well, let's be honest," Isaac offered. "It's a bit of a forced vacation. However, I do know this about Virgil, and that is that he's resilient. He's tough." She tittered quietly. "He's also quite rich now, too."

"I suppose so," I commented. "But that's only one piece of the puzzle."

"What else is there?" Isaac's tone turned sharp.

"Well, for one, corroboration."

"What does that mean?"

I bit my lip, unsure how far I dared to push Isaac, but my hesitation was only momentary. I led with collaboration. "Since we're being honest with each other, consider this: from my perspective as a Special Agent, I'm fully aware that a phone call is just that. It's a discussion between two voices. There's no way I can know that the number I dialed wasn't rerouted to someone else. Or rerouted somewhere else. How do I know I was connected to a phone in Jamaica? Furthermore, there's no way I can know that you actually gave me Virgil Preston's number. And finally, without voice analysis—which, by the way, is not foolproof on its own—I can't know if I was really talking to Preston."

I assumed that Isaac would jump defensively at my skepticism, but to my surprise, she said, "You'd make a very good investor, Ben. What you are doing, what you are saying, is what we would label, in business jargon, as due diligence. You're checking and rechecking." The connection made a whiffling noise as if she'd switched ears, and she added, "How do you go about doing that verification work?"

*Volkov, aboard* Almaz, *would already have it done, if I was with her*, I thought wistfully.

Facing my reality, I replied to Isaac, "I have a very good technical resource in the FBI's Boston Field Office—an Intelligence Analyst with an alliterative name of Louis Lewis. He is world-class with this sort of research. He's my next call, and then he'll connect his computers to my phone. Ultimately, he'll be able to establish a trace."

"Fascinating," Isaac said approvingly. "How long does that take?"

"I'm not exactly sure. The technology stuff is pretty opaque to me. But not long, really. It's pretty simple work with the appropriate tools."

Isaac hummed. "Hmmm. Well, I wish I could assist you with the task, but, obviously, in that regard, there's little value that I would add. Nevertheless, I applaud your attention to detail." She cleared her throat as if she was satisfied with the conversation and outcome, and she added with a note of finality, "Is there anything else I can help with?"

I hesitated. *Louis Lewis was good, and he could do the work, but would he? Would he jump on the project—especially since our once mutual boss Jennifer Appleton was no longer in the SAC's office?*

I decided on attempting an end-run, or, at least, creating a backup plan—another lesson I'd learned over and over. I lobbed praise before getting to my request. "I appreciate your cooperation very much," I began. "I also recognize that what I'm about to ask for is contrary to what you said yesterday, about the FBI doing its job. But you clearly have a direct connection to—"

I flipped frantically through my notes, looking for the name. "Special Agent Marianna O'Toole. The agent you met with at the Elm Tree Club."

Isaac snorted. "Let me guess. You want me to reach out to her, and then get you in front of Barbutero."

"You claimed yesterday that he was connected with O'Toole."

"Yes," she confirmed. "I assume that's still the case. But, let me ask this—both O'Toole and you work for the same team. Am I not correct? Wouldn't it be better—no, not better, um, more impartial—if you went directly to her?"

As I framed my pitch, even as she spoke, that question had already occurred to me, and I was ready with an answer. "It would be better for me, yes, in terms of procedure and protocol. However, it would not be good for you, because there's a risk that this gets flagged to the Attorney General. It's my understanding that you'd prefer to leave him aside at the moment."

Silence.

Finally, Isaac breathed, "I hadn't thought of that."

I waited for her to continue and—nothing. She remained quiet. I began to speak, "I propose we—"

"No, you're correct, Ben," Isaac said, once again speaking over me. "I wanted to think it over, and yes, that's a risk. Too many ears. Therefore,

I'll see what I can do. But—I have terms."

I scoffed, "Naturally. This is Washington, after all."

Isaac guffawed with a loud laugh that caught me off-guard. "Ben, you're a piece of work. You're in the wrong line of business. You should toss away that badge and come work for me. I'd make you a shit-ton of money."

"That's actually tempting," I said—because it was. Isaac's decisiveness and clarity were a fresh contrast to the normally murky world of investigations. "Perhaps, someday. But I do like to finish what I start. Someone once called me tenacious." I didn't tell her that it was the AG who used that word.

"Well, let's finish it, then," Isaac said curtly. "But I want my name out of it, and I want your assurance of absolute discretion."

"Okay. And?" My voice trailed off, leaving just the question hanging.

Isaac spoke slowly. "I'll set you up with Barbutero. You meet with him alone, you don't take notes, and you leave your phone and all your devices behind. No weapons, either. This is strictly off the record."

I looked down at my pad, buying a second to think, before countering, "That doesn't work. If it's off the record, what's the use?"

"It's called deep background," Isaac explained. "I'm not going to let you compromise my position. I like you, Ben, but I gotta protect myself, too. I can't risk that you'll, say, record the discussion, and then pass on the recording to the AG so that he can bury it."

I nodded affirmatively. "I understand. Makes sense."

"We have an agreement?"

"Yes. Agreed."

"Good," Isaac said, drawing out the word. "Hang on. I'm putting you on hold, and I'm calling O'Toole."

The connection went silent, but the time counter continued to tick upward, indicating that the call was still active. Finally, three minutes later, I heard a soft click, and Isaac's voice announced, "O'Toole says we can make this happen. She'll send Barbutero to Washington late tonight. You'll meet at five in the morning tomorrow, as we have no time to spare, nor can we be visible, so you're meeting at the Lincoln Memorial. You'll have an hour, max, with Barbutero."

"What about this O'Toole? Will she be there? Will she escort Barbutero?"

"Oh, Ben, so many questions," Isaac sneered. "First, I'll remind you—O'Toole is not holding Barbutero. He's a witness, not a suspect. He'll travel on his own recognizance."

"Got it," I replied. I did have more questions, of course, about a zillion of them, but I sensed I was pushing the limit of Isaac's patience.

She continued, again barely waiting for my response, "Ben, you've only begun to see how effective I can be. I don't waffle on petty details."

"You don't waste time," I said, with a clear note of admiration in my voice.

"Frankly, the EPIC vote is in two days, and I've got Aximerva to run. Right now, I am treading water, and I want all of this behind me."

The connection ended abruptly.

"Wow." Lin finally spoke, wide-eyed. "You've got some sort of magnetism. And you've got some pull. Are you really capable of getting this Lewis guy to backtrace Preston's number?"

"Yeah, that's straightforward," I muttered, distracted as I scribbled a quick recap of the call with Isaac on my pad.

"How long does it take?"

I shrugged. "If I can convince Lewis to start immediately, I'd guess a few hours."

"That's all? That means there's no immediate rush."

Annoyed that my notetaking was interrupted, I placed my pen on the pad and eyed Lin. She was batting her eyelashes at me, and she stood, grinning. Coquettishly, she looked me up and down and said, "You should enjoy a proper shower. Care to join me?"

She pirouetted and pranced to the bedroom. I didn't make a move to follow as I heard the shower hiss. First, I wasn't in the mood for Lin's taunting games. And second, more importantly, having her isolated alone in the shower worked to my advantage, as I had a phone call to make.

There was no way I was so naïve as to meet with Barbutero alone. I needed backup. I just hoped I'd have enough time to set it all up.

# CHAPTER
## 45



**REFRESHED AND PROPERLY DRESSED,** Lin and I stepped out of her Foggy Bottom pad into a seasonally warm, sunny, November, Tuesday morning to begin the seven-minute walk to the New Hampshire Avenue office building.

As soon as we set foot on the sidewalk, Lin asked, "Can we detour?"

"Lewis usually gets in at nine. I want to grab him before he gets distracted by whatever's going on in the Boston field office."

She nudged my shoulder to the right as she said, "Five minutes. I want to stop at the coffee shop on I Street. Five minutes extra, tops."

I looked at the time display on my phone. It was 8:48 A.M.

"Sure. I'm suitably coffeed, but I could use a muffin or something."

Cutting through a pedestrian-only plaza adjacent to the George Washington University School of Medicine and passing the Foggy Bottom Metro station, she pointed ahead. "It's the next block. Just past the Whole Foods."

Antsy to get started with tracing the call to Preston, while Lin went inside the coffee shop to place our order, I waited outside and placed a call to Louis Lewis, the well-regarded, Boston-based Intelligence Analyst that I'd worked with several times previously. I visualized the spiky, blond-haired, computer whiz wobbling on his latest ergonomic gizmo—he'd foregone the standard-issue imitation Aeron chair for a standing desk with a balance board—but the call went to voice mail. My message was brief and to the point: "Hey, Louis. It's Ben Porter. Call me. This is an urgent, like 9-1-1, situation. Thanks."

I waited impatiently for Lin to rejoin me on the sidewalk, but all the same, I was grateful for the proffered brown paper bag containing a sugary, cinnamon, crumble-topped muffin. And, we made our schedule, stepping into the elevator to our fifth-floor office precisely at 9:00 A.M.

The elevator dinged our arrival on the fifth floor at the very same moment that my phone chimed with a text message notification. Hoping for a response to the call I had just made, instead, I saw a text from Attorney General Bart Williams:

> I'm told you've been busy. I'm calling you
> in 10 for an update. Ok?

*How does the AG know I've been busy?*

The answer hit me in an instant. *It must be Lin, communicating with him on her own. Reporting back to her boss. Maybe while I was getting dressed? Maybe from the coffee shop?*

At a loss for words, I merely sent a tapback thumbs-up, considering again that it would be nice, sometimes, to be able to send a middle finger tapback. Though, I realized, I wanted to send that sentiment not to the AG, but to Lin, who was most definitely not being transparent with me.

My immediate issues with Lin were compounded, though, by another problem as I considered, *I'm gonna be dancing on a pinhead to update the AG without compromising my deal with Isaac.*

Stepping distractedly into the fifth-floor foyer, I realized that our useless associates had beaten us to the office, perhaps to impress, and the duo of Toonin and Kinnar-Hering greeted Lin and me with mumbled "Good mornings." Grumpily, I dismissed them with a curt, and I confess, an impolite wave even as I beckoned Lin to follow me to my office.

I closed the door behind us and settled into my Aeron desk chair. Pointing, I motioned Lin to one of the so-called visitor's chairs opposite my desk, two hard-looking, stick-figure affairs that looked like they were supremely uncomfortable. As she sat, I asked, without preamble, "What are you up to? Whose side are you on?"

She looked back at me wide-eyed. "What do you mean?" Her voice was plaintive. Almost whiny.

"You're plugged in with the Attorney General. You worked at Main Justice, at least until this assignment. We haven't seen head or tail of the two other fellows—Toonin and, uh, something with a hyphen, until just this morning. We don't know what, if anything, they did yesterday, because we dismissed them so we could meet with Isaac in private. And yet, the AG just texted me, saying that he wants an update because I've been busy. You'd be the only source of that intel for the AG."

My tone was cutting, but I rushed on. "I can't believe we haven't discussed this yet—you're on a first-name basis with the two people that we are investigating. You've got 'em on speed dial or something. Two powerful, busy people, and yet, you call them, and, bam, they show up. Coate on Sunday, Isaac yesterday, and all of a sudden, we're cozy besties?"

"I don't think I like this line of questioning," Lin complained. "I thought we were a team. Maybe . . . even more than that." She batted her eyelashes suggestively, exactly as she'd done earlier this morning.

"I thought so, too," I replied, dialing my tone down to try and be more agreeable. "Therefore, if we're a team, what aren't you telling me?"

She shrugged. "Nothing."

I let the word hang in the air. She wasn't being defensive, but she was definitely acting cagey. I decided to wait her out.

Lin squirmed in the chair—either because she was nervous, or perhaps because the chair was inherently uncomfortable. After an awkward moment of silence, she began, "Isn't it obvious? I'm on the AG's investigating group because I know Coate and Isaac. Remember, I did my undergraduate work at Stanford. My parents are rich." She pointed her chin at me and added, "Adds up, doesn't it? I enjoyed pretty good access in California, and I got to know the Senator and his wife." She straightened up and concluded defiantly, "Because of my connections, I am a strategic asset to the Attorney General, *especially* in this investigation."

She was peeved. But she could have told me that, earlier, as I argued, "I didn't know that, obviously. That would have been critical intel to have before meeting with Coate and Isaac. You've put me in a blind spot, intentionally."

"No. I disagree," Lin countered. "You would have acted differently. More deferentially, possibly, had you known of my personal connection to them."

"Maybe."

The word hung in the air damply, as if a fog suddenly descended.

*It's a metaphor for this case,* I thought. *Foggy.*

At that very moment, I made a decision: I couldn't trust Lin. I let my breath exhale with a whoosh. I thought I had a partner, and instead, I'd come to realize that I'd been quite literally sleeping with the enemy. Well, maybe not the enemy, because I couldn't figure out exactly who the enemy was—and that made it all the more depressing.

I was on my own. But—in the interests of deflection, for now, I offered an olive branch. "Sorry. Came on a little strong there, I think. I really do appreciate the introduction to the Senator and his wife. You do have some high-level connections!"

I hoped my renewed friendly enthusiasm took the edge off my attack, and Lin bought it. "Yah. You think? Gee, Ben, settle down." She grinned happily—and then my phone rang, right on schedule. "Who's that?" she asked sharply.

Instead of responding, I placed the device on the desktop and tapped to accept the call on speaker. "Porter. And Lin."

"Ah, good," boomed Bart Williams. "Thank you for taking the call on short notice."

I fake-laughed. "No problem, sir. You're the boss, after all."

"Indeed, I suppose. But at this moment, you, Porter, hold my interest. Lin tells me you've met with both Coate and Isaac. What are your impressions? What did you learn?"

As typical, the AG didn't waste time with preambles and small talk. Yet, he confirmed my suspicion: that Lin had already been in touch with him, without me knowing. *Foggy.*

I didn't want to answer his question directly, so instead, I replied, "They are an impressive couple. Charming, engaging, and they appear to be quite transparent." I paused briefly before dropping the bombshell—having no idea whether Lin had already passed on Isaac's revelations. "Also, Virgil Preston is alive."

"What?!"

"Isaac claimed that Preston is alive and that she communicated with him on Sunday."

"That's impossible!"

*Either Lin didn't reveal that to him, or he's genuinely surprised. But I don't know who I can trust. Foggy . . .*

"I'm not finished, sir. Isaac facilitated an introduction, and I spoke with Preston himself, not more than two hours ago."

At that moment, I decided to play both sides, and I purposely omitted a very salient detail—that Isaac bought Aximerva. Instead, I focused on the missing person, presumed deceased by the FBI. "Preston is very much alive, and Isaac also offered an introduction for me and Barbutero. Tomorrow, at five, first thing in the morning."

"That's also impossible," the AG blurted. "The FBI can't find him, so how on earth can Isaac set up a meeting with him?"

I watched Lin's face from an oblique angle as I constructed an answer that was close enough to the truth to pass future muster. "What do you mean, the FBI can't find him? Barbutero is remaining in contact with the FBI in New Haven."

The AG grunted. "That's very concerning. I knew it. No, I suspected that there's a splinter within the Bureau. This is exactly why I wanted to engage you, Porter, and Appleton. I can't have this sort of dichotomy within the agency. But there it is."

"Yes."

Lin's unlined face didn't change in the slightest. She manifested no emotion. No concern, no fear, no joy.

*She told the AG about our meetings with Coate and Isaac, but she didn't tell him the whole story. Why is she withholding details from the AG? Foggy . . .*

The AG demanded, "Who are you meeting Barbutero with? Lin? Isaac?"

"Alone, as per Isaac's conditions."

The AG hummed loudly. "Hmm. I don't like that at all. It could be dangerous, Porter."

"No, I disagree, sir," I lied, even as I continued to subtly study Lin.

The AG continued, "I don't trust Isaac. I doubt very much that Preston has conveniently chosen these few weeks to be silent. Where is he?"

"Jamaica, sir. Playing golf. But—that's as of yet unverified. I'm working on corroboration."

"Working with who? How do you intend to accomplish that task? Wait—"

I thought I heard something, and I squeezed the side of my phone to increase the speaker volume. It was the AG, breathing loudly. Wheezing.

After a moment, he huffed, "This is all disturbing. Lay it out step-by-step, Porter. What is your plan?"

*Well, ain't that the question of the day?*

I decided I would proceed very methodically. If there was really a scandal afoot, and this all really had something to do with the EPIC vote in two days, that gave me forty-eight hours.

It was a turning point.

I took a deep breath. "First, sir, I will utilize an FBI resource, who I might add can be trusted to be discreet, to confirm that indeed, Preston's phone was in Jamaica this morning. I didn't record the call, so I cannot do a voice analysis, but once we ID the phone, we can track its movements. Are you with me so far?"

"Yes. Proceed," Williams ordered.

"I've spoken with both Coate and Isaac, with credit going to Lin for expediting those meetings." I smiled at Lin; she grinned back, presumably happy that I'd elevated her to her boss.

"Yes, yes, yes. That's why Lin is on this case. She's quite valuable, as you've seen."

Lin was beaming as I continued, "However, despite speaking with the couple, we're still missing one angle. That is, of course, Barbutero. It's critical I meet with him, and it's helpful that will take place first thing tomorrow." I sniffed and concluded, "I am confident that we will be able to piece the puzzle together by end of day tomorrow."

Lin nodded encouragement as the AG said, "That's a workable plan and timeline. I want an update by noon on Wednesday. That will give me a window before the EPIC vote on Thursday morning."

"Window for what, sir?"

"I'm going public. We are working on a press release, and we will schedule a press conference. I will disclose the improprieties of the Coate and Isaac collusion, and that revelation is certain to at least delay the EPIC vote. I'll do that tomorrow afternoon—unless you give me reason to hold—by noon tomorrow," he repeated.

"Understood. Noon tomorrow," I confirmed.

The AG wasn't finished, apparently, as he added, "I am disturbed that Isaac knows where an FBI suspect is located, and yet, I don't have that intel. But we have no choice but to pull at this thread. You'll take precautions when you meet with Barbutero?"

I shrugged casually, mostly for Lin's benefit. "I don't think I need to worry, sir. I'm quite certain it will be a productive conversation."

Lin's right eye twitched ever so slightly.

The AG's voice rumbled once more. "I should hope so. In the meantime, I want constant contact on this. Every detail. Call me, or at least call Lin, as soon as your conversation with Barbutero concludes, Porter. No matter what the time. Understood?"

"Yessir."

The connection was terminated, and I grinned cheerfully at Lin. "We've got a report to write. Let's get started with Toonin and Kinnar-Hering, and let's order in lunch. I'm buying."

"Sure," she exclaimed—and with that one word, I knew my hunch was correct.

# WEDNESDAY
# NOVEMBER 2, 2022

**THE DAY BEFORE** *THE VOTE*

## *EARLY MORNING — WASHINGTON, DC*

**AT FIVE OF FIVE** on a windless, chilly, thirty-eight-degree Wednesday morning, I began to ascend the eighty-seven steps from the Reflecting Pool to the chamber where the 175 tons of white marble, quarried in the state of Georgia, form the almost universally recognized statute of Abraham Lincoln. The figure appears on paper currency and is even faintly visible, though tiny, on a penny coin.

The Washington pre-dawn skies were dark and overcast, but the nineteen-foot-tall statue was brightly illuminated, with Lincoln's gaze peering, as it has done since 1922, just over two miles to the east at the United States Capitol building. Only the 555-foot-tall obelisk of the Washington Monument obstructs the sixteenth President's view of the Capitol.

From his great height, Lincoln wouldn't have seen the slightly stocky, somewhat overweight, and moderately out of breath me, alone on the vast platform, clad in a dark jacket, dark jeans, and black sneakers, but someone else did, and from the shadows to the south, I heard a hissing call. "Porter. Over here."

I turned my body to the right, first doing a simple visual reconnaissance sweep from facing Lincoln to the west, then turning north, where a solitary man dressed in a Washington bureaucrat's uniform of a blue blazer and carrying a briefcase ambled toward the northeast, aiming away and in the direction of the Vietnam Memorial. Continuing my rotation, I peered east over the length of the Reflecting Pool, usually surrounded by a throng of tourists but now, at five in the morning, entirely unpopulated. Finally turning south to the source of the voice, I responded cryptically, "Hanna sent me. Who are you?"

"Oh, for fuck's sake, Porter, cut the theatrics," the voice growled with a heavy New York inflection. "We're the only ones here. It's Rocco."

"Rocky Balboa?"

"You think you're funny, eh?"

I pulled my hands from my jeans pockets and held them out, palms up, toward the figure dressed in a tan trench coat who lurked by the southeast corner column—one of the thirty-six, forty-four-foot-tall Doric columns that surrounded the structure and which inclined slightly to the middle, thus creating the illusion of a symmetrical building when seen in a perspective view.

Indeed, I was a fount of knowledge about the 22,800-square-foot edifice, a necessary component of the pre-operation outline that I'd worked on yesterday in the office. I assigned the research task to Toonin, who'd proven himself quite useful, adept at going beyond Google to provide me with every detail that I required of the Lincoln Memorial. Meanwhile, Kinnar-Hering showed his value by scribing, as Lin and I dictated, the reports of our various meetings over the past two days. I ensured that the written material was recorded solely on my password-protected and fingerprint-secured laptop computer—which I'd disconnected from WiFi and Bluetooth, and which was secured in the locked fifth-floor turret, accessible only by elevator with three unique ten-digit passcodes.

A disappointment of yesterday was a lack of a return call from Louis Lewis, but I would have to work around that.

Returning to Lin's pad in the evening, we talked over the various questions that I'd have for Barbutero before retiring early to bed in advance of my early morning. I intended to get a good night's sleep, but Lin had other plans—and I demurred, to her annoyance.

After the strong words in the office the day before, I anticipated that the tenor of our relationship would change, and my expectations were met by Lin's pettiness when she didn't rise with me. Alone, I had slipped from the warmth of Lin's home an hour ago.

"Okay," I said as I walked toward the figure, "let's try Rocco Barbutero. I suppose it would be polite to say something like, nice to see you again."

"That was quite a bump you gave me on the Acela," he replied, grinning lopsidedly, exposing coffee-stained, crooked teeth.

"Don't take it personally."

"Of course not." He pulled a small box of cigarillos from his coat pocket, extracted one, and lit it with a gold lighter, the brief flame lighting his leathery skin and pockmarked complexion.

"I don't think they allow smoking here."

"You're an FBI agent. Arrest me."

I snorted. "Smells good, actually."

He wiped his mustache and waved toward the rear of the memorial, toward the west. "Probably better not to attract attention. But first, eh, lift your arms."

"You gonna frisk me?"

"No weapons, no phone, no wires, no nothin'. You get that memo?"

"Yeah. Want me to strip?"

He grunted. "That won't be necessary." His movements were efficient and, dare I say, professional, as he poked, prodded, and slid his hands in all the correct places, ensuring that I was clean. He paused at my right hand, tapping the black ring that I wore on my index finger. "What's this?"

"It's a fitness ring. Sleep tracker, counts steps, monitors pulse, that sorta thing." I grinned sheepishly. "Trying to get in shape, ya know."

He puffed his cigar. "Oh, yeah, I've heard of those rings. Never gonna bother. It's a useless effort, if you ask me. You're gonna die anyway. What's the point?" He continued his search, and when he completed his task, he politely tugged at the lapels of my coat, smoothing it carefully, as if he was a tailor who'd measured me for a new suit. "Okay. You're clean. Let's walk around back."

We matched paces westward, aiming toward the Watergate Steps that led to the shoreline of the Potomac River. From the height of the

Lincoln Memorial, the vista was splendid even by night; to the south and soon behind us, lights glittered at the Martin Luther King, Jr. Memorial and ahead, the vastness of Arlington National Cemetery was spread out across the river. Barbutero swept his left arm outward and turned slowly, saying, "What a view, doncha think?"

I smiled my agreement but thought otherwise. *He's not admiring the scenery. He's making sure we're alone.*

Figuring I might as well move things along, I asked, "Can we get started? Isaac told me I had only an hour with you, so I don't want to waste any more time. Are you going to explain your connection to the Attorney General? To Isaac? To Virgil Preston?"

We reached the southwest corner of the Lincoln Memorial, its back wall blank and unadorned but, along the perimeter, the Doric columns continued their precise spacing. Below us were three tiers, like extra-large steps, that led to a narrow grassy area and then to the fourteen-foot-tall retaining wall that surrounded the backside of the edifice.

Barbutero sucked at his cigarillo, the tip glowing a fiery orange, before answering. "Lemme take those names in order. The AG is a very clever manipulator who has aligned the interests of his political aspirations with that of his nation. His success will be my ticket, too, when he kills the semiconductor bill for his own gain."

"Which is what?"

He shrugged; his cigarillo clenched in the right corner of his mouth as he shoved his hands in the pockets of his tan trench coat. "He will crush the EPIC bill and Coate's career when the AG charges Isaac for ordering Preston's murder."

"That doesn't make sense," I complained. "Isaac told me that Preston is alive."

Barbutero laughed with derision. "She's lying. Preston is dead."

"Wait . . . what?" I rubbed my hands together as if I was worried and confused. "I talked to Preston yesterday."

Barbutero pulled his hands from his trench coat pockets. In his left hand was a black suppressor, and in his right, a pistol. With practiced, smooth motions, he brought the pieces together and twisted the suppressor to mate with the pistol.

As he brought the pistol up, he said mockingly, "Since you somehow started to unravel this thing faster than anyone believed possible, we're covering our tracks, just as sure as your body will be covered by those bushes below the retaining wall."

I clutched my hands together as Barbutero sneered, "Porter, you shoulda taken me out on the Acela."

# CHAPTER
# 47

**WITH MY HANDS** clutched together, I tightly squeezed the simple black ring that I wore on my right index finger, and in an instant, Barbutero and I were illuminated by the white-bright glare of a high-intensity, focused spotlight.

A split second later, a man's Boston-accented voice commanded, "Lower the pistol, or you're going to be missing your head, Mister Barbutero."

Barbutero's eyes darted back and forth, and his lips parted. The cigarillo dropped to the marble platform and flared slightly.

He slowly complied, angling his pistol to the marble as a tall, somewhat pale man, with thinning gray hair combed over his temples approached from the north.

"Where the fuck did you come from?" Barbutero snarled, eying the menacing pistol in the gray-haired man's right hand.

"That's not germane to your present situation, Mister Barbutero. I will, however, inform you of what should be important to you, which is the second weapon that is aimed at you from the opposite direction."

"That's right," Jennifer Appleton's voice called out. She was invisible given the glare of the spotlight, but I could identify that her voice sounded out from just beyond a low bush that bordered the Memorial's southern retaining wall. "Now, Mister Barbutero, if you'd kindly dissemble your piece and return the components to your trench coat pockets, please."

As soon as Barbutero's grip shifted to unscrew his suppressor, I knew I was safe, and I exhaled—and the spotlight was extinguished, forcing me to blink rapidly as my pupils adjusted to the dim light.

Barbutero was similarly afflicted, and he fumbled with his trench coat, finally slipping the pieces of his weapon into the captivity of the tan trench coat.

The gray-haired man ordered, "Retrace your steps, please. Try anything, and I'll fire at the back of your left knee—so that you don't topple off the retaining wall and instead fall toward the walkway."

Barbutero turned and began to walk toward the front face of the Memorial. "That's very precise."

"Should you live long enough, you'll discover that I'm nothing if not exacting," the gray-haired man replied. With his free left hand, he adjusted the half-Windsor knot of his navy blue and leaf-green striped tie, tastefully matched with a starched, light blue button-down shirt, a navy-blue blazer, and sharply creased charcoal dress trousers.

I looked sideways at my companion. "Where's your briefcase?"

"Appleton has it."

We reached the face of the Memorial and descended the steps to the plaza above the Reflecting Pool. Turning to our right and to the south, we circled the Memorial a quarter-turn until we reached what I immediately recognized as Appleton's bug-out vehicle: an older, dusty, dented, maroon-colored Ford F-250 pickup truck.

Opening the passenger side front door and then the suicide-style rear door of the extended cab truck, Appleton commanded, "In the back, right here, Mister Barbutero. Apologies for the lack of legroom, but it's a short drive."

"Wait," I commanded. I reached into the pickup truck and withdrew a pair of latex gloves from a box in the passenger-side front door bin. Snapping the gloves on, I frisked Barbutero, pulling the pistol and suppressor plus a flip phone from the pockets of his trench coat. I laid the evidence in the passenger side front footwell and ordered, "Now, get in."

Wordlessly, Barbutero climbed into the truck, prodded along gently with the gray-haired man's pistol. As Appleton circled to the driver's side, the gray-haired man seated himself next to Barbutero, I closed the rear door and hoisted myself up to the shotgun seat.

Appleton started the truck, and its meticulously maintained engine hummed as she accelerated, winding around the Memorial and carving a path northward, back toward the heart of Foggy Bottom.

*Progress*, I thought. With a conspirator in custody, I might be able to confirm several suspicions, one of which had become obvious to me.

# CHAPTER
# 48

**ELEVEN MINUTES LATER,** Appleton deftly parallel-parked the big truck on 28th Street Northwest. Recognizing the location from a previous case, I stated, "Ah—the Georgetown University law professor's pied-a-terre. We're using it again?"

Appleton turned off the F-250's motor. "The professor retired, and I bought the place. Not in my name, of course. I was going to offer it to you for your residence when the AG dispatched you to Washington, but then you, ah, um . . ."

"Shacked up with Lin?"

The former SAC rolled her eyes. "Something like that."

One by one, we followed Appleton into the red-brick-clad, two-story townhouse, the gray-haired man in the rear, pistol still encouraging Barbutero to follow orders as we made our way to the home's wood-paneled library, where Appleton commanded us to sit. "No talking, please. I don't want to miss anything, but I'd like a cup of coffee."

"Let me give a hand," I offered, though my intentions were otherwise.

I tailed Appleton to the home's tidy, tiny galley kitchen, immediately pulled out my phone, and swiped to the contacts screen.

Appleton demanded, "Who are you calling?"

I held up a single finger on my free hand to "shh" her and said to my phone, "Hey, Sara. He ghosted me."

I angled the device slightly, and Appleton leaned in to listen in as Lin replied, "Barbutero didn't show? That's crazy. I wonder what happened."

"Yeah, I dunno. I hung out for almost an hour. I'll call Isaac later, at, you know, a respectable hour. Anyway, while I was waiting, Appleton texted me," I lied. "She drove through the night to DC." That part was true, at least. I continued, "I'm meeting her for a coffee." Also true.

Appleton's expression evolved from suspicion to impressed.

Lin asked, "Are you going to bring her by our office later?"

"Yeah, definitely." I tried to sound convincing but, at that point, I wasn't the slightest bit sure. "I'll see you or call you later. Bye."

Appleton turned her attention to fuss with the coffee pot. "Can you explain why that was necessary?"

"In a minute," I assured her as I watched her spoon ground coffee from a bag into the machine's maw. "Couple more scoops, please."

She eyed me. "Really? Super high test?"

"I suspect it's gonna be a long day."

Appleton grinned wryly. "It was a long night, too. You didn't give me much time. But it was a brilliant call."

"Did you have any trouble with Gansett's security?"

"I flashed my FBI ID and relieved two guards of their duty. There will be hell to pay for those two today, and for me, too, eventually, but I think we have a bit of time. Though, I'd like to know not only why you just lied to Sara Lin, but also better understand your conclusions in detail."

I pursed my lips as the coffee machine wheezed. "Can we discuss freely? In front of Barbutero?"

"I think we must. He has intel and is a corroborating witness. Ultimately, we're gonna have to broker a deal," she stated with her usual clarity.

The coffee machine's drip quieted, and Appleton placed four mugs on a tray. We returned to the library, and I poured myself a cup. Taking a sip, I started, "First, introductions." With a little flourish, I waved at the gray-haired man as I addressed Barbutero. "Rocco—can I call you Rocco? Mister Barbutero is a mouthful."

"Uh, sure," Barbutero grunted.

"Very well. Rocco, this is JJ Gansett. He was previously known as the Central Intelligence Agency's most deadly contract assassin, but he was recently removed from their service. He'll be rejoining the workforce in a new capacity alongside me and Jennifer Appleton." I motioned at Appleton for clarity and added, "Appleton is a former Special Agent in Charge of the FBI's Boston field office."

I paused briefly. "You see, Appleton and I are currently working for the Department of Justice under the sole authority of the Attorney General of the United States. We have quite a few questions for you, Rocco. Shall we get started?"

# CHAPTER
## 49

**IN THE TOWNHOUSE** that previously belonged to a Georgetown law professor, I took in my audience: former FBI Special Agent in Charge Jennifer Appleton, ex-CIA assassin JJ Gansett, and New York fine foods purveyor and alleged hitman Rocco Barbutero.

My mom would be proud. Or dismayed by the company I kept. Or confused. Or, possibly, all of the above.

Appleton crossed her skinny-jeans-clad legs, showing off a tasteful suede boot, and asked, "Porter, may I begin?"

I nodded, relieved a bit that my boss would set the tone.

Appleton cleared her throat and said, "Yesterday morning, Porter texted me to the effect that he required backup and requested Gansett, which, given that he's under FBI-secured house arrest for previous crimes against the United States, seemed quite unusual. Nevertheless, I put the wheels in motion, literally, and I drove to Cape Cod to retrieve him. That's when Porter called me with a situation report." She lifted her coffee cup to her lips but, before sipping, jutted her chin at me and passed the baton. "Your turn, Porter."

I nodded a second time, having received Appleton's message by way of the details that she revealed. *Nothing is off the table.*

"You see, Mister Barbutero, I began to have grave suspicions that Sara Lin was playing the role of a double agent. On one hand, she's an attorney working directly for Bart Williams in Main Justice. And yet, on the other hand, she's cozy with two people that the AG is investigating, namely Hanna Isaac and Senator Coate. That became obvious pretty quickly."

Barbutero shrugged, his hands clasped tightly together, but he remained wordless. Maybe Gansett's pistol pressed into the New York hitman's gut had that effect.

I continued, "I wasn't certain where Lin's allegiance lay. I figured she was feeding intel to both Isaac and to the AG. Then, she became worried when I told Isaac that I could trace my call to Preston—with help from the Bureau, of course."

Appleton demanded, "Who in the Bureau?"

"I called Louis Lewis, but he hasn't called back yet."

"I'll get him," Appleton offered.

"I'm not sure there's any need, anymore, though the data would be useful in prosecution. Because, then I had a call with Lin and the AG. Lin was totally non-plussed by the concept of Isaac masterminding a meeting with me and you, Barbutero, alone, in the dark of the dawn, with no protection. Ergo, I figured she knew that I wasn't going to return from that meeting. Send the lamb to slaughter, as it were."

I turned my gaze to Gansett. "Unfortunately, I think Lin suspected that I was on to her duplicity. She stuck to me like glue yesterday. Finally, in the evening, Lin caved to use the bathroom, and I seized that opportunity to call Appleton for a fast situation report. By that time, she and Gansett were en route to DC in Appleton's truck, so we laid out the plan to entrap you."

Barbutero side-eyed Gansett. "You mind, buddy, if I have some coffee? Or you gonna shoot me?"

"Be my guest," Gansett offered, but he didn't alter the pressure of the pistol the slightest.

Barbutero reached a hand for a mug of coffee and sipped it eagerly. Pursing his lips, he grunted, "Hmm. Good enough. A little bitter, though." He looked at me. "Clever, with that ring. When did you get it?"

"Gansett pulled it out of his briefcase and handed it to me this morning as I walked from Lin's place to the Memorial. A little toy that the CIA developed. GPS tracking, audio transmitter with remote recording, and even video, though the angle makes it less than optimal. Anyway, we have our entire conversation memorialized." I raised my hand to show him the black ring. "I'm still wearing it, as you can see, and it's recording this discussion, too."

Barbutero groaned in dismay. "Lin didn't say nothin' about it, nor did you have it on in any of the photos she took of you and sent to me. I missed the significance of it when I patted you down. Nice touch," he added grudgingly.

"Thank you," I replied politely. "That confirms without a shadow of a doubt that Lin is untrustworthy. Also, just to let you know, while Appleton and I were in the kitchen preparing coffee, I called Lin. I told her that you were a no-show. That subterfuge on my part will cover me for a while, since obviously, I don't know what your protocols were to be after you killed me. Care to share? Were you also supposed to dispose of the body?"

"Nah. Would have just let your corpse drop into those bushes next to the retaining wall. Not too many people go back there, and the wall is what, twenty feet high?"

"Fourteen."

Barbutero twitched. "Figures you did the research. Anyway, your body might have been found during the day. Would take a little while for it to start to smell at these temps." He cocked his head to the side. "Wouldn't have mattered. The DC police would eventually be called, and it would take a little time to ID the stiff."

"Well, fortunately for me, Gansett and Appleton's intervention saves them from that trouble." I sipped at my coffee and asked, "Speaking of stiffs, Rocco, what was the play with Preston?"

"Ahead of time, I knew that Isaac didn't want to be seen with Preston. At the end of the meal, I told Preston I'd take him out the back, through the kitchen."

"And can you tell me what happened next?"

"Yeah," Barbutero grunted. "Preston reached into his pocket to pay, you know, uh, kinda confused 'cuz he's thinking the lunch was on Isaac. So we had this moment of, you know, jocularity." He chuckled at his cleverness.

"Hysterical," I deadpanned.

"So Preston is bitching about the food, you know, 'cuz he wants somethin' more substantial than a plate of spaghetti. He goes, hey, how 'bout a steak sandwich? I said sure." Barbutero was snorting his laughter as he concluded, "Shit, I even said, hey, man, I'm good with a knife—I used to be a butcher!"

I was worried that Barbutero's gut heaving in his peals of self-congratulatory sniggers would cause Gansett's gun to fire, so I waited until the hitman calmed himself down before asking, "You killed Preston in the kitchen?"

"Yeah," Barbutero admitted. "Unfortunately, there's evidence on the scene. Blood. DNA. In the kitchen. I saw the splatter hit the butcher block and I thought to myself, shit, I'm not gonna be able to sanitize that." He turned to Gansett. "You seem like a man with that sorta experience. Wanna back me up on that?"

Gansett grunted, "Sloppy." Without taking his attention from the pistol he still held steadily in Barbutero's side, he glanced at Appleton, then me. "But he's accurate. He would have been able to wipe down the floor and any stainless steel in that setting in short order. Ridding a wooden surface, even the dense wood of a cutting board, of embedded, soaked-in cellular matter without leaving a trace would be difficult even with the proper tools and materials."

"See what I mean? Yeah, it was messy. And the knife I used had a wooden handle, but that was small enough to dispose. That item is with the body." Barbutero frowned. "Chef types are usually possessive of their knives, so I bet they noticed a blade missing from the kitchen."

"Correct, again," I confirmed.

"Yeah, figures," the hitman mumbled. "Someone probably found those two fuck ups. NYPD or FBI, I dunno." He brightened. "But nobody 'cept me knows where the body is, and you need a body, dontcha, to prove the crime."

Appleton interjected, "We know about the block and the knife. There was a complete forensics inspection of the bistro as well as a full investigation." She didn't reveal that we already knew, from neighborhood cameras, that Barbutero had already been placed at the scene. Instead, she added politely, "Any additional data and details that you can provide will be helpful to the FBI."

"I'm not new at this, lady," Barbutero protested. "This is the part when I turn state's witness and give the AG the deets in exchange for immunity. That data, as you call it, is worth a deal."

"That's not my decision," Appleton cautioned. "But we will transmit the offer. You'll have to provide more."

"Such as?" Barbutero's voice cracked slightly in confusion.

"Hold that thought," I grumbled. I reached into my pocket to pull out the Nokia flip phone that I'd liberated from Barbutero's trench coat. "This is yours, right?"

"Yeah."

I flipped the phone open, guessing that this older phone would not have any security measures baked in. Satisfied that I had full access to his device, I set it on the coffee table and pulled out my phone.

I dialed Preston's number and waited.

Nothing happened.

I frowned. "Huh. That's interesting." I lifted my eyes to stare at Barbutero. "Where is Preston's phone? I want that, too."

Barbutero's eyes darted back and forth, until finally, his gaze dropped to the floor. "I don't have it with me." He looked back up at me. "How'd you know?"

"You laid on the fake accent way too thick and too inconsistently. You hesitated when I asked where you, or, rather, Preston, was. And most damning, Preston doesn't smoke or drink. He wouldn't have a cigar or a Red Stripe beer on the golf course."

"Oh." The hitman's bluster deflated considerably. He reached for the coffee mug and then changed his mind, apparently, as his hand fell to his lap.

"Moreover," I added, "when I told Isaac that I was planning to trace the call, she played it cool, at first, but then offered up you. At five in the morning—alone. Who does that?"

Appleton leaned in, "Someone arranging a hit, but clumsily. She took some risk, though."

"She had no choice," I ventured. "Isaac is accustomed to business risk, and in this case, she was forced to take the chance that I couldn't get the phone traced—but she tightened up the timeline considerably with the pre-dawn meeting time. Or, essentially, the fastest realistic schedule to get Barbutero transported from Connecticut to Washington while allowing some wiggle room in case she met with resistance in New Haven. She bet the farm, correctly as it turns out, that I couldn't get the trace done in one working day."

Barbutero's face brightened. "Well, I'll disclose the location of the phone, which will become real evidence, as opposed to a computer trace—assuming I get my immunity deal."

I leaned forward and tilted my almost-empty coffee mug slightly at Barbutero. "You're too confident, in my estimation. What makes you think you shake a murder rap plus a conspiracy to commit murder—of me—and you walk free? You might get a reduced sentence."

Barbutero met my stare and replied with a sneer, "This case is too valuable for the AG not to let that happen. He'll paper it over and hide me as a confidential informant."

I turned my attention to Appleton. "Seems anti-climactic, doesn't it? If this all checks out, and the AG agrees to a deal, we've cracked the case."

"That's what concerns me," Appleton replied.

"Exactly," I agreed. "It's too easy."

Barbutero argued, "Eh, typical FBI. You'se all are stuck on conspiracies and complications. It is that easy," he groused. "Run the deal over to the AG, and we're done."

Appleton scoffed. "You're remarkably confident."

"Remember, I did business with him before," Barbutero said. "I know how he moves."

Appleton said nothing, and Gansett also remained mute, focused on his pistol, ensuring that Barbutero did nothing aggressive.

The hitman's statement gave me pause. "Speaking of moves, why did you follow me in the Azores?"

Barbutero froze. "What?"

"That was you, right?"

"Who told you that?"

"The Attorney General came to that conclusion. I suspect you were on my flight, too, but I didn't know anything about you, so I didn't look for you."

Barbutero scoffed. "Didn't think to run a flight manifest, did you?"

Appleton held up a hand. "I ran manifests, and your name didn't appear. Not a surprise since we assume you have multiple identities. Facial recognition scans at Boston's Logan Airport don't show you in the terminal, so we came up empty on that front."

"That's 'cuz I got no clue what you two are talkin' about," Barbutero claimed, his eyes boring into mine. "What flight? When? I haven't left the United States in years. I never been to the Azores. Haven't been on a plane in years. So on that question, Porter, you got the wrong mark."

I slowly turned to Appleton and exhaled. "If it wasn't him, then who was it?"

# CHAPTER
## 50

**I DRAGGED APPLETON** to the kitchen of the Georgetown townhouse as the day brightened significantly outside, mirroring my mood. *A new day. A new hope.*

Wait. Part of that is the name of a movie, right?

Never mind. It works here in this context, so let's go with it.

In the privacy of the kitchen, I attempted to confer with Appleton, but she was already shaking her head back and forth. "Don't go there, Ben. I know what you're thinking."

"Back in Salem, the Attorney General and you were confident it was Barbutero tailing me in the Azores. If not him, then who?"

She countered, "We can't prove it wasn't him, yet. You can't take him at his word."

"You said it yourself—facial recognition didn't put him in the terminal. Therefore, he must have flown private, taken off after I departed, and landed in time to make the 5:05 Acela. What are the odds of that?"

"They're excellent," she protested. "Isaac, for one, owns a Gulfstream jet."

"I don't buy it," I complained, eyeing the empty coffee pot—which gave me an idea. I turned to face Appleton. "Give me some leeway, please. How 'bout this: you trade places with Gansett, and I game it out with our CIA man? Let's see if he has a fresh take."

Appleton grinned. "Creative. You're correct; he'll see it differently." She began to return to the library but called over her shoulder, "Have Gansett rustle up some breakfast while you talk. Fridge is stocked, and I'm starving."

My head was deep in the refrigerator when Gansett entered the galley kitchen asking, "Appleton said I was supposed to make breakfast?"

"Something like that," I agreed. "Do you know how to cook?"

"Step aside, son."

I chuckled. "Can you cook and talk at the same time?"

Gansett was significantly taller than me, and from his height, he glared at me in a patrician manner. "I'm very talented, Porter. I can do many things."

I followed his order and shrank myself into a corner of the kitchen. Gansett was familiar with *Almaz* and knew that part of the story, so there was no need to rehash it for him. Instead, as the ex-CIA man swirled and stirred a pan of ingredients that eventually became a sort of *huevos rancheros*, I was able to limit my briefing to an explanation of my trip to the Azores, a retelling of my evasion of the tailing vehicle, and ultimately my receipt of the cryptic text message.

Gansett worked efficiently and silently, and I was frustrated. I felt like I'd been talking to myself until Gansett began plating his culinary composition. With four, empty white plates ready on the countertop, and a wooden spoon in hand, he froze, mid-motion. "It's quite simple."

"What's simple?"

"Your recall is excellent, and the details are crucial," the ex-assassin explained. "But it's all there. When was the last time you used your American Express card?"

"What?"

"Answer, please."

I thought for a moment and replied, "I didn't come to DC with much luggage, so I bought some clothes over in Georgetown. A few days ago, on Saturday. Oh, and yesterday. I bought lunch."

"Were you alone?"

"No. Every time I was with Sara Lin." I inadvertently gasped. "You think it was it her, in the Azores?"

Gansett prepared two plates in silence as I stewed. He stopped his work again and said quietly, in a professorial tone, "Porter, set aside your feelings for Lin. You think you've been used, or whatever. Let it go and focus because you're still missing it. You used your personal American Express card to pay for the rental car in the Azores. You even said there was a momentary pause in the processing. It's being monitored. That sort of work is child's play with the right tools and access. Someone is watching your movements via your personal credit card."

The CIA's most deadly assassin, now retired, completed plating the fourth dish. He folded a towel over his arm and, with the deft motions of an experienced waiter, lifted all four plates while saying, "I'll cover you when you swipe that card, somewhere in public, and then remain in the establishment—alone. Your tail may materialize."

# CHAPTER
# 51

**EAGER TO PUT** Gansett's theory to the test to smoke out my tail, I barely tasted Gansett's breakfast. Even the coffee lost its kick, at least as far as I was concerned. I was primed for action and ready to bolt from the Georgetown townhouse.

Appleton, on the other hand, was true-to-form cautious. "Porter, don't you remember the threatening tone of the text message? I'll get you eventually, it said. Right?"

"Yeah," I was forced to agree.

"I know what you want to think," Appleton protested, "but remind yourself that you are a trained agent of the FBI. Look at your proposed op from that perspective. Manage the risk and the unknowns."

"I've got a location in mind. A café. It's got an outside patio with excellent sightlines and plenty of opportunities for cover as well as only two approach points, which means it's got only two escape routes."

"Sounds promising," Gansett grumbled, his eyes closed in concentration as the CIA agent envisioned a proposed arena of operations.

"We can map it out on Google Maps with satellite images and then do a dry run. The chance of being spotted by my tail as we're doing recon is extremely unlikely since I won't swipe my credit card until we are in position," I explained. "With two of you at opposite angles flanking me, I've got cover on infil and exfil. Essentially, it's the same op that we ran this morning with Barbutero, except that this time, we have the benefit of daylight and practice."

"Even without a dry run, that worked out good," Barbutero mumbled in a defeated voice. His tone became more positive as he complimented the chef. "This is a good meal, Gansett. Where'd you learn to cook? You know, I'm in the food service business, and—"

"Enough," Appleton interrupted. "Porter, despite Mister Barbutero's unsolicited endorsement, there's a flaw in your plan."

I hung my head slightly and admitted, "I know. If we've got two on overwatch, that leaves no one behind with Rocco, who I'm quite sure won't sit here demurely and wait for our return."

Appleton eyed Barbutero wryly. "Hmph. Well, Porter, it's a good thing that I anticipated this." She paused. "Well, not *this* exactly. However, I knew I'd want local backup in case we were successful in entrapping Barbutero because I didn't want to be his babysitter." Glancing at her silver wristwatch, she announced, "It's almost seven-thirty. Reinforcements are due any moment now."

As if on cue, the doorbell chimed, and Appleton set her plate aside. She disappeared to the front door, and a moment later, reappeared in the library—now accompanied by a red-headed pale man, tall and skinny, with a spotty ginger beard, the unruliness of the facial hair contrasted with a well-tailored navy suit, and a fastidiously Windsor-knotted, black necktie patterned with little, red pirate skulls.

I jumped to my feet. "Paxton Parr! I hoped our paths would cross again, and here we are." I nodded at Appleton with appreciation; the wily former SAC had introduced me to Parr on a previous case, and with her usual, impeccable foresight, knew that he'd be the perfect addition to our little team.

"Ah, yes, the infamous Ben Porter," Parr drawled in his Southern accent. "Somehow, I knew that you'd be involved in this little caper."

Appleton pointed at Barbutero and said, "Here's your assignment. Meet Rocco Barbutero. He's not on our side, he's dangerous, and yet he's very important to us. Keep him safe, please."

"Ah, that won't be a problem, ma'am," Parr assured her. He looked at Gansett, who had stood politely after carefully aligning his fork and knife, business edge inwards, at a precise four o'clock angle on his plate. Parr asked, "And who do we have here?"

"My name is JJ Gansett."

"And your occupation, sir?"

Gansett smiled thinly. "That's up to Appleton to reveal." He cocked an eyebrow in curiosity. "Yours?"

Parr pursed his lips and directed his words not toward Gansett, but at Barbutero. "My specialty is sanitation. As in, cleanin' up somebody else's mess."

"And," I added, pointing to his shiny, alligator-skinned boots, "fashion icon."

"That feller got a bit ahead of me," Parr admitted, raising his left hand and showing that it was missing the pinky and ring finger. "Fortunately, I shoot and cut with mah otha hand."

Barbutero spoke for the first time. "Cut, huh? I was a butcher. I'm good with a knife."

"I doubt you'll have occasion to show off yur skills, ace," Parr scoffed.

Appleton sighed with obvious contempt. "Are you boys done with your posturing? We've got an op to run. Let's go."

# CHAPTER
## 52

**ARRIVING AT** the District Donut shop on the Potomac waterfront at 8:39 A.M. on a breezy and gray, fifty-one-degree Tuesday morning, I was ready for my mission.

My little squad and I had reviewed satellite images and done, without entering the shop and by casing the outdoor patio, a dry run.

Unfortunately, though, when the pieces were in place, the plan seemed foiled, as it started to drizzle. I hoped it was only a passing shower as I pulled the door open to the smell of rich coffee and freshly baked bread.

Approaching the counter, I opened my mouth to place my order with the barista when, to my surprise, she spoke first. "I recognize you. From, like, springtime."

She was correct; I'd been in the shop back last March, and I belatedly remembered that her recollection of faces had been helpful to me. I dredged out her name from the depths of my brain. "Hey, Jolene."

No, that's not true; I'm exaggerating the acuity of my memory. I can't lie to you. She was wearing a nametag. But I did recognize her.

Jolene asked, "Four coffees, black, and a dozen glazed donuts?"

*Wow. With that kind of recall, we should hire her as an agent*, I thought.

"Not quite," I grinned. "Just two coffees, please."

Jolene efficiently prepared the simple order, her brown ponytail bouncing as she pointed at a light brown carry-out tray. "Need one?"

"Nah," I replied as she swiped my Amex through a slot on the side of the cash register monitor.

With the transaction complete, I decided to double down on the tradecraft. "Sorry, um, but I changed my mind. Can I get those dozen glazed donuts?"

Jolene adjusted her baseball cap and rolled her eyes, but without a word, boxed the donuts and, for a second time, accepted my proffered Amex.

Tipping her generously, I took my coffee to a condiments counter, where I decided to follow Hanna Mo'Nique Isaac's example as I cut one of the coffees with oat milk. Carrying the two cups and the box of donuts precariously, I shoved the door open with my hip.

Overlooking the Potomac River, the patio outside was dotted with black, wire-mesh metal tables and chairs—all of which were empty and slightly wet.

*At least the rain stopped*, I thought, setting my cups and box on a table and wiping a chair with my hand. I sat, and I immediately felt a dampness through my jeans. *Another glamorous moment in the life of a real-life agent. A fictional Bond would be wearing linen trousers, seated at a bistro with pastel-colored umbrellas, waiting for his contact while perched on a terrace overlooking a Venetian canal. Maybe someday, I will too . . .*

I sipped my coffee slowly, my mind frantic as I looked over the steel-gray, wind-ruffled waters of the Potomac.

My over-addled brain came to no conclusions except to admit that coffee with oat milk was pretty damn good.

Twenty minutes later, my coffee was empty. Eyeing the box of donuts, I cracked the cellophane tape seal on the edge and angled the lid up, inhaling the scent of sugar. The donuts were still warm, and I carefully selected one.

*Just one donut, Ben*, I reminded myself.

"How about a donut for me?"

I jumped—literally jumped, startled from my chair—at the sound of a voice that I instantly recognized.

It was Anastasia Volkov.

# CHAPTER 53

**A LIGHT DRIZZLE BEGAN** but my spirits were undampened as Volkov and I held each other in a tight embrace.

My mind raced. *I was correct! I knew it!*

I had a zillion questions but, for a moment or three, I was satisfied with my cheek pressed into Volkov's caramel blond hair; a pose that would disguise the tears that I felt in my eyes.

I didn't care, though, that I was crying. For those sweet, precious minutes, I didn't care about Isaac or semiconductors or Coate or Attorney General Bart Williams or justice.

I cared only for Volkov.

Catching movement in my peripheral vision, I loosened my grip on my friend ever so slightly, enough to raise my gaze to see Appleton approaching from her overwatch location. With a sniff and with wetness on my cheek—from my tears or from the rain, or both—I pulled my head back so that I could look into Volkov's blue eyes.

Those eyes smiled at me.

Except, in the soundtrack of my mind, I heard the infuriating screech of a record needle being dragged across vinyl as I did a mental one-eighty from happiness to guilt.

*I shouldn't have fled the Azores. Shouldn't have been a coward. Should've stood firm and investigated. I should have been more forceful; should've pressed harder to get Appleton and the others to accept my discoveries in the Azores. To accept my theory.*

"Don't do it, Ben," Volkov whispered, her voice lilting with just a hint of a Russian accent, an effect left over from her upbringing in her native Ukraine. "I know you well enough to guess what you're thinking. Don't go there. At least not now. Besides, we have a lot to talk about."

I spoke to her for the first time, my words and thoughts jumbling together. "It is a lot. We have a lot—I have so many—I can't believe—but I knew—I knew—I—"

"It's okay," she said reassuringly, but then her body tensed as if she felt an electric current. Her face darkened, and to my disbelief, she shoved me aside, shouldering her body in front of mine so that our backs touched.

I spun so I could see what startled her, and I laughed lightly, repeating her words but now in a new context. "It's okay."

"That's—that's—" Volkov sputtered.

"JJ Gansett. I'm impressed you remember him," I said with a steady tone. "It's a long explanation, which we'll get to, but he's on our side now."

Volkov appeared skeptical. "Our side? Who is our?"

"I hope you remember me, too," Appleton called brightly.

Volkov spun, wide-eyed, to take in the sight of her former boss from the Boston Field Office. "Oh, my," was all she could manage.

"The gang is back together," Gansett said, trying, I think, to introduce himself to Volkov in a positive manner.

It backfired.

Volkov's eyes sank, and her expression clouded. "Not really."

Appleton acknowledged Volkov's meaning with a solemn nod. "No, you're right, I'm afraid. Not really. And believe me, their absence haunts me—but all the same, I am thrilled to see you." She looked over at me. "And I owe Porter an apology."

"None needed," I protested.

Appleton hummed, "Hmm. We'll see about that. For now, how about we get out of the rain?"

Ever organized, Gansett disposed of my empty coffee cup, grabbed the full one and the box of donuts, and led us toward the F-250, parked some distance away out of sight.

I tentatively reached for Volkov's olive-skinned hand. The hairs on the back of my neck, even damp as they were, tingled as she accepted my invitation.

Our fingers interlaced, and I swore I would never let go.

# CHAPTER
# 54

**BACK AT THE GEORGETOWN TOWNHOUSE,** we found privacy in the wood-paneled library. Parr had relocated Barbutero to a second-floor bedroom where the hitman slept soundly, lulled, perhaps, by the twang of a country and western tune that sounded at low volume from Parr's smartphone.

Gansett dispatched himself to the kitchen to prepare more coffee to warm us from the damp drizzle while Appleton sat solo in a club chair, opposite Volkov and me on the sofa, our hips pressing together.

Appleton and I both waited in quiet anticipation as Volkov took a deep breath and began. "The raft drifted for days. It was stocked with some basic emergency supplies, but I was parched and weak when it landed on a rocky beach. I climbed out and, despite my unsteady legs, I dragged the raft away from the swell."

"The raft was found above the tide line," I said. "That should have been the first clue that someone was in it."

Volkov shrugged. "It's circumstantial. A storm could have moved it."

"There were no storms, according to the investigation," I countered.

"Easy, Porter. We now know you were correct—but that clue alone could not possibly mean that someone survived," Appleton chided. "There were no other indications of life."

Volkov smiled demurely. "That's because I scrubbed them. Porter's correct, though. I wasn't thinking clearly when I hauled the raft further than it could have gotten naturally." She paused and blinked. "I eventually figured out where I was when I discovered the little chapel on the bluff above the beach. Critically, I found fresh water there—and I found paperwork, an address, that sort of thing. And then, I met—"

"Santiago Botelho," I guessed.

"Exactly. I borrowed some clothes from the chapel, made myself presentable, and made his day. His life, maybe. I found him working on the farm that surrounded the chapel."

"You bought him off, didn't you," I theorized. "Shiny new car, new clothes, maybe some dental work? His teeth were brilliantly white."

"I did," Volkov admitted.

Appleton was shaking her head. "It's impossible. Bought him off with what?"

Volkov raised her left arm. "With this." She tapped the silver wristwatch with the Cyrillic characters that she always wore. "It's not just a watch. It's a ruggedized flash drive. I stored critical data on it—case files, passwords, back doors for access and hacking, alternate identities, and—"

"Bank accounts." This time, I wasn't theorizing. I now understood.

She nodded in affirmation. "Yes. As you might recall, at one time, we apprehended a criminal with substantial assets, and we used those assets to fund several operations."

It was my turn to grin. "And you retained access. The Bureau assumed access to those assets disappeared when *Almaz* sank."

"Yes," Volkov said. "And, initially, I planned to disappear as well."

Gansett carried a tray of fresh coffees into the room. Each of the four mugs was filled to exactly the same depth, and to designate who got which mug, he'd somehow drawn each of our first initials with milk froth floating atop the rich, brown coffee. He'd also prepared a small plate of tea sandwiches—slices of cheese, cucumber, and tomato on tiny toasts.

Volkov examined Gansett's offering. "Impressive. Is that to wow me, to trick me, or to distract me?"

Gansett chuckled. "D. None of the above. Just who I am. If it's worth doing, it's worth doing correctly."

"I can see how you were so effective in your former endeavors," Volkov said without irony or inflection. Her tone was matter-of-fact.

"I also have excellent hearing," Gansett announced. "I picked up most of the conversation. Why did you want to disappear?"

I was grateful for Gansett's direct question, for it was one that I didn't have the guts to ask when she had revealed that only moments before.

Volkov's reply was delivered in her usual, even, analytical tone. "What was left for me? My team was gone. My home sank. And Lockwood . . ."

I asked, almost in a whisper, "What happened to Lockwood? We know he reached the raft."

Blinking twice, Volkov answered my question using her analytical tone—signaling that she was setting her emotions aside and merely reporting facts, perhaps insulating herself from the memory of being there. "I had made it aboard the raft when I spotted him in the water, paddling toward me. I tried to pull him up but I—I couldn't. I was weak with exhaustion and so was he, and he slipped away."

She turned away from me and sank into the upholstery, her head back and her gaze at the ceiling. Pensive for a moment, she finally spoke. "It was terrible, and initially that's why I wanted to disappear. To move on . . . and to create a totally new life." She paused. "But as some time went by, I felt like I was in some sort of stasis. Indecision. And I realized that I also wanted someone to know what happened. Ultimately, I think I always knew I wanted the Bureau to know someone may have survived when the boat sank. And yet, I knew that I could evade detection. With my ability to access plenty of money, with the alternate identity stored on my watch's flash drive, I could go anywhere or be anyone."

I whispered, "What changed your mind?"

"You," she answered simply.

She let the comment hang between us before elaborating, "After I was comfortable that Botelho would stick to the story about finding the raft, I set myself up in a secluded, little home overlooking the ocean, a couple of miles east of where the raft was discovered in the village of Achada. Quaint, you know. Basalt stones, tiny windows, barrel roof tiles, and satellite internet. Pretty much all I needed. Through a back door, I logged into the Bureau's servers and watched from afar as the file on the loss of *Almaz* was built, and I finally understood what really happened. And I wondered what would happen next, so using the data on my flash drive, I tagged a few credit card accounts to monitor, among them Appleton's and yours, Ben."

She pursed her lips and added, "When you rented a car at the Ponta Delgado airport, I was happy, because at long last, someone whom I cared about came to look for me—and cared enough to come to the Azores in person."

Grabbing both of my hands, Volkov whispered, "Thank you for leaving that memorial stone. That was a beautiful gesture, Ben."

I fumbled for words. "It was the, um, you know, the least . . . anyway, you climbed down the bluff and saw it?"

"Yes," she said wistfully, releasing my hands.

"It's obvious, now," I said, a tinge of embarrassment in my voice. "It was you in the black car. And to think I would have known all this so much earlier, had I just confronted the driver of the car with the beady headlights. Instead, I bolted, flushed the tail, and hid."

"Good tradecraft, though," Volkov grinned. "I was certain you'd show up at the hotel that you drove into. And when you didn't, I finally realized that you skunked me. I searched the town for your rental car. I even got Botelho to help. But you became a ghost."

"I returned the car at the airport and walked back to town," I explained. "Got an off-beat hotel room, paid cash, and went to the airport the next day. And then when I boarded the plane—it was you who sent the text!"

I paused for a half second before asking, "Why didn't you just say it was you? Why the cryptic message?"

Volkov narrowed her eyes. "It wasn't cryptic. I thought it was friendly. You know, like, we'll catch up later. And then you didn't respond."

Gansett chuckled dryly. "And this is why I don't like texting. There's no emotion. No inflection. Therefore, the other side sees what they want to see."

I felt foolish, but I deflected by saying, "It never occurred to me to reply to the message. I interpreted it as a threat." I shrugged and added, "Well, at the very least, this confirms that Barbutero wasn't lying."

Volkov straightened. "Who's Barbutero?" She looked at her audience—Appleton, Gansett, and me—and said, "You guys are working on something other than just exposing Ben's tail. What is it? Can I help?"

With that, I knew that my team was complete, and I knew exactly how to deploy.

# CHAPTER 55

**"ALRIGHT,** here's what we're gonna do," I began, simultaneously pulling out my phone. Looking at the screen, I stated, "It's 9:32 A.M., which means we've got just over twenty-four hours to unwind this thing."

Appleton immediately raised a hand to question, or possibly object, and she asked, "Unwind what, exactly?"

"Well, we've only got one fact, but we need to prove it," I replied. "Barbutero admits to killing Preston. But all we've got are allegations. We need proof. Therefore, let's get the body. Appleton, you take Parr and Barbutero to wherever he stashed Preston's corpse—and dig it up."

"Lovely," Appleton carped sarcastically. "However, one problem— Barbutero told us he wanted a deal with the AG before disclosing the location of the body. How do you get around that?"

"I don't. Paxton Parr does."

Appleton smiled grimly. "Extraordinary times call for extraordinary measures."

"Yup," I confirmed. Turning to Gansett, I said, "You're my shadow. Where I go, you go, but invisibly. And my first task is to smoke out Lin. It's my theory that she's working for Isaac, but we don't have proof of a connection."

"Okay—but I'm going to need technical help, then," Gansett requested.

I pointed at Volkov. "You'll find no one better."

Volkov shook her head negatively. "I didn't bring any of my gear with me. It's all in the Azores."

Appleton offered, "I've got a MacBook here. Top of the line. Plus, two burner phones if we need them, as well as a handful of weapons."

"The computer is all I need," Volkov said. "I can tap into the local surveillance networks, and I can cover Ben remotely."

"I'll take one of the burners," Gansett said. "I can improvise a protection detail for Porter."

Appleton rolled her eyes. "Great. Not only have I sprung you from FBI custody and given you a gun, Gansett, but now I'm gonna give you an untraceable burner phone." She sighed. "In for a penny, in for a pound."

"Works for me," I agreed. "I'll get into the office and try to understand what Lin is up to." I turned my attention back to Volkov. "In the meantime, I'm leaving you this."

I tapped at my phone to remove the facial recognition and password protection measures. Passing the device over to Volkov, I explained, "It's unlocked. With that, along with Appleton's MacBook, can you do what I wanted Louis Lewis to do? Trace my call to Preston's number and track the phone. Find out where it is."

"Lewis? He's tangled up in this, too?"

"No," I clarified. "I wanted his help, but he's not responded, yet."

"And if he responds, don't answer," Appleton interjected. "We don't need him anymore, and we definitely don't need someone else involved."

"I can easily trace the location of the phone that you called. That will be done by noon, if not way earlier," Volkov stated with confidence. "Trying to backtrace more data from the phone you called will take longer, and I'll still need this," she explained, gesturing at my device. Then, she pointed at the Nokia flip phone. "Whose is that?"

"Barbutero's device."

Volkov frowned. "Too old to have GPS location services, but I'll be able to triangulate location from the cell towers it connected to. Want me to track that one, too?"

"Yes, definitely," I replied. "But focus on Preston for now." I turned to Gansett. "Back on my security, don't forget that I've still got the ring," I said, twisting the black circle on my finger.

Gansett apprised me. "In all my years and all my ops, I've never seen a plan built so quickly. I must admit, though, it's all workable. You've got one oversight, though." He didn't elaborate; he merely stared me down with a critical expression.

I instantly realized what he was referring to. I touched Volkov's hand—the hand that was holding my phone, and maybe the hand that made the mark on the fire-charred raft on an Azores beach. "I'm gonna need to borrow that phone back for a sec," I whispered.

Gansett rewarded me with a wink as I tapped out a text to Sara Lin:

```
Appleton is going to freshen up at her
hotel. She drove all night and will meet
us sometime later. On my way to the office.
Want to meet me there?
```

In a fraction of a second, my phone blooped with a tapback reply tone and a little thumbs-up icon popped into the corner of my text bubble.

"Let's go," I said to Gansett. "By the way, do you have any other CIA toys in your briefcase?"

"Perhaps," he replied. "What do you have in mind?"

"Wait!" Volkov exclaimed. "When are you going to enlighten me with the big picture? What are we unwinding? Who is Parr? Who is Lin?"

Mid-step to the door of the Georgetown townhouse, I paused my departure. *I should explain my, um, relationship with Lin to Volkov,* I thought.

Instead, I blurted, "I gotta go, but Appleton will bring you up to speed before she heads out."

And I bolted.

*Ben, you're a coward.*

# CHAPTER 56

**I WAS FIVE PACES** out the door of the Georgetown townhouse with JJ Gansett when I reconsidered.

*You've waited too long for this, Ben,* I thought, grinding my teeth in angst. I didn't want to lose what I'd just found, nor did I want to risk a future.

*A future that looks like what, Ben?*

"Why are you turning around?" Gansett's voice broke into my reverie. "We don't have any time to waste."

"I gotta clear something up with Volkov," I explained hastily. Reaching the door, I made a thinly veiled order into a request. "Can you see if Parr needs any, um, inspiration?"

Gansett's expression indicated that he could see right through me, but true to form as a gentleman, he merely nodded and climbed the stairs to the second-floor room where Parr was, to use Appleton's word, babysitting our hitman suspect.

"You're back," Volkov announced. She barely looked up from her perch on the sofa as she leaned over the coffee table, her attention focused on Appleton's smoke-gray MacBook. Her silver wristwatch was tethered to the computer, and my phone lay face-up on the table beside the watch.

I plopped into the sofa beside her—and a thought popped into my addled brain, a logistical exercise that would prove useful in cutting through my emotions. Pointing at my phone, I asked, "Can I use that?"

"Sure," she confirmed. "I'm just setting up. Haven't done anything yet, so do what you need to do."

I sensed her looking over my shoulder as I hefted the device and began to tap out a text to Lin, so in the interest of disclosure, I ensured Volkov could see the screen clearly by angling it toward her face.

```
Still with Appleton. She wants another
run-through of details again. Probably
will take some time so I'll be at the office
in a while.
```

Volkov could see that the message was being transmitted to Lin, who, unlike before with the thumbs-up tapback, replied with a little red heart. Volkov noticed, of course, but she didn't mention it, instead asking innocently, "What's up with the delay tactic?"

"You asked earlier about Sara Lin and Paxton Parr." I inhaled deeply and began, "Parr is one of Appleton's resources. He's a fixer. She can tell you more if you want, but I think I should tell you more about Lin."

"Okay," she muttered, remaining focused on the MacBook.

"I met Sara Lin toward the end of March last year, first by phone, courtesy of an introduction by the Attorney General, and then in person, at the apprehension of the mastermind of the case we were working on."

Volkov looked up at the ceiling. "End of March, huh? That was when *Almaz* sank."

"Yeah. It was all related, actually." I paused to make sure my recollection of the timeline was exact. "Lin and I had dinner on the second-to-last day of March, so before the raft was discovered."

Volkov probed gently, "Is that relevant?"

"It shouldn't be. But, I guess, maybe it is, because . . ." My voice trailed off.

"Because it was presumed that there were no survivors of the *Almaz* wreck." In a contemplative tone, Volkov completed my thought accurately.

"Yeah. I guess."

"And then what?"

I shrank myself into the sofa, literally pushing back on the stuffed upholstery with my shoulder blades, before chastising myself, *Don't be that coward, Ben.*

Pulling myself up so my spine was straight, I replied, "Then last week happened. Not even a week ago, really. Saturday, I walked into a conference room at Main Justice, and there Sara was." I shrugged. "I kinda thought it was fate, you know. Serendipitous. Because then we, um, you know."

Her face was stone. "No, I don't know, Ben." She paused for a beat. "Well, I can guess. But you can say it."

"We hooked up."

There was a moment of dead air. An awkward moment. And then—

Volkov began to laugh. "You are such a fool, Ben. An adorable, nerdy, dumb-ass fool."

I was taken aback. "What?"

"Ben, there's like, almost ten thousand lawyers at the DOJ. Did it ever occur to you that this was not a coincidence? That it was not serendipity?" She voiced the last word mockingly.

"I'll be damned," I whispered. In my usual volume, "Knowing what I know now, what I want to prove—and this is a piece of that proof—it was a—"

"Honey trap." Volkov chorused the words with me, and her voice matched mine exactly.

*We're finishing each other's sentences*, I thought, my fears of this discussion dribbling away like flowing honey.

That's too much, eh? Sorry. It fits, though.

Let's just go with, I was happy—and I was relieved and happier as Volkov took my hand, saying, "Look, Ben, I fell for Lockwood. I pushed you away, I guess, because he's this cool dude, this confident, good-looking guy, and—"

"Are you saying I'm not good-looking?"

She snorted. "You're, uh, well, you're not at Lockwood's level."

"You mean by height? Yeah, for sure, he's taller than me."

There was a new brightness to Volkov's eyes as she looked directly into mine. "Ben, Lockwood is a stud, but he's not you. He doesn't have your humor, your brains, or your charm." She whooshed out a breath before adding, "I didn't make a mistake with Lockwood, and you didn't make a mistake with Lin. It is what it is. What it was. You know?"

"We're good, right?"

"Yes," she agreed, those eyes still smiling.

I grinned, but then I rolled my eyes to the ceiling. "Except for the part about me sleeping with the enemy. Honestly, I don't know how to unwind that. The moment I see her, in the office later this morning, she'll see it, I think. Then what?"

Instead of answering, Volkov reached forward and disconnected her watch from the computer. Sliding the timepiece onto her wrist, she picked up my phone and snapped the cord into the device, and then she tapped the face of it several times, her thumbs moving in a blur. A screen that I'd never seen before materialized, and then she set the tethered device down. Her fingers flew across the MacBook keyboard until, with a flourish, she used her right forefinger to stab the Return key. "The trace sequence is running, and with your vague text to Lin, you've bought us some time. Why don't you explain this case to me? Maybe I can offer some ideas."

Like a flashback montage in a feature film, my brain visualized the day in 2017 when I'd first spoken to Anastasia Volkov. As a lowly Information Management Specialist back then, I was awed by the introduction to the legendary Information Analyst, surrounded by computer screens in the high-tech Boston field office operations suite. I remembered the sensation exactly—I was smitten, and here, in the Georgetown townhouse, I was smitten anew.

It was a good feeling. A great feeling.

And, as I began to tell Volkov about the case, and Isaac, and Coate, and EPIC, I knew she'd contribute.

I didn't expect, though, her startling conclusion.

# CHAPTER
## 57

ANASTASIA VOLKOV RECLINED on the sofa of the Georgetown townhouse, eyes closed, face angled to the ceiling. Before her, on the coffee table, the computer and tethered phone rested unattended, running some sort of routine that Volkov had initiated for the trace of the call to Preston's phone. As eager as I was for that intel, it was Volkov's voice that lit a path.

"You know, Ben," she began, "here's the part that doesn't make sense. We assume that Isaac wanted to silence Preston's opposition so she would smooth the way for an upvote on EPIC. Right?"

"Yes, and—"

I stopped, distracted by the sound of footsteps on the stair. Appleton appeared first, then Gansett, followed by Barbutero, who was tailed by Parr. Appleton announced solemnly, "We've reached an agreement with Mister Barbutero. We're headed to New York."

"Hold that for a sec, please," I requested. Turning my attention back to Volkov, I prodded, "Go on. And yes, that's the theory—Isaac buys off his silence."

"A piece of it doesn't add up. Preston is this self-made guy, this model citizen, as you said the AG called him, and he's ready to build the first future-tech chip foundry in America. Even if EPIC passes, he's way ahead of the competition. He's in a very strong position." She paused and straightened her frame to emphasize her concluding question, "There's a fragment of data missing. Why would Preston sell Aximerva?"

"Isaac told me that they negotiated for a while, and ultimately, he agreed. She said she was able to make—what was the word she used?—a compelling offer."

I shrugged, thinking at first that was where it ended, and yet Volkov's line of questions and her curious expression caused me to focus. "You're right. There's something else," I mused. "What would have compelled him?"

"Cash," Barbutero barked. "A sackful of cash. Ain't that how it always works?"

"Nah, I don't think so," I said contemplatively. "Preston was not poor. He owns the largest, private computer company in America. He's got access to resources, even if he has to borrow money. And, if he's really the model citizen that the AG makes him out to be, he's not going to compromise his principles for greenbacks."

A solution eluded me, and Volkov didn't contribute further, so I asked Appleton, "Why are you going to New York?"

Appleton grimaced. "Mister Barbutero has agreed, thanks to Parr and Gansett's very convincing terms, to reveal the location of Preston's body."

"Do I want to know what those terms are?"

"For deniability, no."

"Gotcha," I said.

Appleton continued, "We will be there in five hours because we have a quick pitstop to make here over in Virginia first. Barbutero will hand over Preston's phone."

Volkov was peering at the computer screen. "The trace is almost complete, but what I can see so far, the phone that Ben called is nowhere near Jamaica."

Barbutero mocked, "No shit. It's probably about two miles away from here."

"We already know that, but we must prove that with evidence," I rebutted evenly.

Volkov held up a hand. "With Preston's actual device, I can get all sorts of data off it, including WiFi networks it connected to, the device's location while it was not making calls, and so forth. I can track Preston's movements from the moment he activated the device, whenever that was. And, of course, we can see who he called, emailed, and texted."

"Seems like we got a plan in place, fellas," Parr said happily.

I think Parr was pleased to be escaping the confines of the townhouse's second floor, but he would be trading the comfort of a bedroom for Appleton's aging F-250. On the other hand, I would have preferred just to hang out with Volkov, instead of having to traipse to the office to confront Lin. Stalling for a moment, I wondered if I should wait for them to return with Preston's phone before I departed the townhouse.

Parr was at the door, Barbutero in tow. "Appleton, you drive. I'll keep my pal Rocco here company in the backseat. Let's hit the road, folks."

*Wait. Hit?*

*Like hitman.*

"Wait," I grunted, jumping to my feet. "Rocco, one question. You obviously searched Preston for his phone so you could snag it. Other than the phone, did you take anything from Preston? Did he have anything else on him?"

"I wanted just the phone," Barbutero revealed. "But, yeah, I patted him down, makin' sure he carried only one device. He had the usual pocket litter. Wallet, pair of reading glasses in a little case, one of them USB things, hotel key card, hankerch—"

"A USB what?" I demanded.

"I dunno what it's called. The thing that, ya know, you stick in the side of a computer thing."

"A flash drive," Volkov announced.

"Yeah, that's it," Barbutero agreed.

"I want that drive," I stated firmly. "Appleton, I hope you have a heavy foot. Up to the City and back—nine hours?"

"Oh, it's gonna take a little longer than that," Barbutero cautioned. "The body isn't exactly, um, accessible."

I wondered, not in a kind tone, "What do you mean by that?"

Barbutero grunted, "It's gonna take some digging."

Exasperated, I threw up my hands—and Barbutero added, "That's right, Porter. Gonna need lots of hands."

"We'll all go, then," I announced, "except Volkov. Once we get Preston's phone, you run it down."

"I can do that from anywhere, so I'll go, too," Volkov offered.

"Whoa," Appleton groaned. "We can't all fit in my truck."

Volkov grinned. "I can fix that." She swept a hand to encompass Appleton, Parr, Gansett, and Barbutero, and commanded, "You four go get Preston's phone. Go—and I'll text you instructions." She turned to me. "Ben, do you have the Uber app on your phone?"

"Yeah," I replied, adding dumbly, "We're gonna Uber to New York City?"

Volkov looked smug. "Not really."

# CHAPTER

# 58

**THREE MINUTES LATER,** a pewter Toyota Prius whirred to a stop at the stoop of the Georgetown townhouse. Carrying one of Appleton's burner phones, the MacBook, and a handful of patch cords, Volkov slid into the backseat while confirming the driver's identity and the destination address. I followed, now armed thanks to Appleton, with my phone in one pocket and with Barbutero's Nokia in the other pocket.

As I clambered into the Prius, I felt, to my dismay, the aging vehicle sagging on its suspension as I sat beside Volkov. I announced, "After all this is over, my New Year's resolution is to lose some weight."

"Yeah, sure, because everyone sticks to those resolutions," she mumbled as she fiddled with the burner phone, tapping out a text.

"Where are we going?"

"Hang on a sec," she snapped, focused on her task. Less than sixty seconds later, she lifted her head to look at me. "Sorry for being short. I sent Appleton the address. They'll be about ten minutes behind us. But we're only—" she glanced at her watch—"now only ten minutes out. Therefore, that gives you only ten minutes to come up with an excuse for Lin as to why you're not going to make it to your office, or whatever, today. Make it a good one."

"Okay," I said, cradling my device but not typing. "I could say a friend came in from out of town."

"That's true. But that's not exactly a reason to take a day off from an urgent investigation."

"Earthquake? Flood? Locusts?"

She apprised me quizzically. "What? That sounds familiar, but . . ."

"Never mind. I watched a lot of '80s movies with my father. Look it up," I said absently. She didn't get the "Blues Brothers" reference, but oddly, the irrelevance allowed my distracted brain to compose the perfect pretext. I tapped out a text:

> Remember Isaac referenced an agent O'Toole?
> Appleton tracked her down in Connecticut.
> O'Toole can lead me to Barbutero. I rented
> a car, and I am zipping up to New Haven.

I showed the sent text to Volkov. "It's a weak excuse," she cautioned. "It doesn't make sense."

"Lin will reply," I predicted. "I'm not done yet, but I want it to look natural."

Sure enough, the phone chimed with a response:

> Why? Isaac said she'd have Barbutero in
> DC this morning. Seems like a wasted trip.
> Let's just contact Isaac.

"Ha!" I exclaimed. "Lin thinks Barbutero ghosted me—because that's what I told her earlier. She wants to loop back in with Isaac. I gotta deflect." I typed:

> But Barbutero was a no-show. I bet
> O'Toole didn't agree to release Barbutero
> from custody. So - YOU CAN'T TELL ANYONE
> what I am doing! If Isaac finds out, then
> they'll know I'm on my way and that gives
> Isaac or O'Toole time to move Barbutero.
> If you tell the AG, he can't do anything
> without ordering O'Toole to be held as a
> conspirator, and that also warns Isaac. I
> need 5 to 7 hours. Okay?

"Excellent," Volkov whispered in admiration. "You've just bought us the day, but you've also backed Lin into a corner. If she's a mole for Isaac, if she warns her, she's exposed herself. If she contacts the AG, she's got to explain why she objects to you doing this."

The phone dinged and a series of emojis appeared in a text bubble—thumbs-up, praying hands, and a red heart, reminding me that I wasn't a fan of comms by icons. However, Lin loved her emojis, and I considered this was good news that she'd replied with her usual string of little pictures. I announced, "She bought it, and yet she isn't digging with more questions. But—oh, shit."

"What?"

"I changed the access code to my private office, so she can't get to my computer which has the case file on it. She might be suspicious . . . but I guess that since it was her who suggested changing the codes frequently, maybe not. All the same, I wish I had a way to track her."

"We could track her phone. Maybe even tap the microphone," Volkov suggested. "We might need to pull in Louis Lewis after all, and Appleton could effort that."

"Wait—why can't you do it?"

"I'll be busy. And so will you."

With my head down and my eyes focused on the text exchange, I was oblivious to the outside scenery. As I asked my question, the Prius slowed to a stop at a metal security gate emblazoned with a sign:

— Authorized Access Only —
Signature Aviation Flight Support
Ronald Reagan Washington National Airport

Volkov rolled her window down. She leaned out and spoke to a guard while simultaneously pointing at a small, twin-engine jet, painted white with a swooping blue-and-grey stripe extending the length of the fuselage, with coordinating accent colors also dabbed on what appeared to be fuel tanks mounted at the ends of each wing.

The gate squeaked open, and the Prius rolled onto the airport tarmac. Pulling her head back inside the vehicle and pressing the button to slide the window up, Volkov whispered to me, "Ben. Act like a pilot."

"What?"

She hissed, "This aircraft is not certified for single-pilot operation. Therefore, you're my co-pilot. Just do what I do and try not to say anything."

The Prius halted gently beside the left wing of the aircraft. I managed one last question before Volkov clicked her door ajar. "Since when do you have a pilot's license?"

Volkov bit her lip and replied, "Well, technically, I don't."

# CHAPTER 59

**I FOLLOWED MY INSTRUCTIONS** exactly. After Volkov dropped the computer and peripherals inside the clamshell door to the plane, she trotted to a nearby building to file a flight plan. I stood mute, hands clasped behind my back, as she settled a bill with a credit card. I heard snippets of conversation, "Tanks filled," "takeoff clearance," "weather report," and I remained wordless. Not that I'd have anything intelligent to add, naturally.

Departing the building, we returned to the jet. Volkov walked around the plane, doing, I guess, a pre-flight check. I tailed her like a puppy, stumbling a bit, wide-eyed, and mostly confused.

I followed, still mute, as Volkov climbed aboard the jet and settled herself into the left-side pilot's seat. She pointed at the co-pilot's seat to the right and handed me a headset with a boom microphone.

As she began flipping switches, I heard her voice through the headset. "Good job, Ben. You played it nice and cool. They bought it. Now, please don't touch anything."

"Uh, yeah, I'm quite certain that won't be an issue." I watched her press buttons on some gizmo in the cockpit. "Can you, um, explain the part about, um, not technically having a pilot's license?"

She paused her work. "Remember that the funds used for the *Almaz* operation were confiscated from a criminal? There was quite a bit of money, about seven hundred million or so, and I had sole access." She tapped her dual-purpose silver watch. "It was my responsibility to change the log-in codes and so forth, and I'd just done so only a few hours before *Almaz* went to the bottom of the ocean. So, with lots of downtime in the Azores and a lot of money at my disposal, last year I decided to learn to fly. I bought this plane and hired an instructor."

"You know," I observed, "most pilots get started, as far as I know, like in propellor planes. You bought a jet?"

"I didn't learn to drive in a go-kart," she snickered. "I figured the same applies to planes. I wanted to pilot a jet, so I purchased a jet. This is a 1982 Lear 35A, completely refit in 2018 and modified for longer range. I paid three million. And in the Azores, let's just say some more money greased the wheels in getting flying lessons and skipping over some of the more, um, mundane instructional levels." She turned to face me completely. "Don't worry. I've got a lot of hours already. In fact, within hours of you swiping your Amex at a series of clothing stores in Georgetown, my instructor and I flew this plane transatlantic, with a stop in Halifax, Nova Scotia to refuel. The aircraft has the range to go to Washington non-stop, but I thought it would be good to get in even more practice."

"Reassuring," I said flatly. "Where's the instructor now? That would be more reassuring."

"I sent him back to Ponta Delgado on a commercial flight."

"Oh." I stared at the high-tech, glass-faced displays in front of me. "But— isn't it illegal for me to even sit in this seat during a flight?"

She laughed. "Well, by decree based on an FBI investigation, I'm deceased, and I got into the country using a false identity in violation of who knows how many immigration and customs laws. Gansett is probably considered a fugitive. I have no idea what Parr's status is, but I'm guessing he operates outside normal legal conventions. And Barbutero is allegedly a hitman. On the other hand, we have an investor who appears to have engaged said hitman to murder a CEO in order to collude with her high-placed Senator husband to pass a $280 billion piece of legislation that will ultimately benefit her and her husband. Pick your poison, Ben."

"Fair point," I admitted.

Volkov turned back to the cockpit. Glancing out the left-side window, she announced, "Appleton is here. Lean back and tell them to close and lock the door once they're on board."

I craned my head to watch Appleton park the F-250. A yellow-vested ground crewman pointed the way to the Learjet, and in moments, Appleton, Parr, and Barbutero boarded. Gansett was last into the clamshell door.

I pulled the headset off and called, "Gansett, close the door, please."

Gansett ducked his tall frame into the narrow and low cabin and turned to snap the door locked with practiced motions. He peered forward into the cockpit and announced, "Barbutero had stashed Preston's phone at a motel in Arlington. We've got it with us now." He looked at me in the right seat and added, with a less confident tone, "Porter, I didn't know you could fly."

"I can't," I disclosed. "I'm no more than a prop to fill the seat."

"Well, I can," the former CIA man announced. "I'm instrument and multi-engine rated, though given my current legal situation, I suspect my pilot's license is no longer valid."

"Fine with me. Take over." I clambered out of the cramped co-pilot seat and found my way to the rear of the cabin, where I was greeted with polished maple woodwork, a tastefully but subtly patterned Oriental-style carpet, and one vacant, imposing, tan-leather throne. Ducking my head, I found myself far more comfortably and appropriately seated.

Patting my pocket, I squirmed to the side to pull out Barbutero's Nokia. Snapping it open, I scrolled through the call log, wishing that Volkov could work her magic on the device and simply download the data.

*I'll have her dig through this thing once she's done with Preston's phone,* I thought, as the engines whined, and the Lear began to roll.

From the overhead speakers, Gansett's voice evenly broadcast, in the calm, steady cadence of pilot-speak everywhere, "We have a priority flight plan to Teterboro airport, twelve miles outside of New York City. Given our routing, it's going to be a steep climb, so please buckle your seat belts and remain seated for the duration of the fifty-two-minute trip."

Minutes later, the engines spooled to take-off power, the brakes were released, and Volkov's Learjet arrowed into the air—aiming for the corpse of Virgil Preston.

# CHAPTER
## 60



**ABOUT NINETY MINUTES** after we departed the Georgetown townhouse, a maroon GMC Yukon XL, on loan from the Teterboro branch of Signature Aviation thanks to a courtesy call from their counterpart at Reagan National, jolted to a stop on Cornelia Street, in the West Village neighborhood of Manhattan. From my perch in the shotgun seat of the Yukon, with Gansett beside me at the wheel, I watched as Barbutero, flanked by his shadow Paxton Parr, disembarked from the Yukon and tapped a code into the keypad next to a tall, arch-topped pair of double doors. The heavy, wormholed, wooden slabs swung open on electric motors, and Gansett piloted the big SUV into a private garage.

In all, the maroon Yukon was visible on the street for sixty seconds, tops. It was the pinnacle of private access in New York City.

The remaining four of us alighted from the Yukon inside the one-car garage. Appleton consulted her phone. "We're good to go. I've been in contact with the case officer out of the New York Field Office who was assigned to Preston's disappearance case. An Agent Peck. He's at a courthouse now getting the warrant signed, and then he'll meet us here.

There's no way anyone outside New York City will get a heads-up that we're here, so let's get started."

We followed Barbutero to an adjoining hall where he pointed at the staircase. "We're on the entry level. Kitchen and living room, one story up on the third floor. Bedrooms and a terrace, fourth floor. And then on top, there's a roof deck."

I held up a hand. "Volkov, go find a place to work. Dig into Preston's phone. Then look at this one." I handed her the Nokia device.

She nodded and trotted up the stairway, carrying the MacBook, Barbutero's Nokia, and Preston's phone, which Appleton had guarded protectively during the flight. It was a shame that Volkov couldn't have gotten started dissecting the phones while on the plane, but, you know, she had to fly it.

As she disappeared upwards, Barbutero continued, "We're going down to the lowest level. Most of it is underground, but it's got a bit of daylight toward the rear, so Isaac calls it the garden level."

The hitman led us down the flight of stairs to the garden level where, to our left, we found a fully equipped gym with an adjoining bathroom. "You'll be able to wash up, later, in there," Barbutero advised.

To the right of the base of the stair, and opposite the gym, we found a cavernous, two-story space, the high ceiling flecked with dancing light reflected from the surface of a shimmering indoor pool.

Beyond, glass doors at the far end of a two-story gallery led to a compact outdoor garden surrounded by high, visually impenetrable wooden fencing.

"Isaac has nice taste," Appleton observed. "Quite a spread here. Later, I'd like to snoop around upstairs and check it out."

"Be my guest," Barbutero grumbled, his stare focused on the glass doors that flanked the two-story fireplace in the gallery.

Parr pointed at the doors. "You buried Preston in Isaac's little backyard garden, didn't ya? Ballsy, ace."

"Not exactly," Barbutero mumbled. "Um, that way." He pointed back toward the gym.

Uncharacteristically, Gansett exploded with laughter, guffawing, "I've got to give you credit, Rocco. Very clever. Where are the controls?"

Brightening at the praise from the CIA man, Barbutero explained, "There's a mechanical room through the gym. The good news is we're not gonna be making a mess of the street. It drains to the stormwater sewer."

Appleton's face showed that she lost her patience. "What drains? Where is the body?"

Barbutero pointed at the shimmering water. "Under the bottom of the pool."

# CHAPTER
# 61



### *NOON — GREAT FALLS, VIRGINIA*

**OVER FIVE YEARS,** Hanna Mo'Nique Isaac bought three adjoining parcels of land along the Potomac River in Great Falls, Virginia, a wealthy commuter enclave roughly a half-hour north and west of the United States Capitol building. The nine-acre property at the center of the triumvirate was raw land, wooded, and pristine, and it was here that Isaac built a 12,500-square-foot residence for her husband's use when Congress was in session. As soon as construction was complete in late 2019, Isaac created two shell companies to purchase the two residences that flanked the new home—and, naturally, she immediately tore them down, creating a nineteen-acre estate with commanding river views and, of course, privacy.

She hated it—secluded, remote, boring.

But, for the time being, the estate served her purposes, close enough to travel to Washington if the need arose, and convenient enough access to three airports for her Gulfstream to make a hasty retreat to the bustle of New York or to the beachfront of Malibu.

With the Senator gladhanding votes in the Senate office building and beyond, and intent on keeping a low profile, Isaac remained at the estate, alone (save for the twelve or so staffers to tend to the grounds, the kitchen, and the laundry). And, with Virgil Preston's antagonism gone, Coate was confident of a landslide approval vote of the Enhanced Production of Integrated Circuits bill—and Isaac would do nothing to interfere with the momentum. She'd bide her time until it became appropriate to reveal she was the new owner of Aximerva, and in the meantime, her team didn't post on social media, and Isaac herself refrained from taking most calls as she carefully selected who she would communicate with—and only if absolutely necessary.

Silent. *Bored*, she thought, dressed casually in jeans and a sweater, barefoot, idly watching the leaves fall outside the triple-paned, floor-to-ceiling windows of her minimalist, white-themed study.

Her phone, on silent mode, vibrated with a notification. At first, she ignored it, until her innate curiosity compelled her to look at the device.

"What—the—*fuccckkkk*." Isaac scrolled through the stop-frame photos sent automatically by the security system at her Cornelia Street townhouse. She could download the video later, but in the meantime, the photos told her enough of the story, and she swiped to a contact screen to dial FBI Special Agent Mariana O'Toole.

O'Toole answered on the first ring. "Good morning, Miss Isaac."

"You're not going to believe this," Isaac sputtered. Her voice and incomplete sentences revealed her frantic concern. "My security system—set to notify me if my place in New York is opened—sent me pictures—it's fucking Barbutero. He's in New York, at my place."

"Slow down," O'Toole commanded. "Sequence it, please."

Isaac inhaled to compose herself. "I have a townhouse on Cornelia Street. It's equipped with a security system, of course. When someone opens the street-side entry door or the garage door, the system sends a notification to my phone along with three images which are culled from the twenty-four-seven recorded video footage. The first image is a freeze-frame recorded thirty seconds before the door is opened, the second is the instant the door is opened, and a final image thirty seconds after. I can download the full video stream if I need to, but it's faster just to glance at photos to establish who's going in or out."

O'Toole quickly concluded, "And Barbutero is at the door. How long ago?"

"There's, like, a little lag, but no more than a couple of minutes."

"Is he alone?"

"No. One other man with him. I don't recognize him. Tall guy, red hair, red beard. Never seen him before. But there's gotta be someone else, because a reddish SUV, like a Suburban or something, rolled into the garage. Tinted windows, but obviously there's a driver."

"Interior cameras?"

Isaac scoffed, "No, I don't spy on myself."

"What about the Capitol Police? Don't they monitor the security system?"

"No," Isaac huffed. "They are briefed when my husband or I am in residence, and then they keep watch. Otherwise, they ignore it. They can't be bothered to check every workman or cleaning person who enters all of my places, and frankly, my staff is none of their business."

"Okay, no problem," O'Toole replied calmly. "Send me the photos. I will immediately dispatch someone from the New York field off—"

"No!" Isaac exclaimed. "You need to go there. Don't send some random."

O'Toole whistled. "I'm in New Haven. Even with lights and siren, I'm at least ninety minutes away."

"Fine. Go. I don't want anyone else in that house other than you."

Beat.

O'Toole's voice was hesitant, almost deferential, as she asked, "Why not? Are you hiding something?"

Beat.

"No," Isaac finally replied. "I've got nothing to hide from you. It's the other, um, less enlightened agents that I worry about."

"Understood. I'm on my way. But—any idea why Barbutero is there? Is he looking for you? Is he setting a trap for you? What's his motive?"

Isaac was quick with a reply. "If I think of something, I'll call you. Go!"

The investor swiped off the call and efficiently texted the photos to the FBI agent. Examining the screen as the messages whooshed into the ether, she noted the time and said to herself, "Almost noon. Less than twenty-four hours and this mess is over."

# CHAPTER
# 62

## *SAME TIME — NEW YORK CITY*

**THE HITMAN** hadn't been kidding. It was messy work.

The pool itself was not large, only about 375 square feet and not quite six feet deep, and the mechanical pumps drained it in short order. With two sledgehammers that Barbutero had stashed previously in the garage, we took turns smacking at the thin layer of gunite that formed the bottom of the pool, where we found a slightly thicker layer of concrete and, below, a waterproof rubber membrane.

Taking a break from my turn with one of the heavy hammers that was quickly nicknamed "sister sledge," I realized that it was almost noon. The AG had demanded an update, and even though I figured Lin was probably ratting on me and keeping him posted, I decided to send him a text myself. I pulled off the work gloves that I'd worn while wielding the sledgehammer, and I yanked off the ring that Gansett had given me earlier; the finger was reddened and swollen. Shoving the ring into my pocket, it took an effort to tap out a message with tired and sweating fingers:

```
    Barbutero was a no-show. I've let Lin
    know. Working with Appleton now; we are
```

expecting significant new evidence shortly.
We both strongly recommend you hold off on
your press conference.

Williams sent a reply almost immediately:

What evidence? I need a timeline. Call me.

Knowing that I was still dancing on the head of a pin, I demurred, using the oldest excuse in the spy-game book:

Can't say with a text or on a call. This
connection is not secure. Give me a couple
of hours.

If, indeed, Lin had relayed the gist of my excuses earlier—that I was traveling to New Haven by car—the timeline would match, and sure enough, the AG replied with a curt,

OK

Refocusing on the pile of debris that accumulated on the still-wet bottom of Isaac's basement pool, I asked Barbutero, "How did you pull this off?"

He handed his shovel to Parr and explained, "Isaac left town immediately after her lunch with Preston. She took her Gulfstream back to her place in Malibu. I had this place all to myself. Once I stashed the body, I pretended I was Isaac's residence management service, and I hired some tradesmen to fix the bottom of the pool."

"How'd you get the body here?"

"I arranged for my delivery business to provision the restaurant on the day of the lunch," Barbutero explained. "My guys brought the goods downstairs to the basement bistro, and then I helped them carry the trash back up to the street level."

"And by trash," I offered, "you also mean Preston's body?"

"Yeah," he admitted.

I'll spare you the foul details of extracting the plastic-wrapped corpse from its muddy, dirty tomb under the pool's rubber membrane. True to form, after Gansett, Barbutero, and I struggled as a team to heft the slippery, ungainly, bagged carcass to the brown, stone pool deck, it was the unflappable duo of Appleton and Parr who enjoyed the honor of slitting the plastic open, both of whom wisely averted their eyes from the bag as the cut was made—not because they were squeamish, but because they knew what was coming.

"Oof," Appleton grunted. "Phew. Okay, we're well past rigor mortis but we've got the usual gas odor as the organs decompose and the bodily fluids leak. The inside of the bag is slick, to say the least."

Parr peered inside the opened bag with the aplomb of an experienced Medical Examiner. "In the first phase of decay, the flesh has a greenish hue. This one's starting to turn reddish from the blood decomposing." He leaned in closer. "Teeth are—" I watched him reach into the bag—"still intact. Hair isn't falling out yet." He paused and looked up, apparently unaffected by the stench. "I'm no expert, but given all that, I'd put this feller at between one and two weeks post-mortem."

The odor of the decomposing body reached my nostrils, and I admit I gagged a little. Fortunately, with the immensely high ceilings, the noxious smell dissipated somewhat.

I'm downplaying it for your sake. It was nasty.

Fearlessly, and with a sort of suspiciously practiced hand, as if this wasn't his first time doing so, Parr continued to paw at Preston's bagged corpse.

Honestly, I kept my distance, angling to get out of the cavity of the drained pool and be as far as I could from the black bag. Distracted, I almost stumbled and fell backward when Volkov's voice surprised me. "Wow, it reeks in here!" She appeared in the doorway to the pool area. "Hey, the pool deck is basalt. It matches the stone at my house in the Azores."

She grabbed my arm and helped me climb the still-slick steps out of the pool cavity as she offered, "I took some time to back up Preston's phone to the computer so that we would have a duplicate copy of the data. Then, I started with location tracking, starting with the device in the Washington area as of late last night. Before that, it was in New Haven for a few days. From what I can tell, Barbutero took a high-speed train from Boston to New Haven. And—"

"Whoa," I interrupted. I barked at Barbutero, "You had Preston's phone on you, on the Acela?"

"Uh-huh," he mumbled.

"It gets better," Volkov proclaimed. "It wasn't just in Boston. It was also in Salem." She turned to Appleton and added, "At or near your residence in Salem."

"We'll get back to questions about that," Appleton decided. "Keep backtracking."

"Before being in the Boston area, the device was in New York City. I've got an exact listing of times and addresses—including corroborating that the device departed Bar Virtuosismo after the lunch on Tuesday the 25th. But here's the best part. On Friday, October 21st, for almost an hour, Preston was at this very address."

"Fascinating," I whispered, as a new thought came to my mind. Peeling off one of the latex gloves that I wore, I dug into my pocket and pulled out my phone. Handing it to Volkov, I instructed, "Take this; it's still unlocked with no passwords, like it was back in Washington. See if any of my contacts—specifically, Isaac, Lin, or Williams—made or received calls to Preston's phone. You've also got Barbutero's Nokia. See if that matches up. Look for any connections between all of us."

"I'm on it," Volkov replied as she accepted the device and rushed from the pool area back toward the stairwell.

I called after her, "How long will it take?"

"Not long," I heard her shout from the stairwell. "It's a simple download from each of the devices. I'll compile a complete log in no time."

I barely heard the end of her sentence as Parr yelled, "I got somethin'!"

At the body bag, Parr straightened and stretched his hand out, and pincered between his latex-gloved thumb and forefinger, I could see a USB flash drive, garishly emblazoned with the name of a big-box electronics chain.

"I'll take that." Appleton snagged the drive from Parr. She palmed it in her gloved hand, bolted toward the stair, and I raced after her.

# CHAPTER
## 63



**HANNA MO'NIQUE ISAAC PACED** restlessly in front of the floor-to-ceiling triple-paned windows in her study. She took no notice of the burnt umbers and blood-red scarlets of the fall foliage outside. Instead, she focused on the time, imagining Special Agent O'Toole weaving in and out of the typically light afternoon traffic southbound on Interstate 95, or perhaps bouncing through the potholes on the bumpy and scarred Cross Bronx Expressway—a roadway that earned the dishonor of holding three of the top ten slots in a study of the most dangerous spots on America's highways by a nonprofit transportation research group.

"No," Isaac said to herself, "she'll be safely on the West Side Highway by now."

Forcing herself to stop the incessant pacing, she stood immobile for a moment, staring at the sliver of the Potomac River, just visible through the tree trunks, visualizing the glimmer of the water as the Hudson River.

For the umpteenth time, Isaac tapped her phone display, fretfully waiting for the call from O'Toole. Nothing.

Her mind required action, but Isaac knew that merely dialing O'Toole would only add to her impatience. Nonetheless, her thumb hovered over the device's glass screen. Her digit twitched, tapped at the screen, and as Isaac invented a stop-gap plan, the thumb called up an entirely different contact card. Isaac smiled at her intuition as she tapped the speakerphone icon.

Calmed, somewhat, she sat at her desk as a ringtone sounded.

Finally, Sara Lin answered with a lilting, "Hello?"

Without preamble, Isaac demanded, "Where are you?"

"At the New Hampshire Avenue office. Why?"

Isaac turned to the flatscreen computer monitor on her desk and linked to the livestream video feed from the street-facing security camera at her Cornelia Street townhouse. The street view remained vacant of vehicles or pedestrians, a typical quiet midday for the narrow alley nestled in the lower-midtown West Village neighborhood. Isaac glared at the scene and explained, "Rocco Barbutero showed up on the security camera at my place in New York. He's got entry access, and as far as I can tell, he's inside. And yet, at five this morning, he was supposed to be meeting with your man Ben Porter."

Lin didn't hesitate with a response. "Porter called me at, like, six A.M., and he said that Barbutero ghosted him. You haven't heard from Barbutero?" Lin's voice climbed an octave. "He's not in Washington— he's in New York?"

"Yes," Isaac confirmed. She manipulated the face of the smartphone as she added, "I'm texting you a picture now. It's definitely Barbutero, and he's with another guy. Do you recognize him?"

The speaker rustled as Lin fidgeted with her device. "The ginger with the beard? Never seen him before. I can send this to some people who will run a facial scan."

"No," Isaac replied. "Don't get anyone else involved."

"I'll call Barbutero," Lin offered.

"No," Isaac snapped. "Not yet. I want to know what he's up to before he gets spooked. O'Toole is on her way to New York." She consulted the clock display at the bottom right corner of the computer screen and said, "She should be almost there."

There was no response from Lin, and Isaac asked, "Are you still there?"

"Yeah," Lin mumbled. "I was just looking at my texts. Porter sent a message that he was meeting Jennifer Appleton for coffee, and then a second message that he was going to be delayed getting to the office because he was reviewing the case with Appleton. You know who she is, right?"

"I've heard the name."

"Appleton is the former Special Agent in Charge of the Bureau's Boston field office. She stepped aside to head up the AG's new investigatory task force. Porter was one of her protégés, which is why he's also on the AG's task force."

Isaac sighed with obvious exasperation. "This is what I warned Porter about. I thought he'd see the inherent conflict of the Attorney General running investigations on his own. There's no accountability. Bart Williams has gone mad with power." She paused and sighed a second time. "Where is Porter now? I could talk some sense into him, and—"

Isaac's phone dinged with a new notification, and she bent over the screen to read it. "Hang on, Sara. I think—yes! O'Toole just arrived at Cornelia Street."

Focusing her attention on the much larger computer screen, she watched the street in front of the garage door as O'Toole, her red hair glinting in the sunlight, stepped down from a black Chevrolet Tahoe with blue-and-red strobe lights blinking in the SUV's grillwork. A half-second later, a second vehicle—a similarly black Ford sedan also equipped with flashing blue-and-reds—pulled to a stop beside the Tahoe.

Hands waving earnestly, O'Toole appeared to be talking with the medium-height man who exited the sedan, his pale, balding head bobbing above a glinting badge of some kind that was prominently clipped to the left lapel of his brown checked sports coat. On the opposite side of the car, another man, stocky and somewhat overweight, swung the passenger door open and laconically joined the conversation.

Isaac muttered to herself, "Who is that?"

"What?" Lin's voice rang out from the still-active speakerphone connection.

"There's someone else at Cornelia Street. Another car, like NYPD, or maybe FBI. Two men. I'll text you a photo in a sec."

"Is it Porter?"

Isaac studied the screen. "No, definitely not. And why would Porter be in New York? You just said he was with that Appleton person in Washington."

"I—I—I don't know. I just—I feel like a lot is happening now," Lin stammered.

"Yeah, I'd say," Isaac mumbled. In a stronger voice, she ordered, "Stay by your phone. I'm calling O'Toole."

# CHAPTER
## 64



**ON THE THIRD-STORY LEVEL** of Isaac's Cornelia Street townhouse, Volkov commandeered the kitchen island for her work. Appleton and I hovered impatiently, at times ogling the view outside the rear-facing, floor-to-ceiling glass windows, but mostly gaping blankly at the screen of the MacBook that rested on the dark gray soapstone countertop. Volkov narrated, "Okay, I installed a copy of my anti-virus program from my watch onto Appleton's MacBook, and it has almost completed examining Preston's USB drive for malware." She glanced at Appleton. "Don't worry, I didn't touch the drive. You can get prints off it later." Returning her attention to the screen, she explained, "Once the routine is complete, I'll copy the contents of the drive to the MacBook, so that we can reserve the USB drive as evidence, and then we'll have a look at what's on it."

Appleton's phone dinged, and she chuckled as she examined her device. "Well, isn't that fascinating?"

She placed her phone face-up on the counter, next to the flash drive pulled off Preston's corpse, and explained, "Special Agent Danny Peck, New York Field Office, the lead agent on Preston's disappearance case—

and he's arrived with our warrant. But he's with an uninvited guest. Guess who also showed up outside?"

I leaned in to read the message. "Well," I said flatly, "the text from Peck says he's with Special Agent Mariana O'Toole. Do I win a prize for reading comprehension?"

Appleton headed for the stair down to the entry floor. "Porter, duck to the garden level and tell the guys to stay put and to stay quiet, and then join me upstairs on the entrance level."

"Got it."

We split at the entry floor, Appleton headed to the garage, and I continued down one flight.

Poolside, or rather, graveside, I passed on Appleton's message to Parr, Gansett, and Barbutero, and then I climbed the stair to the entry floor, where Appleton was leading a trio upstairs to the third floor. I tagged along.

Appleton halted in the street-side living room—strategically keeping Volkov, in the kitchen behind a wall dominated by a fireplace—out of sight. As I entered, she announced, "As I said at the garage door, I'm Jennifer Appleton, former Boston SAC and now head of a new DOJ task force. Let me introduce Special Agent Ben Porter. He works for me." I nodded, and Appleton continued, pointing at a balding man, "Porter, that's Danny Peck, and his partner Marty Farnman. Both New York Field Office."

Farnman was a stocky and somewhat overweight dark-skinned man with short, black, cropped hair and a suspicious expression; his eyes were darting left and right, and his nose was wrinkled. "Smells a little funny in here."

Appleton made a show of sniffing and shrugged. "Yeah, maybe a little musty." Having brushed off Farnman's concern, Appleton turned to the red-headed woman and asked, "And you're Special Agent O'Toole? What are you doing here in the Big Apple?"

O'Toole glanced at the ringing smartphone that she held in her right hand and squeezed it, silencing the ringtone. Pushing her shoulders back, she glared at Appleton. "The question, Appleton, is rightfully—what are you doing here? This is a private residence."

"Oh, sorry, is this your place?" Appleton's voice was mocking.

O'Toole scoffed. "Cut the posturing, Appleton. You know who owns this residence. How's that gonna look?" She was clearly agitated as she paused to wipe her mouth. "Let's see—the FBI raids a home owned by a Senator's wife? How dare you even be here?"

Appleton angled her head toward Peck. "Seems like you're very vigilant of citizen privacy, O'Toole. I agree with your perspective, but all the same, I have a warrant to be here."

Peck reached inside his brown-checked sport coat and withdrew a sheaf of paper folded into thirds. "Signed a short while ago." He handed the documents to Appleton. "To be specific, now you have the warrant."

Folding her arms across her chest, O'Toole didn't back down. "What are you looking for?"

"Not a *what*, Agent O'Toole," Appleton clarified. "A *who*. Virgil Preston."

"That's ridiculous," O'Toole replied snidely. "He's not here. Preston is out of the country, in Jamaica, playing golf."

I held up a hand and interjected myself into the stand-off. "Agent O'Toole, I met with Hanna Isaac on Monday morning, and I've been in contact with her since. I am aware that you—along with Isaac and a gentleman by the name of Rocco Barbutero—all met on Saturday, as I recall, at a private club in New Haven."

"Yeah, your name came up, Porter," O'Toole said, her tone far less sharp with me than it had been with Appleton. "Seems like you're the only one here with a clue. Care to fill me in?"

"Sure," I agreed. "Let's have a seat. But—I have one condition."

O'Toole grimaced slightly. "What's that?"

"Phones go in the kitchen, behind that fireplace, out of reach. We're going off the record, and nothing I say leaves this room."

"Fine by me," O'Toole grumbled, handing me her phone.

In turn, I collected devices from Appleton, Peck, and Farnman. "Be right back," I called as I stepped around the fireplace wall into the kitchen area.

As I set the stack of devices down on the soapstone countertop, Volkov greeted me with a barely audible whisper. "Ben. You've got to see what's on Preston's USB drive." She pointed at the screen. "This is a PDF; one of many. Read it."

I began to skim the document as Appleton called from the living room, "Porter?"

"Yeah, um, hang on," I sputtered. "I'm just getting a, uh, glass of water. Anyone else want one?" Before waiting for a reply, I rushed on, merrily announcing, "Never mind! I'll just get everyone a glass. Make yourselves comfortable."

I tore my eyes from the screen and hissed to Volkov, "Please get five glasses of water. Make some noise. Let me skim this stuff as fast as I can."

"I'm on it." She began to bustle about the kitchen, slamming cabinet doors and running the kitchen sink tap water. She ducked her head close to mine and purred, "The files on this USB are the missing link."

"Yeah," I murmured, trying to digest the material. "Question is, how do I play it?"

# CHAPTER
## 65

**VOLKOV ARRANGED FIVE** glasses filled with water on a tray that she'd found in Isaac's contemporary kitchen. The sun on this November afternoon was already low in the sky, and the water shimmered festively in the bright light of the kitchen space before darkening as I carried the tray to the living room. I carefully placed the tray on the low, oblong coffee table that was the centerpiece of a seating area featuring two opposing, long, curved-front sofas. Peck and Farnman were splayed on the sofa to my left, the men taking up far more space than was necessary, and O'Toole and Appleton were perched opposite them—though each at the opposite far ends of their sofa.

Save for the fact that my guests were all armed with some sort of weapon, it looked like a middle school dance. Well-dressed girls primly poised on one side, slouchy boys lounging on the other side trying to look cool—and no touching.

I hated middle school dances. Core memory; not a good one; let's not go there.

I picked up one of the glasses and chose to stand in front of the fireplace. Taking a sip, I licked my lips and began, "Fresh information has come to light on the Preston case. I believe that it is sensitive, and therefore, before I proceed, we've got to agree on a gag order."

"You've already got my phone," O'Toole stated.

"We need to go beyond that," I replied evenly. "Agent Appleton and I are going to have to depart shortly, and, frankly, I'm not certain I can trust the rest of you to stay put. You're all sworn agents of the Bureau, but I recognize that you'll feel compelled to, um, act."

O'Toole was shaking her head. "Are you always this opaque, Porter?"

Turning to my left, I said, "Agent Peck, I'm not sure you remember me, but our paths have crossed twice before."

"Nah, I figured it out," he replied, rubbing his balding scalp. "First it was the thing with the box, and then I finally put two-and-two together after the thing with the bridge."

*Good*, I thought with relief. *I might have an ally.*

"Well done. In other words, I don't have to rehash my credentials with you." Moving away from the fireplace, I brushed by Appleton's knees and lowered myself into the sofa next to O'Toole. Turning to my new colleague, I announced, "Virgil Preston is not in Jamaica. He's dead."

"That's incorrect, as I've already stated," O'Toole retorted.

"That's a reasonable position, Agent O'Toole, given the set of facts that you've been privy to. However, in this instance, I know more."

"How can you be so certain?"

I sipped my water before placing the glass back on the tray, the remaining four glasses so far untouched. "We've located the body."

O'Toole wouldn't back down, and I appreciated that she was being tenacious when she asked the obvious question, "Where?"

"That's the part I'd rather not disclose," I offered, "until you agree to keep the intel quiet until I have an opportunity to charge the individuals involved. Otherwise, we may be looking at a flight risk."

"Reasonable. Fine. Where?"

I looked at my shoes, which I'd done my best to clean after the excavation exercise. "About twenty feet below us."

O'Toole shot to her feet. "Bullshit."

"Follow me," I invited as I followed suit, standing.

I heard Appleton whisper tentatively, "Porter?"

"We're okay," I reassured her. "I got this. You too, gentlemen."

The agents tailed me down the stairs to the garden level, and from behind, I heard Farnman mutter, "That funky odor is getting stronger."

"Yeah," I called over my shoulder, "you were correct before. The smell gets worse."

We entered the pool area, and I could only imagine their thoughts as they processed the seven-foot-long scar at the bottom of the drained pool, the black body bag, and the three men seated next to it—Barbutero wedged protectively between Gansett and Parr.

Barbutero puffed out his chest even as he ran a finger across his mustache. "You get used to the smell after a while." Then, he caught sight of the red-headed agent, and the bluster evaporated. "Uh, O'Toole, what are you doin' here?"

"I don't believe this," Peck muttered. "I assume that cadaver is Preston."

"Yeah. You're welcome to take a look," I said.

"Nah. I'll take your word for it," he replied, leaning on the wall.

O'Toole was braver and approached the bag. She swallowed and made a face as she looked inside, Parr helpfully holding the bag wide for her inspection. Finally, she choked out, "I guess that's Preston," and she retreated.

"Now you see our problem," I suggested, purposely using the word *our* in an attempt to gain her support. "I don't want this getting back to Isaac."

O'Toole narrowed her eyes. "That's not the problem," she said, using an even, thoughtful tone for the first time since entering the Cornelia Street townhouse. "Isaac already knows you are here. Well—not you, Porter." She swept a forefinger from Parr to Barbutero. "But she knows that guy and Rocco are both inside."

I involuntarily gasped. "How?"

A new voice sounded from the stairwell—it was Volkov, announcing, "There's a security camera outside. I can hack it, I suppose."

At the sight of the caramel blonde at the doorway, O'Toole reached for her service weapon and spat, "Who the hell are you?"

Appleton stepped forward on the basalt pool deck. "She's an Intelligence Analyst that I've assigned to my task force." She turned to me. "But this is another challenge. Any ideas, Porter?"

I grinned. "I know exactly what to do."

# CHAPTER 66

**IN SHORT ORDER,** I'd given out my assignments. Peck and Farnman agreed to remain in the townhouse with O'Toole. Indeed, Peck even whispered, for my ears only, "I don't like this O'Toole. She's up to something no good. She ain't going anywhere, and she ain't calling anyone." He clutched O'Toole's mobile phone in his hand, waving it to and fro for emphasis. "You've got my number, you've got your phones back, so don't hesitate to call me if something comes up."

"You're going to send me your report of the Preston investigation, right?"

"Already done," Peck replied. "You should see a link on your phone."

"I'm grateful for that, Agent Peck," I murmured, as Volkov appeared walking down the stairway from the third floor. She sandwiched the MacBook, Preston's phone, and Barbutero's Nokia in one hand and, in the other, I could see the USB drive dangling in a clear Ziploc bag. Turning back to Peck, I nodded and said, "I'll read the report on the way back to Washington."

Inside the garage, O'Toole watched skeptically as we piled into the Yukon. Volkov handed me the Ziploc bag, and I hopped into the shotgun seat, Gansett once again to the left of me, behind the wheel. Appleton, Volkov, Parr, and Barbutero crammed in the rear.

Over the growl of the Yukon's V-8 engine starting, O'Toole shouted, "Isaac is in Washington. You're gonna drive to Washington, and you're expecting me to sit here on my ass for what, four or five hours? She's gonna be calling me non-stop." She held up her hands and protested, "I can't dodge the calls for five hours."

Rolling my window down, I assured her, "We got that covered." Wishing, a little, that I was at a middle school dance, I flexed my superior stature. "Our task force has its own jet. We'll be there in an hour." Enjoying O'Toole's dumbfounded expression, I ordered, "Farnman, open the garage doors, please."

I hit the switch to roll the window up as Farnman pressed a bulky button mounted on the interior wall of the garage, adjacent to the door to the hallway. Gansett reversed the big SUV outside into the long-shadowed light of the setting sun, and once the snout of the Yukon was clear of the door, I said, "Stop."

Swinging the door open, I stood on the running board of the Yukon, steadying myself with my right hand on the door frame, and I looked up at the brick-clad townhouse. Spotting the camera that I should have seen earlier, I raised my left hand, where I carefully held, between my thumb and forefinger, the clear bag containing Preston's USB drive.

I counted to ten and slipped back into the Yukon. "Let's go."

Appleton called from the third-row seat in the rear area, "Are you sure that was wise?"

"Yep," I mumbled, reaching for my phone, hoping that Peck would be true to his word and was keeping O'Toole's device away from her.

I found Isaac's contact card and dialed, tapping the speakerphone icon. "Muzzle Rocco, please. The rest of you, don't say anything. Just listen."

Parr instantly headlocked Barbutero, making it impossible for him to talk, and probably making it difficult for the hitman to breathe.

Isaac picked up after two rings and dispensed with a greeting or preamble. "What are you doing at my house, and how did you find out about that USB stick?"

"I dug it out of Preston."

She spluttered, "That's—that's impossible. I simply don't believe he would tell you about it."

I didn't take her bait, instead adding, "Furthermore, Barbutero is in my custody, and we're on our way back to Washington. We need to meet. You, me, and the Senator."

"Fine, fine," Isaac stuttered. "Let's clear this mess up once and for all. Um, I will text you our home address. It's in Virginia, and it's a bit north of the city, so therefore it's maybe a half-hour shorter drive from New York."

"That won't be necessary," I replied. "I have my own plane."

I caught a glimpse of Gansett rolling his eyes as he coaxed the Yukon faster toward Teterboro.

I continued, "Meet me at my New Hampshire Avenue office in ninety minutes. And if you don't do that, because you're thinking of bolting, know that I will have a warrant for the arrest of Senator Coate and you out to all federal and state law enforcement and to the national media in ninety-one minutes."

"That's preposterous," she spat. "An arrest on what grounds? Do you know who you're dealing with? What bogus charges have you and your pal Bart Williams concocted?"

"Oh, that should be obvious, especially to you," I deflected. "Do you remember where the office is, or do you need me to text you the address of the New Hampshire Avenue building?"

"That won't be necessary," Isaac hissed coldly, parroting my words back to me.

"Right, right, of course. You could always get that info from Sara Lin." Before she had a chance to respond, I stabbed *End Call*.

From the backseat, Appleton cautioned, "I'm not sure that was a wise move, Porter. You've just given her room and opportunity to wiggle."

I twisted in my seat to face my boss. "She's run out of space."

"Hmm." Appleton paused, running a hand through her hair as she thought. "It's inconceivable to me that she's still hanging onto the ruse that Preston is alive. How much longer can she continue to bluff?"

"Well," I noted, with a confidence that I felt but wasn't quite certain of, "if she's bluffing, she's playing poker. And yet, I'm playing chess."

# CHAPTER 67



**THE EVER-RESOURCEFUL** JJ Gansett tapped a contact from his former CIA career to secure a landing slot at the Ronald Reagan Washington National Airport. As the wheels of Volkov's Lear 35A squawked onto the tarmac and the jet braked to slow, I turned to Appleton, seated across the narrow aisle from me in the confined cabin, and asked, "Did you finish reading the files from Preston's USB drive?"

She sighed, and her eyes were cast downward to the space-gray MacBook balanced on her knees as she replied, "Yes. It's disturbing. Did you read Peck's crime scene investigation report?"

I waggled my phone, which I'd studied through the entire flight, and confirmed, "Yes, and I've gone through the phone logs that Volkov put together. I don't have time to explain," I said as the plane taxied. "We must invite the Attorney General to our meeting with Isaac and Coate. I know the AG is waiting to hear from me, but strategically, I want it to come from you. Would you mind arranging that?"

She pulled out her phone. "Consider it done."

The Lear lurched to a stop, and the engines whirred slower and slower into silence. As Volkov completed the shut-down routine,

Gansett clambered out of the cramped cockpit and cracked the clamshell door open.

The efficient ground crew, accustomed to the demands of their elite clientele, were already moving Appleton's F-250 toward the Lear, parking the pickup next to a compact, white Nissan SUV with the Signature Aviation logo stenciled on the hood. Gansett explained, "I called ahead and arranged a second vehicle. The driver has the address."

"Excellent," I said, angling toward the Nissan. "Let's move out. We've got no time to spare."

As before, Appleton hoisted herself behind the wheel of her truck, with Gansett and Parr squeezing Barbutero's flanks in the backseat. Volkov and I boarded the Nissan, also taking the rear seats behind the baseball-capped driver. With a glance at my partner, I signaled that we'd remain silent for the thirteen-minute drive into The District as I continued to study the documents on my phone.

Distractedly gnawing on the fingernail of my right thumb, I looked up briefly through the Nissan's windshield as we drove across the Arlington Memorial Bridge with a view of the brightly lit Lincoln Memorial to our right. Volkov, to my left, placed a reassuring hand on my left thigh. I was grateful for the gesture; it calmed me, and I focused on the task at hand: entrapment.

The Nissan rolled to a stop before the familiar door below the fifth-floor turret, and Volkov and I waited for a moment as Appleton wheeled the F-250 into the narrow confines of a curbside parking spot. Tapping the requisite codes into the keypads, I herded my group into the elevator, and we rode up in silence.

The elevator doors parted with a wheeze, and I stepped into the foyer—and faced a crowd.

Toonin, Kinnar-Hering, Lin, and Isaac gaped as the elevator discharged five passengers. As the elevator doors slid closed, I watched Barbutero sneer at Isaac.

It was Isaac who broke the hushed standoff, demanding, "Where's O'Toole?"

I crossed my arms and revealed, "She's at Cornelia Street, but she is incommunicado at the moment, in the company of two FBI agents from the New York Field Office." I paused, making a show of scanning the attendees, and I glared at Isaac. "Where's the Senator?"

Isaac stepped forward a half-pace and snarled, "He's not here. Nor will he be."

"That was not my instruction." I closed the distance between Isaac and me with a step of my own, blustering, "The deal was *both* of you."

"Are you always this impertinent, Porter? He's a Senator. You're a— what—a lowly agent?" Her voice was venomous as she growled, "Besides, my husband has no part in any of this. Believe what you want, but I have *always* insulated him from my work. I am quite certain you have nothing—not a shred of anything—that connects him to me other than our marriage."

I bit my lip. "That's true," I confessed, annoyed with myself at the consequences of not anticipating her objection and therefore immediately losing round one of the matchup.

*Focus on the evidence you have, Ben,* my inner monologue chided. *The Senator isn't involved, so stay on point and keep away from theatrics.*

Isaac's head swiveled back and forth as she examined the two women who had stepped off the elevator with me. Settling on Appleton, Isaac said thinly, "I believe you are Jennifer Appleton—yes?"

Appleton bowed her head with exaggerated politeness. "I am."

Isaac jutted her chin in Volkov's direction. "And who are you? And who are these two other men?"

It was Appleton's turn for drama as she stepped forward from the line-up, explaining obliquely, "This is the team that I have assigned to my task force. Their identities are of no concern to you."

Isaac spat, "Well, Appleton, are you going to rein in Porter? Who is in charge, anyway?"

In a monotone, Appleton replied, "In this room, me. However, my superior will arrive imminently, and then the Attorney General of the United States will preside over our discussion." Her phone chimed, and Appleton added, "In fact, he's here now, on the sidewalk outside."

A moment of silence passed, and no one moved. Finally, Isaac threw up her hands. "Well, are you going to go get him? Escort him up here?"

I grinned, making sure Lin could see my expression. "I'm quite certain he has the access codes. Isn't that right, Sara?"

Sure enough, the elevator dinged, and the doors parted to reveal Bart Williams, flanked by two men of his protective detail. "Hold the doors, please," I commanded, and Gansett reached back to place a palm on the elevator jamb to prevent the door from sliding shut. Pointing at Toonin and Kinnar-Hering, I demanded, "You two—out." Addressing the AG, I requested, "Sir, I'd prefer if your detail waited at the street level, if that's okay with you."

"Fine," the AG boomed, first staring at me, and then slowly turning his head to take in the rest of the crowd, and finally facing Appleton. "What is this all about?"

In response, and with all my chess pieces on the board—or at least gathered in one place—I wordlessly ushered the group into my fifth-floor turret, thinking, *Showtime. Shit, I hope I've correctly seen through the fog of this case, otherwise, my career is over.*

# CHAPTER
## 68

**LIKE AN ORCHESTRA CONDUCTOR,** I shooed my audience into seats reflective of their status. I motioned Isaac, Lin, Appleton, and the AG to the four barrel chairs. Pointing at the two uncomfortable-looking, stick-like seats on the visitor's side of my desk, I instructed Barbutero and Parr, "Sit." I nodded to Gansett and then in the direction of the office door; he received the message and swung the door closed and then stood beside it, sentry-like. Finally, I pulled out the tall back of the Aeron chair at my desk, rotated it slightly, and offered it to Volkov, who sank into it. She placed the space gray MacBook on the desk. Beside it, she laid out Preston's phone, Barbutero's phone, and the bagged USB stick.

I took my time to precisely position the phones and the flash drive so that they were visible to Isaac and the AG, and for that moment, the only noise in the fifth-floor turret was the faint sound of traffic far below on New Hampshire Avenue. The windows were dark as rain clouds gathered above Washington, blocking any glimpse of the moon or stars.

I remained standing, facing the assembled audience. With my hands clasped behind my back, I addressed Lin, "Sara, you're quite the enigma. Let's start with you and your duplicity."

As usual, Lin attempted to play the innocent victim. "I don't understand. What are you accusing me of?"

I didn't reply. Instead, I consulted the AG and asked, "When you formed your task force, did you inform your staff that Appleton and I were both tapped to be involved?"

"I did," the AG confirmed.

"And then, once she became aware that Appleton and I agreed to serve the so-called Q-Group, did Lin ask to participate?" I watched as Lin's eyes narrowed at my use of her surname instead of her first name.

"She did," Williams said. "Her request made perfect sense to me since you two worked together so successfully last March."

"But she's not independent, like Appleton and I," I stated. "She reports to you."

"Of course," the AG replied smugly. "I wanted to be fully informed."

"And Lin was aware of your opposition to the EPIC act?"

"That's no secret."

"Right," I agreed. "Nor should it have been a secret that Lin knew both Coate and Isaac personally."

"It was a strategic decision on my part. I offered Sara an ideal seat on the inside, assuming she would utilize those personal connections toward the work of the task force—which, by the way, she did, by coordinating meetings between you, Porter, with Senator Coate, and with Miss Isaac," the AG explained defensively.

I crossed my arms over my chest and aimed a question at the AG. "Did you know Lin was spying on you?"

The Attorney General's eyes narrowed, and he hissed, "What?"

At the same time, Lin sat forward in her barrel chair and protested, "That's quite a reach, Porter." She emphasized the P to make it obvious to me that she, in turn, would now refer to me by surname.

*We're past the point of pretending to be friends*, I thought with some relief.

"Is it?" I countered. "Indeed, what's your motivation? It's not money—you have plenty of that. You were brought up in A-list society, and I suspect you realized that relationships are far more lucrative than only your parents' fat checkbook. You collect connections, and you squeeze them for favors, for rumors, for gossip, and for leverage. On the face of it, you worked for Bart Williams. But you colluded with Hanna Isaac. Did either of them know that you were playing both sides?"

Both Isaac and the Attorney General remained stone-faced. Lin, on the other hand, pouted, "I was on *your* side, Porter, trying to help you and your task force. But I guess you're too infatuated with *her* to see that now," she snarled, scowling across the room at Volkov. "I've seen a photo from the files, and I'm guessing that you're the famous Anastasia Volkov?"

Volkov chuckled meanly. "I am. And—try as you might, pretending that this is some sort of a love triangle gone bad to deflect the attention that's on you isn't going to work. Porter is quite capable of managing by himself. As he tells it, he was on top of you days ago."

*I wish she picked a different phrase*, I thought, feeling my face flush.

I managed to regain my composure and explained, "By that, Volkov means that I was onto Lin's deception."

"What deception?" That question came from Isaac, and she was hesitant; she'd lost the self-assured composure that she carried when the meeting started.

"The deception that led to the discovery of this item," I replied, dramatically stepping toward my desk and lifting the bagged USB drive for all to see.

"I demand to know how you got your hands on that," Isaac insisted. "And what gave you the right to be at my home in New York?"

The AG pointed at the Ziploc bag that I dangled. "What is that thing?"

"Evidence," I purred smoothly. "Evidence recovered from Virgil Preston."

Placing the bag back on the surface of the desk, I pointed at the two phones. "These two devices are Preston's iPhone and Barbutero's Nokia. We'll come back to the Nokia. Let's start with the iPhone that once belonged to Virgil Preston, which somehow ended up in the custody of Rocco Barbutero."

Isaac's eyes darted to Barbutero as I picked up Preston's phone. "I couldn't understand, initially, why Barbutero carried this with him—

until I realized that he needed to keep it close in case anyone tried to reach out to Preston. And by anyone, I mean you, Hanna." I addressed Isaac directly. "You never called Preston; you only texted. And you were texting a dead man."

Isaac's mouth drooped in obvious shock. "What?"

"There's more, I'm afraid," I said firmly. "Virgil Preston's corpse was buried at your home at Cornelia Street, and because of that, the Attorney General will likely charge you as an accessory to Preston's murder."

Hanna Mo'Nique Isaac's face transformed that instant, from confused yet approachable, to fierce anger and denial. Her cheekbones stood out prominently as her jaw tightened and her eyes narrowed. She bolted to her feet and cried out, "I'm calling my lawyer. I'm done here."

**AS HANNA MO'NIQUE ISAAC TRIED** to shove her way past JJ Gansett's tall frame at the doorway of my fifth-floor turret office, I cautioned, "Not so fast. I'm not finished."

The Attorney General of the United States rose slowly to his feet. He stepped toward the investor and said with disdain, "I've been wondering, and so has much of the media and many lawmakers, why Virgil Preston—once so adamantly opposed to your husband's EPIC bill—suddenly went quiet after lunching with you privately. Not a word from him or from his company. And here we are, on the eve of the vote of the bill that's surely going to pass tomorrow, we find out why—and you're bold enough to dispose of the body on your own property?" He folded his arms across his chest and muttered, "This is shocking. Disgraceful."

Isaac spun on her heel. "I didn't have anything to do with a murder," she hissed.

"That's technically true," I offered in a pleasant tone. Pointing at the barrel chair that she'd vacated, I addressed her with eye contact and explained, "Immediately after your lunch with Preston at Bar Virtuosismo, Preston was killed by Barbutero. He stabbed him in the kitchen. Unfortunately, a bit of blood splattered onto a butcher block, so while Barbutero could dispose of the knife with the body, he couldn't hide that error. But he could get the body out of the restaurant. It was taken out with the trash, loaded in a waiting truck at the street level, and then the truck wandered around Manhattan until the wheels of your Gulfstream lifted off from Teterboro and flew you, Hanna, back to Malibu. That gave Barbutero the opportunity to bury the body in the place most damning to you—under your basement pool at Cornelia Street."

Wordlessly, Isaac returned to her barrel. She sank into it and asked, "How do you know all that?"

"I've seen the body, I've read the FBI's report from Bar Virtuosismo, and I have Barbutero."

Barbutero grumbled, "I ain't sayin' nothin' till I get my deal."

I barely glanced at him as I noted, "You've said quite enough. Sit tight."

The Attorney General rumbled, "I've heard plenty." He moved toward the barrel chair that he'd vacated and sat, feet planted on the floor. Placing his hands on his knees, he stared straight at Isaac and said, "I'm calling an emergency press conference, and I will go to Congressional leadership to do two things, immediately. We're postponing the vote on your husband's pet bill, and we will censure him, if not impeach him, for your impropriety."

The AG sat back and crossed a leg. "Very good work, Porter. It's terrible that Virgil is dead, but—" he exhaled and painted his face with a sad but haughty expression—"we will get him the justice that he deserves."

Isaac opened her mouth to speak, and then clearly changed her mind, her eyes downcast to the floor.

I allowed a moment of silence to pass before dropping the bomb. "Sir, don't you want to know what's on that USB drive?"

The AG's self-righteous expression vanished when I said, "The drive was Isaac's leverage to compel Preston to consider her offer for Aximerva, and sir, you didn't know of the existence of the drive. Preston told you that he was running out of options, but he didn't tell you about the documents on the USB stick that Isaac gave him, did he?"

The AG eyed me with a blank look as I continued, "You see, Attorney General Williams, Isaac and Preston met at Bar Virtuosismo that Tuesday so that he could sign the papers to sell Aximerva. And if Isaac owns Aximerva, and Preston no longer has reason to oppose the EPIC act, what motive does Isaac have to kill him?"

No one moved a muscle, nor did anyone attempt to answer my question.

"That's right—your collective silence means you reached the same conclusion as I did. Isaac has no reason to murder Preston." I stepped to the desk and picked up Preston's iPhone for emphasis before I turned to the Attorney General. "However, you and Preston exchanged texts before that lunch. You knew that Preston was considering selling out, and that was a problem for you, wasn't it? After all, if Preston is out of the picture, you no longer have leverage over Isaac and, by definition, no longer have a mouthpiece to battle EPIC and to discredit Coate."

Finally, I knelt on one knee beside the four-chair grouping, and I stared directly into the Attorney General's dark eyes. I spoke slowly, emphasizing each word, "What's shocking and disgraceful, sir, is your attempt to frame Isaac by ordering Barbutero to murder Preston, and then, when I started to unravel your ruse, by ordering Barbutero to murder me."

# CHAPTER
# 70

**THE ATTORNEY GENERAL'S** vacant expression did not change the slightest as I accused him of conspiring to commit murder.

Instead, he cavalierly dismissed it. "That's a long putt, Porter."

I was so surprised by his statement that I stuttered, "Wh—wha—what?"

Unfazed the slightest, the AG rumbled patronizingly, "Oh, you don't play golf, do you? The phrase means that you're really stretching. The odds are against you. And frankly, this accusation is absurd."

Shaking off his deflection, I stood and began to pace the room, laying out the case against the Attorney General. "Let's start at the beginning, which as far as this case is concerned, was on Friday, October 21$^{st}$, when Virgil Preston met with Hanna Isaac at Cornelia Street." I gently shook Preston's iPhone, which I still held in my hand. "His phone puts him at that location, which is when Isaac handed him this." I placed the phone down on the desk and, once again, picked up the bagged USB stick. "The contents were saved to the drive just that morning. While a fingerprint analysis hasn't yet been done, it's a reasonable assumption that a computer forensic analysis will match it to one of Isaac's computers."

With a relieved expression, Isaac exclaimed, "It will match! I created that thing myself, and I cannot believe that it's now exonerating me from this ridiculous murder accusation."

"I wouldn't get so excited," I cautioned. "The USB stick suggests intimidation, coercion, and extortion." I placed the bag down on the desk. "The documents on this drive were collected by Sara Lin and sent to Hanna Isaac. They evidence that the Attorney General and Preston colluded for years. The AG greased wheels for Preston and for Aximerva to expedite import clearances for the machines that make advanced chips. The AG's office facilitated land acquisition deals, even going so far as being prepared to invoke eminent domain so that Aximerva's plant on the mutual Texas-Mexico boundary could be built straddling an international border. The AG would be instrumental in creating the border-free zone within the plant that would permit Mexican nationals to work inside a US factory, at Mexican wages, and with no US tax or citizenship."

Pausing my monologue, I made sure my audience was raptly engaged before continuing, "It's not entirely one-sided to the benefit of Preston and Aximerva, though. Via the Attorney General, Preston obtained the financing for the plant—debt sourced not from banks, but from the AG's web of contacts in hedge funds, government pension funds, and private equity firms." I glowered at the highest lawyer in the land. "It's quite an intricate web, indeed. It's no wonder that you didn't want Preston to sell Aximerva, as it would have unwound all your promises to a number of powerful people. You'd be tottering on thin ice or flailing in quicksand. In fact, that's your motive—if Preston is murdered by Isaac, you're off the hook for all those deals, and a side benefit is that by incriminating Isaac, you also destroy Coate's credibility, thus elevating your stature significantly."

Williams scoffed. "You cannot prove that I directed a murder."

"I can. We have established your motive, and we have material evidence within the phone logs and the text messages. Let's go over the timeline, shall we?"

Volkov pointed at the Nokia and began, "Barbutero's phone links you all together, showing calls connecting to Hanna Isaac and to Sara Lin." Consulting her screen, Volkov stated, "On the night preceding Preston's disappearance, Isaac called Barbutero."

Isaac exclaimed, "I didn't call Rocco to order a murder!" She exhaled audibly with exasperation. "I called him to request his usual assistance to serve at a private lunch meeting."

"As you'd done several times before," I affirmed. "The FBI report includes their interview with Chef Isola, and he confirmed that you'd booked the restaurant four times previously. He also verified that Barbutero, or at least a person matching his description, since he didn't know the name, gigged as your waiter."

I faced Lin and continued, "But, seconds after your conversation ended, Barbutero dialed Lin." I stepped to the side slightly and leaned in to speak. "Like Lin, Barbutero is playing both sides. He has no allegiance to anyone, and I'd imagine his motive is the simplest of all—money and connections from Isaac, and immunity plus protection from prior sins, courtesy of the Attorney General. Isn't that right, Rocco?"

Barbutero only shrugged; this time, the wise guy was wise enough not to speak.

I didn't need Barbutero to verbalize an answer to my question, as I could prove it otherwise with the call history. "Indeed, Barbutero is as much a double agent as Lin. He serves at Isaac's whim, both figuratively and literally, acting as a waiter for her private meals at Bar Virtuosismo. Then he switches sides—on the spot!—and kills Preston. Why, I wondered, until I ran through the texts on Preston's phone and then matched up the timing to Barbutero's phone."

I pointed at Volkov's screen. "On the morning of Preston's disappearance, Preston's phone was at The Pierre hotel in New York City, and he was texting with the Attorney General. Preston knew he was in trouble. His deals to build his plant were teetering in the face of the EPIC vote. And, he'd seen what Isaac had on his secret, possibly illegal collusions with the AG—and if Isaac exposed that, he was done. Preston had no choice but to sell out in the face of coercion. But the AG told Preston, in a text message, 'You've got to protect Aximerva,' yet he didn't offer a solution, nor did Preston disclose his apparent intention to sign the papers hours later to sell the company to Isaac."

I moved my finger from Volkov's screen to Barbutero's phone. "A few minutes after that text exchange ended with Preston proposing a call with the AG at 2:00 P.M. that day, Barbutero's phone shows an incoming call from Lin." I made eye contact with Williams. "You'd had enough, eh? Via Lin, you ordered Barbutero to kill Preston, because you've concocted your plan to frame Isaac and to discredit her and her husband, figuring—correctly, as it turns out—that Appleton and I, operating as your new task force, will certainly find the clues that incriminate Isaac."

The Attorney General remained silent, but I could tell from his expression that I was beginning to needle him, to shake his resolve. A vein on his neck was pulsing, and try as he might, he couldn't disguise an elevated heartbeat.

I continued, "But Isaac, however, doesn't know Preston is dead. She remains concerned that the AG will continue his efforts to kill or pause the EPIC vote. Thanks to her inside intel from Sara Lin, Isaac learns that Appleton will be taking on a role at Main Justice on the AG's private task force and that they'll be meeting in Salem on Thursday night. Two days after the lunch, Isaac called Barbutero, and shortly thereafter, Preston's iPhone—because it's being carried by Barbutero—begins to move from Barbutero's warehouse in Jersey City toward the Boston area."

Appleton interjected, "All of this is happening invisibly, by the way. Until we recovered the two phones, that is, and we could begin to track movements and calls. We'd be able to do this by getting the data from the carriers and commencing a reconstruction by our Intelligence Analysts—but having the devices in hand drastically speeds up the process. Volkov did most of this work while sitting at Isaac's kitchen counter at the Cornelia Street townhouse earlier today."

"Let me pick back up on the timeline," I suggested. "In our interview, Isaac disclosed to me that she dispatched Barbutero to Boston to reason with the AG. Isaac told me that she had been working with FBI Special Agent Marianna O'Toole. Indeed, it was also O'Toole who was concerned that the AG's new task force would give him too much power. Isaac sees the meeting in Salem as an opportunity to disclose to the AG that she's bought Aximerva, and Preston isn't going to oppose EPIC any longer."

I confronted Lin. "However, unbeknownst to Isaac, Lin must have been sharing everything that Isaac is doing with Williams, so the AG is aware that Barbutero is in Salem, outside Appleton's house. Williams seizes this as an opportunity."

I leaned over Volkov's shoulder to check the times that she'd logged. Straightening, I outlined, "We've got a record of Barbutero calling Isaac late at night Thursday, October 27, sometime shortly after I arrived, via Uber, at Appleton's house." Holding my left hand up, I extended my forefinger. "That's call number one to Barbutero that night."

After pausing for emphasis, I continued, "Several minutes after that call was logged, Isaac dialed Barbutero's number. That's call number two." I paired my middle finger with my forefinger and said, "And then, hours later, at 1:24 A.M., Lin calls Barbutero. Call number three."

With my ring finger up, I waved my three-digit left hand in the air. "I remember the exact moment, too, because I was sitting there, literally twiddling my thumbs while Appleton was in her kitchen, making coffee, and Williams stepped into the restroom. His phone had been dinging with notifications for at least an hour. I'd be willing to bet Isaac's house in Malibu that Lin was relaying whatever Isaac and Barbutero were scheming via text. Williams found an opening to duck out of the room, he called Lin, and then Lin immediately called Barbutero."

As I dropped my raised hand, Isaac asked, shaking her head in confusion, "Why?"

"Excellent question," I said. "Recall that I said that Williams seized this circumstance as an opportunity— an opportunity to manufacture an alibi to insulate him from this whole mess." I smirked in Barbutero's direction. "Our hitman shoots out the back window of Appleton's Tahoe, and yet the AG is entirely unfazed. Then, Barbutero makes Williams look like he's an assassination target on the 5:05 Acela."

"You can't substantiate any of this nonsense," Williams rebutted.

"Isaac's interview supports it. She said that Barbutero's gun was triggered when I bumped him. At least, that's the story that Barbutero tells Isaac, but that's not what happened. In fact, Barbutero fired at the ceiling before I reached him. And, had I not been there, the AG's undercover protective detail would have intervened, as they eventually did. Williams was expecting Barbutero, and he reacted calmly, as if he planned the whole episode ahead of time. That's because he did—the whole thing in Salem and then on the train was nothing more than a circus act."

Volkov picked up the exposition. "The acting gets further entwined on Tuesday morning when, at 8:49 A.M., Barbutero's phone receives another call from Lin." She looked at the four barrel group and said, "Lin called Barbutero on behalf of Williams to set up the hit on Ben."

"Ah, yes," I said. "Our other double agent, Sara Lin." I glared at Lin as I recited her name. "We were walking to the office, and you had a sudden need for a detour—an urge, you told me, to buy a coffee. Except that subterfuge allowed you an opportunity to do Williams' bidding and to arrange for Barbutero to eliminate me. That's when the fog began to lift. You knew I'd be meeting with Barbutero, alone, and yet you did nothing. But I'd already figured out that Barbutero was impersonating Preston. You knew that, too, because you knew Preston was dead. Care to comment?"

"Fuck you, Porter," Lin spat.

"No thanks," I said dismissively. I faced Barbutero. "When we intercepted your attempt at the Lincoln Memorial, you became cooperative awfully easily. I couldn't understand why—you made little effort to resist, and you were open with information. That's when I realized that you were a pawn in something far larger. You clearly weren't working for Isaac because you quickly gave up the location of Preston's corpse. I bet you thought you were doing the AG a favor by closing the loop and setting up Isaac for the fall with the discovery of the body. Instead, you inadvertently led us to the USB drive, which exonerates Isaac and implicates the Attorney General."

"This is ridiculous," Williams protested meanly. "For the last time, you can't prove that I had anything to do with this charade—with this house of cards that you've constructed."

"True, true," I said agreeably. "I cannot." I pointed at the bagged drive on the desk and put my hand on Volkov's shoulder. "But she can."

Volkov reclined in the Aeron chair. "The digital footprints will prove everything. They'll prove the phone calls, the texts, the provenance of the USB documents utilized to pressure Preston when they were created by the AG, and the transmission of those documents from Lin's phone or computer to Isaac, who ultimately saved them on the drive." She smiled. "The binary breadcrumbs never lie, and when we subpoena Lin's, Isaac's, and the Attorney General's devices, I am quite sure I will be able to definitively prove Ben's theories."

Appleton stepped in, and she revealed, "I read the files on the USB drive, too. The one that fascinated me the most was that Williams played both sides, just like Lin and just like Barbutero." Glancing in Isaac's direction, Appleton explained, "Indeed, the AG went so far as to negotiate a lucrative employment deal with Aximerva as its chief legal counsel, to take effect as soon as the plant was constructed and operational. Certainly, that private sector gig would pay far, far more—in your case, at least ten times more—than your Level 1 position in the Executive Schedule of government pay scales."

I followed Appleton's gaze and addressed Isaac. "And you knew, Isaac, that if you went public with this information, you'd crater the future fortunes of both Aximerva and Bart Williams. Those documents would be scrutinized, and the deals would be unwound. You gave Preston no choice but to sell his company to you."

Isaac's expression dimmed as she scolded, "You don't know the first thing about business, Porter. I presented Preston with a set of facts and, faced with dealing with those facts or selling, he chose the latter. *Freely* chose, I might add."

"Or," I continued, as if she hadn't said a word, "The alternative, your backup plan, in the event Preston didn't agree to sell was that you go public, and you look squeaky clean, burnishing your image brighter than it is now. If EPIC passed, your husband's approval rating also goes up. There's no downside to you, is there? In either outcome, you have zero motive to kill Virgil Preston," I announced, attempting to sound triumphant.

"Precisely," Isaac exclaimed.

"However, Preston did sell out. It's no wonder that the Attorney General worked so quickly to get the task force going. He knew that

Preston's position was tenuous, and once he ordered Barbutero to execute Preston, the AG waited for the task force—for me—to pin Isaac for the crime. To keep Isaac in the dark, the AG has Barbutero impersonate Preston while Appleton and I conducted our investigation. All the while, the AG looks as if he is independent—ironically, the very same pitch that he made to us to form the task force would shield him from liability. Not only that, but he also adds in the attempted hit on the train to make himself look like a target."

I glared at Williams. "I guess you underestimated my tenaciousness . . . and my resolve not to naïvely accept the facts that you wanted me to see."

Gansett spoke for the first time. "Nor did Mister Williams expect you to turn to me when you saw through the subterfuge surrounding your meeting with Barbutero."

"Speaking of which," Appleton offered, "Williams even knew that it wasn't Barbutero in the Azores, since he knew Barbutero was sitting outside my house in Salem. And he knew that Porter wouldn't have his usual support from his former team." She nodded in Volkov's direction. "Except Porter never let go of that thread, either. I'm sorry that I didn't recognize that earlier."

Volkov grimaced. "Yeah, well, me too. While I'm happy that I showed up in time to help, this would have been a lot more straightforward if I'd been more forthright in the Azores with Ben." She looked into my eyes and added softly, "I'm sorry, but not sorry. At least we're together now."

Williams guffawed. "Oh, this is rich. Unreal, in fact. You've got nothing that links me directly to any of it, do you? It's all conjecture and unsubstantiated conclusions."

"Wrong," I said flatly. "Your man Barbutero sold you out. Indirectly and with an innocent comment, but one which proves you knew what happened at Bar Virtuosismo."

I turned to Isaac. "What did you have for lunch that day?"

"I—I—what?" Isaac scowled. "Why does that matter?"

"It's in the FBI report that Agent Danny Peck wrote, so actually, I already know, because I read the report. But humor me."

She shrugged. "I had a kale and beet salad."

"Right," I said agreeably. "Your usual, according to the statement that Agent Peck took from Chef Isola. You customarily ordered that entrée at each of the private lunches that you hosted at Bar Virtuosismo. And what did Isola serve Preston?"

Isaac scoffed, "Virgil didn't like the food. He pushed it away. Pasta Bolognese."

"Very good," I confirmed. Turning to Appleton, I said, "When the Attorney General met with us in Salem, however, that's not what he reported. He claimed that Preston had a steak sandwich. Remember?"

Appleton nodded. "Yes."

I pointed at Barbutero. "When Rocco directed Preston to leave through the kitchen, Isaac thought it was so they would not be seen together exiting the building. Rocco, however, had another agenda, and he offered to make Preston a proper meal—a steak sandwich. At least, that's what he told the AG when he reported back to him, and it's what Rocco told me after he tried to kill me at the Lincoln Memorial. Only the AG and Barbutero knew about the steak sandwich. Oh, and Preston, too, but he's not talking."

"You can't possibly try a case based on recollections of a menu," the AG said mockingly.

Appleton stood. "It's another piece of the puzzle, and I've heard enough. Barbutero gets his immunity in exchange for testimony which will support the digital evidence. Lin will be prosecuted for breaches of confidentiality and as an accessory to murder. Her legal career is over. Isaac will be prosecuted for extortion." Appleton glared at Isaac. "You're going to jail, Isaac. I hope you look good in orange."

"She likes tangerine," I mumbled, but only Volkov heard me.

Appleton was already facing the Attorney General. "Sir, you'll be prosecuted for collusion, treason, as a conspirator to the attempted murder of Ben Porter, and as a conspirator to the murder of Virgil Preston. The instant this conference is over, I am forwarding these findings to the FBI Special Agent in Charge in New York. Jacinda Burns will go to the press tonight, and the EPIC vote scheduled for tomorrow morning will be postponed, I'd imagine. After all, how will it look if the backer of the bill is bailing out his wife while the Attorney General is being detained for crimes against the United States?"

Williams placed his hands on the arms of the barrel chair and pushed himself upright. With his jawline set, he scowled tensely at Appleton, the vein in his neck visibly pulsing. "Impressive, Appleton. Your Q-Group managed to uncover quite a conspiracy."

"Per our terms, sir, don't begin to think that you can exert influence over me. My task force will survive your incarceration."

"It will," the AG rumbled. "Yes, yes, indeed it will."

He clicked his tongue. "Absent my imprisonment, our relationship will be dicey, though. I'd imagine that the pressure of still having to deal with me might shake even you, Appleton, despite your reputation for being imperturbable."

The AG's comment created a stare-down standoff between Williams and Appleton. After a beat, she said, "You're delusional if you think you're remaining in office."

"Hmm," Williams grunted, with sort of a throaty chuckle. "We'll see about that." He glanced pointedly at Appleton and then returned his attention to me. "You see, Porter, you've overlooked one critical component of this so-called puzzle."

# CHAPTER 71

**I RACKED MY BRAIN,** running over the details frantically. I was so focused inwards that I barely noticed a bolt of lightning flashing outside the dark windows of the fifth-floor turret as a late fall thunderstorm neared Washington.

*One critical piece?* I couldn't come up with a single omitted part. Granted, it was complicated—especially given the duplicity of both Lin and Barbutero. *But the evidence is clear. The binary breadcrumbs don't lie, Volkov said. Barbutero can't lie, either; he would only impeach his own credibility and risk his immunity deal.*

"Would you care to sit, Porter?"

The AG's supercilious voice cut through my fog.

"I'm good," I retorted, shifting my weight, not willing to be scolded into submission as if I was an errant child.

Appleton, too, remained standing, asking, "If you're so confident, lay it out. What's missing that proves your innocence?"

The AG chuckled wickedly. "Well, nothing, in fact. You're not missing anything. I'd say you're spot on in your deductions. Isn't that right, Hanna?"

Isaac hesitated. "I'm not sure I want to answer that."

"Fair enough," Williams boomed. "Let's start with Appleton and Porter's steps out of bounds. For example, with that guy." He pointed at the doorway where Gansett casually leaned against the frame, still blocking the exit. "I know who you are. You're JJ Gansett, and you are supposed to be detained under house arrest by the FBI—and yet, here you are." He scowled at Appleton. "That reckless step alone disqualifies your so-called case."

"My methods by employing Gansett might be atypical but all the same, I'm protected by the charter of the task force that you yourself signed," Appleton argued.

"And her?" The AG pointed at Volkov. "When it comes time for testimony about these digital breadcrumbs, you're going to somehow produce a woman who drowned at sea? How does that play out, Appleton?"

She didn't back down in the slightest. "There are plenty of people who can replicate her work. I'm not concerned."

"It clouds the evidence. It taints the chain of custody of that evidence," the AG cautioned.

"I appreciate the lesson," Appleton said, the sarcasm evident in her voice. "I'll prepare for that contingency at trial."

"Ho, oh, no," the AG chuckled, sounding a bit like Santa Claus. "We're not going to trial. We're not even getting to the part where Jacinda Burns and the New York office are notified."

"Really?" I stepped forward. "Why not?"

"Other than these irregularities—and not counting that man, who I don't even know," the AG said, inclining his head toward Parr, "you're not going to go any further because Isaac and I don't care. Do we, Hanna?"

Isaac was examining the AG carefully as he settled into the barrel chair next to her. He leaned forward so that he was face to face with Isaac, and he rumbled smoothly, "If EPIC passes, your husband will certainly gain support far and wide, especially with the midterm elections next week. Imagine what he could do, stumping on behalf of candidates after his EPIC victory. There's too much peril if we reverse course on the EPIC vote tomorrow. Wouldn't you agree?"

Hesitating, Isaac nodded and quietly said, "Yes, that's for certain."

"Mmm, yes," Williams murmured. "You've seen my deals with Preston on that USB drive. Are you prepared to honor those terms now that you're the owner of Aximerva?"

Isaac perked up visibly. She nodded a second time. "Absolutely."

"Very good," Williams intoned. "While it is unfortunate that Mister Preston has been waylaid, I do think the future of Aximerva is bright, especially if its new owner accepts support from EPIC subsidies. Ultimately, Virgil will be proud of what the company that he founded becomes as it prospers with our leadership." He extended his right hand toward Isaac and concluded, "I look forward to doing that work with you, Hanna."

The investor accepted the gesture and shook hands with the Attorney General. "I, too, anticipate a long and mutually beneficial relationship, Bart."

Releasing his grip, the AG leaned back in the barrel and crossed his legs. "You see, Porter, Appleton, this is how things are accomplished here in Washington. We take setbacks and work around them. Hmm. Lemons into lemonade, as Senator Coate might say."

"We'll see about that," I countered with a fierce tone. I held up my phone. "You're forgetting about Preston's body, stinking up Isaac's townhouse. The FBI isn't going to let that slide."

The AG uncrossed his legs and placed his feet firmly on the floor, glaring at me. "That's incorrect, too. You forget, Porter, that I was the New York DA some time ago. Jacinda Burns and I have a collaborative relationship. In the end, after all, the only person with dirty hands in this whole affair is Rocco Barbutero."

Parr made no move to restrain Barbutero as the hitman shot to his feet, toppling his sticklike chair. "What the fuck? What about my deal?"

The AG flicked at an imaginary spot on the carpeted floor with his black wingtip shoe. "The deal you made with Appleton? Hmm. As of now, overruled as invalid by her superior. By me. Because, after all, Rocco, it's your word against mine. Remember, I never called you directly—it was always Sara Lin."

Appleton grimaced. "You're not going to get away with this."

"Get away with what?" The AG's tone feigned blasé innocence. "I control access to the media. I can spin a story the way it must be presented to align with my desired outcome. Sure, you can go to some off-brand outlet and try to undermine me, but all you'll be doing is destroying your own credibility by appearing as a disgruntled crackpot." He cackled meanly. "I'd almost like to see you attempt that, as it would surely be entertaining to watch. Though I'd admit, it would be a distraction."

With a self-assured expression, Isaac contributed, "You also overlook my standing in the media. My mastery of social channels means that I get my message out first to my fans. They've got a fifteen-second attention span. They're not interested in your tales of complicated conspiracy. They don't have the appetite nor the patience to care."

Williams grunted, "Hmph. So, you see, Appleton and Porter, despite your best efforts, all you've managed to accomplish is to wed two unlikely partners. Dare I speak for Hanna, but she and I are both far more sophisticated in these matters than you, and we will seek the most pragmatic path to power and profit."

I shook my head sadly. "That's what it's always about, isn't it? Power and profit to those who have it, and epic injustice to the have-nots." I gritted my teeth and spat, "You're both an insult to morality."

Appleton was more specific as she threatened, "You established my task force with a five-year term, and I'm going to stick to you like glue." She hissed menacingly, "One slip-up, and I'm there, and I will demand your accountability. I will get justice."

"Oh, please. Spare me the theatrics." The AG's expression remained unfazed. He pulled a phone from his suit coat inside breast pocket and tapped on it. "I've summoned my detail. They'll take custody of the suspect, Mister Barbutero, and I'll ensure that his story matches mine— or else," he added vaguely, somehow signaling a threat.

Williams stood. He offered a hand to Isaac, who clasped it and also rose as Williams said, with a syrupy tone, "Let me walk you out, Hanna. Would you care to join me for a late supper?"

"Thank you, Bart," Isaac said sweetly. "I would."

Williams turned to Appleton and me, standing shoulder to shoulder. "That critical component? The one piece of the puzzle that you overlooked? Let me explain as clearly as I can," he lectured. "This is Washington. We deal in power. From power comes money." He grunted meanly. "In pursuit of those two goals, we look out for ourselves first and foremost. And then we look out for those who can be useful to us, knowing full well that they are doing the same. Ultimately, loyalties shift and boundaries blur as we seek bedfellows in pursuit of our own success and stability."

I laughed scornfully. "Ha. Do you even listen to yourself? Do you hear what you're saying?" I shook my head bitterly. "Remember our discussion back in Salem? About our old friend Lord Acton. 'Power tends to corrupt; absolute power corrupts absolutely.' You're a fine example of that, don't you think?"

Williams rolled his eyes upward. "Not in the least. You're mistaken again, Porter. I merely deploy the power of my office in creative ways, which, admittedly, tend to protect my position. But to suggest I am corrupt? Hardly," he scoffed with derision.

I chided, "You can't see it, can you? You're blinded by your arrogance."

"Or you're merely ignorant, Porter. You simply don't understand how the system functions." He jutted his chin at Sara Lin. "Sara, you've been invaluable to Hanna and me. I appreciate your intuition and your inventiveness to expand your influence by partnering with Hanna, and even though you did so behind my back, I'm impressed. Care to join us?"

Lin glanced at me with a dark pout, and then she turned and winked coquettishly before visibly swooning toward the AG. "That sounds lovely."

Williams shoved his way past Gansett and flung the office door open. I heard the elevator bell ding, and a moment later, the AG's two security men rushed into my office. One of them handcuffed Barbutero, who attempted to resist—but his efforts were futile. They pushed the hitman to the elevator.

Arms linked, Williams and Isaac followed Lin into the elevator carriage. As one, they pivoted on their heels to face the still-open door, and the Attorney General boomed, "Appleton. Porter. You assumed that I have your interests at heart, with some sort of nationalistic patriotism guiding me. I don't. I have *my* interests in mind, and mine only. I don't have some sort of aspirational moral compass to play it by the book. We don't play parlor games here. No poker, no chess, nothing silly and insipid like that—because those games have rules. Here in Washington, those in power—like me—we make the rules as we see fit, to benefit us first, foremost, and forever."

# THURSDAY
# DECEMBER 1, 2022

**ONE MONTH AFTER** *THE VOTE*

# CHAPTER 72



**THERE IT IS,** once more. *The rules.*

"The Rules" demand that these stories open with a hook: a catchy first sentence, first paragraph, first chapter, and that they end with the bad guy losing and with the good guy winning.

I broke the rules again, I guess. The villains got away with the crime.

After Isaac and Williams conspired and waltzed out of my fifth-floor turret with arrogance and impunity, I revisited that outcome again and again over the course of a month.

I mean, was Isaac really all that bad? It was Preston who had colluded with the AG; Isaac merely capitalized on inside knowledge. For her own gain, sure—but is that a crime? I mean, when the AG proposed that she would get off the hook if she only kept quiet and honored Preston's deals, why wouldn't Isaac agree?

And what about Preston? His motives were good; he wanted Aximerva to succeed without government assistance, and he made side deals with the AG to protect his goal. Do the ends justify the means?

*Possibly*, I thought, watching from the north-facing terrace of Volkov's brown basalt cottage on the bluffs of Achada as the last rays of a setting sun cast over the endless, glittering waves of the North Atlantic Ocean.

Indeed, real crimes were committed by the duplicitous pair of Barbutero—the murder of Virgil Preston—and by Lin, ordering that murder.

Bart Williams shrewdly insulated himself through the power and standing of his office—pulling at the puppet strings from above as he worked the system to his advantage. Yeah, ultimately, he was responsible, but he was enabled by a two-faced system of politics and dealmaking that rewarded injustice—a system that benefits those who are in power without any tangible accountability except for an infrequent cycle of votes by an uninformed electorate trained to have a short attention span and swayed by slick press and media selectivity. That's the real villain here.

I'd turned my back to Washington and left it all behind. Sitting in a wooden chair on a terraced bluff high above the rocky beach and sipping a glass of Especial beer, crafted on-island by local brewer Melo Abreu, I felt detached—far more relaxed than I was in Washington, or anywhere, in fact. I'd become accustomed to the slow pace of the island, my days filled with flying lessons at the controls of a Cessna 172 single-engine propellor plane, seated beside the pilot whom Volkov had summoned, the day of the EPIC vote, to help her bring her Learjet back to the Azores—with me as the sole passenger in the cozy cabin.

The EPIC bill passed, naturally, by a bipartisan vote that signaled broad support of Senator Merritt Coate. In his down-homey way, he didn't gloat, but he did trot himself out on every television program possible for his victory lap, hinting at his upcoming presidential campaign.

Four days after the vote, the New York *Times* headlined the homicide of Virgil Preston, with FBI New York SAC Jacinda Burns taking credit for the investigation that fingered Rocco Barbutero. Burns was quoted as saying, "The suspect attempted, unsuccessfully, to frame investor and influencer Hanna Mo'Nique Isaac for murder. A joint FBI effort by our field office in New York, supported by agents in Washington, DC and in New Haven, Connecticut, led to the discovery of Preston's remains. As a lethal threat to society and pending trial arrangements, the suspect will be held without bail at Riker's Island jail complex."

Barbutero hung himself in his jail cell within days of his incarceration. Volkov commented, "Shades of Jeffrey Epstein. I don't buy it."

I didn't either, for the obvious reasons, assuming that Barbutero was silenced by decree from above—or more specifically, by Main Justice, especially when Barbutero's final visitor was revealed to be a female lawyer of Japanese descent who was interviewing the suspect on behalf of the US Attorney General's office.

Two weeks later, bored with their coverage of the midterm elections and ready for a fresh round of clickbait and new news, the breathless press drooled over the savvy acumen of investor Isaac, who finally revealed, at a press conference on the site of Aximerva's proposed plant on the Texas-Mexico border, that she was the sole owner of Aximerva. A reporter from the New York *Post* lobbed the only intelligent question at the carefully scripted, media-friendly event, asking, "The purchase and sale agreement was dated the day of Preston's death, but this is coming to light now, weeks later. How do you explain that?"

Her hair tousled by a prairie breeze, Isaac confessed, "I was in disbelief that my partner, my friend, and my mentor Virgil Preston disappeared after we celebrated our deal at a private lunch. I couldn't bear the thought of going public with the news. My advisors recommended discretion, in the hopes that he would be found, so that we could—"

She stopped, catching her breath, and she dramatically wiped a tear from her cheek. "So that we could announce the transaction together. It's—it's heartbreaking that he's not here now, standing beside me. It's just terrible. Horrible that he was murdered so brutally." She sighed heavily. "No further questions at this time. Thank you for your understanding. It's just too difficult."

Volkov and I had watched the live-streamed press conference from our cottage in the Azores while on a conference call with Appleton, in Washington, and Gansett, at his home on Cape Cod. "Isaac needs no training as an actor. It was an Oscar-worthy performance," I commented dryly.

"Look at the backgrounds," Gansett suggested, his voice crackling through the international connection. "Close-ups of national flags and the state flag, camera pans showing a carefully selected multi-racial audience, and a drone shot of the vacant land that will become North America's most advanced chip foundry. This is no run-of-the-mill press conference. It's a Hollywood production."

"Isaac has the financial resources for that kind of show, and as she told us in Washington, she has media expertise," Appleton said. "She's played it perfectly. She played us perfectly."

I asked, "What's going on in Washington? Any backlash from Williams?"

"Not yet," Appleton replied. "Fortunately, I negotiated an ironclad agreement with him before I took this job—I knew it would be a risk to naïvely move on from my position as SAC, and therefore I took precautions. My position is secure, I'm using your turret office, Porter, and I will be building a staff for the Q-Group." Attempting to make it sound like an afterthought, a note of disappointment was evident when she added, "Though I thought I had one."

"We're not ready to come back there," Volkov said cheerfully. "Ben and I deserve some time together."

"I know," Appleton conceded pleasantly. "In the meantime, I have a deal pending for Gansett's release from home arrest so that he can come to DC and work with me. You know I'm holding two spots open for you guys."

"Thanks," Volkov replied, but in a distant tone.

I jumped in, not willing to have *that* conversation with Appleton quite yet. "Where's Paxton Parr?"

"Among other things, Parr is shadowing Sara Lin. She'll slip up. Eventually," Appleton predicted, before offering pleasantries and ending the call.

Since that conversation two weeks ago, Volkov had been fixated on what I assumed was a throwaway, self-evident comment by Appleton:

that Isaac had the financial resources to pull off an impeccably packaged publicity stunt. When the conference call had terminated, Volkov asked me, "Where'd Isaac get all that money?"

"Investments," I had replied. "She built her fortune from scratch."

"That's the story scripted for public consumption that you're supposed to buy," she argued. "I wager that there's more to it."

I knew better than to bet against Volkov's investigatory skills, so I didn't respond. She spent the better part of the last two weeks on her computer. I spent the time in the air by day, and on the terrace by night, and tonight, with no flight lessons on the calendar for tomorrow, I decided that it was time for another Especial.

I could hear the staccato tickety-tackety of Volkov's fingers on the keyboard as I reached into the fridge for a cold bottle of beer. Padding, barefoot, into the wood-trimmed, white stucco walled study that Volkov used as her office, I passed silently through the arched doorway.

With the taste of the chilled, hoppy beer on my lips, I held the cold, brown bottle in my left hand as I placed my right hand on Volkov's shoulder.

"Hey," she said. "Hang on. I have something here."

"Okay," I replied, looking not at her screen, but at her long, caramel hair.

*I have something here, too,* I thought. *I will definitely hang on to this.*

An epiphany came to me in a flash as I realized, *The villains might have gotten away with the crime, but . . .*

"In the end, actually, I *did* win," I whispered, the words unintentionally slipping out audibly.

"What? Just wait a sec."

"I don't need to wait any longer," I said, leaning over and nuzzling her head with my own. "I've got everything I've ever wanted."

She turned her face and looked up from her chair, keyboarding paused. "What do mean?"

"The problem with our gig is that we see only the dark side of life. The criminals, the conspiracies, and the corruption." I sighed. "The injustice that sneaks into everything that happens in lawmaking, in media, in business." Sipping my Especial, I concluded, "It can be depressing, and yet here I am, as happy as I've ever been."

She smiled, but there was something—a tic in her cheek—that I recognized, after a month of living together, the most idyllic month of my existence, as a warning sign.

I wanted to brush it off. I didn't want to spoil the moment. Instead, I held up my bottle and asked, "You want one? Come sit outside with me."

"Sure," she agreed, grinning again. This time, I could tell the expression was authentic. No subtext.

I stopped at the fridge to grab her a bottle, and we settled into side-by-side wooden chairs on the stone terrace. The December night had settled over the Azores, but the temperature remained pleasant, and at first, we drank our beers in convivial silence. We no longer needed to fill the dead air with conversation. We were comfortable with quiet, with just being together, and I was blissfully content.

Volkov finally broke the stillness. "Over the past week, I discovered something about Hanna Mo'Nique Isaac. I've run it down again and again, looking at my suspicion from multiple angles and using numerous sources. It checks out."

"What checks out?"

"You know, I've been wondering about her. She started with nothing, and fifteen years later, she's a billionaire. I backtraced every detail of every public transaction that she was involved with, and it doesn't add up. She simply could not have built her wealth as she said she's done."

I asked, "Like a Madoff thing? Like he faked investment returns?" I referred to, of course, the sixty-five-billion-dollar Ponzi scheme that came crashing down in 2008, orchestrated by disgraced and now-deceased financier Bernie Madoff.

"Not exactly. That was all hot air disguised with falsified statements and abetted by inept oversight. You know, typical government oversight." She swigged a gulp of beer and licked her lips before clarifying, "No, Isaac's wealth is backed up by real assets. The question that I've been working on asks, because there is no possible way that she could have accumulated her wealth organically, did she have outside help? In other words, was she or is she bankrolled by someone?"

I turned to face her as I set my empty brown bottle on the stone terrace with a clink. "I'm gonna assume you have an answer to that."

"Mhhh hmm," she mumbled, putting her bottle down next to mine. "I'm concerned, though, because I've spent two weeks digging and prodding into sensitive areas. Like, state secret stuff. I hope I didn't trigger any alarms." She twisted her back to stretch it after a long day of computering, and she revealed, "Isaac was, and still is, backed by a Chinese citizen who lives in Hong Kong and who has strong ties to the Chinese state."

I let that sink into my brain. Volkov said nothing; I could hear only her quiet breathing and the faint crash of the North Atlantic waves far below the bluff.

"That's—that's—that's astounding," I managed. "China?"

Remembering the tiger-patterned Chinese silk scarf that Isaac wore the morning we first met, the regular beat of the waves below became louder in my imagination as I put two and two together and realized, "This whole thing is circular, then. Senator Coate proposes the EPIC bill to nationalize advanced semiconductor production, so the United States does not have to rely on imports from Taiwan and China. Meanwhile, Isaac buys control of the first mover, and now effectively, Aximerva is controlled by the Chinese?"

"Yeah, and Aximerva's future general counsel and the person who will protect the company at all costs is none other than the United States Attorney General," Volkov noted with contempt in her tone.

My eyes downcast to the stone patio, I was shaking my head in dismay. "We gotta go back to DC. As much as I love it here, with you, we can't sit idly by and let them get away with it all." I lifted my eyes to Volkov with trepidation, fearing her reaction.

To my immense and immediate relief, she met my hesitant gaze with a smile. "We can always come back to visit. But, yeah, we've got work to do."

My head up, and with one ear angled to the edge of the bluff, to my shock I realized that it wasn't the beat of the regular waves that I'd heard before—as the noise of the repetitive *whomp whomp whomp* got louder and louder.

"Helicopter," I shouted, bolting to my feet.

Volkov shot upright beside me and clutched my arm. "Oh, no. No! My research work *did* trigger something!"

A menacing, black, attack helicopter, bristling with weaponry on each flank, suddenly crested the edge of the bluff. The rotor noise and downdraft blasted us as we were rudely lit in the glare of a superbright spotlight. We both spun on our bare heels, and I barely heard the tinkle of the beer bottles toppling like bowling pins onto the stone terrace as I grabbed Volkov's hand just before she screamed, "Run!"


## THE END

# THANK YOU

**I AM VERY GRATEFUL** that you've spent your time reading my story.

Dare I ask you to take a few more moments now to share your assessment of my book on Amazon, Goodreads, or any other book review website you prefer? Your opinion will help the book marketplace become more transparent and useful to us all, and like all authors, I rely on online reviews to encourage future readers. Your opinion is invaluable.

If you are new to Ben Porter's world, please check out the prequels to this story, *False Assurances*, *Threat Bias*, *Subversive Addiction*, and *Vital Deception*, available in print or e-book via Amazon, Apple Books, or Barnes and Noble, in print by order through your local bookstore (distributed by Ingram), or in audiobook format on Audible, Amazon, or Apple.

For insight into my world, please check out my website and social media presence. You may not know this, but I'm an independent author. I am not backed with the resources of a ginormous publishing house, nor am I insulated by layers of staff, agents, and hangers-on. It's just me—and you.

And I have a small but loyal team behind me. I'm grateful to them, too.

First and foremost, to my family—who have always supported this adventure. My wife Meghan has both infinite patience and boundless love, and without that, none of this book stuff would be possible. Keilan, Maggie, and Connor (my three children, and in each one of these sections, I try to list them in a new order!) also put up with my bouts of writing and my mood swings when that writing comes slowly (yes, writer's block; it happens). And my parents, Jeanne and David, were the first fans of Ben Porter.

Speaking of firsts, as what has become custom, the very first draft was read by my Dad, my son Connor, and my good friend Doctor Phil Dickey. After I send the draft, I wait with eager trepidation for their feedback, and they've always delivered thoughtful critiques and excellent suggestions. Then the manuscript gets run by Ryan Steck; his reply started with, "Dude!!!! I just finished the new book. Wow." I was tempted to put that on the cover (which, like Book Four, was designed by Sarah Shropshire).

Also as custom, the audio version of this book is narrated by the duo of Christopher Boucher and Jessica Threet. I hear their voices—of Ben, of Appleton, of Volkov, and of the AG—even as I write. (Yes, I admit, I hear voices in my head.)

And last but certainly not least, James Patterson took the time to read the penultimate draft, and his insight and advice are, of course, invaluable. Jim is gracious and generous, and I am deeply thankful for his mentorship.

I took risks with this story, in terms of structure, pacing, and by placing Ben in a setting not typically associated with a "thriller" novel. I wonder if it worked, and I wonder who is in that helicopter . . .

Thanks for reading!

- Christopher Rosow, Southport CT, April 2023

www.RosowBoooks.com

Instagram, Facebook, and Twitter: @RosowBooks

# ABOUT THE AUTHOR

Christopher Rosow is an independent author who has self-published five novels. He decided to forge his own path after being rejected by the mainstream publishing houses—and he proved them wrong when the book they turned down, *False Assurances*, became a best-seller. Four sequels continue the story of Rosow's unique and compelling protagonist, Ben Porter.

When not writing, Rosow still works full-time in his "day job" in the design and construction space. And, when not working or writing, or enjoying time with his amazing family, he's probably found out on the water somewhere, sailing. He lives in Connecticut with his family, his dogs, and way too many boats.

www.RosowBooks.com
Facebook, Twitter, and Instagram: @RosowBooks

The Ben Porter Series by Christopher Rosow:
*False Assurances* — Book One (2020)
*Threat Bias* — Book Two (2020)
*Subversive Addiction* — Book Three (2021)
*Vital Deception* — Book Four (2022)
*Epic Injustice* — Book Five (2023)

www.ingramcontent.com/pod-product-compliance
Lightning Source LLC
Chambersburg PA
CBHW021021310726
48969CB00006B/1493